About the Authors

Marion Lennox is a country girl, born on an Australian dairy farm. She moved on because the cows just weren't interested in her stories! Married to a 'very special doctor', she has also written under the name Trisha David. She's now stepped back from her 'other' career teaching statistics. Finally, she's figured out what's important and discovered the joys of baths, romance, and chocolate. Preferably all at the same time! Marion is an international award-winning author.

Initially a French/English teacher, **Emma Darcy** changed careers to computer programming before the happy demands of marriage and motherhood. Very much a people person, and always interested in relationships, she finds the world of romance fiction a thrilling one and the challenge of creating her own cast of characters very addictive.

Helen Lacey grew up reading *Black Beauty, Anne of Green Gables*, and *Little House on The Prairie*. These childhood classics inspired her to write her first book when she was seven years old, a story about a girl and her horse. She continued to write with the dream of one day being a published author and writing for Mills & Boon True Love is the realisation of that dream. She loves creating stories about cowboys, horses, and heroines who get their happily ever af

Postcards from Paradise

Postcards from Paradise:
Australia

MARION LENNOX

EMMA DARCY

HELEN LACEY

MILLS & BOON

First Published in Great Britain 2023
by Mills & Boon, an imprint of HarperCollins*Publishers* Ltd,
1 London Bridge Street, London, SE1 9GF

www.harpercollins.co.uk

HarperCollins*Publishers*
Macken House, 39/40 Mayor Street Upper,
Dublin 1, D01 C9W8, Ireland

Postcards from Paradise: Australia © 2023 Harlequin Enterprises ULC.

Saving Maddie's Baby © 2016 Marion Lennox
The Incorrigible Playboy © 2013 Emma Darcy
The CEO's Baby Surprise © 2015 Helen Lacey

ISBN: 978-0-263-31911-8

SAVING
MADDIE'S BABY

MARION LENNOX

To Meredith and Alison, who make
my writer's life fun.

PROLOGUE

HEROES AND HEROINES don't choose to be brave, Maddie decided. Mostly they have bravery thrust upon them. In her particular case, a heroine was created when vast chunks of rock trapped one doctor in an underground mine, a mine she should never have been near in the first place.

This heroine wasn't brave. This heroine was stupid.

Everyone knew the mine was dangerous. Ian Lockhart, the owner, had left Wildfire Island weeks ago, with salaries unpaid and debts outstanding. The mine had been closed for non-compliance with safety standards not long after Ian's disappearance.

So whose bright idea had it been to see if they could tap one of the seams close to the surface?

There were reasons this seam hadn't been tapped before. The rock was brittle. Without salaries, though, and desperate for income, the islanders had cut through the fence and quietly burrowed. No one was supposed to know.

But now… The call had come through an hour ago. A splintered piece of shoring timber and a minor rockfall had left one of the islanders with a fractured leg.

If it hadn't been badly fractured they might have

brought Kalifa down to the hospital, keeping their mining secret. Instead, his mates had had the sense to ring Maddie, asking her to come across the mountains to the overgrown mine site.

Maddie—Madeline Haddon—was heavily pregnant but she was the only doctor available. The miners had told her there were shards of bone puncturing Kalifa's skin, so transporting him by road before assessment meant the risk of cutting off the blood supply.

She'd had to go.

Once at the mine site, it had taken work to stabilise him. Kalifa needed specialist surgery if he wasn't to be left with a permanent limp, and she was worried about the strain on his heart. She'd just rung Keanu, the other island doctor, who was currently on his way back from a clinic on an outer island. She'd been asking him to organise Kalifa's evacuation to Cairns when there was an ominous rumble from underground.

The mouth of the mine had belched a vast cloud of dirt and dust.

She'd thought Kalifa and the two friends who'd called her had been working alone. She'd never imagined there were men still in there. Surely not? But out they came, staggering, blinded by dust.

She'd been helping lift Kalifa into the back of the jeep—her jeep was set up as a no-frills ambulance, used in emergencies for patient transport. She'd turned and gazed in horror as the miners stumbled out.

'How many of you are down there?' The guy out first had a jagged gash on his arm. She grabbed a dressing and applied pressure.

'Tw-twelve,' the guy told her.

'Are you all out now?' When they'd rung about Kalifa she'd assumed... Why hadn't she asked?

'Three still to come.'

'Why? Where are they?'

'Malu's smashed his leg,' the guy told her. 'He's bleeding like a stuck pig.'

'Is he stuck? Has the shaft caved right in?'

'Just...just a bit of a rockfall where Kalifa fell against the shoring timber. Malu got unlucky—we were trying to shore it up again and he was right underneath where it fell. Macca and Reuben are helping him out but they had to stop to tighten the tourniquet. But the shaft's clear enough in front of the fall. They'll be out soon.' His voice faltered. 'As long as they can stop the bleeding.'

She stared at the mine mouth in dismay.

The dust was settling. It was looking almost normal.

Bleeding out...

Oh, help.

She'd done a swift, sweeping assessment of those around her. No one seemed in immediate distress. Men were already helping each other. The nurse who'd accompanied her, Caroline Lockhart, was taking care of a miner who looked like he'd fractured his arm. He was still standing, not in obvious danger. A couple of the men were crouched on the ground, coughing. They should be checked.

Triage.

One broken arm. Bruises, lacerations, nothing else obvious. Kalifa was waiting to be transferred to hospital.

Bleeding out...

Triage told her exactly where she was needed.

But she was pregnant. Pregnant! Instinctively her hand went to her belly, cringing at what she was contemplating.

What was the risk?

This had been a minor rockfall, she'd told herself. The shaft was still clear.

Along that shaft, Malu was bleeding to death. She had no choice.

'Help me,' she snapped at an uninjured miner. She grabbed his hand, pressing it onto the pad she'd made on his mate's bleeding arm. 'Push hard and keep up the pressure until Caroline has time to help you. The bleeding's already easing but don't let go. Caroline, can you radio Keanu?'

'He's on his way in from Atangi.'

'Tell him to land the boat on this side of the island and get here as fast as he can. Meanwhile, don't move Kalifa. He needs a doctor with him during transfer. The blood supply to the leg's stable, as long as he doesn't shift. But he has enough pain relief on board to keep him comfortable. Meanwhile, give me your torch,' she snapped at another miner. 'And your hard hat.'

'Y-you can't go in there,' the miner stammered. 'Doc, you're pregnant. It's dangerous.'

'Of course it's dangerous. You've been working in a mine that's supposed to be closed, you morons. But what choice do I have? Malu's got two children and his wife's my friend. Caro, you're in charge.'

And she picked up her bag, shoved on a hard hat and headed into the shaft.

'Doc, wait, I'll come with you,' one of the miners yelled after her.

'Don't even think about it. You have children, too,' she snapped back. 'We now have four idiots in the mine. Don't anyone dare make it five.'

CHAPTER ONE

DR JOSHUA CAMPBELL was so bored with solitaire he'd resorted to cheating to finish each game faster. It defeated the purpose, but he'd read every journal he could get his hands on. He'd checked and rechecked equipment. He'd paced. He was driving the rest of the staff at Cairns Air Sea Rescue Service nuts. He was going out of his mind.

No one in Northern Queensland seemed to have done so much as stand on a spider for the whole week. He'd been rostered for patient transfers, and every one of them had been routine. Patients had either been heading home, or were being flown from the city hospital to the country hospitals where they could continue recuperation among friends. There'd not been a single emergency amongst them.

'If this keeps up I'm joining the army,' Josh grumbled to Beth, his paramedic colleague. 'Maybe there's a place for me in the bomb squad. Do you suppose there's any call for bomb disposal any place around here?'

'You could try cleaning our kitchen as practice,' Beth said morosely. 'School holidays and three teenage boys? I'd defy a hand grenade to make more mess. You need to try a touch of domesticity if you want explosions. Consider marriage.'

'Been there, got the T-shirt,' he muttered.

'That's right, with Maddie, but that's ancient history.' Beth and Josh had joined the service at the same time, and after years of working together there was little they didn't know about each other. 'You hardly stuck around long enough to feel the full force of domestic bliss.' And then her smile faded. 'Whoops, sorry, Josh, I know you lost the baby, but still… It was so long ago. You and Karen, you think you might…?'

'No!' He said it with more vehemence than he'd meant to use. In fact, he startled himself. They were in the staff office, in the corner of the great hangar that held the service planes. The door was open and Josh's vehemence echoed out into the vaulted hangar. 'No,' he repeated, more mildly. 'Domesticity doesn't interest either of us.'

'And you're seeing less of each other,' Beth said thoughtfully. 'Moving on? Seeing we're quiet, you want to check some dating sites? We might just find *the one*.'

'Beth…'

'You're thirty-six years old, Josh. Okay, you still have the looks. Indeed you do. It drives me nuts, seeing the way old ladies melt when you smile. But your looks'll fade, my lad. You'll be on your walker before you know it, gumming your crusts, bewailing not having a grandchild to dandle…'

'I'm definitely applying for the bomb squad,' he retorted, and tossed a sheaf of paper at her. 'Just to get away from you. Sort these for a change. They're already sorted but so what? Give me some peace so I can download a bomb squad application.'

And then the radio buzzed into life. They both made a grab, but Beth got there first. She listened to the curt instructions on the other end and her face set.

The tossed papers lay ignored on the floor. Josh was already reaching for his jacket. He knew that look. 'What?' he demanded as she finished.

'Trouble,' Beth said, snagging her jacket, as well. 'Mine collapse on Wildfire Island. One smashed leg, needs evac to the orthopods in Cairns. Plane's leaving in ten.'

'Mine collapse?' He was snapping queries as he got organised. 'Just the one injury?'

'He was injured at the start of it. One of the supports collapsed. Fell on this guy's leg but the rest of the idiots didn't see it as a sign they should evacuate. But now...' She took a deep breath. 'The collapse looks serious. We're working on early information but one of the local doctors is trapped, as well.'

One of the local doctors.

Wildfire.

And something inside seemed to freeze.

Beth stopped, too. 'Josh? What is it?'

'You said Wildfire. Part of the M'Langi group?'

'Yeah.'

'That's where Maddie's working.'

'Maddie?' Her eyes widened as she understood. 'Your Maddie?'

'We're not married.' It was a dumb thing to say but it was all he could think of.

'I know that. You haven't been married for years. So how do you know she's there?'

'I sort of...keep tabs. She's working fly in, fly out,

two weeks there, one week on the mainland. Her mum's still in a nursing home in Cairns.'

'Right.' Beth started gathering gear again and he moved into automatic mode and did the same. There was a moment's loaded silence, and then...

'You mean you stalk her?' she demanded, but he knew it was Beth's way of making things light. Making a joke...

'I do not stalk!'

'But you keep tabs.' There was little to add to their bags, only the drugs they kept locked away or refrigerated. 'It sounds creepy.'

'We keep in touch. Sort of. Christmas and birthdays. And I take note of where she's registered to work. In case...' He hesitated. 'Hell, I don't know. In case of nothing.'

Beth's face softened. She clipped her bag closed, then touched his shoulder as she straightened. 'I know,' she said. 'I've been married twice, remember. Once your ex, always your ex. Unless it's nasty there's always a little bit of them under your skin. But, hey, there's a sizeable med centre on Wildfire. The trapped doctor doesn't have to be Maddie.'

'Right.' But suddenly he was staring into middle distance. He knew... Somehow he knew.

'Earth to Josh,' Beth said, not so gently now. 'The plane's waiting. Let's go.'

The crash had come from nowhere. One minute Maddie was working efficiently in the dim light, worried but not terrified.

Now she was terrified.

She needed to block out the dust and dark and fear.

Where was her patient?

She'd lost her torch. She'd fallen, stumbling in terror as the rock wall had crashed around her. She was okay, she decided, pushing her way cautiously to her knees. There was still breathable air if she covered her mouth and breathed through a slit in her fingers. But she couldn't see.

Somewhere in here was a guy with a life-threatening bleed.

Where was the torch?

Phone app. She practically sobbed with relief as she remembered an afternoon a few weeks ago, sitting on the hospital terrace with Wildfire's charge nurse, Hettie, while Caroline had shown them apps they could put on their cell phones.

Most she had no use for, but the torch app had looked useful for things such as checking it was a gecko on her nose and not a spider in the middle of the night. The disadvantages of living in the tropics. But now... Yes! Her phone was in her jacket pocket. She grabbed it and flicked it on.

One push and a surprising amount of light fought through the dust.

She could now see the big torch, lying at her feet. She grabbed it. The switch had flicked off when it had fallen. Not broken. She had light.

Next...

The guy she'd come in for.

She'd met them halfway in. Blood had been streaming from Malu's thigh and he'd been barely conscious.

The miners with him had tied a tourniquet but it wasn't enough.

'He needs more pressure,' she'd snapped. 'Put him down.'

And then she'd felt the rumbles. She'd felt the earth tremble.

'Run!' she'd screamed at the two guys who'd been carrying him, and she still seemed to hear the echoes of that yell.

They'd run.

She hoped they'd made it. Fallen rock was blocking the way she'd come. Please, let them have made it to the other side.

It was no use hoping. First things first. She was raking the rubble-strewn floor with her torch beam, searching for Malu. The combined beam of torch and phone only reached about three feet before the dust killed it.

He must have pulled himself back.

'Malu?'

'H-here.'

A pile of stone lay between them. She was over it in seconds. It hurt, she thought vaguely. She was eight months pregnant. Climbing over loose rock, knocking rock in the process, was maybe not the wisest...

She didn't have time for wise.

He was right by the pile. He was very lucky the rocks hadn't fallen on him.

Define luck, she thought grimly, but at least he was still alive. And still conscious.

Dust and blood. A lot of it.

He had a deep gash on his thigh where his pants were

ripped away. The guys had tried to tie a tourniquet but it had slipped. Blood was oozing…

But not pumping, she thought with relief. If it'd been pumping he'd be dead by now.

She was wearing a light jacket. She hauled it off, bundled it into a tight pad, placed it against the wound and pushed.

Malu screamed.

'I'm so, so sorry,' she told him, but there was no time to do anything about the pain. She had to keep pushing. 'Malu, I have drugs but I need to stop the bleeding before I do anything else. I need to press hard.'

'S-sorry. Just the shock…'

'I should have warned you.'

Go back to basics, she reminded herself, desperately fighting the need to cough, and the need to breathe through the grit. Desperately trying to sound in control. Don't start a procedure before explaining it to the patient, she reminded herself, even if she was trapped in a place that scared her witless.

Malu had relapsed into silence. She knew Malu. He was a large, tough islander from the outermost island of the M'Langi group.

He had a wife and two small children.

She pushed harder.

She had morphine in her bag. If she had another pair of hands…

She didn't.

His pants were ripped. Yes! Still pressing with one hand, she used the other and tugged the jagged cloth. The cloth ripped almost to the ankle.

Now she was fumbling one-handed in her bag for scissors. Thank heaven she was neat. There was so much dust... Despite the torchlight she could hardly see, but the scissors were right where she always stored them.

One snip and she had the tough fabric cut at the cuff, and that gave her a length of fabric to wind. The miners had tried to use a belt as their tourniquet but it was too stiff. The torn trouser leg was a thousand times better.

She twisted and wound, tying the pad—her ex-jacket—into place. She twisted and twisted until Malu cried out again.

'Malu, the worst's over,' she told him as she somehow managed to knot it. 'The bleeding's stopped and my hands are now free. I'll make us masks to make breathing easier. Then I'll organise something to dull the pain.'

And get some fluids into you, she added to herself, saying silent prayers of thanks that she had her bag with her, that she'd had it beside her when the collapse had happened, that she'd picked it up almost automatically and that she hadn't dropped it. She had saline. She could set up a drip. But in this dust, to try and keep things sterile...

Concentrate on keeping Malu alive first, she told herself. After so much blood loss she had to replace fluids. She'd worry about bugs later.

Malu was barely responding. His pulse... *His pulse*... Get the fluids in. Move!

Five minutes later Malu had morphine on board and she had a makeshift drip feeding fluids into his arm. She'd ripped her shirt and created makeshift masks to keep the worst of the dust from their lungs. She sat back and held the saline bag up, and for the first time she thought she might have time to breathe herself.

She still felt like she was choking. Her eyes were filled with grit.

They were both alive.

'Doc?' Malu's voice was a whisper but she was onto it.

'Mmm?'

'Macca and Reuben... They were carrying me.'

'I know.'

'Reuben's my uncle. You reckon they've made it?'

'I don't know.' There was no point lying; Malu would know the risks better than she did. She grasped his hand and held. There was nothing else she could do or say.

The thought of trying to find them, trying to struggle out through the mass of rubble... Even if she could leave Malu, the thing was impossible. The rubble around them was unyielding.

Malu's hand gripped hers, hard. 'Don't even think about trying to dig out,' he muttered, and she thought that even though his words were meant as protection to her, there was more than a hint of fear for himself. To be left alone in the dark... 'It's up to them outside to do the rescuing now. Meanwhile, turn off the lights.'

'Sorry?'

'The lights. We don't need 'em. Conserve...'

'Good thinking,' she said warmly, and flicked off her torch. Then she flicked off the torch app on her phone. But as the beam died, a message appeared on the screen. When had that come in?

She wouldn't have heard.

The message was simple.

Maddie? Tell me you're not down the mine. On way with Cairns Air Sea Rescue. Josh.

Josh.

Josh was coming.

Her phone was working. Help was on its way.

It was amazing that the signal had reached down here, but this was a shallow tunnel, with ventilation shafts rising at regular intervals. The simple knowledge that she had phone reception made her feel better. And Josh was coming... All of a sudden she felt a thousand per cent lighter. She told Malu and felt the faint relaxation of the grip on her hand. Cairns Air Sea Rescue would be the forerunners, she knew. The cavalry was heading this way.

She gripped her phone hard, as if it alone was a link to the outside world. Help. Heavy machinery. Skill, technology, care. All the things needed to get them out of here.

Josh was coming.

It shouldn't make one scrap of difference that Josh would be one of the rescue crew. Their marriage had been over for years. They talked occasionally as casual acquaintances. Friends? Probably not even that.

But still... *Josh was coming.*

'So you still got reception?' Malu whispered, sounding incredulous, and she looked at the one bar out of five signalling a really weak link to the outside world.

'Just.'

'Tell 'em to hurry,' Malu muttered. 'And tell them if there's one single camera at the mine mouth then I need a new pair of trousers before they bring me out.'

She even managed a chuckle. He was so brave.

His pulse was so weak...

'I'll tell them,' she said and ventured a text back.

Yeah, we're underground. There's a bit of rock between us and the entrance. We're not very respectable. If you're coming in we'd appreciate a change of clothes. There's a distinct lack of laundry facilities down here.

She read it to Malu and he managed a chuckle. She should say more, she thought. She should give a complete medical update but for now it was enough that she was breathing and Malu was breathing.

She just had to keep it that way until Josh…

Until the cavalry arrived.

The plane was taxiing out onto the runway. 'Phones off now,' the pilot snapped, and Josh went to flick off his phone—and then paused as a message appeared.

If you're coming in we'd appreciate a change of clothes. There's a distinct lack of laundry facilities down here.

He swore. Then he swore again.

'Josh?' Beth was watching, all concern.

'She's down there,' he said grimly. 'Maddie's trapped.'

'Then all the more reason to turn your phone off so we can take off.' But she took the phone from his hands and stared at the screen, and her face tightened. This team were used to horror, but when it affected one of their own…

'Wait thirty seconds,' she told the pilot, and she started texting.

'What?' He tried to grab his phone back, but she turned her back on him and kept typing. Then the text sent, and she handed it back.

He looked down at what she'd written.

We're on our way. With Josh in the lead. He'll be in there with you, even if he has to dig in with his bare hands.

'Beth…' He could hardly speak.

'Truth?' she queried, and he tried to swallow panic. And failed.

'Truth,' he muttered, and he flicked his phone off and they were on their way.

CHAPTER TWO

WHAT BLESSED FAIRY had made her run into the mine with a fully loaded medical bag?

What bad goblin had made her run in at all?

In the hours that followed, Maddie tried to get a grip on what had happened.

There should have been systems in place to stop her, she decided as the darkness seemed to grow blacker around her. There should also have been barriers to stop the mine's ex-employees gaining access in the first place.

But who was in control? Where was Ian Lockhart? He owned this mine, or at least his brother did. So much on this island was running down. Lockhart money had dried up. There'd even been mutterings that the medical service would have to close.

At least the service had still been operating this morning, she thought, grasping at any ray of light she could find in this nightmare. The good news was that she'd been here. Yes, she'd been dumb enough to run into the mine, but she'd carried three units of saline and she'd only used two on Malu. The bleeding had slowed to nothing and his blood pressure was rising and...

And she was still trapped underground. A long way underground.

Her telephone beeped into life again. Ringing. Not a message.

A real person! But first she frantically sought settings to turn the volume down. The dust was still settling around them, and it seemed to her that any little sound might cause more rock to fall.

Malu was no longer aware. She'd given him more morphine and he'd fallen into an uneasy slumber. The ringtone hadn't woken him.

'H-hi.' It felt eerie to be calmly answering the phone in such conditions. She had to stop and cough. 'H-hold on.'

Let it be Josh.

Why did she think that? Josh was coming from Cairns. He couldn't be here yet. The coughing eased and she managed to focus again.

'Maddie?' The voice at the end of the phone was growing frantic. Not Josh.

She recognised the voice—Keanu, one of the other two island doctors. Sam, the island's chief permanent doctor, had decided to take leave before she had her baby, which meant she and Keanu were currently the only doctors on the island.

'What's happening?' he demanded. 'Are you okay?'

'We seem to be trapped but we're okay.' She glanced down again at Malu. 'You and me both, aren't we, Malu?'

Malu didn't respond but she didn't expect him to. The wound on his thigh was ugly. Without morphine he'd be writhing. She released the pressure from his makeshift mask a little, trying to get a balance between stopping the grit and making it harder for him to breathe.

Oxygen would be good. Why hadn't she lugged in an oxygen cylinder, as well?

She should have brought a wheelbarrow.

'Maddie?'

She jerked herself back to focussing on the call. 'Keanu? Malu has an impact injury, thigh.' She suspected broken ribs, possible internal injuries as well, but it was no use saying that in Malu's hearing. 'I suspect he'll need surgery when we get out of here, evac to Cairns, but I've stopped the bleeding and he's stable. Two litres of saline, five milligrams of intravenous morph…'

'You had that stuff down there?' He sounded incredulous.

'I was a girl scout,' she said dryly. 'I'm prepared.'

There was a moment's silence. Then…

'Are Macca and Reuben with you?'

'They ran when the second collapse came. They're not with us now.'

He must have her on speaker phone. She could hear sobbing in the background. He'd be in the operations room of the mine, she thought. The sobbing would be Macca's and Reuben's families.

Malu's family would be there, too.

No one belonging to her.

But then… Josh was coming. He'd said he would.

Josh wasn't her family, she reminded herself. In truth, he never had been.

'That last rockfall…' She was almost afraid to ask, but she had to. 'Was anyone else hurt?'

'Everyone's clear but you four.'

'Kalifa?'

'Maddie, worry about yourself.'

'Should I worry?'

There was a moment's silence.

'It might take a while to reach you,' Keanu said at last. 'How's the air down there?'

'Dusty.'

'But?'

'But otherwise okay.' She sniffed. 'I can feel a bit of a draught. Do you reckon there might be some sort of escape hatch?'

'It's probably from a ventilation shaft. Thank God that's still working.' He hesitated. 'Maddie, we need to bring experts and machinery from the mainland.'

'The mainland... Cairns.'

'Yep.'

'Is that coming on the mercy flight?'

'How do you know about the mercy flight?'

'Josh told me.'

There was another silence. 'Your Josh,' he said at last.

'He's not my Josh.' And then... 'How do you know he's *my* Josh?'

'Hettie told me. She relayed the message from Cairns Air Sea Rescue. But... You've been talking to him yourself?'

'Yes.'

'Maddie?'

'Mmm?'

'You need to conserve your phone. It's probably not the time for chats with your ex.'

'He texted. I also have three battery backups in my bag. That's enough for two days.'

'That might not be enough.'

'You have to be kidding.'

'I hope I am,' he said. 'But for now…two days or not, conserve your phone.'

Two days or not, conserve your phone.

Maddie sat back on her heels and tried—really hard—not to panic.

Two days?

There'd been an incident, not so long ago, where miners had been trapped…where? Tasmania? The miners had been successfully brought to the surface after how many days? Fourteen? She couldn't remember the details but she remembered watching the rescue unfold on television. She'd been mesmerised by the tragedy of the mine collapse but even more mesmerised by the courage shown by the miners trying to keep their sanity as the appalling endurance test had stretched on.

Neither of them had been badly injured.

Malu was suffering from shock and a deep laceration, she thought, but what else? She wanted X-rays. She wanted him in hospital. She wanted a sterile environment and the necessary surgery for his leg.

She couldn't even see him.

Two days…

The darkness was absolute.

Her fingers were on Malu's wrist. His pulse was settling. There was no need to turn on the torch.

She flicked the torch on anyway, just for a moment. Just to see.

Their chamber was about eight feet in diameter. The roof was still up there, and there were shoring timbers above them. Where their tiny enclosure ended, the shoring timbers had splintered like kindling.

The floor was rock-strewn. She needed to clear it a bit to get Malu more comfortable.

She could do it without the torch. She had to do it without the torch. She flicked it off again and the total darkness was like a physical slap.

Her phone gave a tiny ping and the screen lit momentarily. She took three deep breaths—because she had been close to panic—and she let herself look.

Landed. You nice and safe down there? Got a couple of good rocks you can use for pillows or are you thinking you might like to come on up? Josh.

She could have kissed him. Except she didn't kiss Josh. Not any more. He'd always been uncomfortable with overt displays of affection. Even when they'd been married... Affection had been an effort, she thought, seizing on the excuse to get her mind off the dust. She'd never been in any doubt that he'd wanted her, but affection had been for behind closed doors. It was almost as if he'd been ashamed to admit he'd needed her.

He didn't need her. He'd figured that five years ago when he'd walked away from their marriage. But right now she needed him. She texted him.

I'm not going anywhere. Just trying to decide which rock pillow to use. It seems I have a choice. Have given Malu morphine. He's suffered major blood loss. Have given two litres of saline. I only have one more and want to hold it in reserve.

For drinking? She didn't say it. She couldn't.

Heart rate a hundred and twenty. Only just conscious.
Worrying.

Damn Keanu and his ban on using her phone, she
decided, as she hit Send. Okay, her battery life was
precious, but Josh was a trauma specialist, a good one,
and she needed advice. If she was going to be stuck
down here with Malu, then the least she could do was
keep him alive.

Which meant texting Josh. Didn't it?

She didn't get the little whoosh as her message sent.
She stared at the single flickering bar of reception on
her screen and willed it to send. Send. *Send.*

The screen went blank again and she was left with
darkness.

Whoosh.

Sent. Delivered. At least she hoped it had been delivered. Josh would be on his way from Wildfire's tiny
airstrip, and he had to cross the mountains to get to the
mine. There were places up there where there was no
phone reception at all.

How long before he saw it?

Did it matter? She was pretty sure there was nothing more she could do medically for Malu, except make
him comfortable.

Comfortable? Rock pillows. Ha!

Josh will text when he can, she told herself, and the
thought was comforting.

Why? Why Josh rather than anyone else?

She had lots of friends on Wildfire Island. She'd been
working as a fly in, fly out doctor here for five years

now, spending two weeks here, one week in Cairns. She was doing okay. She'd put her marriage behind her. This next stage of her life... Well, it was a gamble but it was something—someone—she desperately wanted.

Unconsciously her hand went to her belly. She'd been hit as the rocks had flown, but surely she'd protected her baby enough?

Why on earth had she risked her baby? It had been a split-second decision but now...it seemed almost criminally stupid.

'I'm sorry. I'm so sorry,' she whispered to the little one in her belly, and she felt like weeping.

She had to talk to someone.

Maybe she could text Hettie. Hettie, Wildfire's charge nurse administrator, was a real friend, whereas Josh was now merely a contact, someone she'd put to the back of her mind like she'd put old school photos to the back of her wardrobe. One day she'd throw them out.

But not yet, she decided as she told herself she couldn't phone anyone and started groping her way around the floor. She was shoving loose rocks to the side, clearing space so she could make Malu as comfortable as possible.

Photos. The thought was suddenly weirdly front and centre. Pictures of her mother before the stroke. Photographs of her wedding day.

They were all history, she told herself. She should get rid of them all. She touched her belly again, lightly, a touch that, all at once, seemed to be almost a prayer.

'I don't need any of it,' she said out loud, even though speaking was impossibly hard through the dust. 'The past is just that. I have a future now.'

But still…

Text soon, she pleaded silently to her phone. Please, Josh?

And she went on clearing rocks.

A truck met them at the airstrip. A chopper would have been more sensible, Josh thought grimly as they transferred gear from the plane to the truck, but the instructions had been explicit. 'We used to keep a solid clearing around the minehead but there's been cost-cutting,' Hettie had told them. The charge nurse at the hospital had put herself in charge of communication. 'The jungle's come back and even the parking lot got so rutted in the last rain it'd take hours to clear a landing site. We'll get you from the airstrip to the mine by truck.'

If they couldn't land the choppers, the injured would have to be trucked back to the airstrip for evacuation.

The injured…

Maddie?

The thought of where she was made Josh feel sick. He couldn't think of her. He had to concentrate on the job at hand—but it was taking too long to reach her.

To reach it. To reach the mine.

Maddie.

With the gear loaded he jumped into the front passenger seat of the lorry. Another jeep took Beth. They turned off the coast road, skirting the plateau to the other side of the island.

He checked his phone.

Nothing.

'There's no reception, mate,' the lorry driver told him. 'Not with the plateau between us and transmission.'

'Do you know anything more?'

'Not more'n you, probably.' The guy's knuckles were white on the steering wheel, but it wasn't because of hard driving. His face was grim as death. 'We haven't heard from Macca and Reuben. They're mates. We know Malu and Doc Haddon are alive but they're trapped.' The man's knuckles gripped even tighter. 'Bloody Lockhart. Rips all the money from the mine and what does he do with it? He's been told those shoring timbers needed replacing or the mine sealed. And where is he? Not here facing what he's done, that's for sure. It won't be him crawling down the mine trying to get them out.'

'That'll be Max Lockhart?' Josh ventured, trying not to think of anyone crawling down the mine to get... Maddie out. He was dredging up stuff he'd seen in the press about this island group. 'Isn't Max Lockhart the owner of Wildfire?'

'Yeah.' The guy spat out the window of the moving truck. 'But we've hardly seen hide nor hair of Max for years. Ian's his brother. He took over day-to-day running of the mine a few years back. He's supposed to be running the island for his brother, but as far as we can see he's just out for what he can get. He's somewhere overseas now. The mine got dangerous, the money stopped and he left. And now this mess... How the hell are we going to get 'em out?' There was a moment's silence and then he swore with an intensity Josh had never heard before and never wanted to hear again.

'And... Doc Haddon?' Josh ventured, not because he wanted to but because he was almost forced to say it.

The knuckles kept their death grip but the lines on the man's face softened. 'She's a great kid. Well, maybe she's not a kid any more but I'm sixty, mate, so she's a kid to me. She's been on the island for five years now. The wife got shingles last year. Doc saw her in the market, saw the bumps. We'd thought they were just bites but before we knew it Doc had her at the clinic. She gave her this fancy medicine right on the spot. The shingles was bad enough but Ally—that's our daughter—she looked it up on the internet and said if Mum hadn't taken the stuff it could have been ten times worse. And every day Doc found an excuse to pop in. When she was off island she got Caroline or Ana to come instead. You know that nerve pain they get? Real bad, it was, but Doc Maddie was right onto it. She cares for everyone like that.'

And then his face hardened again. 'They say she just ran in. Everyone else was running out and someone shouted that Malu was bleeding so hard the guys carrying him had to stop. She grabbed her bag and ran. She's a hero.'

And his voice cracked with emotion as he swiped his arm across his face and sniffed.

Josh's phone pinged. He glanced down, trying not to hope, but the word on his screen read *Maddie*.

He couldn't read the message. For some dumb reason his eyes were blurry, too. He had to do a matching swipe before he could make it out.

I'm not going anywhere. Just trying to decide which rock pillow to use. It seems I have a choice. Have given Malu morphine. He's suffered major blood loss. Have given two litres of saline. I only have one more and want to hold it in reserve. Heart rate a hundred and twenty. Only just conscious. Worrying.

How long since that'd been sent? While he was in the air? He swiped his face again and turned into doctor. Texted back, hoping whatever sliver of reception he had would last.

You're doing great. Heart rate will be high considering shock. Do what you can to keep him warm, cuddle him if you need to. If it's his thigh, see if you can get him sloped so his legs are higher than his heart. But you know this, Maddie. Trust your instincts. Love you.

And then he paused.

How many times in the past had he texted his wife and finished with the words *Love you*?

'You've never really loved me.' He remembered Maddie saying it to him in those last dreadful days when he'd known their marriage was over. 'Love shares, Josh. Love gives and takes and you don't know how.'

Love you?

She was right, of course. He hadn't loved her. Or not enough.

He stared at the screen for a moment and then he deleted some characters. Then hit Send. Without the love.

'I can't imagine what the wives are going through,' the truck driver said, almost to himself. 'And Pearl... Malu's wife... She's another who thinks the sun rises and sets with Maddie. Y'know, our local mums are supposed to go to Cairns six weeks before bubs are born but the docs can't make 'em so Pearl didn't. Maddie had to be choppered out to Atangi in the middle of the night. Breech it was, and Doc Maddie did an emergency Caesarean, right there in Pearl's kitchen. Pearl won't go to any other doctor since. And now Doc's trapped with Malu. Doesn't bear thinking of.'

Josh tried to think of something to say—and couldn't. He didn't trust his own voice.

'Married yourself, are you?' the guy asked at last. They were heading downhill now, through dense tropical rainforest, presumably towards the coast. Josh was trying to consider the terrain, thinking of what he already knew: that the rainforest had reclaimed most of the cleared land round the minehead, and how hard it was going to be to get machinery in.

He wanted to worry about machinery. About technicalities. He wanted to worry about anything but Maddie.

Married yourself? The guy's question still hung.

'No,' he said at last. 'Not now.'

He didn't deserve to be married. He hadn't protected...

He'd failed.

Born to useless, drug-addicted parents, Josh had been the protector since he could first remember. The strong one.

He remembered a social worker, one of the early ones, walking into their house to find Holly curled on the bed and whimpering. There hadn't been food in the house for days.

He'd been eight and Holly five. Josh had been big for his age, confused, helpless, as hungry as his little sister, but he hadn't been whimpering. He'd learned early not to cry.

And the woman had turned on him, shocked into an automatic attack. 'Why didn't you come for help?' she'd demanded. 'You're big enough now to protect your sister. Why didn't you at least tell a neighbour?'

He'd never made that mistake again. He'd protected and protected and protected—but it hadn't worked. He remembered the helplessness of being torn apart from Holly, placed in separate foster homes. The nightmares.

He'd learned to disguise even those. His job was to protect, not to share his pain. Not to add to that hurt.

And now? Once again Maddie was hurting and he was stuck on the far side of a mountain.

'Partner?' Maybe the guy was trying to distract himself. Surely he was. They were his friends underground.

And that was what Maddie was, he told himself. His friend. Nothing more.

'I guess… A girlfriend,' he told the guy and tried to think of Karen. They'd only been dating for three months but that was practically long-term for Josh. Karen was fun and flirty and out for a good time. She didn't mind that his job took him away so much. She used him as he used her—as an appendage for weddings and the like, and someone to have fun with when it suited them both.

Maybe she wasn't even a girlfriend, Josh thought. But that didn't matter.

Whereas Maddie…

'Here we are,' the truck driver said, turning off the main road—if you could call it a main road—into a fenced-off area. The main gates were wide open. The sign on the fence said Mining Area—Keep Out, but there was no trace of security.

There were a few dilapidated buildings nestled among the trees. Only the cluster of parked vehicles, an ancient fire truck, a police motorbike and a jeep with the Wildfire Medical insignia, told him that anything was wrong.

'Best place for the chopper's round the back,' the truck driver told him. 'The guys were starting to clear it when we left.' He pulled to a halt outside the first of the buildings and turned and clamped a hand on Josh's shoulder. 'Good luck, mate,' he told him. 'Thanks for coming. We sure need you.'

Josh climbed out of the truck and as he did his phone pinged. Maddie again.

We're warm enough. Could use a bit of air-conditioning. Do you think you could arrange it? Also a couple of fluffy pillows, two mattresses and Malu reckons he could handle a beer. I could handle a gin and tonic, though I suppose I'm stuck with a lemonade. Actually lemonade sounds brilliant. I'm happy to make do. That's my 'needs' list, Dr Campbell. Could you get onto it, stat?

A pillow would be nice. A pillow would be magnificent. Instead, Maddie lay on her back, with her hands behind her head, trying not to think how hard the rock was. And how much of a dead weight Malu's legs were.

See if you can get him sloped so his legs are higher than his heart.

That was easier said than done. She could have put rocks under his thighs—yeah, that'd be comfy. Instead, she'd emptied her soft leather medical bag and given that to him as a pillow. She'd given him a couple of sips of the water—not as much as he wanted but she was starting to figure that if Keanu said two days then she might need to ration. Then, out of options, she'd lain down and lifted his legs onto hers.

It helped. She had her hand on his wrist and she could feel the difference.

He'd objected but not very much. In truth, he was drifting in and out of consciousness. He could hardly assess what she was doing.

She wouldn't mind a bit of unconsciousness herself. She ached where she'd been hit by flying debris. She had a scratch on her head. Blood had trickled down and it was sticky. And grimy.

She'd kill for a wash.

Her back hurt.

Cramps?

That was her imagination, she told herself fiercely. It had to be.

Lie still and think of England.

Think of Josh? He's out there.

Josh. Her husband.

He was no such thing, she told herself, but for now, in the dust and grit, she allowed herself to think it. She'd married him. She'd made vows and she'd meant them.

When she'd signed the divorce papers it'd broken her heart.

'Josh…' She couldn't help herself. She said his name aloud, like it was some sort of talisman. She didn't need him, or at least she hadn't needed him until now. Josh hated to be needed.

But that wasn't true, she conceded. He loved to be physically needed, like he was needed now, flying off to the world's emergencies, doctor in crisis, doing what he could to help in the worst possible situations. But when she'd needed to share emotional pain?

That's when he'd been…divorced.

'Who's Josh?'

Malu asked his question sleepily. He stirred, winced, swore then settled again. His legs were so heavy. She couldn't do this for much longer, she decided, but she'd cope as long as she could.

'Josh is my ex-husband,' she said, more to distract herself than anything else. Doctors didn't reveal their personal lives to their patients, yet down here the lines between professional and personal were blurred. Two days? Please not.

'He's a trauma specialist with Cairns Air Sea Rescue,' she said, and the words seemed a comfort all by themselves. 'He's texted. He's on his way.

'Because of you?' Malu's words were slurred, but strong enough to reassure her.

'It's his job.'

'So not because of you.'

'We've been divorced for five years.'

'Yeah?' Malu must be using this as a means to distract himself from the pain, from the fear, from the difficulty breathing, she decided. It was so hard to talk through the dust.

She couldn't tell him to hush and conserve his energy. Maybe she needed distraction, too.

'So he's not the dad?' Malu asked.

'No.' She wasn't going there and it seemed Malu sensed it.

'I can't imagine being divorced from my Pearl,' Malu managed, moving on. 'So…five years ago? What happened? Wrong guy in the first place? He play fast and loose?'

'I guess…first option. He was always the wrong guy.' She thought about it for a bit and then suddenly she found herself talking. Talking about Josh. Talking, as she'd never spoken of it to anyone.

'Josh had it tough,' she said, softly into the dark. 'He had a younger sister, Holly. His parents were worse than useless and that the two of them survived at all was a miracle. They were abandoned as kids and went from foster home to foster home. Sometimes they were separated but Josh fought battle after battle to keep them together. To keep his sister safe. Their only constant was each other.'

'B-bummer...'

'Yeah,' she said softly. 'It was a bummer. But Josh was tough. He got a scholarship and made it into medicine, then worked his way through university, supporting Holly while he did it.'

'Where'd you meet him?'

'Just after I finished university. I was a first-year intern. We became friends and...well, one thing led to another.'

'To marriage.'

'That's right,' she whispered, thinking back to the precious months before that nightmare time. Lying in the dark, holding Josh. Feeling him hold her. Feeling his love unfold, feeling that they might have a chance.

'B-but?' He coughed and coughed again and then moaned, and she did a recalculation of morphine dosages and figured she could give him more in half an hour. She daren't give it sooner. She couldn't drug him too deeply, not with this amount of dust in the air.

So distract him. Tell him...the truth?

'I'm still not sure the reasons for marriage were solid,' she told him. 'My mum...well, maybe you already know? I told Pearl about her when she asked why I don't stay on Wildfire all the time. My dad took off when I was six. I'm an only child. We were incredibly close—and then she had a stroke. Major. She's unable to do anything for herself. She's permanently damaged. Anyway, as I said, Josh was my colleague and my friend, and when the stroke happened he was amazing. He cared for me when I was gutted. He cared for Mum—in fact, I think sometimes he still visits her. He did…everything right. And I thought…well, I fell so deeply in love I found myself pregnant.'

'Hey, that happens,' Malu whispered. 'Like me 'n Pearl. Never a better thing, though. So, your Josh. He was happy about it?'

'I'm not sure,' she whispered. 'He told me he was. But there's one thing Josh is good at, and that's hiding his emotions. All I knew was that he seemed happy about the baby, and he said he loved me. So we married. He still felt a bit…distant but I thought…maybe…'

'So what happened to the baby? What broke you up?'

'Knowledge,' she said bleakly. 'Learning Josh knows how to care, but not to share. Do you really want to listen to this?'

'Pearl says I'm a gossip,' Malu whispered, and grabbed her hand and held on. A link in the darkness. 'Tell me.' And then, as she hesitated, his grip tightened. 'I know it's not my business, but honest, Maddie, I'm scared. You could tell me it's all going to be fine but we both know that's not true. Distract me. Anything that's said in the mine stays in the mine.'

She almost smiled. 'That seems a really good arm twist to give you more gossip.'

She sensed a half smile in return. She was friends with his wife, but she barely knew Malu. Though maybe that was no longer true, she decided. There was nothing like hurling you down a mine and locking you in, with the threat of rockfalls real and constant, to make you know someone really fast.

And what harm to talk about Josh now? she asked herself. Somewhere he was out there, worrying. Caring. Caring was what he was good at, she thought.

Caring wasn't enough.

Tell Malu? She might as well. He needed distraction and she...well, so did she.

'They say troubles come in threes,' she said finally into the dark. 'So did ours. Mum had her stroke. We got married, which was the good bit, but there were two more tragedies waiting in the wings. We lost the baby—Mikey was born prematurely—and then Josh's little sister died.'

'Oh, Maddie.' What sort of doctor–patient relationship was this? she asked herself. It was Malu doing the comforting.

As Josh had comforted.

'You know, if it had been my sister and only my baby, like it was my mum, I'm guessing Josh would have coped brilliantly,' she said, and now she was almost speaking to herself. Sorting it out in her mind. 'But it was Josh's pain and he didn't know how to cope with it. It left him gutted and his reaction was to stonewall himself. He just emotionally disappeared.'

'How can you do that?'

'Normal people can't,' Maddie said slowly. 'But Josh had one hell of a childhood. He never talks about it but when I met him his sister was doing brilliantly, at uni herself, happy and bubbly. She told me how bad it had been but Josh never did. He used to have nightmares but when I woke him he'd never tell me what they were about. Sometimes I'd wake and hear him pacing in the night and I knew there were demons. And then came baby Mikey, too small to live. And Holly. One drunk driver, a car mounting the footpath. So after all that, Josh's care came to nothing and he went so far into himself I couldn't reach him. He finally explained to me, quite calmly, that he couldn't handle himself. He didn't know how to be a husband to me any more. He had to leave.'

She shook her head, trying to shake off the memory of the night Josh had finally declared their marriage was over.

There was a long silence, for which she was grateful. And then she thought…

These *are* cramps. Stomach cramps.

Back cramps?

And that thought brought a stab of fear so deep it terrified her.

She was lying on a rock floor, supporting Malu's legs. Of course she had cramps.

Of course?

Please…

'I can top up the morphine now if you like,' she managed at last, and at least this was an excuse to turn on the torch. She needed the phone app torch, too, to clean the dust away and inject the morphine. She held the phone for a bit too long after.

The light was a comfort.

The phone would be better.

No word. No texting.

Cramps.

Josh…

Malu's grip on her hand gradually lessened. She thought he was drifting into sleep, but maybe the rocks were too hard. The morphine didn't cut it.

'So your Josh abandoned you and joined Cairns Air Sea Rescue?' he whispered at last.

Oh, her back hurt. She wouldn't mind some of that morphine herself...

Talk, she told herself. Don't think of anything but distracting Malu.

'I think that other people's trauma, other people's pain, are things he can deal with,' she managed, struggling to find the right words. Struggling to find the right answer. 'But losing our baby... It hurt him to look at me hurting, and when Holly died, he didn't know where to put himself. He couldn't comfort me and he thought showing me his pain would make mine worse. He couldn't help me, so he left.'

'Oh, girl...'

'I'm fine,' she whispered, and Malu coughed again and then gripped tighter.

'I dunno much,' he wheezed. 'But I do know I'm very sure you're not.'

'Not what?'

'Fine. You're hurting and it's not just the memory of some low-life husband walking out on you.'

'I'm okay.'

'I can tell pain when I hear it.'

'I got hit by a few rocks. We both have bruises all over.'

'There's room on my pillow to share.'

'It's not exactly professional—to share my patient's bed.'

'I'm just sharing the pillow,' Malu told her with an

attempt at laughter. 'You have to provide your own rock base.'

She tried to smile. Her phone pinged and she'd never read a text message faster.

Hey, you. Quick update? Tell us you're okay. Josh.

'Is that telling us the bulldozers are coming?' Malu demanded, and the threadiness of his voice had her switching on the torch again. 'Hey, it's okay,' he managed. 'You tell them…tell them to tell Pearl I'm okay. But I wouldn't mind a bulldozer.'

'I wouldn't mind a piece of foam,' she told him, and tried to think of what to say to Josh. Apart from the fact that she was scared. No, make that terrified. She hated the dark and she was starting to panic and the dust in her lungs made it hard to breathe and the cramps…

Get a grip. Hysterics were no use to anyone.

She shouldn't have come in in the first place, she told herself.

Yeah, and then Malu would be dead.

Josh wanted facts. He couldn't cope with emotion.

Yeah, Josh, we're fine.

CHAPTER THREE

JOSH WASN'T ON Wildfire to dig into a mine and pull people out. Not even Maddie. Josh was there to assess medical need, perform triage, arrange evacuation where possible and then get his hands dirty dealing with injuries needing on-the-ground treatment.

And there was a need. The locals were doing all they could, but the medical team here consisted of one doctor and two nurses. It had apparently taken the doctor—an islander called Keanu—time to get there, and the guy who had been injured first was taking up his attention. A fractured leg followed by a cardiac arrest left room for little else.

But there was more medical need. Apparently, before Keanu had arrived, the miners had fought their way back into mine, frantically trying to reach their injured mates. It hadn't worked. There'd been a further cave-in. Further casualties. Keanu barely had time to acknowledge Josh and Beth's arrival.

There was still a sense of chaos. Keanu had ordered everyone back from the mine mouth but no one seemed to be in charge of rescue efforts.

'Where's the mine manager?' Josh snapped as he surveyed the scene before him. A group of filthy miners were huddled at the mouth of the mine, with pretty much matching expressions of shock and loss. Keanu had organised the casualties a little way away, under the shade of palm trees. He and the nurses were working frantically over the guy with the injured leg, but he shook his head as Josh approached.

'We have everything we need here. It's touch and go for this guy and there's others needing help. The guy with the arm first.' He motioned across to where a miner was on the ground, his mate beside him.

'No breathing problems?'

'They've all had a lungful of rock—we could use a tank of oxygen—but...'

'I'll get Beth to do a respiratory assessment. Beth?'

'Onto it.' She was already heading for the truck, for oxygen canisters. 'Okay, guys,' she called. 'Anyone want a face wipe and a whiff of something that'll do you good? Line up here.'

'What's happening down the mine?' Josh asked.

'Hettie's called the mining authorities in Cairns. We need expertise. They're sending engineers and equipment now.'

From Cairns. It'd take hours.

Maddie was down there.

Keanu was adjusting a drip, watching the guy's breathing like an eagle watched a mouse. A tiny thing, the rise and fall of a chest, but so important. 'So you're the ex-husband,' he managed.

'Yeah.'

'Yeah, well, we all love Maddie, but she's in there now and it's up to the experts to get her out. Meanwhile, sorry, mate, but there's more work here than we can handle. We're still trying to stabilise. We have a suspected ruptured spleen, a guy with an arm so crushed he might lose it, a fractured leg with shock and breathing problems and more. Could you look at the spleen for me?'

And somehow Josh had to stop thinking of Maddie underground, Maddie trapped, Maddie deep in a mine where there'd already been two major rockfalls. He needed to focus on the here and now.

Triage...

He headed across to the guy with the suspected ruptured spleen. As long as he wasn't going into shock—which he could be if the rupture was significant—then the arm was the first priority. If he could save it.

Four underground. Including Maddie.

'Who's the mine manager?' he snapped, asking it not of Keanu, who was committed to the patient under his hands, but of the miners in general.

'Ian Lockhart,' one of the men ventured. 'At least, he's supposed to be in charge but he lit out when the debt collectors started sniffing around.'

'Was he in charge of day-to-day running of the mine?'

'That used to be Pete Blake. Max Lockhart owns the island but he's never here. He put Pete in charge but Ian reckoned he knew it all. He sacked Pete last year and took over the day-to-day stuff himself. Reuben Alaki's acting supervisor now but...' He hesitated and his voice cracked. 'Reuben's one of the guys stuck down there.'

'Is Pete still on the island?'

'He'll probably be out fishing.'

'Get him,' Josh snapped. 'Use one of the island choppers to bring him here—do an air drop.'

'What, pluck him off his boat and drop him here?'

'Exactly,' Josh snapped. 'We need expertise now.' He bent over the guy with the fractured arm. Compound. Messy. 'Okay, mate, let's get you assessed and see if we can do something for the pain. Meanwhile let's get things moving to get your mates out from underground.'

And then a nose wedged its way under his arm and he almost froze with shock. It was a great, bounding golden retriever.

Bugsy.

It was so long since he'd seen the dog it was all he could do not to shed a few tears into his shaggy coat. The big dog recognised him. That was amazing all by itself.

He'd given Bugsy to Maddie after their honeymoon, just before he'd gone back to work. His job was search and rescue. He spent days at a time in remote places, coping with emergencies like this one.

He'd been aware just how alone Maddie had been— that was one of the reasons he'd married her. Puppy Bugsy had been a great idea. He'd been their one constant when things had fallen apart, but when things had really fallen apart it had been logical that Maddie take him.

That he was here… On the island…

He couldn't focus on the dog, though. The fracture was severe. On first assessment he thought enough blood was getting through to keep the hand viable, but suddenly…it wasn't.

And behind him Keanu had the CPR unit set up on the guy with the fractured leg.

'Go find Maddie,' he said to Bugsy, pushing the great head away with a wrench that almost physically hurt. 'I can't go to her but maybe… Go fetch Maddie. Go!'

* * *

The cramping was hurting. Really hurting.

It's only my back, she told herself. It has to be only my back. I must have wrenched it when I fell.

The cramps were fifteen minutes apart...

Or more like ten.

Uh-oh.

'Josh, I need you here.'

Keanu wouldn't be calling if the need wasn't beyond urgent. He elevated the arm he'd been treating and called for Beth to hold it steady, as straight as possible. Please, let enough blood get through to keep it viable until he got back. The man needed two of him.

At least it stopped him thinking about Maddie.

'So tell me how you met Pearl?'

Malu might be her patient, Maddie thought, but the distinction between doctor and patient was getting blurred. The blackness was closing in, and her only link to reality seemed to be Malu's hand. But it was she who was doing the comforting, she told herself. Of course it was.

She'd asked the question to distract him from pain and fear. And she needed him to answer, because she needed to be distracted from pain and fear right back.

So she listened as, in a faltering voice that sometimes paused for long enough to make her worry, Malu told of growing up on the island, of diving, of fishing, of learning to show off to the girls.

Of being in sixth grade and kicking a ball between the desks with his mates. Of being punished by being made to sit next to a girl.

Of watching Pearl write a story about watching the boys dive, then listening to the teacher praise it and saying, 'You boys might dive any time you can, but by writing it down, Pearl keeps it forever.'

Of deciding right there and then that she was his woman.

Of it taking ten years before she finally agreed.

Then babies. Domestic drama. Love…

Maddie was blinking as Malu's voice finally trailed off and she realised he'd drifted into sleep.

Love, she thought. You didn't realise how rare it was until you lost it.

She'd lost her baby. Born so prematurely… Mikey. He'd lived for two hours.

And she'd lost Josh.

Actually, she hadn't lost him, she told herself harshly. She'd never had him. And now she had a baby to love on her own.

She'd brought her baby into a collapsed mine. How could she have done something so stupid? Even to save Malu… To risk her baby…

Josh was out there, she told herself, and, as if on cue, her phone rang.

It rang, didn't ping for an incoming message, and when she answered, miraculously it was Josh!

'Hi!'

Do not cry, she told herself. *You will not.*

'Maddie?'

She took a couple of deep breaths—or as deep as she could manage—and tried to talk.

'J-Josh.'

'Hey…'

'No. Sorry. I'm scaring you.' She was fighting to

get a grip, immensely grateful that Malu was sleeping. 'There's nothing to scare you for. Malu's settling. His blood pressure's rising. I think we can manage without the third bag of saline.' No need to mention why she wanted to hold it in reserve. 'Raising his legs seems to have helped. I've given him an additional five milligrams of morphine. He's... We're as good as we can be.' And then she cracked, just a little. 'Any idea when we might expect help?'

'We're working on it. Pete Blake's just been choppered in. He was out on the reef, fishing. He knows the old seams backwards.'

'P-Pete's good.' He was, too. She—and the rest of the islanders—had been appalled when he'd been sacked. 'But...'

'But he can't get you out on his own,' Josh told her. 'There needs to be careful appraisal before we do anything. I think you need to face staying where you are overnight.'

Overnight. Right. At least that was better than Keanu's two days.

'How will we know it's bedtime?' she managed, striving for lightness.

'The time will be on your phone, Maddie, but I'll ring you and tell you anyway. If you like, I'll even sing you a lullaby.'

'You!'

'My voice is improving with age,' he said, sounding wounded. 'You want to hear?'

'No!'

'No taste,' he said mournfully. 'I don't know why I married you.'

'I don't know, either,' she said, and suddenly it was

serious again. The past was flooding back—but also the present. 'Josh?'

'Mmm?'

'What's happening out there?'

'We've just saved a hand.'

She drew in her breath. 'Whose?'

'Max Stubbs.'

'Oh!' She thought back, remembering the stream of miners emerging from the mine mouth. Max had been there, staggering but on his feet. 'His blood supply was compromised? I missed it.'

'You're going to blame yourself?'

'If I'd stayed on top...'

'You made a call. Malu's need was greater.'

'I didn't even assess...'

'It wasn't compromised when you saw it. It was an unstable fracture and it moved. It's okay. We got it in time.'

She hesitated but she really wanted to know. 'What else did I miss?'

'Nothing.'

'Then why the sag in your voice? What aren't you telling me?' She knew this guy. He hid his emotions, but not well enough. Maybe that was why he'd had to walk away from her; because somehow she'd seen behind the wall.

'Maddie...'

'If you don't tell me I'll assume there's some sort of gas leak and it's on its way in here now, creeping in, inch by inch, ready to swallow—'

'Maddie!'

'So tell me!'

He hesitated again, but finally conceded. 'We lost a patient. The first guy out.'

'Kalifa?' She was incredulous. 'He had a broken leg.'

'Cardiac arrest. Sixty-seven years old. Overweight. He should never have been down the mine in the first place.'

'None of them should,' she said bitterly. 'But Kalifa… His heart… Oh, no. I should have—'

'Cut yourself some slack,' he said curtly. 'You were one doctor in the middle of a disaster. You did what you could. There were a couple more injuries from guys trying to be heroes after you disappeared but we're thinking they'll be fine. How's the battery on the phone?'

Her battery was okay. It had to be. This link to Josh seemed the only thing keeping her same. 'I have backup but I'll be careful. Josh?'

'Mmm?'

'You need to go back to work.'

'I do. We're stabilising, then we'll get everyone we can to the hospital here or out to Cairns. But I'll be staying at the mine mouth.'

Why did that make her feel a thousand times better? Why did his voice make something inside her settle, something that had been unsettled for years?

'Bugsy's been here,' he said tangentially. 'I saw him when I first got here. How come you get to keep him on the island when you're fly in, fly out?'

'He's become our hospital dog. Everyone loves him, but officially Hettie looks after him when I'm in Cairns. Hettie's our nurse administrator. She's tough on the outside, marshmallow on the inside.'

'Like me,' Josh said, and she heard his smile and why it made her want to weep again she didn't know.

Still that strange feeling. But she was over Josh, she told herself. She had to be.

'You're okay?' he demanded, and she struggled to make herself sound okay. The cramps… The pain in her back… But what was the point of worrying him? It wasn't like he could wave a magic wand and get her out of here.

'I'm fine.'

'You don't sound fine.'

'Okay, I'm sure my lipstick's smudged but I can't find a mirror.'

She heard him chuckle, but she knew the chuckle was forced. 'I'll ring you again in an hour, if Keanu's not watching,' he promised, and she managed to smile, and managed to tell herself the cramps weren't bad and she wasn't going to cry and she didn't need Josh here, now, holding her.

'And if he is?' she managed.

'I'll ring you anyway. I promise.'

She was trying not to think of Josh. She was also trying not to think of contra—of cramps. If she lay very still the cramps weren't so bad.

If only they weren't so regular.

They were every ten minutes or so, sweeping through her entire body. She had to fight not to gasp. Not to cry out.

If I lie very still…

She lay very still.

She lay in the dark and stared at nothing and her hands cradled the swell of her belly.

'I'm so sorry,' she whispered. 'I should have thought of you first.'

'Maddie…'

'Mmm?' Malu was stirring.

'Time for another of those wee jabs?'

'Pain scale, one to ten?' she asked, and he thought about it.

'Eight,' he said at last. 'And you?'

'I'm not—'

'Lying? I'm damned sure you are. You want to take your legs out from under mine?'

'No, I—'

'Or I'll shift 'em myself.'

'Malu…'

'There's two of us in this mess,' he said morosely. 'We keep things fair.' And then he hesitated. 'Though that's not true, is it? There's three.'

'Don't…'

'You are hurting. I can hear it in your breathing.'

'I told you, I got bumped.'

'How many weeks are you?'

'I… Thirty-four.' She was lying. Stupid, stupid, stupid. She'd gambled and she'd lost, big time.

Not catastrophically, though, she pleaded. Please…

'Maddie!'

'It's okay,' she managed. 'We just need to be patient. You want another sip of water?'

'Yeah.' But there was a world of meaning in that word. A sip… What they both wanted was a river. Or six.

'Pearl says you don't know who the daddy is.'

'Leave it, Malu.'

'You don't want to talk about it?'

'I don't want to think about it.' She'd just got through another cramp and her fear was building by the minute. 'I don't want to think about it at all.'

* * *

'No one's going near the mine until the engineers arrive from Cairns.' Pete, the sacked mine manager, had been lowered by chopper. He was still in his fishing gear and smelled of bait, but he was competent and authoritative. He was also adamant. 'The seam they're in…well, suicidal's not the word for it. Even Lockhart… He was greedy for every ounce of gold the mine'd give him. He knew it was a rich seam but the ground's unstable granite. Burrowing into it's like burrowing into rocky sand. It's a miracle the shoring timbers have stayed up as long as they have.'

'But we have two alive and two don't-knows in there,' Josh said bleakly. 'How—?'

'We worry about getting them out when the engineers arrive.' Pete was standing in front of the mine entrance and his body language said that anyone who wanted to go in there had to go through him. Which would maybe take a bulldozer. 'But initially we can check the ventilation shafts. There's a possibility we might be able to get lines through, enough to check air supply and to get them water.'

While they waited for rescue that might never happen? That might be too dangerous to even consider? The words were left unsaid but they didn't have to be said. They were so loud in Josh's head that everything else seemed muted.

The initial rush of trauma-related work had abated. The guys with the fractured arm and the suspected ruptured spleen were on their way to the airstrip, and then to Cairns. A doctor who'd been conducting research out on Atangi had been on the fishing boat with Pete. He'd agreed to fly back to Cairns as acting medical officer.

That was Josh's job, but Josh wasn't moving. Instead, he was pacing, like a trapped, caged animal with nowhere to go.

There was nothing to do.

Engineers were due to arrive at any minute. They had another couple of hours of daylight.

How much air was down the mine? How to get fluids down?

And then there was a shout.

'Hey, someone's down there. Someone's coming up.'

There was a surge towards the mine entrance but Pete was still in blocking mode. He spread his arms so no one could get past him—and then Pete saw who it was and forgot about security, making a surge himself.

And two minutes later he was helping Macca support Reuben for the last few yards. As the dust cleared, and the surge of miners parted, Josh got a clear view. Two miners, both islanders. An older man, in his fifties, staggering, dragging a leg behind him. A younger guy, tall, filthy, supporting his mate.

The younger guy's hand holding... Bugsy. Maddie's dog. Though it was kind of hard to tell—the usually gold of the retriever's coat was now matted black.

The big dog was wagging his tail, but even as Josh watched him he tugged sideways, looking back at the mine entrance.

'Hold, Bugsy,' he snapped. He was fifty yards away and he could see exactly what the dog intended to do.

And Pete was quick. He snagged the dog's collar and handed him over to the nearest miner before helping lower the injured guy to the ground. 'Doc...'

All Josh wanted to do was go to Bugsy, figure out how he'd done what he'd done and, more importantly, figure out if he could do more, but his attention had to be on the men.

Caroline, one of the island nurses, was with him, and judging by the fleeting embrace he'd witnessed between them, she was involved with Keanu. She had scissors out already, even as Pete was lowering Reuben to the ground.

Please, let him not need me.

It was silent prayer as he started work. Another compromised blood supply or similar would take all his attention.

But this leg was good. This leg was great.

Or…actually not. It'd hurt like the devil for a week or more but it wasn't broken. It needed careful cleaning, debridement, but it wasn't urgent.

The urgent stuff had been dealt with. And Keanu was here.

'You'll be okay,' he told Rueben. He glanced at Caroline, then at Bugsy, then back to Reuben again. 'We'll give you something for the pain and get you to the hospital but this looks like bruising and lacerations, not a break.'

And then he looked at Bugsy again.

'Do you think Bugsy could find Maddie?' Caroline whispered. He and Caroline were still kneeling over Reuben, but Caroline was following his gaze. 'He's Maddie's dog…'

He wasn't the only one thinking it, then. He glanced at Caroline and saw her fear.

'You're her friend?'

'Yes, not only am I her friend but I'm a Lockhart. My uncle was supposed to be taking care of this mine and these workers. He clearly failed at that. He's gone and now Maddie's in danger. This is partly my fault. I ordered the closure of the mine but I should have seen that the workers would be in desperate need. I just can't believe that Maddie went in there...'

She looked sick. This was bad for the outside rescue workers, he thought. How much worse would it be for those who'd lived and worked every day with those trapped underground?

And as if on cue, Caroline's phone rang. She flicked it open.

'Maddie. Oh, my God, Maddie, are you okay?' She cast Josh an uncertain look and then flipped the switch to speaker so he could hear. But all he heard was silence.

'Maddie, you've rung the duty phone,' Caroline said urgently into the silence. 'This is Caro.'

'I wanted...' Maddie's voice faltered. 'Caro, I wanted Hettie. I forgot you'd have the phone. Can I...? I need...' Her voice broke on a gasp.

It was too much for Josh. He took the phone from Caroline's hand and spoke.

'Maddie, what's wrong? We can get Hettie to ring you but it might take a few minutes. You sound distressed. Can you tell us what's happening?'

There was another gasp from the end of the line. Pain. Maddie was hurting, he thought. Worse. Maddie was terrified.

'Maddie...'

'I need Hettie,' she whispered. 'I need...'

'Hettie's doing the communication for transport. She's based at the hospital. We'll have her ring you as soon as we can, but you need to tell us why you're hurting.'

Silence seemed to stretch forever, or maybe it was

the fact that Josh wasn't breathing. The whole world seemed to be still. And finally Maddie answered.

'Hettie's the island midwife,' she whispered. 'I need… I need someone to talk me through this. My baby's coming. I think I'm in established labour.'

There were noises around them. Keanu was giving orders in the background. A truck was backing up, ready to transport patients. Beth was talking to someone on the phone.

All Josh could hear was white noise.

Established labour.

There was more silence. He could hear Maddie gasping through the phone. Breathing through a contraction? He knew she couldn't talk.

'How pregnant?' he demanded of Caroline, and it physically hurt to say the words. It physically hurt to wait for the answer.

'She says thirty-four weeks,' Caroline whispered, sounding terrified herself. 'But I suspect… She needs the money to support her mother in that gorgeous nursing home. I know she wants to work for as long as possible. She's due to finish here at the end of this week but I looked at her yesterday and thought the baby's dropped. There's a chance she's a couple of weeks further on.'

Thirty-four weeks. Maybe thirty-six.

Who's the father? But he didn't say it. He hardly even thought it.

Maddie. Underground. In labour.

Thirty-four weeks. A premature baby?

'Maddie,' he said, more urgently, but there was still no answer.

He thought suddenly, searingly, of Maddie five years

ago. Maddie lying in the labour ward, holding her tiny son. Mikey had been born impossibly early, never viable from the moment they'd recognised placental insufficiency. But the grief...

Maddie had held their son—*their son*.

He'd walked away. He'd been unable to share his grief and he hadn't been able to help her.

'Maddie?' And this time she answered.

'Y-yes?'

'How far apart are the contractions?' Somehow he kept his voice calm. He was desperately trying to sound like a doctor, when all he wanted to do was to drop the phone and start heaving rocks from the collapsed shaft.

'T-ten minutes. Maybe a bit less.'

'Thirty-four or thirty-six weeks, Maddie? Honest.'

'Thirty-six.'

He breathed out a little at that. It made a difference. For a prem baby, underground, with no medical technology at all, two weeks could make all the difference in the world.

'Malu,' he managed. 'The guy down there with you. Is he your partner?'

There was an audible gasp, and then, unbelievably, he heard the trace of a smile in her voice. 'No. Malu's married to my friend. He has two kids.'

'Can he help you?'

'No.' The sliver of humour disappeared as fast as it had come. 'I need... I need to talk to Hettie. She'll talk me through—'

'I'll put you back to Caroline,' he said in a voice he knew sounded strangled. 'She'll try and organise a line to Hettie. Hold on, love, and—'

'I'm not your love.' It was said with asperity.

'No.' He took a deep breath and somehow steadied himself. Asperity was good, he thought. Asperity meant she still had spirit, strength, the grit he knew and loved. 'The important thing is not to panic,' he told her, but he was all for panicking himself. There wasn't a shred of him that wasn't panicking. 'Hold on, Maddie. We need to do some fast organising.'

He handed the phone back to Caroline.

'Keanu,' he managed in a voice he hardly recognised as his own.

'Yeah?' Keanu was with him in an instant, thinking from Josh's voice it was something urgent, something medical.

It was.

'I want refills of morphine, saline, electrolytes,' he snapped, grabbing his bag then reaching for Keanu's and helping himself. There was a coil of thin rope lying nearby. He slung it over his shoulder. How much stuff could you cart down a collapsing mine? Not enough, but maybe enough to make a difference. 'Can you take over here?'

'What the—?'

'I'm heading down,' he snapped.

'You're going nowhere.' Keanu's hand landed on his shoulder. 'No one goes down that mine.'

'Bugsy's been down and come back again,' Josh snapped, reaching for one of the massive torches one of the miners had set aside. 'If he can, so can I.'

'Bugsy's a dog.'

'Yeah, he's a dog. He has no dependants and he's expendable if necessary. Mate, that's what I am. No one's waiting for me at home and I might make a difference. We have a pregnant woman in labour, an injured miner and the possibility that I might be able to reach them. I'm not trying to dig like the other idiots did. I'm following the path Bugsy's already found. I'm fit and I'm used to tight places. I'm asking no one to come in and rescue me—the responsibility's mine.'

'There's no way.' Keanu growled. 'I can't allow it.'

'You don't have a choice. As I don't. This is my wife.' And suddenly that's exactly what it felt like. He'd walked away from their marriage vows five years ago but she still felt…

Like part of him.

He wasn't married, he thought grimly as he sealed his bag. He didn't do marriage. He hadn't been able to help Maddie in her grief when he'd been unable to handle his own, and it'd almost killed him.

'Pete says the mining engineers are due here in the next half-hour,' Keanu said, urgently. 'They'll assess the risk.'

And he knew exactly what they'd say. They'd seal it. They'd work in inch by painstaking inch. They'd take days to reach her.

Reach *them*.

They'd have the manpower and the authority to stop him. Keanu did, too, if he gave him time to call Pete, to block the mouth by force, to muster all the sensible reasons why he shouldn't try.

'Sorry, mate.' He grabbed a discarded hard hat with attached head lamp and shoved it on his head. 'But this is my wife, my call. Clean things up here. Reuben, I'm leaving you in the best of hands. Oh, and if my boss calls, tell him I'm on family leave. Starting now.'

And then, before Keanu could respond, before another argument could be mounted, he grabbed Bugsy's collar from the miner who was holding him.

'Come on, Bugsy,' he told him, looping the collar hard under his hand. Bugsy had obviously figured the direction to go. He'd gone straight to the injured miners, and then, reluctantly, it seemed, accompanied them to safety.

'Come on, Bugsy,' he told the dog again, and he was at the mine mouth, heading in before anyone could move fast enough to stop him.

CHAPTER FOUR

'MADDIE?'

She'd had to disconnect from Caroline to try and reach Hettie but it hadn't worked. Hettie was manning the phone at the hospital and the line was continuously engaged. She grabbed the phone now, hoping it was Hettie, or, weirdly, hoping even more it was Josh.

That's crazy, she told herself. Just be grateful that you get reception down here, that you have any connection at all.

It wasn't Josh.

'Keanu?'

'Caroline's trying to get a message to Hettie to clear the line so you can talk to her,' he told her. 'Meanwhile, progress?'

'Things are stable. Nothing's changed.' She'd kill for a drink. The contractions were still steady at ten minutes. She ached. Malu was drifting in and out of his drug-induced sleep.

Yes, things were stable.

'Blood pressure?'

'Mine or Malu's?' It was an attempt at humour but it didn't work.

'Both,' he snapped, and listened as she told him.

'That's sounding okay.' But there was serious tension in Keanu's voice—deep tension—tension that told her something else was going on.

'You're about to tell me the sky's going to fall on our heads? If so, it already has.' She caught herself then and directed her beam upwards. 'Actually, no. No, it hasn't. Bad idea.'

'Can you see any light at all?'

'Um…no.'

'We were hoping you'd be near a ventilation shaft.'

'In which case we'd see light.'

'Not if it's blocked. No.'

'So…' There was still something he wasn't telling her. 'Anything else I can help you with?' She tried to make her voice chirpy, sales assistant like.

'You said you were feeling air.'

Another contraction. She gasped and forgot the sales assistant act. Keanu just had to wait.

'There is the faint whiff of air,' she admitted as she surfaced again.

'It's blowing hard out here, straight into the mouth of the cave. You have the torch? Can you shine it at the rocks, look for gaps?'

She shone. The torch beam simply disappeared into the dust and blackness.

'I can't see anything. Even if there was a way out, I could hardly wiggle. And not with Malu…'

'So if we got someone in to you…'

'No one's to come in.' She must have sounded shrill because Keanu didn't answer for a moment and when he did he sounded deeply concerned.

'Maddie?'

'It's just there's still stuff…settling,' she told him. 'Can't you dig us out from the top?'

'We're working on it. Maddie, you sound like you're in pain.'

'I'm not. I'm worrying. Keanu, no one else is to risk…' And then she stopped. She knew Keanu well. 'Someone's already trying, aren't they? Of all the… There's no room in here. Drill a hole down. Get us out from the top. We can't drag Malu out. There's no room for a stretcher and there are rocks still falling. Burrowing's impossibly perilous. I was an idiot to come in, but I've managed to keep Malu alive. There's no point in me doing that if someone else dies.'

Silence.

'What?' she said, feeling the weight of the silence. 'What aren't you telling me?'

'It's Josh,' he said heavily. 'And Bugsy.'

'What the…?'

'Bugsy went haring into the mine. He found the first two miners, the guys who were helping Malu when you went in. They came out, with him leading. It was almost as if Bugsy knew what he had to do. He got them to the surface but he was heading in again.'

'And Josh?' She could scarcely breathe.

'Josh has gone with him. We couldn't stop him. The guy's either a hero or an idiot and I can't decide which.'

'Idiot,' she said, but only half of her meant it.

The other half of her unashamedly wanted Josh.

Torches were almost useless in the dust. The cabled lighting that usually lit the shafts had obviously been knocked out by the fall. The floor was covered with rock litter. Josh wasn't too sure where the roof was, and his torch beam seemed to disappear.

He kept his hand on Bugsy's collar. Bugsy was whining a little, but heading inward and down. He seemed to know exactly where he was going.

If Josh hadn't been holding him he'd have surged ahead. To Maddie?

Who knew? But the fact that he'd found the two miners was an excellent sign. The mine branched out in half a dozen different directions a little way in from the mouth. The miners had been in the tunnel Maddie was in, so he had to assume that was where Bugsy was heading.

To Maddie.

He stumbled on a loose rock and dropped to his knees. Bugsy whined and turned and licked his face, then tugged again.

'You need to go at my pace,' he told the dog. 'Four legs and half my height would be good.'

He tugged. Okay, there was no use sitting around waiting to shrink or grow new legs.

His phone went.

What was it with communications in this place? All the way across the mountains there'd been no signal, yet here…

Maddie. The name popped up on his screen as soon as his fumbling hand hauled his phone from his pocket. He almost dropped it in his haste to answer.

'Hey.' He tried to make his voice normal but the dust was too heavy. He ended up coughing instead.

'You're down the shaft.' Her voice was dull, dread-filled.

'Only a little way down,' he told her. 'Me and Bugsy.'

'Well, turn yourselves around and go back up again.'

'Bugsy won't and I don't know the way without Bugsy.'

'Bugsy took the miners out. They knew enough to say "jeep" and she obeyed. The whole island knows "jeep" to Bugsy means head back to the jeep and stay there. You can't have a dog trailing after you on every island emergency without a few ground rules.'

'So if I say j—' He stopped. 'If I say the name of your car...'

'Say it, Josh.'

'We're coming to find you. Me and Bugsy.'

'You'll kill yourselves and where will that leave us? The engineers will drill in from the top. It's not so deep. They'll find us.'

'It'll take days. Maddie, I'm disconnecting now. Bugsy's eager to keep going.'

'Josh, I don't want this. I didn't expect... You can't risk...'

'You know I always risk. It's what I do.'

'You're trained to swing from helicopters and abseil down cliffs. You're trained in emergency rescue. But for every single scenario you trained and trained. I'm betting not once have you ever trained to dig into a collapsing gold mine when even the experts are saying it's crazy.'

'I'm training now,' he said briefly. 'I'm coming, sweetheart.'

'I don't want you to die!' And it was a wail. She couldn't help herself. Her beautiful Josh...

She loved him. She always had and she always would. He wasn't marriage material. He'd never been her husband, not properly, and years ago she'd stopped hoping for that, and yet she still loved him. The thought of him being down in this appalling place was unbearable.

And then another pain hit. She whimpered before she could stop herself. She bit it off fast, but he'd heard.

'What the...?'

'I just moved on the floor. Sharp rock,' she lied, and heard silence on the end of the line. 'Josh, go home.'

'Conserve your phone batteries, love,' he told her. 'Any minute now you'll get to talk to me in person.'

'I'm not your love,' she repeated.

'Go tell that to someone who cares. I'm coming in anyway.'

He was coming.

She should be appalled. She was appalled.

But...he was coming.

'Help's on its way,' she whispered to Malu, but he was sleeping too deeply to hear.

He needed more fluids. Would Josh be carrying fluids?

'He won't get here.' She said it out loud, trying to suppress the flare of hope, of belief, of trust. 'Okay, Bugsy made it to where the last rockfall took place but there *was* a rockfall.

'It can't be too thick.' She was talking out loud to herself. 'Those guys were with us when it started falling and they ended up safe on the other side.'

She crawled across her little cavern to where the mound of fresh-fallen rock blocked the exit. At least, she thought this was the mound in the direction of the exit. It could be the one behind her.

She was pretty disorientated.

She was in pain.

Forget the pain, she told herself, fiercely now. Concentrate on ways out of here.

Ways Josh could get in.

The rocks were big. The fall wasn't packed with loose gravel, but rather a mound of large boulders.

Dear God, they'd been lucky.

Define luck.

'We have been lucky,' she said out loud. 'If any of these mothers had hit us we'd have been squashed flatter than sardines.'

They could still fall. Above her head was a mass of loose rock, and the shoring timber was cracking.

Don't go there.

Was there a way through the rocks? Was she even looking in the right direction? She played her torch over the mass. There were gaps in the boulders—of course there were—but there were more boulders behind. To try and crawl through...

'He's an idiot to try,' she said out loud. 'Ring him again.'

She knew it'd make no difference.

And for the first time a wash of fear swept over her so strongly, so fiercely that she felt as if she'd be physically ill.

Josh was out there.

There was nothing she could do. She crawled back to Malu and put her head next to his on his makeshift pillow. She pressed her body hard against his. She'd done this before when he'd needed comfort.

She was doing it again now but it was she who needed comfort. It was she who needed to escape fear.

'He's coming,' she whispered, and she linked her hands under her belly and held. Her belly was tight, hard.

Her baby...

'He'll come,' she said, and this time she was talking to her baby, talking to someone she'd barely been brave enough to acknowledge as a separate being until now. Was this why she'd been dumb enough to rush into the mine? Because she'd hardly had the courage to acknowledge that this baby could be real?

She'd lost one baby. Mikey's death had left a huge, gaping hole in her life, and it had been a vast act of faith, a momentous decision, to try again. Once the decision had been made, she'd gone through the process of finding a sperm donor, the months of hope, the confirmation of pregnancy...

But once that confirmation had come, joy hadn't followed. Terror had followed, that once again she could lose the baby.

She'd coped by blocking it out. She'd not bought any baby clothes. She'd hardly let herself think about it. It was as if by acknowledging she really did have a baby in there she'd jinx it. She couldn't let herself believe that she could hold a little one who might live.

But, belief or not, this baby had rights, too, and one of those rights was not being buried in a collapsing mine before he/she/it was even born.

'I'm sorry,' she whispered as another contraction started to build. 'I'm so sorry I got you into this mess. And I'm even more sorry we're depending on Josh to get us out.'

She was in labour.

The thought was unbelievable. The knowledge was doing his head in.

Somehow he had to put it aside, focussing only on

keeping his grip on Bugsy. He was inching ahead, making the big dog slow. Staying safe. He'd be no use to anyone dead. He was taking no unnecessary risks.

In labour.

Who?

Of all the stupid questions? Did he need to know who the father was?

They'd kept in touch. Theirs had been a civilised divorce, born out of grief. Maddie had understood why he couldn't stay married.

She'd said she felt sorry for him.

Why did that slam back now? That last appalling conversation as he'd tossed random stuff into his kit bag, ostensibly heading for a flood in Indonesia. The Australian government had offered help and Cairns Air Sea Rescue had asked for volunteers.

Maybe a month, they'd said.

They'd both known it would be longer. The pain of loss was so great Josh had curled inward inside. He couldn't bear seeing his loss reflected on Maddie's face. He couldn't help her. He couldn't help himself.

'You'll never heal by running away,' Maddie had said sadly, and even then he hadn't been truthful.

'I'm helping others heal. That's why I'm going.'

'You're hiding from the pain the only way you know how,' she'd said. 'But I can't help you, Josh, so maybe it's better this way…'

And then she'd walked out because she couldn't bear to watch him pack, and he was gone before she'd returned.

The end.

Who was the father of her baby? Why hadn't she told him?

This was important.

They got in touch on Christmas and birthdays. Formal stuff.

Babies weren't formal?

New partners weren't important?

He swore.

And then he reached the rock face. The tunnel ended with a mass of fallen boulders and loose gravel.

He raked the floor and saw evidence of the miners who'd been flung apart from Maddie and Malu. A tin canteen. He snagged it and opened it—sandwiches! Worth holding on to? If he could.

If there was anyone to eat them.

He stared at the massive rock pile. It was such a jumble—how could he ever get through?

But Bugsy was nosing forward, whining, clambering up and over the first couple of rocks. He'd let him go—now he made a lunge and grabbed him before he got down the hole he was intent on investigating.

Hole.

Bugsy.

Maddie would never forgive him if he risked her dog.

But contractions… What choice did he have?

He knelt and hugged the big dog close, and he knew what the choice had to be. If this was possible…

Please.

He hauled his coiled rope from his shoulder and tied an end to Bugsy's collar. Then he carefully unrolled the rope so Bugsy felt no pull. It was a light line. It shouldn't cause much friction.

But the chance of a collapse…

Don't think it, he told himself. He couldn't.

He hugged Bugsy one more time, thinking of him

all those years ago, thinking of Maddie's joy when he'd put a warm, wriggling bundle of puppy into her arms.

'I'll love him forever,' Maddie had said.

Dared he risk...?

How could he not?

'We're both risking,' he told Bugsy, and he sat back and let the dog go. 'For Maddie.'

And one minute later Bugsy had crawled his way across the first pile of rocks, pushed his nose into a crevice—and then his whole body.

He was gone.

Maddie lay in the dark and worried. A lot.

He could be anyone and I'd be terrified, she told herself. If he was some unknown rescuer putting his life on the line to save her, she'd be appalled.

But, then, no one else would have done it, and she knew it. To head into a mine shaft where the shoring timbers were collapsing, where the shaft was known to be unsafe, where a mass of rock was already blocking the way, was just plain lunacy.

'Idiot hero.' She said it out loud and Malu stirred beside her and she bit her lip.

But still... 'Idiot hero,' she said again under her breath.

But he'd be in his element. She knew that. Josh would do anything for anyone. He was brave, clever, fearless, giving...

But not taking.

If it was Josh stuck in the mine he'd be pulling down more rocks so no one could save him, she told herself, speaking under her breath. Josh being saved? Ha. No one saved Josh.

That was the trouble. When they'd lost Mikey, the

giving had been all one way. She'd sobbed and he'd held her but he hadn't wept, as well. He'd held himself close.

And then, when Holly had died, he hadn't even let her hug him. She knew how much he'd loved his little sister, but he'd held himself rigid within his grief and despair, with no way of letting it out.

I don't need help. That was Josh's mantra. How could he live like that?

He did live like that, which was why she couldn't live with him.

I don't need help?

Yeah, if that was the case for her then she should be over at the rock face, reinforcing the rubble so no one could get through. She should be telling Josh that the moment he emerged into her cavern she'd toss rocks at him.

As if.

I don't need help?

She was stuck in a collapsing mine shaft with a guy who was perilously ill. She was in labour. Caroline hadn't been able to put her through to Hettie.

Slowly but surely the contractions were building.

I don't need help?

Some things weren't even worth aiming for.

It was a good thing that Bugsy wasn't a fox terrier. Josh was very, very pleased that the dog was large.

Josh's current plan, albeit a weak one, was to let Bugsy see if he could find a way through the rocks. Bugsy wasn't much smaller than he was across the shoulders. If Bugsy could find a way, then he might be able to follow.

There were, however, a whole lot of unknowns in that equation. And risks.

The best-case scenario was that Bugsy would find a safe passage through, tugging the cord behind him. He'd find Maddie. There'd be a happy reunion. Josh could then follow the rope and get through himself.

The more likely scenario would be that the whole thing was completely blocked and Bugsy would have to back out.

A possible scenario was that Bugsy would become impossibly tangled and stuck.

Or there'd be a further collapse.

Both the final scenarios were unthinkable but beyond the mass of rock was Maddie, and Bugsy seemed as desperate as he was to get through. So there was nothing he could do now but sit and wait and watch the rope feeding out.

There was an initial rush of feed as Bugsy nosed his way past the first few boulders. Then the feed slowed.

And stopped.

Josh's heart almost did the same.

'Bugsy?' he called, but there was no response. And the line started feeding out again.

Was he going straight through? Dear God, had he turned? Could he trap himself?

He could cut the line at this end, as long as the dog didn't get impossibly tangled first.

Whose crazy idea had this been?

The line fed out a little further. And further.

Please...

He'd never pleaded so desperately in his life.

She could hear scrabbling.

It was almost like there were mice in the cave with her, but...scrabbling?

She moved away from Malu's side, almost afraid to

breathe in case she was wrong. Then she flicked the torch and searched the rock pile.

She could definitely hear scrabbling and it was getting louder.

It was high up where the rocks almost merged with the ceiling. Or what was left of the ceiling.

If it fell…

She couldn't breathe. She had no room for anything but fear.

Where…where…?

And then there it was, slithering down the face of the cave-in, a great, grey ball of canine dust, a wriggly, ecstatic ball of filthy golden retriever.

And Maddie had the presence of mind—just—to put the torch down before she had an armful of delirious dog, and she was hugging and hugging and pressing her face into Bugsy's filthy coat and bursting into tears.

He was going crazy. Or maybe he already was crazy. There'd been one last, long feed of line, like Bugsy had made a dash—and then nothing. Nothing!

According to the line, the dog didn't appear to be moving.

If he'd killed Bugsy…

Of all the stupid, risky, senseless plans. He'd worked for search and rescue for years. There was no way a plan like this could even be considered.

He knew the rules. You played it by the book. You got in the experts, you did careful risk assessment, you weighed up your options. You never, ever put people's lives on the line.

Or dogs'.

Maybe his bosses would okay dogs, he thought bleakly, but surely not Bugsy.

What was happening? Dear God, what was happening?

And then his phone rang.

'Josh.'

She was crying. He could hear her tears. His heart seemed to simply stop.

'Maddie.'

'I have a dog,' she managed. 'I have a whole armload of dog. He's here. Bugsy's here.'

His heart gave a great lurch and seemed to restart. 'Does he still have a cord attached?'

'I...' There was a moment's pause. 'I'll see. It is dark in here.' She said it almost indignantly and he found himself grinning. His lovely, brave Maddie, who always rebounded. 'Yes. Yes, he does. But Josh, what the—'

'I'm coming through, then,' he said. 'Are you hugging Bugsy?'

'Yes, but—'

'Sandwich hug,' he promised. 'Stat.'

'Josh, don't you dare.' He heard her fear surge. 'We have a line through now. Wait for the experts.'

'How far apart are the contractions?'

'I don't... Josh, no!'

'How far, Maddie?'

'I'm not saying.'

'Then you don't need to say. I'm coming in.'

CHAPTER FIVE

JOSH WASN'T A DOG. Dogs were smaller than Josh and they bent more. He was carrying a backpack, necessary if he was to be useful in there, but it made things harder. After a while he tugged it off his back, looped the straps round his ankles and towed it. It was better but still hard.

The fallen rocks were large and angular. Where were smooth river rocks when you needed them? These seemed to have broken with almost slate-like edges, flat and sharp, fine if you walked over a nicely laid path of them but murder to crawl up and around.

But Bugsy had made it through and he would, too. He just had to be careful. Ultra careful. He was following Bugsy's cord, using the head lamp to see, but he was feeling his way, as well. He was testing every rock before he touched it, feeling the rocks above him, trying to take the fewest risks possible. Hauling his pack behind him with his feet. Halting whenever it snagged.

It was so dark. And sharp. And hard.

It was also really, really claustrophobic. He didn't get claustrophobia, he told himself, but another part of him was saying that in this situation claustrophobia was just plain sensible.

At the other end of the cord lay Maddie. Maddie, who was in labour.

He had to be so careful not to pull on the cord so it didn't become dislodged. He was feeding out another line behind him with the idea of ultimate rescue. These cords were lifelines. Meanwhile he was keeping his hard hat on, getting his body through the next crevice, figuring how Bugsy could possibly have got through. Every fibre of his body was tuned to survival.

Bugsy had done it in fifteen minutes. After half an hour Josh was still struggling...

How long could she bear it?

She wanted to ring him but how could she? How could Josh do what he was doing and calmly take time out to answer the phone? He couldn't. She wanted every ounce of his concentration focussed on keeping him safe.

She wanted him out of there.

And she could hear him. That was the worst part. For the last twenty minutes she'd been hearing him hauling his way through the rock. She could hear the occasional shift of earth, the silence as he waited for things to settle. Once she heard the echo of a muffled oath.

She sat and hugged Bugsy. Bugsy whined a little, tugging forward as if he'd go to him—after five years did Bugsy still feel loyalty?—but Maddie was holding tight.

Josh was trying—against all odds—against all sense—to haul himself through impossibly tight, impossibly dangerous conditions. Bugsy had been truly heroic but the last thing Josh needed now was a golden retriever in there with him, licking his face, blocking his way.

She was saying silent prayers, over and over. *Please, let him be safe. Please...*

She'd be saying them for anyone, but for Josh...

She couldn't even begin to understand what she was feeling.

He was her husband.

He wasn't her husband. He was...an old friend?

Liar.

She was no longer curled up by Malu. There was no way she could disguise the contractions now; they were so strong if she lay beside him he'd feel them.

Some doctor she was!

Malu was restless and she knew the pain would break through again soon, leaving him wide awake.

How could she ask a man with such injuries to help deliver a baby?

How could she deliver herself? To put her baby at such risk? This little one who she'd longed for with all her heart and yet hadn't had the courage to acknowledge might be real. This baby who had every right to live.

Could she depend on Josh manoeuvring through these last few yards? Could she dare hope?

Another contraction gripped and she stopped asking stupid questions. Only the one word remained.

Please...

This...had been...a really, really, really...dumb idea. He'd be trapped in here forever, a skeleton, hanging by his fingernails to a stupid rock that, if he could only find purchase, he could use to drag himself up and over.

Bugsy had done it but Bugsy had more toenails than

he did. Bugsy's back half wasn't nearly as heavy. She hadn't been hauling a backpack. This thing was imp—

No. He had it. He hauled and felt himself lift.

The cord now seemed like it was running downwards.

Please... It was a silent prayer said over and over. Let this be the last part. Let it open up.

Let me see Maddie.

He gave one last heave, up and over—and suddenly he was slithering, head first, downwards. He hadn't realised it was so steep. He almost fell, sliding fast on loose shale, the backpack slithering after him.

And then suddenly his head and then his torso were free from the tunnel. He saw light that didn't come from his head lamp.

Torchlight swung towards him, almost blinding him. 'J-Josh?'

And suddenly he was clear. He was on the floor of a cramped cavern that was still a tunnel but after what he'd been in seemed as wide as a house.

But he wasn't noticing. Nothing mattered except that he'd made it and he was holding Maddie in his arms. Holding and holding and holding.

Maddie. His woman.

She'd always felt like that. She'd always been that, from the moment they'd first met, but how much more so in this moment?

He could feel her heart beating against his. She was breathing almost as heavily as he was. He was hugging her and she was hugging right back, maybe even crying.

He wasn't crying. Crying wasn't his style, but holding was.

Why had he let this woman go?

It didn't matter now. Nothing mattered except that she was in his arms, she was safe and they were together.

'Maddie...'

He would have tilted her face. He would have kissed her.

But then there was the slight hiccup of the dog.

Bugsy wasn't letting interpersonal relations get in the way of his needs. He'd orchestrated this rescue and being left out now wasn't going to happen. The dog was wedging his way firmly in between both of them, turning a hug into a sandwich squeeze.

And then, from behind them, a voice.

'Have we got company? I wouldn't mind a hug myself.'

Malu. He put Maddie away from him, just a little, still holding her but loosely so he could see the man lying on the floor.

'Hey, how's the patient?'

'So who's the patient?' Malu managed. 'My Pearl's had two babies, with me beside her every step of the way, so I pretty much know my current treating doctor is well into labour. And her newly arrived backup seems to be one filthy doctor who looks—to my untrained eye, I'll admit—to be bleeding. You'd best fix him up, Maddie,' he told her. 'And then he can fix both of us up next.'

Malu was right. The first priority was actually him. The rocks had been hard and sharp. He'd sliced his arm on that last uncontrolled descent. It wasn't serious but it was bleeding hard and the last thing any of them needed was to lose fluids.

So he tolerated—barely—sitting back while Maddie put pressure on it until the bleeding subsided. She cleaned the cut, pulled it together with Steri-Strips and slapped on a dressing. He made a fast call to Keanu while she did it.

'I'm in.'

Keanu wasted no words. 'Is there a safe way to get them out?'

'No.' He thought about the way he'd had to clamber though. There was a good chance he couldn't get out himself.

If Maddie hadn't been here, maybe he wouldn't have made it. That tunnel was practically suicidal.

But he was here, with Maddie, who was calmly dressing his arm. Between contractions.

'We'll depend on the engineering boys to get us out,' he told Keanu. 'Short of another collapse, we're safe enough for now. But, sorry, mate, I have work to do. I'll ring as soon as I have things under control.'

Under control? That was a joke.

'It's not my neatest work,' Maddie said, a bit breathlessly, as she finished. 'But you'll do.'

She was breathless and her breathlessness didn't come purely from the dust. 'When was your last contraction?'

'Over ten minutes ago. I'm slowing down. Stress, do you think?'

'So you really are in labour?' Malu's speech was easier now, his body language showing how much it meant to him that someone had been able to get through. 'You didn't admit—'

'There wasn't a lot to admit,' Maddie said with asperity. 'You're not moving and there's no way we can boil water and switch on humidicribs.'

'So you're thirty-six weeks?' They were sitting on the ground. Josh had his arm cradled in front of him. The more he rested it now the less likely it would be to bleed again if...*when* he got busy. 'Tell me why you're still on Wildfire?'

'I'm due to leave on Friday.'

'You know the rules for fly in, fly outs. Thirty-four weeks and then only under strict conditions.'

'I wanted every day of my family leave to be spent with my baby. Leaving six weeks before was a waste of time.'

'Says the woman stuck underground in labour.'

'I didn't intend to get stuck underground,' Maddie said—and sniffed.

The sniff echoed.

'You make our Maddie cry, injured or not, I'll get up and shove you back in that tunnel,' Malu warned. 'And I'll shove a rock back in after you.' He hesitated and his voice faltered a little. 'I don't suppose... Maddie, you can't get out that tunnel hero-boy just came in through.'

'No.' Josh and Maddie spoke together. Maddie, because the thought of crawling through rocks with the massive bulge she had underneath her was unthinkable. Josh...well, pretty much the same for Josh. He'd been incredibly lucky to get here, he conceded. He could well have got himself stuck at any number of places on the way.

'They'll dig down from the top,' he said with more confidence than he felt. He crawled across and lifted Malu's wrist. 'Pain... Scale of one to ten.'

'I'm okay.'

'Answer the question.'

'Seven,' Malu said, reluctantly. 'But I can cope.'

'Forget coping. I have drugs.'

'Maddie has drugs.'

'I have more drugs. Nice drugs.'

'I'd give more for a mouthful of water.'

'I can do that, too. I have a backpack, fully loaded.' He helped the man drink, holding him up a little and then easing him back on his makeshift pillow. Noting the fierce effort it took him not to cry out.

He was in pain, Josh thought, but not from his leg. Ribs?

His breathing was a bit scratchy.

Fractured ribs? Pierced lung?

There weren't a lot of X-ray facilities down there.

'How long since you gave the last morphine?' he asked Maddie.

'I… Half an hour ago. Five milligrams.'

He cast a quick look back at her. She sounded strained.

She was strained. She was leaning against the rock wall, her arms were holding her belly, she was arched back and she was trying not to scream.

He flicked the torch away from her fast, so Malu couldn't see.

Triage. He'd like to do a very fast pelvic examination but Malu was breathing too fast. The pain would be making his breathing rapid and his heart rate rise.

The priority was Malu, but Malu got the world's fastest injection. He set up another bag of saline. Then he hesitated.

'Go to her,' Malu whispered. 'I'm imagining a nice

cubicle partition in my mind. I'll close my eyes. Those drugs you gave me…they'll make me sleep, right?'

'They will, but not for ten or fifteen minutes.'

'Tell you what,' Malu said. 'Those empty saline bags… Prop 'em up against the side of my face. Then tell Doc she has all the privacy she could ever want to get that baby out.'

'She's not… It can't be soon.'

'You're the doc and I'm the miner,' Malu whispered. 'But, hell, Doc, I'd go take a look if I were you.'

'I can't have my baby down here.'

That was pretty much what Josh was thinking. He had nothing. Nothing!

Well, that wasn't exactly true. He had basic sterile equipment.

Forceps, not so much. Equipment for an emergency Caesar? Not in his wildest dreams.

'Sweetheart—'

'I'm not your sweetheart.'

'Sorry,' he said, chastened. 'Maddie, I need to examine you.'

'I know you need to examine,' she moaned. 'And I heard what Malu said. Malu, thank you for the privacy but if a vacuum cleaner salesman could stop this pain right now I'd say go ahead, look all you like.'

Malu gave a dozy chuckle.

'Lie back,' Josh told her.

She lay back. He desperately wanted a decent bed. He was asking her to lie on rocks.

He could tug off his shirt to use as a pillow but he was already thinking ahead. If…*when* this baby came he needed something to wrap it in, and things to wrap it in were few and far between.

'So where's your layette?' he demanded, striving for lightness.

'Layette?'

'One of the mums we brought down from Weipa to Cairns last month had a suitcase with her she explained had a full layette. Her mum had knitted it for her. All white. Matinee jackets, bootees, christening robe, tiny wool dresses with pink roses embroidered on them. She went on to have a boy but at least she was prepared.'

'To live in Weipa?' She was gasping, trying to breathe as she obviously knew how to breathe when things got hard. 'With the red dust up there, everything will be pink at first wash.'

'So you don't have a layette.'

'Not here.'

'In Cairns?'

'Not…not even in Cairns,' she admitted. 'I have four weeks to shop.'

He'd helped her tug off her pants, laying them under her hips. That give her a tiny amount of protection from the rocks but not much. Her bra gave her a modicum of privacy, but there wasn't enough of that, either.

Four weeks…

'You're six centimetres dilated,' he told her. 'How many weeks does that give you in the layette-buying plan?'

'I can't…'

'Okay, don't think about it now. Keep doing the breathing. You know how. And stop fighting.'

'Josh, I can't.'

'You and Malu thought you were going to keep this

neat little cave a secret, didn't you?' He shifted so he was against the wall as well, then tugged her across him. She protested, but not too much—she was pretty much past protesting. She leaned back against him instead of the wall. He was holding her and that seemed sort of right. His arm was hurting, but in the scheme of things it was nothing. 'And then along comes Bugsy,' he continued, as if this was a completely normal conversation in a completely normal setting. 'And then Josh arrives—and now it seems someone else is coming, too.'

'Josh, you can't. Your arm. You can't hold me. Oh, my…' Her next words were lost in a silent scream. He felt that scream. He felt the contraction take hold of her. He felt her whole body spasm and he held her because it was the only thing he could do.

The contraction eased. She fell back against him with a gasp and his arms tightened.

'You're doing brilliantly. Has anyone told you lately that you're awesome, Dr Haddon?'

'I have.' It was a slurred interjection from Malu in the shadows, and he felt Maddie smile.

'And Bugsy tells me all the time,' Maddie managed.

And then another contraction hit and he thought, How did that happened? Didn't the texts say the rate increased gradually? That had been all of thirty seconds.

'I'm not pushing yet,' she said through gritted teeth as the contraction passed.

'Good for you. You show 'em. This baby comes on your terms or not at all.'

She even managed a wry chuckle.

'Maddie?'

'Mmm…?'

'Is there a dad out there who'll be frantic?'

There was silence at that. He wasn't sure if the silence meant she didn't want to answer, or she couldn't.

The next contraction rolled by without a word, just more of the silent screaming. This woman had courage. There was no way she'd scream.

Come to think of it, this really was a situation where she might literally scream the roof down. The vibrations of a woman in full labour might even be enough to...

Um...don't go there. Not.

Bugsy was whining a little, obviously sensing Maddie's distress. He was nestled as close to them as he could get. Josh had set one of the torches up, just one, aiming it off centre so it wasn't shining directly at them. They were in shadow.

He was still holding her. This was the strangest feeling...

To hold Maddie.

He'd loved holding Maddie. Holding her had been the only time in his life when he'd felt totally at peace.

But... He'd held her the night their baby had died. Or he'd tried to. He remembered the fierce struggle not to sob himself. Something had clenched inside, some hard knot of despair that he still didn't dare unravel, and the same knot had formed when Holly had died.

He hated it. They were two leaden weights he'd carry forever.

But what was he doing, thinking of the start of his marriage, a marriage that had never worked? Focus on now, he told himself. He had no choice. Maddie needed him.

'Just keep the breathing going,' he told her. 'Deep and even. You know the drill.'

'The drill's different when it's me,' she gasped.

'Breathe, sweetheart.'

'Don't call me sweetheart! Just get me out of here.'

He almost smiled. He'd heard that line before, from so many women in labour. *Take me home.*

Where was home?

He and Maddie used to have…

Don't go there, either.

'There's no father,' she muttered through clenched teeth. 'Or at least no one to slug right now. If it was you I'd be knocking your teeth out the back of your head.'

'Hey, it's not the guy's fault.'

'Who else's fault is it? I want someone I can sue.' She was beyond reason now, he thought, caught in pain and trying to find any way through it. 'Hold me tighter,' she demanded. 'Ohhh…'

He held her tighter. Her fingers clenched on his forearms. It was just as well it was his upper arm he'd injured. He'd have marks from her fingernails, he thought. Maybe she'd even draw blood.

But donating his arms seemed the least he could do. He so wanted to be needed.

If you don't need me then I don't need you. She'd thrown that at him that last appalling week. *You give and give and give, and you never take, not one inch. And what you give…it's all surface stuff, Josh. You hold yourself so tight, like you're in armour, and I can't get in. I don't want to be the taker forever. I can't be. You need to go.*

And he had. He'd walked away because he'd known she was right.

He couldn't let her in. He couldn't let anyone near the pain he was feeling.

'It was a test tube,' she muttered now. Her whole body

was straining, and the fingers were digging even tighter. 'A vial. Tall, black hair like yours, athletic build, smart, a university student doing his good deed for humanity— for me—by donating semen... What was he thinking? Oooh...'

And she tucked her chin down into her throat and pushed.

'Hey.'

He wanted nothing so much as to stay where he was, holding her. Someone had to hold her, but it could no longer be him.

He was needed at the other end. Someone had to catch.

He needed lights.

He had two torches, one head lamp and Maddie's phone app. He set them all up but still there wasn't enough.

It'd have to do.

He wanted towels. He wanted clean.

He ripped his shirt off but laid it aside. It was thick, serviceable cotton. It was filthy but it was the best he could do. But for a newborn baby with a freshly cut umbilical cord to be wrapped in such a thing...

'I used...I used my shirt for Malu...' Maddie gasped, and he gripped her hand and held.

'That's why I came. To bring you mine.'

'You always did...like an excuse to show your six pack...'

'There are a lot of people to admire it down here,' he told her, and then she moaned and pushed again and he had to deal with what he had: a woman lying in dirt he couldn't protect her from.

The head was crowning. A tiny dark head had

emerged at the last push, then gone back as the contraction had eased.

He'd grabbed lubricant from his bag, and gloves. And checked.

The cord... The cord!

'Maddie, I need you to back off.' He tried to make his voice normal, matter-of-fact. 'If you push any harder you'll tear.'

'I need... I need...'

'You don't need to push. Breathe through it, Maddie, and don't push. Don't!'

And she got it. She was a doctor. She knew.

'The cord...'

'It's fine. I just need a little space down here to get things organised. You have to breathe. Hold it, Maddie. Hold.'

And once again that little word was front and centre. Please...

The next contraction hit and he could feel the massive effort it took for Maddie to hold back. To somehow control her body.

The courage of this woman... He had to match it.

One dead baby... There would not be another, he swore. Please.

He had to wait until the contraction eased and it almost killed him.

'H-hurry,' Maddie muttered, and then she swore. 'Hurry, damn you.'

'Do you mind?' he said. 'There are patients present.'

'I'll swear, too, if it helps,' Malu muttered from the shadows, and Josh knew the big miner was feeling as helpless as he was.

Please.

The head had retreated. He had so little time. Where...?

There. He had it. Careful, careful, there was no way he was ripping it...

Hold that contraction.

Now! And somehow it came, slipping seamlessly up and over. The cord was clear and he felt like shouting.

Somehow he made his voice muted but the triumph was there. 'Houston, we have lift-off,' he said in a voice he couldn't possibly hold steady. 'Maddie, the cord's free. Next contraction, go for it.'

And she did. The contraction hit and, risk or not, fear of vibrations or not, there was no way Maddie could keep it in. She hugged her knees and she screamed, a long, primeval scream that echoed and echoed and echoed.

And ten seconds later a tiny, perfect little girl slipped out into that strange new world.

'You have a daughter,' Josh managed, and he couldn't stop himself. He was staring down at the slip of a baby in his hands and tears were streaming unchecked down his face.

'Let me...let me...'

What was he thinking? Every textbook in the land said bring the baby straight up to the mother, place the baby on the mother's breast while you cope with the umbilical cord, even let the mother discover the baby's sex for herself.

He slid the tiny scrap of newborn humanity up to her mother. Maddie's arms enfolded her.

Josh laid his shirt over the top of both of them—he wanted no dust or scraps of rock falling on this little one. He'd cope with the umbilical cord soon. It was good to leave it for a minute or two to stop pulsing, he told himself. And besides…

Besides, there was no way he was cutting anything through tears.

'A daughter.' It was Malu, whispering again from the shadows. 'Hey, a little girl. Congratulations to you both.'

And that was what it felt like, Josh thought. *Both.*

This little girl was nothing to do with him. She was the daughter of his ex-wife and an unknown donor. She had no biological connection to him at all.

But he glanced down at the woman cradling her newborn in her arms, at the look of unimaginable awe on Maddie's face, and he knew…

Biological connection or not, he'd defend this little family to the death.

There were so many emotions coursing through Maddie's mind that she had no hope of sorting them.

She was beyond trying. Josh had laid her tiny daughter on her breast. She was lying on her mother's naked skin, a tiny scrap of humanity.

Her daughter.

Josh had settled his shirt over the pair of them, but under the shirt she was cradling her daughter. Her hands enfolded her, feeling the warmth, the wetness, the miracle.

The tiny girl hadn't cried but she was making tiny, waffling grunts, as if she wasn't the least bit scared but rather she was awed at the amazing world she'd emerged into.

Her daughter.

She'd had the cord around her neck…

The tiny part of Maddie that was still a doctor let that thought drift.

If Josh hadn't been here…

He was. Her Josh, riding to the rescue.

It was what he was good at. It was what she most loved—and hated—about him.

But for now she was no longer capable of processing the whys and the wherefores. Too much emotion, too much pain, and now…too much wonder?

'She's snuffling,' Josh said, and she could hear him smiling. 'I can guess what she's looking for.'

'My bra… It unclips at the front…'

'Great forethought,' he said, but he had to use the torch again to help her unclip it, and he smiled and smiled as her baby girl figured exactly what was going on. He stroked the tiny face, she turned in the direction of his stroking finger, found what he was directing her to…and made her connection.

Maddie gasped and gasped again. How could this be happening? Something so wonderful?

She had a daughter.

A memory flashed back, or maybe not a memory. It was the bone-deep truth that she'd held Mikey like this. That she'd loved her son.

She glanced up and she saw in Josh's face that he knew it, too. It was a bittersweet moment, but strangely it didn't hurt.

And it was good that Josh was here to share it with her, she thought. Josh had never admitted how much Mikey's loss had hurt him, but she knew it had, and somehow, right now, it was important that he was here. Whether he'd admit it or not, this was a joy to be shared, but it was also the remembrance of sorrow. Somehow, Mikey was with them. Somehow, right now, she felt... married?

'Th-thank you for being here,' she whispered to Josh. 'Oh, Josh.'

'Hey,' he said softly into the shadows, and he touched her cheek, a feather touch, a caress, a gesture of love and admiration and...awe?

And then, because he couldn't help himself, or maybe it was her doing, maybe she'd turned her face to him, maybe because it seemed right, inevitable, an extension of this whole amazing moment... For whatever reason, he bent and placed his lips on hers. He kissed her.

'Josh?'

The phone was ringing. Maybe it'd been ringing for a while. No one had noticed and he didn't want to notice now.

The kiss was magic. The kiss was like putting back a part of his body he hadn't known had been removed. The kiss was...right.

But Maddie was stiffening a little and she'd managed to get his name out. She was right. The kiss had to end.

Obstetrician kissing mother?

He hadn't felt the least bit like an obstetrician. There were no foundations for how he'd felt, but still... For a few amazing moments he'd felt like a man in love with his wife. Remembering his son. Welcoming his daughter.

But that wasn't reality. Reality was that the kiss was over. Reality was that he was stuck underground in a mine. He was officially part of the rescue team and making contact had to be the first priority.

He was here to work.

Still, he'd missed the call and Keanu had to ring again, and by the time he answered, Keanu's first word was a shout.

'Josh!'

'I'm here, mate. There's no need to burst my eardrum.'

'What the hell's going on? We heard a scream. Hell, Josh.'

It had been quite a scream. It must have echoed up and out through the shafts.

If he'd been out there he'd have been going out of his mind.

He wasn't. He was in here.

All was quiet in the confines of the tiny cavern. He had a sudden, almost unbearable urge to cut the connection and keep the world at bay.

There was a dumb thought.

'What's happened?' Keanu was demanding. 'Another cave-in? Why haven't you been answering?'

Had the phone been ringing for a while, then? 'We've been busy.'

'The tunnel. Is it safe for me to come in?'

'No.' He knew that absolutely. He'd had amazing luck to get through himself.

'Hell, Josh. We're going out of our minds out here. Why didn't you answer?'

'Triage. We had a bit of a medical emergency but it's okay.'

'Medical emergency?' Keanu's voice was sharp with worry. 'It was a woman's scream. Was it Maddie? Is she hurt? What's going on?'

'Women's business,' he said, and he allowed himself a smile. 'We're on the other side of it now.'

'Women's business…'

'Yeah, and, Keanu…you know you were thinking there'd be three people and a dog to dig out?'

'Yeah?' Keanu sounded dazed.

'Make it four. We have a new arrival. Mother and daughter are doing fine. Malu and I could use cigars but if cigars aren't forthcoming a ruddy great bulldozer with a bit of finesse will do fine.'

CHAPTER SIX

A RUDDY GREAT bulldozer took time to organise. The experts had now arrived from the mainland. There'd be no more heroics. Things were being done by the book.

But because of Josh's forethought there was a further link to aboveground.

Josh had attached a cord to Bugsy when he'd sent the dog to find his mistress. When he'd come in himself, he'd hauled in another behind him. That meant they had two cords running through the caved-in rocks, cords that could be linked, like a raft fording a river. One cord got pulled in, with something attached. The attached thing was removed, the other cord was used to pull it back out. Back and forth. Josh had used the system in tight spots before, though never for himself.

Their team had bags designed for the purpose, tough and slippery. While the team from Cairns started their work aboveground the bags started their cautious way back and forth.

The first bag they tried contained tougher cable. The important thing was not to break the link. Then, with both cords set up as slippery cable rather than nylon, Keanu started sending in supplies.

First came fluids—not much on the first pull, as they

didn't want to risk anything getting stuck. But Keanu also risked sending in wipes and a blanket in which to wrap the baby.

Also a diaper.

There was also a card, very makeshift, written on the back of a mine safety notice.

A big welcome to Baby Haddon, the card said. *From all of us on the surface. But isn't the stork supposed to go down chimneys, not mine shafts?*

He read it to Maddie and it made her smile. Or smile more.

'That'll be Hettie,' she said, sounding a bit choked up. 'She's such a friend. I have so many good friends here.'

She had a whole life he knew nothing about, Josh realised as he retied the empty bag to the cord and sent a text for the guys out there to pull.

Then they went back to the waiting game while Keanu organised more stuff to come in.

Malu had finally let the effects of the painkillers take hold and was deeply asleep. Bugsy was also dozing, pressed close to his mistress. The baby had taken her first tentative suckle and drifted to sleep, as well.

Josh flicked the torch off and moved again to sit behind Maddie. She tried to object. 'I don't mind hard…' but he was having none of it. He was her pillow and they were alone in their cocoon of darkness.

It felt right. He was meant to hold her, he thought. His body thought so.

Danger or not, cradling this woman felt wonderful.

'So when did you decide to have a baby?' he asked into the silence, though he had no right to ask such a question and she had every right to refuse to answer.

Silence.

'Sleep if you want,' he murmured, letting her off the hook, but he felt rather than saw her shake her head.

'I don't feel like sleep yet. I know this is an appalling situation but all I can feel is happy. If you knew how much I wanted this...'

'I guess... I did know.'

'But you didn't want it.'

And there was a game-changer. The peace dissipated from the darkness and he let her accusation drift. Had he wanted this? A wife? A baby?

Not enough to take risks. Not enough to risk the pain he'd felt last time.

'I'm sorry,' she whispered. 'That was uncalled for. It's okay, Josh, I'm not about to dredge up the past. The truth is that I reached thirty-four last birthday and I thought if I don't do something soon I'll end up without a family. I know that sounds selfish but there it is. I wanted it so much.'

'Not enough to remarry?' He tried to say it lightly—and failed.

'I hardly have time for marriage.' She was trying for lightness, too, he thought. 'I work here fourteen days straight and then I have a week back in Cairns. I spend most of that time with Mum.'

'Wouldn't it have been better to get a job in Cairns?'

'Maybe.' This was none of his business and he could almost hear her thinking it, but she didn't say it.

'You know, it's really hard to say goodbye,' she said at last, hesitatingly, almost as if she was thinking it through as she spoke. 'The stroke damaged Mum mentally, but she still knows me and she still loves me visiting. But if I only have an hour, she clings and sobs when I leave. If I use a whole day, though… I take her out for walks, I give her meals and I read to her. Finally she goes to sleep happy. The nurses say the next day, when I'm not there, she's peaceful, not distressed. So if I worked in Cairns, I couldn't just pop in and out. It'd be too upsetting for all of us. But this way there are hardly any goodbyes. It's a private nursing home. It costs a bomb but fly in, fly out doctors get paid a bomb. This is the only way I can keep her there, and it works.'

'I told you I'd help!' It was an exclamation of anger, reverberating round the tunnel, and he felt rather than saw her wince.

'I told you, Josh. I'm done needing you.'

'You needed me today.'

'I did,' she said, and shifted a little and cradled her daughter just a wee bit tighter. 'And I'm so grateful.'

'So why won't you let me do more?'

'We've had this out,' she said, wearily now, and he flinched. The last thing he wanted was to make her tired.

'I'm sorry. We can talk about this later.'

'No, we can't. I shouldn't have kissed you.'

'You still…love me.' Why had he said it? But it wasn't a question. It was a statement of fact, and he waited for her to refute it.

She didn't. She was his woman, and he was cradling her with every ounce of love and protection he was capable of.

'Yes, Josh, I still love you,' she said at last, even more wearily. 'And I'm guessing… You're thinking you still love me.'

'I always have.'

'Within limits.'

'Maddie...'

'But loving's not for limits,' she whispered into the darkness, as if she was suddenly sure she was right. 'Look at my beautiful Lea.'

'Lea?'

'After a friend, here on the islands. And Lea Grace for my mum. I can't wait to show her to Mum. I know Mum's damaged but you know what? She'll think the sun rises and sets from her granddaughter. Unconditional love. That's what I'll give my Lea, from now until eternity.'

'I would have loved you...'

'If I let you. You said that. But your love had conditions.'

'It didn't.'

'It did,' she said, steadily and surely. 'As long as love is one-directional it's fine by you. You're allowed to love me all you want. But me...'

'Maddie...'

'No, let me say it,' she whispered. It was weird, sitting in this appalling place, locked in by total blackness. By rights they should still be terrified, but Lea's birth had changed things. This seemed a place of peace. Even Malu's breathing had settled, reassuring them all.

'Josh, when Mikey died it broke your heart.' She said it steadily into the stillness. 'I know it did, but you couldn't show it. You couldn't take comfort.'

'I didn't need to.'

'Yes, you did,' she said, still surely. 'But you were afraid if you showed it you'd break. You comforted me but when I cried you couldn't cry with me. You were my rock but I didn't need a rock. Mikey had two parents. Only one was allowed to grieve.'

'Maddie…'

'And then when Holly died it was worse,' she whispered. 'Because you were the one who was grief-stricken, but how could you let it out? How could you share? I could see the war you were waging but there wasn't a thing I could do to help. You have this armour, and it's so strong there's no way I can get through. And I can't live with armour, Josh. Just…loving…isn't enough.'

He didn't answer. Guilty as charged, he thought, but what could he do about it?

'It's okay,' she said, steadily now, and he wondered how she could sound so strong after what she'd been through. But she was strong, his Maddie.

His Maddie?

She wasn't his Maddie. They'd decided to end their marriage for the most logical of reasons and those reasons still stood.

His arms were around her. She was cradling her tiny new daughter and he knew if anything happened to either of them his heart would break.

But he couldn't share. That way… To open himself to such pain, to let the world see him exposed.

Maddie called it armour and maybe it was.

And, yes, he still needed it.

Out there be dragons.

She was right. He did have armour, and without it he had no weapon fierce enough to face them.

His phone rang. Thank you, he said silently as he answered. Thinking was doing his head in. Thinking while holding Maddie was doing his head in.

Keanu.

'Another bag coming in,' Keanu told him. 'This

one has air mattresses and a pump. It's safer if we pull in tandem.'

Which meant moving away from Maddie. She'd heard what Keanu had said and was already shifting slightly so he could move.

He hated leaving her.

But air mattresses... To lie on air rather than solid rock... It was imperative for both Malu and for Maddie.

'I'll miss my Josh cushion,' Maddie said, and he knew she'd said it lightly. But to Josh, right then, it didn't sound light at all.

Air mattresses. Dust masks. Food packs and drinks.

All the essentials to let them live.

And then Malu decided he might not.

He'd seemed okay. Josh had even let him use the phone to talk to Pearl. Pearl's terror had resounded through the shaft—there was no room for privacy here—but after a couple of moments the calm, gruff voice of her miner husband seemed to have settled the worst of her fears.

'We're looking after him,' Josh had told Pearl before they'd disconnected. 'He has two doctors dancing attendance every moment. He wouldn't get that sort of attention in the best city hospital.'

'Oh, but you have a baby.' Pearl was so weepy.

He had a baby? Not so much.

'Maddie has a daughter, yes,' he told her, and he couldn't help himself, he had to flick on his torch and let light fall on the woman holding her tiny bundle. No woman could look more contented.

You have a baby? No. This was Maddie's baby. They were separate.

Because he was afraid?

This was hardly the time to think about that. 'Are you telling me Dr Maddie can't cope with a newborn and any medical emergency that could possibly arise?' he demanded of Pearl. 'She's a superwoman, your Doc Maddie.'

And there it was again. *Your Doc Maddie.*

Not his.

'I…I know she is.' Pearl faltered.

'But we don't need her,' Josh said firmly. 'Malu's recovering. He'll emerge battered and bruised—we all will. But for now we have air beds, we have plenty of supplies, we have a new baby to admire and we seem safe. Pearl, we're okay.'

Except they weren't.

How late was it—or how early—when Malu's breathing changed?

Josh must have dozed but Maddie touched him and he was wide awake in an instant.

'What do you need?'

'Listen to Malu.'

She would never have woken him if there wasn't a worry. Maddie was a seriously good doctor. He flicked on the torch and was at Malu's side in an instant.

And he heard what Maddie was hearing.

He'd checked Malu before he'd allowed himself to sleep and Malu had been breathing deeply and evenly. The morphine was effective. He had an air mattress and pillow, and a light mask to keep the dust at bay.

Josh had checked him thoroughly, knowing the bruises and pain from his chest signified probable fractured ribs. There had, however, been no sign of internal problems.

There were problems now. Malu's breathing was fast and shallow. He was staring up at the roof, his eyes wide and fearful. As Josh's torch flicked on, he turned and gazed at Josh in terror.

'I can't... I can't...'

Pneumothorax? Haemothorax? The words crashed into Josh's mind with a sickening jolt.

His mind was racing through causes. Probable broken ribs... The ribs had caused no problems until now, but maybe in his relaxed state, with the morphine taking hold and giving Malu's body a false sense of security, the big man had shifted in his sleep.

And a fractured rib had shifted. If indeed the lung was punctured, every time Malu breathed, a little air would escape into the chest wall. And then a little more, and a little more...

There was no open wound. The air couldn't escape. The pressure would finally collapse first one lung and then the other.

Was he right? Almost before he'd thought it, he had Maddie's stethoscope in his ears, listening at the midaxillary line. Normally he'd listen at the back as well, but there was no way he was shifting Malu and risking more damage with those ribs.

Unequal bilateral breath sounds. Diminished on the right.

Very diminished.

If Malu had presented in an emergency room with suspected fractured ribs, he would have been X-rayed straight away, but up until now his breathing had been fine. That was all Josh had had to go on.

'What...what's happening?' Malu gasped, and Josh

took a moment to regroup. He needed to move fast, but panicking Malu would speed his breathing even more.

'I reckon you've somehow scraped your lung and made a small tear,' he told him. 'It's not too big or it would have caused problems before this, but if we're to get you breathing comfortably again we need to do something about it.'

'What…?'

Behind him Josh sensed Maddie reaching for the phone. They had two doctors, he thought, and the knowledge was reassuring, even if one was only hours post-baby.

'Keanu? We have a slight problem.' Maddie's voice was calmly efficient, as if a tension pneumothorax was something she saw twice a day before breakfast. 'We need a bag in here, with equipment…'

She knew that they didn't have the right equipment with them. She'd hauled her bag in when she'd run in. He'd brought in a bit more but now they needed specialist gear.

Part of his job was road trauma—actually, any kind of trauma. He had what he needed at ground level, in his emergency bag, the gear he'd packed so carefully back in Cairns.

'Let me speak to Keanu,' he told Maddie, and then he summoned a grin for Malu. 'Maddie's better at the bedside manner than I am. Is Lea asleep? Praise be. Our Maddie's just had the world's fastest maternity leave, and she's ready to move on.' And he held his hand out for the phone.

And Maddie had it figured, exactly what was needed of her right now. She edged forward—gingerly—who wouldn't edge gingerly so few hours after birth? Josh dragged his air bed to Malu's side so she had something soft to settle on.

'Let me tell you what I think's happening inside you,' Maddie said to Malu. 'It's really interesting. But, hey, I want you to even out your breaths while I talk. Nice and slow, nice and slow. I know it feels like you're a fish out of water, but we have time not to panic. Do you know what a pneumothorax is?' And she kept on talking, calm and steady, and Josh thought if he didn't know better he might even feel calm and steady, as well.

She was some doctor.

She was some woman.

But there wasn't time for focussing on Maddie. Keanu was on the end of the line, waiting with almost rigidly imposed patience. Maddie had said there was a problem. He'd know better than to demand details until they were ready to give them.

'Malu's developed a tension pneumothorax or hae-mothorax,' he said curtly, while Maddie's reassuring tones made a divide between Josh and his patient.

'Tension… Hell, Josh, are you sure?'

'Sure. A slight shift must have caused a leak. Un-equal bilateral breathing. Subcutaneous emphysema and tenderness, shortness of breath and chest pain. I'm thinking fractured rib is the only answer. Mate, I need gear in here fast. We need oxygen, plus local anaesthetic and equipment to get it into the intercostal space. I need a chest tube for drainage.'

'Mate—'

'Yeah,' Josh said, cutting him off. He knew exactly what Keanu wanted to say—that operating in conditions like this was unthinkable. How to keep a wound clean, a tube clear? 'But there's no choice. Send down a flutter valve but I'm thinking this place is too messy to rely on that alone. We'll use an underwater seal drain. I haven't used one for years but you'll find a three-chamber unit at the bottom of my kit. Also more saline. A lot more saline. Start getting it in now, drugs first. We have gloves and basic equipment here to keep things almost sterile.'

'Do you have enough light?' Keanu still sounded incredulous.

'Our Maddie will hold the torch while I operate. She's a hero, our Maddie. The lady with the lamp. Florence Nightingale has nothing on our Maddie.'

And Maddie heard. She turned a little and gave him a lopsided grin.

'Did you hear that?' she asked Malu. 'Josh reckons I'm great. Well, I reckon he's great so that's settled. We have two great doctors and one patient with a teeny, tiny tear in his middle. Nothing to this, then. Piece of cake.'

'What else do you need?' Keanu snapped, and Josh could hear the tension in the island doctor's voice. It was all very well playing the hero in the middle of hands-on action, he thought, but standing helplessly at the mine-head, knowing there was nothing you could do to help, would be a thousand times harder.

But he needed to concentrate on practicalities. Thinking of others' distress only muddied the waters.

Focus.

'I need a fourteen-gauge angiocath and at least a four-centimetre needle,' he told Keanu, hauling himself back from the brink as he always did in a crisis. If there was urgent need, he had to block everything else out. 'We need anaesthetic, tubing, more antiseptic, more gloves. I need a good clean sheet—when this is done I want Manu and his drainage tube protected from grit. If you can get it in fast, we're good to go.'

'That's all?'

'Plus anything else you can think of,' Josh replied. He wouldn't mind a clearer head to think things through. His arm was throbbing. His own breathing was a bit compromised—the grit was working through the mask and there was still that piercing knowledge of the danger they were in. That Maddie and her baby were in...

Do not go there.

'Actually, a ruddy big hole for lifting everyone out would be great,' he added dryly, and was dumb enough to feel proud he'd kept the emotion from his voice.

'We're working on it,' Keanu told him. 'Is Maddie okay?'

'I'm a whizz,' Maddie said, hearing Keanu's sharp query and taking the phone. She even managed to grin happily down at Malu, as if popping down mine shafts and doing emergency surgery right after childbirth was part of her normal working life. 'I'm practically boring Malu to sleep now, but we might need to up the anaesthetic a bit. Keanu, just tie everything up with pink ribbons as my baby shower and send it right down.'

'What are their chances?'

In the clearing at the mine mouth the men and women were looking grim.

Caroline had been efficiency plus since she'd arrived at the site, but she'd suddenly broken down. Beth was crouched beside her, hugging her.

In the background things were happening. There could be no bulldozers here. One hint of heavy machinery and the entire shaft could crumble.

The odds were being spelled out to all. Caroline had been washing out grit from a miner's eyes. She'd finished what she'd been doing, calmly reassured the guy she'd worked on—and then walked to the edge of the clearing and sobbed.

Beth had been watching her. Helpless R Us, Beth thought. Usually in a disaster such as this there were things she could do. Work was the best medicine, the best distraction from fear.

Here, though, the work for the medical team had dried up. Keanu was acting as communicator, organising the bags that were being carefully manoeuvred underground.

Caroline and Beth were left with nothing to do.

Except fear.

'We have the best team possible,' Beth told Caroline now. 'The best engineers… We've been on to Max Lockhart—apparently he owns this mine. He, like all of us, assumed it was closed, and he's appalled.'

'He would be,' Caroline whispered. 'He's…he's my father.'

'Your father?'

'He lives in Sydney. My uncle Ian's been in charge here. Dad…Dad has problems.'

'No matter,' Beth said soundly. 'Whatever he is, he's moving heaven and earth to get resources here. There's a massive mining operation just north of Cairns. He's been on to them. See those guys over there? That's where they come from and this is what they do, deal with mine collapses. They're saying they'll drill side on to the collapsed shaft where the rock's more solid. Then they'll pick their way across to our guys.'

'But it'll take so long... And Maddie...' Once the tears had come, Caroline was no longer able to stop them.

'We have time.' This was what Beth was good at—that and shimmying down rope ladders and hauling people out of overturned cars, but, hey, she had a few skills, and reassurance was in her bundle. 'The bag pulley system seems to be working well.'

'But how can they stay there? Keanu says the blocked area is no longer than ten feet long. A woman who's just given birth...'

'They have food, water, air and light,' Beth said solidly, maybe more solidly than she was feeling. 'We even have little bathroom bags, like they have in spaceships. We pull 'em out every time the pulley comes this way. We can even send in deodorant if it's needed. Not that your Maddie would smell, but Josh and Malu in a tight spot... All that male testosterone... Come to think of it, I will send in some deodorant. Maddie must be just about ready to pass out.'

And Caroline chuckled. It was a watery chuckle but it was a chuckle all the same.

'But this operation...' she whispered. 'With the rock so unstable... You really think they can be okay?'

'We have two skilled doctors underground and the best mine experts on top of the ground,' Beth told her. 'Of course they'll be okay. You'd better believe it.'

And then Keanu came over to talk to them, to hug Caroline, to add his reassurances.

Of course they'll be okay.

You'd better believe it?

'Please, let me believe it, too,' Beth muttered to herself as she moved away. 'Please.'

CHAPTER SEVEN

THEY HAD ALL the gear. Malu was as settled as they could make him. The pneumothorax had to be fixed now.

There was one slight problem.

Josh's right hand shook.

Maddie had cleaned the gash on his arm and pulled it together with Steri-Strips, but it ran almost from his elbow to his shoulder.

He hadn't lost sensation. There was no reason why his hand should shake.

It shook.

Maddie had prepped and draped Malu's underarm. She'd used ketamine as an adjunct to the morphine, making Malu dozy but not soundly asleep.

What was needed now was local anaesthetic. It was a procedure that needed care, knowledge and a steady hand. The anaesthetic needed to be infiltrated through the layers of the chest wall, onto the rib below the intercostal space. The needle then had to be angled above the rib and advanced slowly until air was aspirated. The last five mils of the anaesthetic needed to be injected into the pleural space.

Josh knew exactly what to do. He'd done it before. He'd do it again—this was his job, trauma medicine.

His hand shook.

'Josh?' Maddie's voice was a soft whisper. She was holding the torch.

She'd have seen the tremor.

'I can do this,' he muttered under his breath, and he closed his eyes and counted to ten, trying desperately to steady himself.

He opened his eyes and his hand still shook.

I can't. But he didn't say it. Malu was still sleepily conscious. The last thing Malu needed was to sense indecision in his surgical team. Instead, he glanced up at Maddie, their eyes locked and held...

I can't.

'Slight change of roles,' Maddie said, without so much as a break in her voice. It was like this was totally normal, first cut one toenail, then cut another. 'Malu, Josh is looking at your ribs and thinking you don't need his great masculine forefinger to be making a ruddy big hole. Not when we have my dainty digits at the ready. So we're swapping. Hold on a second, Dr Campbell, while I scrub and glove. It now seems I get to play doctor while Josh plays the lady with the lamp.'

And Malu even smiled.

She was amazing, Josh thought as he took the torch from her. She'd made what was happening sound almost normal. She was stunning.

She was hours after giving birth. How could she?

'Maddie, can you?'

'Steady as a rock,' she said, smiling at him with all the assurance in the world, and she held up her hands to show there wasn't the hint of a tremor. There should have been. After what she'd gone through. 'Though we're hoping Malu's not rocklike. Malu, if you've been working out I might need to get a drill rather than a teeny, tiny needle. Why you guys think you need muscles is beyond me. Give me a guy with a one pack rather than a six pack any day.'

She was still distracting Malu. He was holding the torch—he could hardly help her on with her gloves but she used the backup method—using one sterile glove to tug on another. It wasted gloves but this wasn't the time to be arguing. Instead…he could do a bit of distracting, too.

'So you'd have loved me better if I'd had a bit of flab?' he demanded.

'The odd sign of humanity never hurt anyone,' she said, turning back to the instruments they'd laid out ready. Dust was still settling. Contaminants were everywhere. There were real risks here, but the alternative was unthinkable. 'I never did have much use for Spider-Man.'

'I guess that's what ended our marriage,' Josh said, managing a grin for Malu. 'Though I would have described myself more as Batman. He was so smooth in his other life.'

'Yeah, six pack in one, smarmy in the other. You ready, Malu? It's going to sting.'

'If he's Batman, I can do the hero bit, too,' Malu managed. 'Do your worst, Doc. Just get this breathing under control.'

He'd thought it would be the hardest thing in the world, to be aboveground, not knowing what was going on.

He was wrong. The hardest thing was doing what he was doing now, which was exactly nothing.

Except holding the torch. If Maddie wasn't totally reliant on the light he was holding maybe he could move behind her, support her a little. What he was demanding of her seemed impossible.

How dared his arm shake?

To have to ask for help... To be dependent on Maddie...

It wasn't him who was dependent on Maddie, he reminded himself. It was Malu. He was under no illusions, Malu's life was under her hands.

But they were steady hands, and there was no doubting their skill. He watched, every nerve attuned to what she was doing, as she carefully, carefully manoeuvred the anaesthetic to where it was needed.

Malu hardly responded as the needle went in. The morphine and ketamine were doing their job—but also, Malu was growing weaker. How much lung capacity did he have left?

To do so much and have him die now...

Stop thinking forward, he told himself. That was the problem with doing nothing—he had time to think.

Josh's work was his lifeline. When things hurt, when emotion threatened to overwhelm him, work was what he did. It stopped the hurt, or at least it pushed it so far onto the back burner that he didn't have to confront it.

They were waiting for the anaesthetic to take hold. Maddie was staring down at the sterile cloth holding her instruments. There was a risk dust would settle on the cleaned tools but there was little they could do about it. Josh was holding the torch with his steady hand. He couldn't do much assisting with the other.

She was practising what she needed to do in her head.

How many times had he watched her skill in a medical setting?

They'd met—how many years ago? He'd been a registrar at Sydney Central's emergency unit. Maddie had been a first-year intern, trying emergency medicine out for size.

She'd been one of the best interns he'd ever met. She'd been calm in a crisis, warm, reassuring and clever.

He'd tried to persuade her to stay, to train in the specialty he loved.

'Emergency medicine's great,' he remembered telling her. 'You live on adrenaline. You save lives. Every time you turn around there's a new challenge.'

'But you never get to know your patients,' she'd said, and she'd said it over and over as his professional persuasion had turned a lot more personal. Soon it hadn't been Dr Campbell trying to persuade Dr Haddon to change career direction, but it had been Josh persuading Maddie to marry him.

'Ready,' she said now, and he shoved the memories away and focussed. Even if his role was minor, the light was still crucial. Her fingers could never be allowed to shadow what she was doing.

But it nearly killed him to watch. What she was doing was so important. He was trained for this. This was his job, whereas Maddie…

This was still part of her job and, unpractised or not, she seemed to know exactly what she was doing. Her fingers were rock steady as she made the incision along the border of the intercostal space. She made it deep and long enough to accommodate her finger.

She glanced up at Josh then, a fast glance that said she wasn't as sure as her actions made out, but then she was focussed again.

'You're doing great,' he told her, but she wasn't listening.

She needed a nurse with swabs. Maybe he could swab, but if the light wobbled...

'In,' she said, and as the tissue was pushed aside by the insertion of her finger he heard the tiny rush of outcoming air.

She had the curved clamp now, using blunt dissection only, using the clamp to spread and split the muscle tissue.

She was in the pleural cavity. She'd be exploring, looking for adhesions. Making lightning-fast assessments.

He wanted to talk her through what was happening, but her face said it all. She was using all her concentration and then some.

'Going great,' he repeated, and then, as Malu flinched, not with pain, he thought, but maybe with tension because breathing was so darned hard, he took the miner's hand with his shaky one and gripped.

They both watched Maddie.

And watching Maddie...

He'd forgotten how much he missed her. He remembered that first time he'd seen her as a newly fledged intern. She'd been comforting a frightened child.

He'd been called to help but he'd paused in the doorway, caught by the sight of her. Something had changed, right at that moment.

Something he'd been denying ever since? That he needed her?

She was putting the chest tube in now, mounting it on the curved clamp and passing it along the pleural cavity. He heard Malu's breath rasp in and rasp in again, like a man who'd been drowning but had just reached the surface. Finally, blessedly, he saw the almost imperceptible shift at Malu's throat. It was imperceptible unless you were looking for it. It was imperceptible unless you knew that the lungs were re-inflating, that what was in the chest cavity was realigning to where it should be.

'Done,' Maddie murmured, and he did hear shakiness now, but it was in her voice, not in her hands. She was still working, but on the exterior, suturing the tube into place. She'd taken a moment to tug off her gloves and put on new ones before she worked on the exterior of the wound. She shouldn't have needed to. If she'd had an assistant...

She didn't. She was working alone.

He could have told her how to operate the underwater seal but he didn't need to. She knew how.

He could have helped her dress the incision area but he didn't need to do that, either.

She was a doctor operating at her best.

She didn't need him.

The words hung. A shadow...

Had he been too afraid to admit he needed her?

The tube was now firmly connected to the underwater seal. He could see the bubbles as air escaped the pleural cavity. The loss of this tiny amount of air wasn't enough to cause Malu major problems. Building up in the pleural cavity, it was lethal. Calmly bubbling out into water, it was harmless.

Job done. The dressing was in place. Maddie sat back on her heels—and he saw the energy drain out of her.

She swayed.

And finally, finally there was something he could do. She did need him. He moved before he even knew

he intended moving. He took her into his arms and
she let herself sag. She crumpled against him, let his
strength enfold her, and let him hold her as if her life
force was spent.

It wasn't spent, though. This woman had the life
force of a small army. She let herself be held for all of
two minutes and then he felt her gather herself, stiffen,
tug away.

And it nearly broke him. For those two minutes he'd
felt her heart beating with his. He'd felt himself melt
into her.

He'd realised what he'd lost.

'Thanks, Josh.' Her voice was still shaky but she was
back to being professional—almost. 'That's what you
don't see in most theatres—doctors cuddling doctors.
But I was a bit woozy.'

'You didn't seem woozy when you were operating,'
Malu managed, and Maddie smiled and touched her
patient's cheek. It was a gesture Josh knew—one of
the things he'd noticed first about her. She was tactile,
touching, warm.

He'd tried it out himself. It reassured patients. He'd
learned from her.

Touching worked.

He wanted…

'I can pull myself together when I need to,' Maddie
told Malu, and Josh knew her attention was back to
where it ought to be—to her patient, to the situation—
to her baby, lying peacefully on the air bed behind her.
'But now, if you don't mind, I'll let Dr Campbell take
over my duty roster. Breathing easier?'

'You better believe it.'

'Excellent. That tube stays in place until we get an

X-ray upstairs, but there's no blood coming out. That's a great sign. It means you have a slight tear in your lung but nothing major. As long as you stay fairly still—no need to make a martyr of yourself but let's not roll over without giving me or Josh forewarning—you should have no problems.'

'I'll need an operation when we get out of here?'

When? There was no if. Even though the walls around them were made of crumbling rock, Malu seemed to have forgotten.

That was down to Maddie, too, Josh decided. She was showing not one scrap of fear. If she'd been a doctor at the end of a long shift in an emergency ward of a large city hospital she couldn't be more composed. She was weary and she was signing off, but she was calmly reassuring her patient before she went.

I'll need an operation...

'You possibly will,' she told Malu. 'One of those ribs must have broken with a pointy bit. Josh and I don't like pointy bits, do we, Josh?'

'No, we don't,' Josh agreed gravely. 'But after what you've been through, an operation to stick two bits of rib together will be a piece of cake. You reckon you might go to sleep now?' With the amount of drugs on board it must be only the adrenaline of what had been happening—plus the terror of breathing difficulties—that had been keeping him awake.

'Going to sleep now,' Malu whispered, his speech already slurred.

'And you,' he told Maddie. He wanted to hug her again but she'd already turned and gathered her baby into her arms, transforming again into a mother. With baby. A brand-new family—of which he was no part.

He tugged an air bed to the far side of the shaft. 'Here,' he said, roughly because emotion was threatening to do his head in. 'Keanu's sent down sheets. Settle. I'll cover you all. You and Malu and Lea. And then you sleep.'

'Yes, sir,' Maddie said, still wobbly, and it was too much for Josh. He did gather her into his arms, but not to hold her as he wanted to hold her. Yes, his arm was weak. No, he shouldn't be doing any such thing, but he lifted her anyway, carrying her bodily across to the air bed, setting her down, making sure she and her baby were safe.

He covered them both with the sheet.

'I need to turn the torch off now,' he told her. Keanu had sent down more batteries but they were both aware that the line into their cavern was fragile and the time until rescue was unknown. They had to conserve everything. 'I'll lie beside Malu so I can feel if anything changes.'

'You're a wonderful doctor, Dr Campbell,' she whispered. 'Thank you.'

Him? A wonderful doctor... He stared down at her, speechless. But she closed her eyes and slept and he was left saying nothing at all.

CHAPTER EIGHT

THE NIGHT CREPT ON, inch by pitch-black inch. It was a relief that Malu needed checking. Every few minutes Josh flicked on the torch and checked the underwater seal, checked Malu's vital signs, checked there was nothing wrong with his patient—and then he checked Maddie.

He never shone the light directly at her. There was no way he was risking waking her. She slept the sleep of the truly exhausted.

Her baby lay in the crook of her arm as she slept. He'd suggested they use his air bed, setting tiny Lea up in a separate space, but the look she'd cast him had been one of disbelief.

'When the roof of the cave could come down any minute? She stays right by me.'

The baby care 'experts' would have a field day, he thought. Mothers in the same bed as their newborn? He'd heard a lecture once by a dragon of a professor...

How easy would it be for mother to roll onto her child?

It wouldn't happen. Every ounce of Maddie's being was in protective mode.

She was instinctively caring.

She was holding her daughter.

And all at once he was hit by a wave of longing so great it threatened to overwhelm him. Family...

He couldn't do family. Families hurt.

He flicked the torch off and settled back on his air bed. Not to sleep, though. Malu's obs were vital.

But things were okay. They were as safe as he could get them. He'd done what he could.

But suddenly things weren't okay. Things were very much not okay.

He was shaking—not just his arm this time, but his whole body.

Why? He was fighting to suppress what was going on, fighting to make sense of it.

He was exhausted—he knew he was. He'd been working on adrenaline for almost twenty-four hours. He was injured. His arm throbbed.

He'd helped his ex-wife deliver her baby. It made sense that it'd affect him. If he could put it into logic, then he could control it.

He'd had to stand back and watch while Maddie had operated. He'd been helpless. He'd lost control.

Think it through logically, he told himself. Keep it analytical. Stop the shaking...

He couldn't.

There was no sound, no movement, and yet he felt like the walls were caving in. His head felt like it was exploding. Sensation after sensation was coursing through him. Black fear... Maddie with rocks raining down around her. Lea with the cord round her neck. Malu gasping for breath...

And more. The past. A dying baby. Maddie lying in hospital, sobbing her eyes out. Looking down at the tiny scrap who could have been his son. A child who *was* his son.

And Holly, his little sister, lying still and cold in the mortuary. A little sister he'd protected and protected and protected.

Until he'd failed.

He couldn't breathe. He couldn't think.

This is a panic attack, he told himself, fiercely, but he couldn't listen. The doctor part of him, the part that had been his all for so long, the Josh who was a crucial member of Cairns Air Sea Rescue was no longer here.

He was a kid lying in the dark, alone and terrified, during the time he and Holly had been separated in two different foster homes. Where was she? What was happening to her? How could he keep her safe when they were apart?

And then…he was a guy bereft, looking down at the body of his tiny son. Seeing Maddie's anguish. Trying to figure how to hide his own anguish so he could help her.

And then Holly's death. Maddie trying to hold him. The cold, hard knowledge that he'd failed. He'd failed everyone.

He must have made some sound. Surely he hadn't cried out, but he couldn't stop shaking. He couldn't…

And suddenly Maddie was there, kneeling on his air bed. Tugging his rigid body close so his head was on her breast. Holding him, despite the rigid shaking, despite the fact that he didn't know why, he didn't know what…

'Josh…Josh, love, it's okay. Josh, we're safe.'

Her words made no sense. The sensation of losing control was terrifying.

Her words faded but her arms tightened.

She held, and there was nothing he could do but be held, to take strength from her.

For the first time ever?

It couldn't matter. He was so far out of control that to pull back was unthinkable. There was no strength left in him.

And gradually the tremors eased. She was kneeling on the air bed, holding him against her, running her fingers through his hair and crooning a little. And as the tremors eased, the crooning turned into words.

'Sweetheart, it's okay. We're safe. The nice men with the digging machines will get us out. This might not be the Ritz but we have comfy beds and Keanu's saying the pulley system's even good enough for hot coffee in the morning. Maybe that's what this is, love, lack of caffeine. You always were hopeless without coffee. But it's okay, Josh. We're all safe. Thanks to you, love, we're fine and we'll stay fine.'

And then she added a tiny rider, a whisper so soft he could hardly hear it.

'I love you.'

And the world settled on its axis, just like that. The tremors stopped. He was a man again. He was Dr Josh Campbell, being held by...his wife.

Needing comfort?

He didn't...need. How could he?

How could he not? It was like he was being torn in two.

He broke away, tugging back, just a little but enough to break the contact. She turned and flicked on the torch, not shining it directly at him but giving enough light to turn blackness into shadows.

She touched his face—and he felt himself flinch.

He raked his hair and then thought he shouldn't have done that. The feel of her fingers in his hair was still with him. He wanted it forever.

He couldn't have it.

To lose control… To stand at the edge of the precipice and feel himself falling…

'Maddie, I'm sorry. I'm…'

'What is it, love?'

Don't call me love. Somehow he stayed silent but he wanted to shout it. Why?

Because he wanted those barriers up. He was in control. He had to be. He knew no other way.

'Maddie, I don't know what happened.' He did, but there was no way he could open the floodgates, explain terror he hardly understood himself.

'This is scary.' She said it prosaically, stating the obvious for the idiot who didn't get it. 'You've spent the day being a warrior, but armour can only hold you up for so long.'

'Yeah.' Like that made sense.

What was he doing, being this feeble? Shame swept over him, a shame so deep it threatened to overwhelm him.

'Sorry.' He spoke more harshly than he intended and he forced his voice to moderate. 'Nightmare or something—who knows? I'm over it. I don't need—'

'Me?'

Yes, he wanted to say. It would be so easy to sink against her again, to take comfort. But beyond that… How could he survive if he needed her?

He couldn't.

'I guess I needed a hug,' he admitted.

'Of course you needed a hug. You're human, Josh. Giving works both ways.'

'But I don't need anything more.'

It was the wrong thing to say. He saw her flinch. 'Of course you don't.' She was watching him, with the expression of a woman who knew everything she needed to know about her man, and it made her sad.

'That's why we could never make it,' she whispered. 'You've never let me share your nightmares. You've never let me close.'

'I can't.'

'I know you can't,' she whispered with desperate sadness, and then Lea stirred and whimpered behind her and she turned away.

'Try and sleep,' she told Josh as she lifted her baby to her breast. 'We'll leave the torch on. I need it to feed and you need it to keep the nightmares at bay.'

'I don't need—'

'And maybe you never will and that's a tragedy,' she snapped. 'Think about it.'

Lea settled. Maddie gently rocked and crooned and loved.

And he lay there in the dark and he felt more lonely than he'd ever felt in his life.

He'd loved loving Maddie. He'd loved holding her, making her laugh, helping her, comforting her.

Wasn't it enough?

But as he watched Maddie's face, as he saw the peace settle over her as her tiny baby settled, he felt like a prism had opened into a world he hardly knew.

Cradling her baby helped. Cradling Lea brought Maddie peace.

She'd wanted to comfort him. The night Holly had

died… He remembered coming out of the mortuary and Maddie had been there, white and shocked. She'd walked straight at him, gathered him into her arms and held.

And he'd pulled away. 'Go home, Maddie. There's no use for us both to suffer.'

To do anything else… To have let Maddie comfort him as she'd tried then…

It was still a precipice, and all he knew was to back away.

CHAPTER NINE

THE EXPERTS CHANGED their minds again. They didn't bore down from the top or the side; rather they cautiously picked their way through the existing shaft, inch by cautious inch, shoring as they came.

For those trapped, the wait seemed interminable, but they had what they most needed. Malu had stabilised and even improved. He slept.

Bugsy seemed resigned. He pinched half of Josh's air mattress. Josh used him as a pillow and he didn't mind. There was something comforting about using a golden retriever as a pillow. Josh slept fitfully while they waited, never for more than an hour at a time, keeping watch, but there seemed no drama. Maddie slept, too, waking only to feed and get to know her new daughter. If there wasn't the risk, Josh could almost imagine she was where she wanted to be. He watched the expression on her face as Lea's tiny mouth found the breast and suckled. He watched as Maddie's arms curved around her with love—and he was almost jealous.

Almost. He had himself back under control.

In the time he wasn't dozing, or attending to his little hospital's needs, he worked, and that was a relief. They now had netting above them, a sort of tent. He'd assembled it with care from materials sent in via the bags, small piece by small piece. It was made of wire mesh, and was supported by a series of triangular, snap-together poles. In the event of a full-scale collapse it'd be useless, but smaller loose stones were now less of a threat.

And the rescuers were on their way. Finally they could hear the miners through the rock.

'We reckon we're within six feet,' Keanu told him on one of their brief calls. Their supply of phone batteries was bearing up. The bag system could pull in more but the slightest rock slip could end their supply. Apart from that first indulgent baby parcel, only the barest essentials were coming in.

Malu was still drowsy but as the miners got closer Maddie stayed awake. Even Bugsy seemed restless. They all knew the last few feet were the most dangerous.

The more Josh thought about how he'd managed to get in here, the more he knew he'd been incredibly lucky—and maybe also incredibly stupid.

If Maddie hadn't been here…

Or not. Beth often told him he was crazy, that he had no fear, and maybe he didn't.

If there was an overturned car at the bottom of a cliff it'd be Josh who abseiled down to attend to an injured driver. He'd swung in a harness over a churning sea. He'd taken risks more times than he could remember.

Why not? It didn't matter if anything happened to him.

But now it mattered. He thought of the people dependent on Maddie and Malu. There were people outside who loved them.

'Do you have anyone back in Cairns you can hug when this is over?' Maddie asked into the silence, and he wondered if she'd been mind-reading.

'I... No.'

'No girlfriend?'

He thought about it before answering. He and Karen dated when it suited them. She was an adrenaline junkie, just like him, and for her birthday last month he'd taken her skydiving.

He remembered their dinner afterwards. She'd spent the night messaging about her awesome adventure to her mates.

No, he thought. She wasn't even his girlfriend.

'Earth to Josh...'

'Bachelorhood suits me.'

'That's fear talking.'

'Since when did you do psychology?'

'I had years to analyse you.'

'So why haven't you remarried?' he growled, and she snuggled down a little farther in her makeshift bed. Despite the earplugs they used during the worst of the drilling, the constant chipping of tools on rock was challenging.

Bugsy had abandoned Josh's air bed and was pressed hard against one side of Maddie, maybe sensing the increasing tension as the sounds of rescue grew closer. Lea was cradled in her arms. It was like she had a small posse of protection and he was on the outside.

'I tried marriage once.' She was speaking lightly, trying for humour, he thought. 'I don't have the courage to try it again.'

'So you'll raise your daughter on your own?'

'No.'

It was said sharply, and her words hung. For a moment he thought she wouldn't continue, but when she finally spoke her voice was reflective again.

'That's why I finally figured I could try again to have a baby,' she told him. 'When I realised I wasn't on my own. I guess...when I started working on Wildfire I was pretty much at rock bottom. I needed a job. The Australian government helps fund the medical services by supplying FIFOs. The pay's excellent and I was determined to keep Mum where she is. And, no, Josh, there was no way I was accepting help from you. But I hadn't been here for six months before I realised what a special place Wildfire is. The people are amazing, and the staff who are attracted to work here seem just as good. I guess all of us outsiders are running away from stuff, saving money, hiding, changing tracks... But the islanders welcome us all. Saying this place is like family sounds a cliché, but it's not.'

'That's why you ran into a collapsing mine?'

'Malu's wife is my friend. So, yes, in a way...'

'They're not your family.' He spoke more harshly than he'd intended. 'You're their doctor and colleague. They need you.'

'It works both ways. I need them.'

'How can you need them?'

'They accept me for what I am,' she said simply. 'When I ache, they ache. Last year Mum had another stroke. I went back to Cairns and had to stay for a month. When I came back, my tiny villa was a sea of flowers. Kalifa met me off the plane. Kalifa was one of the tribal elders, and he and his wife have practically been grandparents to me.'

She paused then and he knew she was thinking of

the eldery man, of a needless death, and of who knew what else waited for them on the surface.

That's what happened when you got attached, he thought. It was like slicing a part of you out.

He didn't have that many parts left.

'I think Kalifa organised it,' she said softly. 'Or maybe it was his wife, Nani, or Pearl, Malu's wife, or Hettie or any one of so many… Anyway, all along the path to my villa were hibiscus, and I think I was hugged by every single Wildfire resident that night. And you know what? That was the night I made the decision to have a baby. Because I'm part of a family. I'm loved and I can love back.'

The last few words were said almost defiantly. As if she expected him to reject them.

And then there was a sound of rubble, falling stones that made them both hold their breath. There was an oath from the far side of the rock and then the steady chipping restarted.

'I can't cope…with them putting their lives on the line for me,' Josh muttered.

'They're putting their lives on the line for all of us,' Maddie said, gentleness fading to asperity. 'You don't have a monopoly on heroism, Josh.'

'I don't—'

'No, that was mean.' She took a deep breath and winced again and he thought she was hurting. She'd given birth not twenty-four hours before. She'd already been bruised in the rockfall. Of course she was hurting. But she took a deep breath and kept on going. 'You know what I've figured?' she said, evenly again. 'I've figured that it's a whole lot easier to be the hero than the one dangling by her fingertips from the cliff.'

'What does that mean?'

'Why are you a doctor, Josh?' she asked, gently
again. 'No, don't answer, because I know. It's because
in medicine you can help. Add to that your search and
rescue job and you can be the hero in every single situation. But when it comes to being rescued yourself, you
can't handle it. That's what killed our marriage and it's
killing you now.'

Silence. He watched her close her eyes and then saw
her wince and put a hand to her neck.

Maybe there was something he could do.

'What's wrong?' he asked.

'Hero again?' she asked wryly, and she even managed a smile.

'Maddie, what is it?'

'I must have ricked my neck in the rockfall,' she con-
fessed. 'I haven't had time to think about it.'

'Would a massage help?'

She thought about it. She looked at him for a long
time in the shadowy light and then slowly she nodded.

'It might,' she said at last. 'But that'd mean accepting—again—that I need help.'

'You do need help. Maddie, being a single mother...
You know it'll be hard. You still have your mother.
You'll be doing a full-time job and trying to care for
a baby, as well.' And then, because the sounds of rescue were growing closer and maybe there wouldn't be
time to say it again, he said what he most wanted to say.

'Maddie, our marriage was good. The chemistry's
still there. Maybe we can make it work again. Maybe
we should try.'

'You'd be a father to Lea?'

'She needs a dad.'

'Need's no basis for a marriage. You must be the first one to tell me that.'

'But you need—'

'Josh, I don't need—at least, not from you. I have the community. I have my colleagues and my friends. Believe it or not, I even have my mum. She still loves me, even though she's so badly damaged, and her love supports me. I have everything I need. Marriage is something else. Marriage is for loving, not for dependency. It's for sharing and I don't think you ever will. I'm sorry, Josh, but I can't let you hurt me again.'

'I never would.'

'You don't understand how not to.' Then she smiled again, trying desperately for lightness, trying desperately to put things back on a footing to go forward. 'But in terms of need… Okay, Josh, more than anything else, I would love a head and shoulders massage. You do the best and I've missed them. That's what I need from you, Josh Campbell, and nothing more.'

Why couldn't she give in to him?

She was giving in to him, she decided as his fingers started their magic. If this was the last massage he ever gave her, she'd enjoy every second.

She'd pretend he was hers?

The first time he'd done this to her had been just after she'd started work. He'd been waiting for her at the nurses' station. She'd been supposedly watching an operation but the surgeon had thought hands-on training was best. The surgeon had stood and watched every step of the way at what should have been a routine appendectomy.

Except it hadn't been routine. The patient had been

a young mum with no history of medical problems, nothing to suggest the sudden, catastrophic heart failure that had killed her.

They'd had a cardiac team there in seconds, they'd fought with everything they'd had, but there'd been no happy ending. Maddie had walked blindly out of Theatre and Josh had been there. He'd gathered her into his arms and held.

He was good at caring was Josh. He was amazing.

They'd been supposed to be going out with friends. Instead, Maddie had found herself on a picnic rug on the beach, eating fish and chips, surprising herself by eating while Josh had let her be, just watched. And waited.

And then he'd moved behind her and started his massage.

It had started as gentleness itself, a bare touching, hands placed softly on her shoulders, resting, as if seeking permission to continue.

She hadn't moved then. She didn't move now.

Permission granted.

And now his fingers started their magic.

First they stroked over the entire area he wanted to massage, her head, her shoulders, her back, her arms and her hands. She was resting against him but as his fingers moved she slumped forward a little, so he could touch her back.

Skin against skin.

How could he do this with an injured arm?

She couldn't ask. Maybe she couldn't even care?

Then his fingers deepened the pressure and she forgot what the question was.

He was kneading the tight muscles on either side of her neck, kneading upward, firm now, pressing into what seemed knots of tension. He worked methodically, focussing first one side then the other. His fingers kneaded, never so hard it hurt, never so hard she felt out of control, but firm enough to make the tension ooze upward and outward and away.

And then to her scalp. Her hair must be full of grit and sweat, a tangled mess, but right now she didn't care. Josh was stroking his thumbs upward, as if releasing the tension that had been sent up there by his wonder fingers. He was teasing her hair, tugging lightly, running his fingers through and through...

She was floating. She was higher than any drug could have made her. Lea was nestled beside her, Bugsy was at her other side, and Josh was turning her cavern of hell into one of bliss.

She heard herself moan with pleasure. She was melting into him, disappearing into a puddle of sensual ecstasy... His fingers... His hands...

Josh.

She drifted and he massaged and she floated, every single threat, every single worry placed at bay.

She loved... She loved...

And yet, as his fingers left her scalp and drifted down, beginning their delicious movements at her shoulder blades, an argument drifted back with them.

A long-ago conversation. After that night. They'd ended up in bed—of course. She'd slept through the night, enfolded by Josh's strong arms, and in the morning she'd woken to her beautiful man bringing her tea and toast.

'Where did you learn...?'

'One of my foster-mothers,' he told her. 'She used to have me do it for her after work.'

'Have you ever had anyone do it to you?'

'No,' he'd said shortly, and she'd set down her tea, looped her arms around his neck and drawn him to her.

'Well, I'm going to learn,' she'd declared. 'We'll massage each other every time we're stressed. Or even when we're not stressed. In fact, with massages like that, we need never be stressed again.'

He'd smiled and kissed her but then he'd drawn away. 'There's no need. I don't need a massage. Any time you want one, though...'

'So if I learn you won't let me practise?'

'As I said, sweetheart, there's no need.'

And there was that word again. It was like a brick wall, a solid divider that kept Josh on one side and the world on another. If he admitted need, then what? He'd fall apart?

She thought he'd crack. She thought if she loved him enough...

She was wrong.

He was stroking down her head now, across both her shoulders. There was grit on her shoulders and the remains of sweat and grime, but it made little difference. The finest oils couldn't have made her feel any more at peace than she was right now.

He was applying gentle pressure, running his fingers down her arms, using both hands, from shoulders to the tips of her fingers. She was totally subsumed by the sensation. If he wanted to make love with her right then...

Right... Less than two days after birth, in a collapsed gold mine, with her daughter, with an injured miner, with a dog...

The whole thing was fantasy. Her head was filled with a desire that could never be fulfilled.

His hands were stroking down her neck and shoulders, down her arms, breaking contact at her fingertips, over and over, but each stroke slower, slower, until finally his fingers trailed away from hers and held still.

Then a feather-light touch on her shoulders, a signal that it was finished.

Silence.

The end.

She wanted to cry.

She wanted to turn and hold him. She wanted to take him into her arms. She wanted him to be her…family?

She did none of those things. You couldn't hug a man with armour, she thought, no matter how much you might want to.

'Thank you,' she whispered into the shadows. 'Thank you, Josh, for everything.' And she gathered Lea back into her arms and held, not because Lea needed her—the baby was deeply asleep—but because she needed Lea.

'You need to sleep,' Josh said, and he held her shoulders while he moved sideways, so he wasn't right behind her, so she was free to settle back onto the air bed with her baby.

'Yes,' she whispered.

'Is there anything you need?'

'Nothing.'

Liar.

But it couldn't be a lie, she thought. She'd made her decision.

Or he'd made his decision years ago and nothing had changed.

And then a puff of dust surged out from the rocks above them and the dust had come from the gap Josh had used to get in, that they'd been using to haul bags back and forth.

'Anyone home?' There'd been scraping at the rocks that had grown so constant they'd hardly been listening—or maybe it was that they'd been just a bit distracted?

'Hey!' Josh called back, and his voice still sounded distracted. Maybe he was just as discombobulated as she was, Maddie thought, and was uncharitable enough to think, *Good!*

'I can see chinks of your light,' the voice called. 'You're eight feet away, no more. We've reinforced up to here. Another hour should do it. You guys almost ready to emerge?'

'You'd better believe it,' Josh said, but once again Maddie heard that trace of uncertainty.

It was as if they'd both be grateful to be aboveground, but neither of them was quite sure what they'd be leaving behind.

CHAPTER TEN

IT WAS MORE like three hours before the final break-through came, because no one was taking chances. By that time, however, there was a solid channel, a shored-up shaft that was deemed safe enough to risk moving them out.

They wasted no time. Safe was relative and any moment the ground could move again, so the move happened with speed. There was the moment's relief when a blackened face appeared, grinning and taking a second to give them a thumbs-up. Then there was skilled shoring work to make the entrance secure before a grimy rescuer was in the shaft with them and Maddie was being told she was to be strapped to a cradle stretcher, whether she willed it or not.

She didn't will it. 'Take Malu first.' She spoke it as an order, in her most imperious tone—a doctor directing traffic in the worst emergency couldn't have sounded more authoritative—and she couldn't believe it when she was overruled.

'Sorry, ma'am, orders are you're first,' the man said, and Josh touched her face, a light reassurance, but his touch was an order, too.

'They get two for the price of one with you,' he told

her. 'You and your Lea. Lea's a priority, even if you're not. Off you go, the two of you.'

And then, because he couldn't help himself, he kissed her, hard and fast, and it was an acknowledgment that being hauled out through the fast-made tunnel had major risks.

As if to emphasise it, another cloud of dust spat down on them.

'On the stretcher,' the man ordered, and Maddie had the sense to submit and then to stay passive, holding tight to Lea as what looked like a cradle was erected over her—the same shape as an MRI machine and just as claustrophobic. Once she was enclosed, the head of the stretcher was hauled up to the guy waiting, and she was lifted and pulled into the mouth of the shaft.

And then along. She didn't know how they did it. These guys were experts but she knew from their silence that they were working far closer to the limits of safety that they'd done before. And all she could do was lie still and hold Lea—and think of Josh left behind...

Josh, who didn't need anyone. Who'd be caring for Malu. Caring and never letting anyone care for him.

And then, amazingly, she was out of the darkness. The light was almost blinding and Lea was being lifted from her. She was being gathered into Hettie's arms and hugged and held, and Caroline was holding Lea and sobbing, and Keanu was there, giving her one fast hug, and she even saw tears in his eyes before he returned to his role as doctor.

They'd rigged up some sort of makeshift hospital tent. 'Let's get you inside,' he said roughly, trying to hide emotion. 'We need to assess—'

'I'm staying out here until the others are out,' she told him, and this time she managed to make them agree.

So Hettie organised washbasins and someone rigged up a sheet for a little privacy, and Hettie and Caroline did their midwife thing, as well as a preliminary assessment of scrapes and bruises, yet she could still see the mouth of the mine.

'She's perfect,' Caroline breathed, as she carefully washed Lea in one of the washbasins and inspected every part of her before wrapping her and handing her back to her mother. 'She's adorable, Maddie. Oh, well done, you.'

Surely Maddie should have beamed with maternal pride—and she sort of did but it was a pretty wobbly beam. She hugged her precious baby back to her, but still she looked at the mine entrance.

Malu's stretcher emerged next.

Keanu was ready to receive him, as was Beth. Hettie moved back to Keanu's side as well, so there was a receiving posse of medics moving straight into ER mode.

And, of course, Pearl was there. Pearl had greeted Maddie as she'd emerged, but even as she'd been hugging her, like Maddie, her eyes hadn't left the mouth of the mine.

As soon as the miners set Malu's stretcher down, Pearl was on the grass beside him, not saying a word, just touching his face, seemingly fearful of the drips, the oxygen mask, the medical paraphernalia Maddie and Josh had organised, but still...just touching.

And it was up to Malu to speak.

'Hey, girl,' he said, holding his wife any way he could. He spoke softly yet every person in the clearing could hear him. 'God help me, girl, I've needed you so much...' His voice broke on a sob and then, tubes or not, mask or not, everything was irrelevant, he was gathering Pearl into his arms and holding.

And Maddie couldn't help herself. Tears were coursing down her face. Happiness tears? There were matching tears on the faces of almost everyone around her, tears of relief, tears of joy, but mixed with that?

What sort of tears?

Jealous tears? To be loved like Pearl was. To be needed.

And then Josh was out, with Bugsy bursting out behind him. Josh had obviously refused the stretcher. He was bruised and battered. His arm needed urgent attention. She knew he'd lost strength so there was a chance of nerve damage, but he wasn't thinking of himself now. When was he ever? He stood blinking in the sunlight, gathering himself, and even as he did so Maddie saw him regroup, turn back into the professional, the doctor he'd become so he could help.

So he could hide?

But only she could see that. He saw her, half-hidden by sheets, lying in the shade, holding her baby. Their eyes locked for one long moment, a moment of recognition of all that was between them—and a moment of farewell?

And then he turned to Keanu.

'I'm fine,' he said roughly. 'We've got them out, now what else needs doing? Beth, what's the priority? What's the need?'

For once, however, Dr Joshua Campbell did not get things his own way.

Beth turned bossy. On his own turf he could have

overruled her, but backed up by the island medical team of Keanu, Caroline and Hettie he'd met his match.

'No one needs you, Dr Campbell. In fact, for the duration you don't even consider yourself a doctor.' Hettie, the island's nurse administrator, was doing the organising. She looked to be in her late thirties and was obviously a woman to be reckoned with. Keanu was testing his arm, making him flex, testing each of his fingers. Together they gave him no choice.

They propelled him into the temporary hospital tent, whether he willed it or not. Malu was on the next stretcher.

Maddie was still outside.

Another of the nurses was at the door of the tent— Caroline Lockhart. She stood, looking a little unsure.

'Caroline?' Keanu said.

'The plane's due to land in twenty minutes,' Caroline told him. 'I've been talking to Beth. There's another doctor coming from Cairns to fly back with the patients. Beth says there'll be room for her and for two patients, but Pearl's desperate to go with Malu. She has a sister in Cairns she can stay with, and another sister here, who'll look after the kids. But a tropical storm's closing in over Cairns and they say this could be the last trip for a few days. If we need to send Josh then Pearl can't go.'

'I'm fine,' Josh growled. What were they doing, sending another doctor? Tending to patients during transport was what he did. 'You don't need another doctor from Cairns. I can care for Malu.'

'The doctor's already on his way,' Caroline said, ignoring his protest, talking to Keanu, not to him. 'And

our little hospital's packed. Which leaves these two…
these three, if you count Maddie's baby…'

'I'm fine,' Josh growled again, but no one was listening.

'Maddie wants to stay here,' Hettie said, still exclud-
ing him. 'She's looking good—there's no medical reason to evacuate her.'

'I'd like them both in hospital,' Keanu growled. 'All
of them. Maddie and baby and Josh. Twenty-four hours'
observation. The conditions underground weren't exactly clean and this is the tropics. Josh, this cut's deep
and needs stitching. You get it infected, you risk long-
term damage. The rest of your scratches need care and
you need rest. So care it is. No one's growing infec-
tions on my watch.'

'Use the homestead,' Caroline said. 'You know we
have six bedrooms. I'll send a message to our housekeeper to make up beds. Keanu, you can do Maddie's
obstetric checks there. Once you've done Josh's stitching and you're happy with them they should be fine. I
can do obs.'

And Keanu stood back and looked at Josh—assessing.
Seeing him not as a colleague but as a patient. Someone
who needed help?

It was all Josh could do not to get up and walk out.
To lie on the examination table and be assessed like this
was almost killing him.

'I want gentle, gradual exercise,' Keanu said at last,
still talking to Caroline. 'Slowly, no sudden movements.
They've been cramped too long with injuries. So gentle movement with support, then food and bed. I'll give
Maddie a thorough check first but if she's okay… I'll
want them watched but the house should work. If we

clear you from hospital shifts, you can look after them, and I can organise one of the night shift to take over while you sleep.'

'And act as chaperone, too.' That was Beth, standing at the entrance to the tent. She had her cheek back. When Josh had emerged from the mine she'd looked whey-faced but now she was practically bouncing. 'These two have been married,' she told the tent in general. 'Josh and your Maddie. Once there were sparks, so separate bedrooms at separate ends of the house.'

'I don't think we need to worry about these two and red-hot sex,' Keanu said dryly, and managed a grin. 'When two sets of bruises unite—ouch—and there's nothing like a one-day-old baby to dampen passion. However, they're consenting adults. Whatever they choose to do or not to do is up to them.' And then his smile widened, and Josh thought for the first time in two days the stress had come off.

'No, actually, that's not true,' Keanu added, still grinning. 'For now Maddie has no obstetrician so I'm it. So, Dr Campbell, no matter what your intentions may be regarding your ex-wife, could you please take sex off the agenda?'

'I have no intention...' He paused, practically speechless. Of all the...

'She's a lovely lady, our Maddie,' Keanu said. 'If I wasn't otherwise engaged I'd be attracted to her myself.'

'Hey!' Caroline said, and everyone laughed, and the tension lessened still further.

Except Josh's tension didn't ease. He was stuck on this island. He was about to spend the night in some sort of private house, even if it was a big one.

If he was at one end of the house and Maddie was at the other—she'd still be there.

No sex… There was no chance of that, but a part of him was suddenly remembering sex from a long time ago, how it had felt lying in Maddie's arms—how it had felt to be needed by Maddie.

That was the only time when his world had seemed right.

His world was right now, he told himself savagely. His world was exactly as he wanted it. All he needed was to get away from this island and get home.

Home? To his base in Cairns? An austere apartment he spent as little time in as possible?

He glanced around the tent at this tight-knit medical community, and then out through the tent flap to where a huddle of women crouched around Maddie. They were readying her for transport to the Lockhart house but this wasn't medical personnel doing their bit. These were friends, and even from here he could tell how much she was loved.

But not by him. He could never admit how much he needed her.

Not even to himself?

But this was exhaustion talking, he thought. This was nonsense.

'You'll be fine.' It was Hettie, washing his already cleaned face again, as if she knew that the grit felt so ingrained it'd take months to feel as if he was rid of it. 'We'll take care of you.'

'I don't need—'

'Need or not,' she said cheerfully, 'you're trapped until the storm front passes over Cairns, so you might as well get used to it.'

* * *

The bedroom was amazing. Luscious. Or maybe luscious was too small a word to describe it. 'It was my parents' bedroom,' Caroline had told her last night. 'Best room in the house.'

'Caro, I can't.'

'Of course you can.' Caroline had helped her shower and tucked her into bed, brooking no argument, and Maddie had been too overwhelmed to argue.

And now it was morning. She lay in a massive bed with down pillows and a crisp white coverlet, surrounded by delicate white lace that served as a mosquito net but looked more like a bridal canopy.

The bed was an island of luxury in a room that screamed of age and history and wealth. Old timber gleamed with generations of layers of wax and elbow grease. Vast French windows opened to the wide veranda beyond. White lace curtains fluttered in the warm sea breeze, and beyond the lagoon and then the sea.

Even her bruises thought they were in heaven.

She did ache a little, she conceded, but this was a bed, a room, a house to cure the worst bruises she could imagine.

And Caroline was standing in the doorway, holding her daughter.

'Sleepyhead.' Caroline chuckled as she set Lea into her mother's arms. At some time in the small hours she'd come in and helped Maddie feed—surely Maddie remembered that?—but the rest... How deeply had she slept? 'Your daughter's been fussing so I took her for a little stroll and introduced her to her world,' Caroline told her. 'She seems to approve. At least she seemed to approve until five minutes ago, when...'

As if on cue, Lea opened her mouth and wailed.

And Maddie felt her face split into a grin. There was nothing she could do about it—she couldn't stop grinning.

And Caroline smiled, too, as she helped Maddie show Lea to her breast—not that Lea needed much direction.

'Hmm,' Caroline said, standing back as Lea started the important business of feeding. 'I don't think you two will need breastfeeding advice.'

'I had a booklet I intended reading before she arrived,' Maddie told her, smiling and smiling down at her tiny daughter. 'Stupidly I left it behind when I went in, but Lea and I figured it out all by ourselves.'

'You left a lot else behind when you ran in,' Caroline retorted. 'Including all our hearts. Maddie, how could you?'

'How's Malu?' Maddie asked, answering Caroline's question with those two words.

'He's okay,' Caro conceded. 'Keanu had a call from Cairns a couple of hours ago. He's settled and stable and sitting up, having breakfast. Thanks to you and your Josh.'

'He's not *my Josh*.' She said it automatically. She was touching her tiny daughter's cheek as she suckled, and she was trying to think about Lea. Just Lea.

Only Josh was in her thoughts, too.

'He seems very concerned, for someone who's not *your Josh*.'

'Josh always cares,' she said carefully. 'It's what he's good at.'

'He wants to see you.'

'I'm sleepy.'

'You mean you don't want to see him?'

She thought about that for a moment. Of course she wanted to see him. She had to see him. After all, without Josh Lea would be dead. The thought made her feel...frozen.

If only he wasn't... Josh.

'How about breakfast first, a shower, maybe even a hair wash and then think about audiences,' Caroline suggested, with a sideways glance letting on that maybe she saw more than her words suggested. 'If I can tell him that, I may be able to bully him back to bed. He has a nasty haematoma on his thigh and Kiera wants him to stay in bed for the day.'

'A haematoma...'

'Cork thigh for the uninitiated,' Caroline said, and grinned. 'Honestly, don't you doctors know anything? He has a ripped and stitched arm, he's bruised all over and we know he hurts. So can I tell him if he's a good boy and stays in bed you'll see him before lunch? A ten-minute visit before you both go back to sleep?'

'Caro...'

'Mmm?'

There was silence while she thought of what to say. It lasted a while.

'He's stuck on the island?' she asked at last, and Caroline nodded.

'We all are. FIFOs are cancelled. Cyclone Hilda's hovering just above Cairns and the weather gurus don't know which direction she'll swing.'

'It's okay here.' There was safety in weather, she thought. It was the only discussion to be had when there was an elephant in the room so big it was threatening to overwhelm her. An elephant by the name of Josh. She made herself look out the windows to where the glassy calm of the lagoon and distant sea gave the lie to any hint of a cyclone. Still, it was the cyclone season…

'You're not really thinking of the weather, are you?' Caroline asked, and Maddie sighed.

'No.'

'So Josh is your ex-husband—only he's not acting like an ex-husband. Do you know how many orders he's throwing around about your care? If he could, he'd swim back to Cairns and swim back, dragging an obstetrician behind him.'

Maddie smiled at that, but absently. That'd be Josh. Caring above and beyond the call of duty. 'I'll see him before lunch,' she managed.

'Can I do your hair?'

'I don't need to be made pretty.'

'It never hurts.'

You have no idea, Maddie said, but she said it to herself, inwardly.

It never hurts?

It still did hurt—so much—after all these years.

She glanced down at her tiny daughter and she knew she needed all her strength and more if it wasn't going to keep hurting forever.

'Ten minutes and not a moment more,' Caroline told Josh as she escorted him along the vast, portrait-lined hallway to Maddie's room. 'Lea's just fed and Maddie is tired. When I trained, it was the baby's dad and the baby's grandparents—immediate family only—in the first twenty-four hours, and that's not you.'

It was said as a warning.

He stopped, which was a mistake. He'd been walking quite well until then. Caroline had wanted him to use a wheelchair. The idea was ridiculous but in truth his leg was weak and when he stopped he wobbled.

Caroline held out a hand to support him but he pulled back. What was happening here? Down the mine he'd coped well, apart from the brief and overwhelming panic attack, but on the surface he was suddenly as weak as Maddie's baby. He was wearing boxers and a T-shirt borrowed from Keanu. His own clothes were ruined, ripped and bloodied. He wanted jeans and a shirt that fitted, but Keanu had had the nerve to grin and tell him clothes would be forthcoming when he, Keanu, deemed Josh fit to leave this makeshift hospital and not before.

For once in his life Josh Campbell was out of control and he didn't like it. Not one bit. He didn't like it that his legs had the shakes—and now this woman was warning him about visiting Maddie.

Only family—and that's not you.

'I may not be family,' he said through gritted teeth 'but apart from a bedridden and confused mother, I'm all she's got.'

'You think so?' Caro said, quite lightly. 'Let me tell you, Dr Campbell, that if you step one inch out of line, if you upset Maddie enough to even make her blink, you'll find out this island is what she's got. The entire island and beyond. The whole M'Langi group. She's loved by us all. Family comes in so many forms.'

'That's not love,' he snapped. 'She's your local doctor. You people need her. She needs someone—'

'To protect her? That's what I'm saying, Dr Campbell. That's what she has. She ran into the mine to protect Malu but if you hadn't gone in after her I can think of over a dozen islanders who would have, including me.

So let's not get carried away with heroics. Our Maddie might have needed saving in the mine, but she doesn't need saving from anything else.'

'Caro?' It was Maddie's voice floating down the hall-way. 'What are you telling him?'

'Just normal midwifery stuff,' Caroline called out cheerfully. 'About not outstaying his welcome and new mothers need rest and not to cough anywhere near the baby. Oh, and there's antiseptic handwash on the bench...'

'He *is* a doctor,' Maddie called, and she was laughing.

'He might be a doctor where he comes from,' Caroline retorted, 'but from where I'm standing he's a patient wearing Keanu's boxers and learning to play by our rules.'

He was wearing boxers and a T-shirt. His dark hair was rumpled, tousled by sleep.

He had an ugly bruise on his thigh and his arm was wrapped in a stark white dressing.

He looked young, she thought, and absurdly vulnerable. She had a sudden urge to throw back the bedcovers and hug him.

He wouldn't let her. She knew it. Letting people close when he was vulnerable was not what Josh did.

She'd just finished feeding Lea. She cradled her close, almost as a shield.

'Hey,' he said, and she managed a smile.

'Have you remembered your antiseptic hand wash?'

He grinned back at her and held up his hands. 'Yes, ma'am. Do you think I dare disobey Commander Caroline? I stand before you, not a bug in sight—or out of sight, either.'

Oh, that grin. She remembered that grin. It did things to her.

Or not. Past history, she told herself fiercely. That grin could not be allowed to influence her in any way at all.

'How are you?' he asked, and it was as if he was holding himself back. He was still standing by the door. Unsure.

Maybe he wanted to hug her, too, she thought, and then she decided of course he did. Josh did comfort in a big way.

'We're both excellent,' she told him, cradling Lea close. Lea was still fussing a little, not hungry, just wide-eyed and not inclined to sleep. 'Me and Lea both.'

'What did Keanu say? Is he worried about infection? You tore a little. Has he put you on antibiotics? And how is Lea? I couldn't clean that cord stump properly. And has he checked both your lungs?'

'You know, if you're going to play doctor you need to find a white coat,' she told him. 'Boxers just don't cut it.'

'Maddie, I'm serious.'

'And so am I. Keanu's my doctor.'

'He's not an obstetrician.'

'Neither are you, though you did do a neat job of filling in,' she conceded. 'I wasn't too fussed about lack of white coats underground.' She smiled, forcing herself to stay light. 'But we're aboveground again now. Normal standards apply. We're both patients for the duration. Keanu's demanding I stay here for a week. I was due to fly back to Cairns today, but with Cairns airport closed I'm stuck. Caroline's been very kind.'

'It's her house?'

'It's her father's house, though it's been used by her uncle Ian. But until she came back a couple of months ago it's been empty. It seems Ian's done a runner. Apparently he's been ripping off money from everywhere. That's why the islanders were down the mine—they haven't been paid for months and they decided to do a bit of gold-mining for themselves.' She shrugged. 'But that's the island's problem, not yours.'

'But you care.'

'About the islanders? Of course I do.' She bit her lip. 'Kalifa died. He had no business…' And to her annoyance she felt tears welling behind her eyes. 'Damn, I'm as weak as a kitten.'

And Josh was over to her bed before she could begin to swipe the stupid, weak tears away, tugging her into his arms and holding. Lea was in there, too. He was cradling them both. His…family?

And it felt right. It felt like home. She could just sink into his shoulder and have her cry out, and let him comfort her as he'd comforted her so often in the past.

'Maddie, we could build again.' What was this? He shouldn't be speaking, she thought. She didn't want him to speak. This was Josh in his let's-make-things-better mode. Let's distract Maddie from what's hurting. She didn't want it but he ploughed on inexorably. 'We could make things right. Neither of us is happy apart. What you've done is extraordinary. You've rebuilt your life and I'm in awe. But, Maddie, I should never have walked away. I should have tried harder. I love you so much, and I love Lea already. We could buy a house with a view of the sea near the air rescue base. It's close to your mum. I can afford a housekeeper. It's near the base hospital, too, if you want to continue medicine. We could share parenting. We could start again.'

He was still holding her. She was still crumpled against his chest. She couldn't move.

She took time to let his words sink in. She needed to take time. The last few days had left her hurt and shocked, and now... Josh's words felt like a battering ram, threating to crumble what was left of her foundations.

To calmly leave here... To go and live in Josh's beautiful house—she had no doubt he'd buy her something special... To have a housekeeper on call...

Share parenting, though... Was that a joke? That'd be where the housekeeper fitted in, she thought. Josh would be flitting in and out in between rescues, playing husband, playing father.

'You don't get it, do you?' she whispered, still against his chest because it was just too hard to pull away. 'You still want me to need you. You want us to need you.'

'What's wrong with that?'

And she did pull away then, anger coming to her aid. How could he be so stupid? How could he be so blind?

'Because love doesn't work one way,' she whispered, and then suddenly she was no longer whispering. She'd had five years to think this through, five years to know she was right. 'Love's all about giving. Giving and giving and giving. And how can I love you if all I can do is take?'

'I don't know what you mean.'

'Of course you do. It's why you walked away. Josh, after Mikey died, you tried to do it your way. You did all the right things. You said all the right things. You supported me every inch of the way. You stood by my side while we buried our son and your whole body was rigid with trying. You had to be everything to me. You couldn't crack yourself because I needed you. You couldn't show one hint of emotion, and you know why not? Because there's a vast dam of emotion inside you, and if you let one tiny crack appear then the whole lot will flood out, and you're terrified.'

'Maddie—'

'Don't "Maddie" me,' she bit out. 'You walked away from me. Sure, you stuck around after Mikey died. You held yourself together, you hugged me and I let myself be hugged because, yes, I needed you, but it hurt even more that you didn't cry with me. You still hurt from losing Mikey. I saw it on your face when Lea was born but you won't admit it. You'll hardly admit it to yourself. And then Holly died and it was worse. You were wooden, as if admitting even a little bit of grief would make you implode. I was so sad for you, but when I tried to get close, when I needed to share, you walked away.'

Hell. He went to dig his hands into his pockets but boxers have a dearth of pockets. He felt exposed. He was exposed. Boxers and T-shirt and bruises and…emotion.

'It was five years ago,' he managed. 'It's history.'

'You mean you have your armour back in place so we'll start again? That'll be fine as long the need all stays one way.'

'Maddie, you care for your mother. You'll care for Lea. You don't need—'

'Another person who needs me? That's what I mean. You still don't get it. Not letting me close hurts, Josh. After five years I should have built my own armour but I don't want to build armour. I love it that my mum needs me. I love it that Lea needs me and I love it that

I have a working life where this community needs me, too. But you know what? I need them, too. I sit and read to Mum and it warms my heart that she can still smile and hold my hand. I cradle Lea and I'm warm all over. The islanders bring me their problems but they also include me in their lives. They share, and when I'm off the island I miss them. Kalifa died when the mine collapsed and I'll go to his funeral and I'll weep. I loved him. I needed him as I need so many.'

'You can't—'

'Don't tell me what I can and can't do, Josh Campbell. You don't have the right.'

And suddenly she was almost shouting and Caroline was gliding into the room and putting herself firmly between Josh and Maddie and giving him a glare that might have turned lesser mortals into stone.

'What do you think you're playing at?' she demanded. 'I told you—you upset Maddie, you upset the whole island. Maddie, you want me to call in a few good men to cast this guy to the fish?'

'I... No.' Maddie choked on an angry sob and fell back on her pillows. Lea whimpered and Josh felt sick.

'What's he been saying?' Caroline demanded. 'Tell Aunty Caroline.'

'He wants to marry me—again.'

There was a moment's stunned silence. Then Caro's lips twitched. It was a tiny twitch. She had herself under control in an instant but he saw it.

'So he proposes in Keanu's boxers and T-shirt,' she managed. 'I can see why that would upset a girl. And where's the diamond?'

'I don't want a diamond.'

But Caroline had moved back into professional mode.

'What you want,' she said, lightly now but still just as firm, 'is a sleep. I'm going to take your obs and then close this room off to everyone. Whatever Dr Campbell has been saying, forget it. What's most important, for you and for baby, is sleep.' And then she lifted Lea from Maddie's arms and turned and handed the tiny girl to Josh.

'Here,' she said, and Caroline might be young but right now she was every inch a Lockhart of Wildfire, with a lineage obviously stretching back to the dinosaurs. No old-fashioned hospital matron had ever sounded more bossy. 'Lea looks like she needs time to settle,' she decreed. 'I need to care for Maddie and if you're proposing marriage then maybe you could take this small dose of domesticity and try it out for size. Keanu wants you to walk, just a little, slowly but getting the circulation moving in those legs. We don't want clots, do we? Can you hold her without hurting your arm? Excellent. I want you to take Lea for a wee walk around the veranda, then settle down outside until I come and get her. You're banned from here, Dr Campbell. Now, Maddie, do you need some pain relief? Yes? Let's get you sorted.'

And she turned her back on Josh, blocking his view of Maddie.

He was left with an armful of baby.

He was left with no choice but to leave.

CHAPTER ELEVEN

HE STOOD IN the hall, holding Maddie's daughter, and he thought...

Nothing.

Maddie's words were still echoing in his head. He should try and make sense of them, but he couldn't sort them out.

In his arms Lea wuffled and opened her mouth to wail.

And at that, the professional side of him kicked in. Caroline had given him Lea for a reason. She knew he was more than capable of caring for a baby. She also knew that Maddie was distressed and needed to sleep, and the one thing that'd stop her doing that was to hear her baby crying. That was the reason she'd handed her over to him. Professional concern.

So be professional. How to stop a baby crying?

He hadn't actually read that in any of his textbooks.

Still, it was a professional challenge and he was a professional. How hard could it be?

'Hush,' he told Lea, and he lifted her onto his shoulder and let her nuzzle into the softness of his T-shirt while he made his way outside.

He walked for a little, as ordered, until the threat

of wails was past, until he heard only gentle wuffling. Then he headed for a mammoth rocker on the side veranda. He settled—cautiously—into the softness of its faded cushions, and rocked.

It was a good place to sit. There were herons wading at the edge of the lagoon, seeking tiny fish in the shallows. The veranda was shaded, cool and lovely. In the distance the sea was a sheet of shimmery, turquoise glass.

There was a cyclone threating Cairns, but here there was nothing but calm.

'There's no threat here,' he murmured to the baby in his arms, but she seemed singularly unimpressed.

She whimpered some more. He lifted her from his shoulder and cradled her in his hands. Why did newborns feel so fragile? He knew from training that babies were born tough but she didn't feel tough.

She felt precious.

He laid her on his knee. He expected to hurt a bit as her weight settled on his bruised thigh, but she nestled as if this was a cradle made for her. Her eyes were drifting with newborn lack of focus but she seemed to be taking in this strange new world.

She looked like Maddie.

Who was the father? he wondered. Who was the unknown sperm donor?

He wished it could have been him.

No. He didn't wish that. Fatherhood… He remembered clearly the agony of loss.

His son and then his sister.

How could he hold himself and not crack? That's why he'd had to walk away. He couldn't help Maddie when he was hurting so much himself. He was no use to anyone.

'If you were mine I'd be useless,' he whispered. 'If you hurt... Or if your mother hurt...'

So why had he offered marriage again? What had changed?

Hope that this time it could be different? Hope that there wouldn't be a time when he was needy?

'Excuse me?'

He turned to see a woman maybe in her late sixties standing at the foot of the veranda. She was short, slightly overweight, breathless. Her soft, white hair was tugged into a wispy bun and her eyes looked swollen, like she'd been crying.

'Excuse me,' the woman said again. 'I knocked on the front door but no one answered.'

'I'm Dr Campbell,' he told her. 'Can I help?'

She'd been climbing the side steps, but as soon as Josh spoke she stopped short, looking at him in shock.

'You're a doctor?'

'I don't look like one, but yes.'

'So... Keanu said...you were helping when my husband died.'

It was a simple statement, said with dignity and peace, like a jigsaw puzzle was coming together in a way she could understand.

'You're Kalifa's wife,' he ventured, remembering the big man, the desperate fight to save him, the hopelessness he always felt when he lost a patient. He'd been gutted, and then the trauma with Maddie had stopped him following up. Normally when a patient died in his presence he'd seek out the relatives and talk them through it.

Too much had happened.

'Kalifa Lui was my husband,' the woman agreed, looking to the baby, to him, then back to Lea. 'My name is Nani Lui. The nurses told me that you and Keanu tried very hard to save him. I thank you.'

'I wish we could have done more.'

'It would seem that you've done more than you could be expected to do,' she said, and the echo of a smile washed across her tired face. 'Did they teach you mine rescue in medical school?'

But then she was interrupted. 'Nani?' It was Maddie, calling through the open window. 'Nani, is that you?'

Uh-oh. 'You're supposed to be asleep,' Josh called back. 'We'll move farther along. Caroline will have us hauled before the courts for disturbing you.'

There was a sleepy chuckle. 'Caroline's gone across to the hospital to get more diapers and, oh, I need to see Nani. Quick, Josh, bring her in.'

'Nani, if you go through that door...'

'No,' Maddie called out, suddenly imperious. 'Come in with her, Josh. I want Nani to meet both you and my daughter.'

He was wearing boxers! 'I'm hardly dressed—'

'Nani won't care. She's practically family and I guess...after all we've been through, so are you.'

So he ushered the elderly woman into Maddie's bedroom—keeping a wary eye on the door. Caroline seemed a woman it was better not to cross. But Maddie's distress seemed to have evaporated. She hugged Nani to her as Josh had seen her hug her mother and he thought...maybe it was true. Maybe Nani was family.

He stood silent, feeling superfluous, until the hugging finished, until Nani stepped back, tears streaming down her face, and turned back to see Lea in Josh's arms.

'And this is your little one,' she whispered. 'They tell me you've named her Lea. For my daughter?' She forced her gaze from the baby to Josh. 'Lea was my daughter,' she whispered. 'She did the cooking at the hospital. She was so full of love and laughter. Then she got the encephalitis. It was so bad, so fast. Maddie worked desperately to try and save her but she died before she could be evacuated. And now... To call your little one for her... My Kalifa would be so proud.'

And Josh looked down at Maddie and saw her eyes fill with tears. It was true, then. She'd named her baby for a patient she'd lost.

Part of her extended family? Surely not. He hadn't asked, though...

He hadn't had the right to ask why she'd decided to call her baby anything.

It hurt that he didn't have that right. It hurt a lot.

'She's beautiful,' Nani whispered. 'A new life from this tragedy. This is joy. And you called her Lea.'

'I wanted to share.' Maddie's voice was weak but determined. 'I know all of you will love her. She'll need you all.'

'And we'll need her,' Nani breathed. 'Oh, Maddie, I'm so happy for you.' She glanced up at Josh. 'Maddie's wanted this little one for so long.'

'I know.'

And Nani's gaze sharpened. She looked from him to Maddie and back again. 'It's true then,' she said forcefully. 'They're saying you two were married.'

'I... Yes.'

'And you walked away.' Her tone was accusing.

'I couldn't help her,' Josh said helplessly.

'Maddie said she couldn't help you.'

'Maddie talked to you about us?' He turned to Maddie, incredulous.

'I'm a grandmother,' Nani said simply. 'Everyone talks to me.' And then she paused, the present crashing home. 'But not my Kalifa. No more. People tell me things and I weep for them, but then my Kalifa holds me…'

'We'll hold you, Nani,' Maddie said. 'You know we will. Whenever you need us. Just as you've always held us.'

And Nani's face crumpled. She stooped and hugged Maddie and she sobbed, just once. And then she sniffed and braced herself and rose and faced Josh again.

'She will, too,' she said. 'Maddie is part of my strength, part of this island's strength. I knew Maddie would be sad about Kalifa's death. She told him to stop smoking. She told him to lose weight. He didn't listen but she tried, and she was there for him when he needed her. As she always is.'

She stopped and stared down at the tiny child and her face softened. 'Life goes on,' she whispered. 'With no blame. With love. This little one…she's our faith in the future. She gives me strength, and, heaven knows, we all need to take strength where we can find it.'

'You find it in yourself,' Josh said, and Nani stepped back and looked at him as if he'd said something that didn't make sense.

'Is that what you think? That you're born with strength enough to hold you up for your whole life?' She groped backwards and sat and held Maddie's hand. 'Is that what drove you apart?'

'Maybe,' Maddie said, and Josh heard exhaustion in her voice.

'We shouldn't be here,' he told Nani. 'Caroline will be after us with a shotgun if she finds us in here. Maddie, go to sleep, love.'

'I'm not your love,' Maddie whispered, and Josh flinched.

But what she said was true. He might love Maddie. She might love him but the chasm between them was still miles deep.

He ushered Nani out. Nani looked as if she was bursting to say more but she held her tongue. Out on the veranda she touched Lea's face again and then gave Josh a searching look.

'There's time,' she said enigmatically. 'You can't be the only one to take care of you.'

She left. Josh looked down at the baby, now sleeping soundly in his arms. He thought of the web of love and dependence and need that held this island together.

He thought he'd head back to his rocker.

Babysitting was easier than thinking, he decided. It was just a shame he could do both at the same time.

She wasn't asleep. She was tired and drowsy, her body was as comfortable as Caro could make it and there was no reason she shouldn't sleep, but she lay in her beautiful bed and looked out at the distant sea and thought about Josh.

He was on the veranda. He'd be rocking back and forth, looking out over the lagoon.

Holding her baby.

He'd called her 'love'. He still wanted her. He even wanted marriage.

The idea was preposterous, crazy, even heartbreaking, so why was there an insidious voice hammering away in her consciousness?

Go on. You know you want to.

And part of her did want to. Despite what Nani had said, this island wasn't her all.

There was still a part of her that ached for Josh.

Down the mine he'd massaged her head and shoulders, and, despite the shock, the danger, the physical battering her body had just been through, his touch had swept back all the memories of the fire between them. He just had to look at her and her knees turned to jelly.

Lovemaking with Josh.

There was a memory she had to suppress. It was still there, though. The perfection.

Five years. Surely she should have moved on by now?

The problem was that she'd made vows.

With my body I thee worship.

Had she made that vow? For the life of her she couldn't remember. Her wedding day had passed in a blur of happiness, and the words she'd spoken, with love and with honour, had blurred, as well.

With my body I thee worship.

If she hadn't said it out loud, she'd said it in her head.

It wasn't enough. It had never been enough. Not when the caring was only permitted one way.

If Josh loved, he protected, and protection for Josh meant never letting her close enough to see his hurt.

'It's impossible,' she whispered into the stillness. 'The island has to be enough. I can't love a man who won't let me love back.'

The only problem was that she did.

* * *

'Josh?'

He'd been dozing a little, the rocking chair stilling as he and Lea drifted towards sleep. His legs made a secure cradle. His hands still cupped her. Lea was peaceful and seemingly content, and for this moment so was Josh.

He had to be. Listening to Nani had left him...discombobulated. He'd tried to figure it out but the effort had left him too tired to sort the tangle that was in his head. For now all he could do was soak in the sun, the peace, the feel of this little girl sleeping between his hands.

Everyone should have a Wildfire Island, he thought sleepily. And a baby called Lea.

'Josh!' It was Caroline again—of course. She was standing in front of him, smiling her approval. 'What a great job,' she told him. 'We'll give you a job in the children's ward any day.'

'Do you have many ill children?'

Why did he ask that? Because he wanted to shift the focus onto medicine? Okay, maybe he did. Ever since he'd arrived on this island, things had been personal and it was time to back away.

'We have too many ill children,' Caroline told him, obviously ready to follow his lead. 'As well as normal kids' stuff we have a vicious ulcer caused by the local mosquitoes. It starts out as a mosquito bite and grows. If left untreated it needs to be cut out and requires skin grafts. What's worse, we also have encephalitis caused by the same mosquito. There's a local remedy—a plant that seems to give immunity—but sometimes parents forget how important it is to use it. We aim to send the encephalitis patients to the mainland but that's not always possible. In the meantime, we need to do the frontline treatment here and the cases are increasing. The island's desperate for more medical staff but there's no money. The government funding's limited and we're running out. And now the encephalitis cases are increasing.'

'Why?'

'Because the money's run out, for education and also for mosquito eradication,' she said bitterly. 'My uncle seems to have been embezzling funds for years. Heaven knows how we can attract any more staff. We're just blessed that Maddie's decided to stay.'

And he'd asked her to leave.

But for her to stay here… With Lea…

Ulcers. Encephalitis…

'You needn't worry. We take very good care of our staff,' she said, seeing him glance at the sleeping baby and guessing his concern. 'And our staff's children. This baby will be cared for by the whole island. But that's not what I came to talk to you about. Keanu's just had a call from Cairns Air Sea Rescue. From Beth. She says to tell you the cyclone's tracking north and the airport's open from dawn tomorrow. So, unless you don't want it, they're flying out to collect you. She wanted to know if Maddie wants evacuation, too, but Maddie's adamant that she stays. Keanu doesn't see any reason why she shouldn't. Oh, and the plane's bringing our permanent doctor back, Sam Taylor, so we'll have a full medical contingent again, or as full as we can afford. Can you be ready to leave at ten tomorrow? Keanu's trying to find you some decent clothes to wear on the way home.'

Unless you don't want it.

In all that she'd said, those were the words that stood out.

Ten tomorrow morning, unless he didn't want it.

His boss would insist he take a break, he thought, at least until the cut on his arm healed. He could…

What? Stay here?

What was the point? He'd only upset Maddie.

'Of course,' he said, and the matter was decided.

She left, taking Lea with her. He stayed sitting on the rocker, staring sightlessly out over the island.

What was the point?

He'd rescued Maddie. He'd played emergency doctor because that was what he did. That was who he was. There was no use pretending he could be anything more.

It was time to move on.

At nine the next morning, Maddie had just finished feeding when there was a knock on the door.

'Come in,' she called, and it was Josh. Of course it was. Caroline had told her he was leaving. She'd warned her he'd want to say goodbye.

He was wearing clean jeans and a crisp, short-sleeved white shirt. He was washed and brushed and almost impossibly handsome. He looked like Josh again. If it hadn't been for the dressing on his arm she'd say he was back to being her invincible Josh. No, not *her* Josh. *The* Josh. The Josh who was in control.

'Caroline says if I promise not to upset you I can have ten minutes,' he said, and part of her wanted to say he could have the rest of her life. But she was sensible and there was no way a sensible woman could say such a thing. Even if he looked like Josh.

'I won't get upset,' she managed. 'You'll be glad to get back to work.' Of course he would. An idle Josh was like a bear with a sore head. Or a sore arm? 'Will they let you work with that arm?'

'Office duties.'

'You won't take a holiday?'

'No.'

'You need to rest.'

'Says you. Are you sure you don't want us to take you to Cairns?'

'I'll go in a week or two, when I'm recovered,' she told him. 'I need to see Mum, but I can't for a little while yet.'

He understood. She couldn't push a wheelchair. She couldn't spend a whole day with her mum.

'I'll go and see her if you like. I'll send word back.'

'That'd be…kind. She'll remember you. She l—'

But then she bit back the word. *Loved.* It was too big to say, and Josh was moving on.

'Going back and forth to Cairns will be hard with a baby.'

'It won't be.' Her chin tilted, a gesture he knew and loved. His brave Maddie. 'It'll be the same as before, only this time I'll have Lea, too. I'm thinking Mum will love her.' And she did say the L word then.

'Maddie, how can you manage?'

'How I can is none of your business,' she said, gently but firmly. 'I'm not asking you to care. In fact, I'm asking you not to care. You've cared before and it almost broke you. You walked away from our marriage because of it and nothing's changed. Lea and I have nothing to do with you, Josh.'

'Yet...'

'There are lots of yets,' she murmured. 'But none of them work.'

'I love you.'

'Not enough.'

'Maddie...'

'When Lea cries, I'll comfort her,' she said, trying to make sense of what didn't make sense at all. But it did—in a stupid, muddly way. 'And you know what? She'll comfort me back. Oh, she won't—she can't—care for me. Even in old age I hope she won't need to care for me, but she'll hug me and she'll be there and just knowing I'm her mum, knowing I'm loved, that's enough. I won't ask for more. But to be there for her when she hurts? What a privilege to be permitted to be so close to someone. And when I hurt and she hugs me...that's a gift, too. A gift you could never accept.'

'You know I can't.'

'I know you can't,' she said, sadly now, and she hugged Lea tightly. 'All I can do is hope that one day you'll meet a woman strong enough to crack that armour.'

'Maddie—'

'It's time to go, Josh,' she said, and her bottom lip wobbled a bit. 'It's over.'

Only it wasn't. He stooped as if compelled. He put his hands on her shoulders and he bent so his eyes met hers.

And, as if she was compelled in turn, her face tilted to meet his. Her eyes were wide, her lips parted, just slightly, in just the way he remembered.

And he kissed her. Properly this time, not like the kiss they'd shared in the darkness and the stress of the mine.

Some things were the same.

Some things were mind-blowing.

He remembered the first time he'd kissed her, the sweetness, the taste, the rush of heat. He remembered the way his body had responded—like here was the other half of his whole.

He remembered thinking it must be something in the water—or what they'd eaten. It had been their first date. They'd bought hamburgers and eaten them on the beach at sunset.

They'd kissed and when they'd finally drawn apart he'd felt like his life had just changed.

He remembered thinking it was ridiculous. She was a colleague. She was just someone…nice.

Nice hadn't come into that kiss.

Nice didn't come into this kiss.

The heat was still there, and the power.

Two bodies, fusing.

They might just as well be naked between the sheets. This kiss said they knew each other as they'd know no other.

Two becom one? They'd made their wedding vows but vows didn't come into this. It was the way he felt.

It was the way she made him melt.

Her lips were parted and the kiss she gave him was all Maddie. Generous. Holding nothing back.

She was soft and strong, warm and wanting.

She gave everything.

He remembered that about her. Her love for her mother. Her generosity to her friends.

The way she gave her body to his.

He'd thought he could lie with this woman forever. He thought he'd found his home, and somehow it was still here, this sweet, perfect centre. This aching, loving perfection.

Her kiss said it all. Her hands were in his hair, tugging him to her, kissing him back with a passion that made his heart twist. That made him want to gather her into his arms and carry her.

To where?

To where he could protect her forever?

She must have felt the discordant note, for suddenly the fierce hold eased and she was pushing him back. When their lips parted he felt as if their bodies were being wrenched apart, but she was smiling.

Sort of. He knew this woman. He could see the glimmer of tears behind the smile. But he could also see the strength—and the decision.

'Time to go, Josh. If I ever need rescuing again you'll be the first person I call on, I swear.'

'I'll come.'

'And if you need rescuing?'

Silence. Her smile stayed, but there was infinite sadness behind it.

'If ever you change your mind…' she whispered. 'If ever you want to hop off your white charger and let me have a turn…' But then she bit her lip. 'No. I won't make a promise like that. I've tried to move on, and I'll keep trying. You go back to your life, Josh Campbell, and I'll stay here with mine.'

'Maddie…'

'No more words,' she whispered, and put a finger
to his lips, a feather touch, almost a blessing. 'Just go.'

He was gone.

She lay in her too-big bed and hugged her baby. Her
body ached.

Her heart ached.

She'd made the right call—she knew she had—but,
oh, it hurt. And it was hurting Josh, too.

'Impossible,' she murmured to herself, but then Lea
wriggled and opened her eyes and screwed up her nose
and told her mother in no uncertain terms that all was
not right with her world.

She was a mother and she was needed.

'But not by Josh,' she told herself. 'I'm on my own.'

Only she wasn't. She had her baby. She had her
mother, her friends, the islanders.

It was only Josh who was alone, she thought bleakly.

He had no choice. With the demons he was carrying
he'd stay alone forever.

CHAPTER TWELVE

'I'M NOT LYING on any stretcher.'

'Honey, we came to pick you up on the grounds that you're a medical evacuation,' Beth told him. 'If we told the powers that be you're fine, apart from a gashed arm, you'd be told to have a nice holiday on Wildfire and come back with the supply boat next week. But you've a gashed arm, a haematoma and shock. Post-traumatic stress disorder is yet to be ruled out. Lie down, like a good boy, and let me give you an aspirin.'

'I'm not lying down,' he said, revolted, and she raised her brows.

'Um…I have backup. The medical opinion on your bruised leg is that sitting upright for the flight is asking for clots and you're not growing clots on my watch. You lie down or we land again and I'll have Sam and Keanu come in here and sit on you. Straitjacket if necessary.'

'You wouldn't dare.'

'Try me,' she said, and grinned and crossed her arms and kept her brows raised. 'Down!'

He had no choice. He lay on the stretcher. She smiled and strapped him in.

'Mind, we could have left you there,' she said serenely. 'We gave you that option.'

'There's no point.'

'Maddie's moved on?'

'I… Yes.'

'Funny things, marriages,' she said. 'Unless they end really bitterly, you always leave a bit of your heart behind.'

'I haven't.'

'No?'

'No,' he said, and then decided if he was to be treated as a patient he could act like a patient. He lay back and closed his eyes as the plane raced down the runway and took to the skies.

He'd have kind of liked to sit up and look down at the disappearing islands behind him.

Saying goodbye hadn't been enough.

It had to be enough. They'd go back to Christmas and birthday cards and that'd be it.

You always leave a bit of your heart behind.

Philosophy of Beth, he thought dryly. After two marriages and four sons, she had an opinion on everything.

She was wrong this time. It wasn't a bit of his heart. It was a lot.

No. It was the whole box and dice. He lay back with his eyes closed, and it felt like he was leaving a part of himself down there. It wasn't just Maddie, either, he thought. He'd delivered Lea. He'd cradled her in his big hands and he'd felt…he'd felt…

Like she was his?

She wasn't, though, and neither was Maddie.

They could have been his wife and his daughter.

He'd walked away.

And all of a sudden it was just as well he was lying

down, as the sweep of emotion flooding through him might have sent him reeling.

He wanted them with a fierceness he'd never experienced before. He wanted to be part of their lives.

He wanted his marriage back.

Marriage... In sickness and in health. Why did that line suddenly slam into his head?

Because he remembered Maddie saying it. To love and to honour, in sickness and in health.

He'd said the words as well, and he'd meant them.

But he hadn't let Maddie mean them.

He'd met Maddie just as her mother had suffered her stroke; when Maddie had been in distress. He'd been able to help. He'd been strong, capable, ready to move heaven and earth if it could make Maddie smile again.

He'd loved helping her and he'd fallen in love.

Because she'd needed him?

Why should he have these insights now, after all these years? It was impossible to understand, and suddenly his thoughts were everywhere.

He remembered the night Mikey had died, trying desperately to hold on to his rigid control. 'It's okay to cry,' Maddie had said, more than once, but he hadn't. He'd held her while she'd broken her heart, and then he'd walked off his pain and his anger where she hadn't had to see.

His job was to protect.

And then, five months later, the policemen at the door. *Your sister, sir...*

He remembered Maddie moving instinctively to hold him, to take him into her arms, and yet he'd backed away.

He'd failed even more. He couldn't protect his sister. He couldn't protect his wife.

They'd been in the air for over half an hour now. Back on Wildfire a funeral would be starting.

Kalifa Lui. Nani's husband.

His thoughts were flying every which way but suddenly they were centred on Nani. Mourning her husband but finding the strength to visit Maddie.

Nani, touching Lea's face, taking strength from a baby.

Maddie, taking strength from Nani.

Loving was all about giving? That had been his mantra, but in Maddie's world loving worked two ways. Giving love and receiving love. Giving comfort and receiving comfort.

Just loving, no strings attached.

Maddie would be at the funeral now, he thought. No matter how sore, no matter how much she'd prefer to be in her magnificent bed with her sea view and her beautiful baby, she'd be at the funeral and no one would send her away.

There'd be no objection from Nani. He knew it. Nani knew that accepting love was the same as giving it.

To accept love wasn't a weakness?

To accept love might even be a strength.

How had it taken so long for him to see it? Was he stupid?

Could he admit he'd been stupid? More, could he act on it?

His thoughts washed on. He lay so silent that finally Beth moved from her seat to check on him.

'Don't you dare die on my watch,' she told him. 'We're only an hour from Cairns.'

'No, we're not.'

'Not?'

'No.' He was trying to unclip the straps holding him in place. 'Give me the radio.'

'What? Why?'

'This is a medical emergency,' he told her. 'I believe Maddie is attending a funeral without proper medical attention. She needs an emergency physician.'

'You're kidding.'

'I would never kid about anything so serious,' he told her. 'But this isn't your decision.'

'Josh...'

And then he softened. Start now, he told himself. Share.

'Beth, I'm in love,' he told her. 'I've been stupid and blind and any number of adjectives you want to call me, but I'm over it. I need your help.'

'You?' she said in disbelief. 'You need my help?'

'I need your help,' he said humbly. 'Dear Beth, please help me unfasten these straps and hand me the radio. And then let's get this plane back to Wildfire.'

The day thou gavest, Lord, has ended, the darkness falls at thy behest...

If there was one thing the islanders of M'Langi prided themselves on it was singing, and the combined voices of what seemed at least half the population was enough to bring tears to Maddie's eyes.

Actually, there were a few things bringing tears to Maddie's eyes right now.

First and foremost was that Kalifa had been a friend and he'd died too soon. If he'd been sensible, stopped smoking, lost weight—if he hadn't decided to embark on a harebrained scheme to make money out of a patently unsafe gold mine—she wouldn't be standing here.

Then there was the sight of Nani, surrounded by her children and her grandchildren. It'd be desperately hard for Nani now, she thought. The elderly woman lived out on Atangi, the biggest of the island group, but her children mostly lived on Wildfire.

She had no money. Kalifa had given it all to his son after he'd lost his fishing boat. He'd mortgaged their house and Nani would have no hope of redeeming it.

She'd lost her husband and her home, yet her shoulders were straight, she sang with fierce determination, and Maddie looked at that sad, proud woman and felt tears well again.

And then there was Josh. Gone.

He'd left five years ago, she told herself. One visit and here you go, falling in love again.

Or still loving?

It's just hormones, she told herself fiercely. She'd given birth only three days ago. Caroline was on one side of her and Hettie was on the other. They both thought she shouldn't have come.

And I shouldn't if I'm going to sob, she told herself. I will not cry.

The hymn came to an end. Kalifa's sons and brothers took up the coffin and carried it out of the chapel into the morning sun. From here it'd be taken to Atangi to be buried in the place of his ancestors.

Maddie wouldn't follow. Burial was the islanders' business. There'd be a wake later on but she wasn't up to a wake yet.

She turned away drearily, immeasurably sad for her friend. But life went on, she told herself. She needed to return to her daughter. She needed to get on with living. She turned towards the hospital—and Josh was right in front her.

Just...there.

'Hi,' he said, and she couldn't think of a single thing to say.

She was facing her husband. No. He was her ex-husband. He wasn't even the father of her child, she told herself desperately. He was someone who had nothing to do with her.

But that was a lie. He was someone who held her heart in his hands.

'I thought you were gone,' she said at last. It was a dumb thing to say but it was all she could think of. But she'd watched his plane take off. He should be in Cairns.

'I had a couple of things I forgot to say,' he said, and then he fell silent.

The hearse drove away, towards the harbour where a boat would carry Kalifa, in all honour, out to Atangi. The islanders followed.

The rest of the mourners drifted off. Maddie stood at the foot of the steps of the little island chapel and felt empty.

'Hey!' It was Caroline, flanked by Keanu and Hettie and Sam. Her people. 'Maddie needs to be back in bed,' Caroline said sternly. 'Thirty minutes tops, Dr Campbell, or we'll set Bugsy onto you.'

'See me terrified,' Josh called back, and Caroline chuckled and linked her arm in Keanu's and said something that made them all laugh—and then they were gone.

Her people.

Her husband?

'What...what did you need to say?' Maddie asked at last, because the silence was getting to her and, in truth, her legs ached and she wouldn't mind sitting down. And as if he guessed, Josh took her arm and led her to a wooden seat that looked out over the headland to the sea beyond.

It really was the most beautiful island. They were facing west, where the sun set. The island's sunsets were where the island got its name, for Wildfire was what they resembled.

Had Josh ever seen a Wildfire sunset?

She was babbling internally. She let herself be propelled to the seat and she tried to empty her mind.

Josh was still holding her arm. How could she empty her mind when all she could do was...feel?

'Two things,' he said into the stillness, and her heart seemed to stop.

'Two?'

'The first is that I'm sorry.' He wasn't looking at her. He was staring out at the distant sea, reflective, sad, almost as if looking back at those five past years. 'I'm sorry I left you. I'm sorry I was so weak.'

'You weren't weak.' She paused and stared down at her feet, thinking of all the times she'd tried to comfort him, all the times he'd held himself back. The bracing of his shoulders as she'd reached for him. The rigidity of his body, the sheer effort of holding emotion within. 'You were so strong I couldn't get near you.'

'But I wasn't strong enough. That was what I didn't see. That admitting weakness, admitting need, takes its own form of strength. That sharing is two-way. And that's the second thing I want to say to you, my Maddie. It's that I need you.'

I need you.

The words hung in the warm morning air.

Need.

He'd never said such a thing. Their relationship had been based on their love and her need. It hadn't been enough.

'How can you need me?' she whispered, hardly daring to breathe, and still he stared out to sea. His hands were clenched, as if things were breaking inside him, as if he was deliberately taking apart something he'd built over a lifetime.

'Because I'll shatter if you don't take me back,' he said, and then he shook his head. 'No. That's blackmail and there's no place for that here. I'll keep on going. I'll stay doing what I'm doing. But, Maddie, something inside me has changed. It's melted. When we were down the mine, when we'd delivered your daughter, when I thought we might die together, Maddie, I wanted to be held. I wanted to admit to you how scared I was. I was terrified for all of us. I was terrified of losing you, yet I couldn't admit it. And then...'

'Then?' How hard was it to whisper?

'Then we were safe and things were as they'd been before. I knew life could go on. I knew you didn't need me. But then I saw Nani come to visit you. She was bereft but she still came, to say to you that she knew you'd done your best, that there was no blame. And I thought, how strong was that? It's the kind of thing I might try—I have tried. When I'm hurt I try to make those around me feel better. It's what's been instilled in me since birth and I don't know any other way.'

'So what's different now?'

'I watched you,' he said simply. 'I watched you admit

that you needed her. That you needed this island. Giving and taking. And all you've said to me… Everything over the years… It was like that moment coalesced it all. Maybe if I could have gone straight back to work, straight back into needed mode, I wouldn't have had time to sort it out, but Beth made me lie on the stretcher in the plane and I stared up at nothing and that moment kept coming back. And I thought…how selfish was I? To not let you care.'

'Josh…'

'I do need you, Maddie,' he told her, simply now and humbly. 'I've always needed you. I just didn't know how. Mikey's death shattered me and all I knew was to try and comfort you. I didn't see that sharing the hurt could have helped heal us both. And then, when Holly died so soon after, I was a mess and I kept thinking I couldn't lay that hurt on you. So stupidly, selfishly I stepped away. I told myself it was protecting you, but all the time it was about protecting my armour. I thought I'd shatter if I admitted need. But, Maddie, I do need. If anything happened to you now, I'd fall apart. If anything happened to Lea…'

And his voice broke.

Enough. She took him into her arms and pulled him to her. And he came. After all these years she felt him melt into her, merge, warmth against warmth. She felt him hold, not in passion but in need.

To take comfort.

To love.

How long they sat there she couldn't say. Up at the house Caroline would be caring for Lea, but she'd fed her just before the funeral. For now time didn't matter. It couldn't be allowed to matter.

All that mattered was that she was holding the man she loved.

'I wouldn't mind a kiss.'

She wasn't sure when she said it, or even why she said it, but suddenly it was needful. Comfort was all very well, she thought, but if she was getting her Josh back... Well, she wanted her Josh back. Bravado and all. Hero, except in the most dire of circumstances. Her knight in shining armour—but with the ability to take off his armour and leave it in the hall cupboard.

But then she was no longer thinking. There was no room for thinking because she was being soundly, ruthlessly kissed. She was in Josh's arms and there was nowhere else in the world she would have rather been.

She was with her Josh. He needed her.

She had her baby. She had her Josh.

She had her family.

Afterwards, when there was room for words again, when the world had somehow righted itself on this new and wonderful axis, she did check the hall cupboard. It took some doing but Josh had been gone for five long years and she wasn't about to let him back into her world on a promise. The sensible side of her—the part that had learned to distrust and could never completely be ignored—wanted to know just what terms that armour would be let out.

'So...' she managed, breathlessly because that kiss had taken energy and she didn't have much energy spare at the moment. 'So how could we work this? Because... Josh, you know that I love you but...'

'But my proposition about a house close to my work didn't make you happy?'

'You make me happy,' she said simply. 'But, Josh…'

'You love this island,' he said, cupping her face and kissing her again, lightly this time, tenderly, as if he had all the time in the world, and kissing her was almost as natural as breathing. 'I can see that. And you love this community and this community needs you. And you love your mum. Your mum needs you and you need your mum. And of course there's Lea, who we both love…'

'You don't…you don't mind that I used a sperm donor?'

'If I ever meet him I'll give him half my kingdom,' Josh said simply. 'He's given me a daughter—if you'll let me share.'

'Oh, Josh.' She could feel the tears. It was weakness, she thought desperately. She hated tears, but Josh smiled and kissed them away and she thought maybe she didn't hate them so much.

'Proposition,' he said simply. 'I've been talking to Keanu.'

'When?'

'Yesterday. When you were faffing about, learning how to feed your daughter. When he was faffing about, worrying about clots on my leg. He talked to me about these islands. He talked about how desperate the islanders are for a full medical service. Apparently the Lockhart money has run dry for the mine, but there's still Australian government funding for doctors—if you can get doctors to come here. They work on a doctors-per-head-of-population ratio, which means the islands are short by at least two, possibly three doctors. So I thought, if it's okay with you, I could come here. This is really tentative—I need to talk to Keanu and Sam—but it seems to me that a couple of doctors settled out on Atangi could work well. I could be part of the emergency on-call roster from there. It's only three minutes by chopper to pick me up. We could run a permanent clinic. We could build ourselves a great house overlooking the sea—'

'Josh…'

'We could be happy there,' he said, urgently now. 'I know we could. Sure, we'd be two doctors dependent on each other for backup, but…' He shrugged his shoulders and gave a rueful smile. 'I guess that's what you already know and I'm finding out. We could depend on each other. I'd need you, my Maddie, and you'd need me.'

'Josh.' Dammit, her eyes were brimming again. It sounded wonderful—it sounded brilliant—but there were still things…complications…

Love.

'Josh, I need to stay flying in and flying out.' It nearly killed her to say it but she had to. 'Or…or leave the islands and live in Cairns. It might need to be in your house near your work. Because Mum…'

'Your mum needs you.'

'I need my mum.' She said it simply. It was two-way, this loving business, and he had to see it. 'I can't walk away.'

'I would never ask you to.' Once more he kissed her. 'It's a whole, complex web. I need you, you need your mum, I need you to be happy and you can't be happy without your mum. But there are needs and needs. There's another thought, as well. Your friend, Nani, loves Atangi and wants to live there, only of course she and Kalifa mortgaged their house to try and get her son out of debt. She loves you. This is early days, there's so much to sort out, but I thought, if we build big with a housekeeper's apartment, maybe we could bring your mother here. And Nani could be our housekeeper-carer. It'd mean your mother would be near Lea as she grows up. You'd have company if I'm called away. Maybe… maybe we could all be happy?'

And that pretty much took her breath away. She sat, astounded, as what he was proposing sank in.

A house on Atangi. No, a home. Her daughter, her mother, Bugsy, Nani…

Her husband.

Maybe even…

'Two or three?' Josh said, and grinned because he knew what she was thinking—he'd always known what she was thinking. 'We wouldn't want to be lonely. And maybe another pup to keep Bugsy company. After all, he saved your life—he deserves his own happy ending.'

'You'd do all that for me?' she whispered, and he cupped her face in his hands and his gaze met hers. He was loving her with his eyes.

'No,' he said softly. 'I'd do all that for me. I'd do it because I need it. I need you. I need family. Yes, I need to be needed, but I can be, and it will be two-way. I promise you, Maddie, love. If you'll marry me again I swear that I'll need you for as long as we both shall live.'

And what was a woman to say to that? There was only one answer and it was a soundless one.

She drew him to her and she kissed him, tenderly this time, lovingly, an affirmation of everything in her heart.

The armour was melting, she thought. Wherever he'd stowed it, she could feel it disappearing.

He had no need of armour.

Her heart was beating in sync with his. She loved and she loved and she loved.

Soon her daughter would need feeding. *Their* daughter.

They'd walk back to the house together, and they'd walk slowly because both of them hurt.

They'd hold each other up, she thought as he helped her to her feet.

They needed each other, and together it didn't hurt at all.

* * * * *

THE INCORRIGIBLE PLAYBOY

PLAYBOY

EMMA DARCY

CHAPTER ONE

THIRTY.

The big three zero.

If ever there was a birthday to inspire the determination to make a change in her life, this was it.

Elizabeth Flippence assessed her reflection in the mirror with a mixture of hope and anxiety. She'd had her long brown hair cut to just below her ears and layered so that it fluffed out around her face in wild waves with bangs across her forehead. It was a much more modern look and softer, more feminine, but she wasn't sure she should have let the hairdresser talk her into the vibrant auburn colour.

It was certainly striking. Which was probably what she needed for Michael Finn to really notice her today—notice her as a woman instead of taking her for granted as his superefficient personal assistant. She desperately wanted their relationship to shift from its consistently platonic level. Two years was long enough to pine for a man who seemed fixated on not mixing business with pleasure.

Which was ridiculous. They were so well suited to each other. Surely Michael knew that in his heart. It couldn't be more obvious. Her frustration over this stand-off situation had been simmering for months, and Elizabeth had decided that today was the day she was going to try smashing down his guard. This make-over should at least capture his attention.

And the hairdresser was right about the auburn tones making her dark brown eyes look brighter. The new hairstyle also seemed to put her rather long nose in better proportion with the rest of her face. It highlighted her slanted cheekbones in a strangely exotic way and even her slightly wide full-lipped mouth looked more right somehow.

Anyway, it was done now and she fiercely hoped it would promote the desired result. When Michael commented on her changed appearance, she would tell him it was her birthday present to herself and maybe…please, please, please…he would suggest celebrating the occasion by taking her out to lunch, or better still, dinner.

She didn't want to be his Girl Friday anymore. She wanted to be his every day and every night girl. If that didn't start happening… Elizabeth took a long deep breath as she faced the unavoidable truth. Thirty really was the deadline for a woman to give serious consideration to finding a life partner if she wanted to have a family of her own. Michael Finn was her choice but if he didn't respond to her differently today, she'd probably be wasting her time to hope for any change from him in the near future. Which meant she would have to move on, try to meet someone else.

She quickly banished the downer thought. It was imperative to be positive today. Smile and the whole world smiled back at you, she told herself. It was one of Lucy's principles and it certainly worked for her sister, who invariably carved a blithe path through life, using her smile to get her out of trouble. A lot was forgiven with Lucy's smile.

Elizabeth practised her own as she left the bathroom. She was just slipping her mobile phone into her handbag, ready to leave for work when it played her signature call tune. Quickly flipping it open she lifted it to her ear, anticipating the caller would be Lucy, who had spent the weekend with friends at Port Douglas. Her sister's voice instantly bubbled forth.

'Hi, Ellie! Happy birthday! I hope you're wearing the clothes I bought for you.'

'Thanks, Lucy, and yes, I am.'

'Good! Every woman should look bold and beautiful on their thirtieth birthday.'

Elizabeth laughed. The beautiful butterfly blouse, basically in glorious shades of blue and green but with the wings outlined in brown and enclosing a vivid pattern in red and sea-green and yellow and lime, was definitely eye-catching, especially teamed with the sea-green pencil skirt. The outfit was a far cry from her usual style in clothes, but under Lucy's vehement persuasion, she had let herself be seduced by the gorgeous colours.

'I've had my hair cut, too. And dyed auburn.'

'Wow! Can't wait to see that! I'll be back in Cairns later this morning. I'll drop in at your office for a peek. Got to go now.'

The connection clicked off before Elizabeth could say, 'No, don't!'

It was probably silly but she felt uncomfortable about Lucy visiting her at work and had always deterred her from doing it. Because of Michael. As much as she loved her ditzy younger sister, there was no escaping the fact that men seemed irresistibly drawn to her. Her relationships never lasted long. Nothing with Lucy lasted long. There was always another man, another job, another place to go.

For several moments Elizabeth dithered over calling her sister back, not wanting this day to be spoiled by a possible distraction from herself. Yet, didn't she need to test Michael's feelings for her? He should value her worth above Lucy's honeybee attraction. Besides, he might not even see her sister drop in. The door between her office and his was usually closed.

She didn't feel right about putting Lucy off this morning. It was her birthday and her sister was happy and excited about seeing her. They only had each other. Their mother had died of cancer when they were still in their teens, and their father, who had since settled in Mt Isa with another woman, wouldn't even remember her birthday. He never had.

In any event, Michael would have to meet Lucy sooner or later if the closer involvement Elizabeth was aiming for came to pass. Accepting this inevitability, she picked up her handbag, slid the mobile phone into its compartment and headed off to work.

The month of August was a pleasant one in Far North Queensland, not too hot to walk the five blocks from the apartment she and Lucy shared to The Esplanade, where the head office of Finn's Fisheries was located. Usually she drove her little car, leaving it in the space allocated for her in the underground car park of her boss's building, but she didn't want to be tied to driving it home today. Much better to be free to do anything.

The thought brought another smile to her face as she strolled along. Michael really was the perfect man for her. Finn's Fisheries was a huge franchise with outlets all around Australia. They not only stocked every possible piece of fishing gear—a lot of it imported—but the kind of clothing that went with it: wetsuits, swimming costumes, shorts, T-shirts, hats. The range of merchandise was fantastic and Michael dealt with all of it. She loved how he never missed a beat, always on top of everything. It was how she liked to be herself. Together they made a great team. He often said so himself.

If he would just see they should take the next step, Elizabeth was sure they could team up for life and make it a very happy one, sharing everything. He was thirty-five. It was time for both of them to start building a far more personal partnership. She couldn't believe Michael wanted to remain a bachelor forever.

In the two years she'd known him his relationships with other women had never lasted long, but Elizabeth reasoned it was because he was a workaholic. It would be different with her. She understood him.

Despite all this positive thinking, her heart fluttered nervously as she entered her office. The door to Michael's was open, which meant he was already in, organising the business of the day. It was Monday, the beginning of a new week. The beginning of something new between them, too, Elizabeth fiercely hoped as she took a deep breath to calm herself and walked purposefully to the opened door.

He was seated at his desk, pen in hand, ticking off

items on a sheet of paper, his concentration so total he didn't sense her presence. For a few moments Elizabeth simply gazed at him, loving the clean-cut perfection of the man; the thick black hair kept short so it was never untidy, the straight black eyebrows that gave slashing emphasis to the keen intelligence of his silver-grey eyes. The straight nose, firm mouth and squarish jaw all combined to complete the look of the alpha male he was.

As always he wore a top quality white shirt that showed off his flawless olive skin and undoubtedly he would be wearing classy black trousers—his customary work uniform. His black shoes would be shiny and... he was just perfect.

Elizabeth swallowed hard to clear her throat and willed him to give her the kind of attention she craved.

'Good morning, Michael.'

'Good morn—' His gaze lifted, his eyes widening in shock. His mouth was left slightly agape, his voice momentarily choked by the unexpected sight of an Elizabeth who was not the same as usual.

She held her breath. This was the moment when the only-business attitude towards her had to snap. A host of butterflies invaded her stomach. *Smile*, her mind wildly dictated. *Show him the warmth in your heart, the desire heating up your blood.*

She smiled and suddenly he grinned, the silver eyes sparkling with very male appreciation.

'Wow!' he breathed, and her skin tingled with pleasure.

'Great hair! Fabulous outfit, too!' he enthused. 'You've done wonders with yourself, Elizabeth. Does this mean there's some new guy in your life?'

The high that had soared from his first words came crashing down. Associating her makeover with another man meant the distance he kept between them was not about to be crossed. Although...maybe he was tempted. Maybe he was just checking if the coast was clear for him to step in.

She rallied, quickly saying, 'No. I've been unattached for a while. I just felt like a change.'

'Super change!' he warmly approved.

That was better. Warmth was good. Elizabeth instantly delivered the planned hint for him to make his move.

'I'm glad you like it. The clothes are a gift from my sister. It's my birthday. She insisted I had to look bold and beautiful today.'

He laughed. 'Well, you certainly do. And we should celebrate your birthday, too. How about lunch at The Mariners Bar? We can make time for it if we get through this inventory this morning.'

Hope soared again. A lunch for two at one of the most expensive restaurants in Cairns, overlooking the marina full of million-dollar yachts...her heart sang with joy. 'That would be lovely. Thank you, Michael.'

'Book us a table. One o'clock should see us clear.' He picked up a sheaf of papers, holding it out to her. 'In the meantime, if you could check this lot...'

'Of course.'

Business as usual, but there was a rainbow at the end of it today. Elizabeth could barely stop her feet from dancing over to his desk to collect the work that had to be done first.

'Bold and beautiful,' Michael repeated, grinning at

her as he handed over the papers. 'Your sister must have a lot of pizzazz.'

It killed the song in her heart. He was supposed to be showing more interest in her, not wondering about Lucy. She shouldn't have mentioned her sister. But there was no taking it back, so she had to live with it.

'Yes, she has, but she's terribly ditzy with it. Nothing seems to stay in her head long enough to put any order into her life.' It was the truth and she wanted Michael to know it. The thought of Lucy being attractive to him in any way was unbearable.

'Not like you,' he said appreciatively.

She shrugged. 'Chalk and cheese. A bit like you and your brother.'

The words tripped off her tongue before Elizabeth could catch them back. The anxiety about Lucy had caused her control to slip. It wasn't appropriate for her to make any comment about her boss's brother. Normally she would keep her mouth firmly shut about him, despite the heartburn Harry Finn invariably gave her with his playboy patter. She hated it when he came into the office. Absolutely hated it.

Michael leaned back in his chair, his mouth tilted in a musing little smile. 'Working behind a desk is definitely not Harry's thing, but I think you might have the wrong impression of him, Elizabeth.'

'I'm sorry.' She grimaced an apology. 'I didn't mean to…to…'

Now she was lost for words!

'It's okay.' Michael waved off her angst. 'I know he seems very casual about everything but his mind is as sharp as a razor blade and he has his thumb on everything to do with his side of the business.'

Charter boats for deep-sea fishing, dive-boats for tourists wanting to explore the Great Barrier Reef, overseeing the resort they'd built on one of the islands—it was playboy stuff compared to what Michael did. Elizabeth's opinion of Harry Finn didn't shift one iota.

'I'll try to see him in that light in the future,' she clipped out.

Michael laughed. Elizabeth's toes curled. He was so charismatically handsome when he laughed. 'I guess he's been ruffling your feathers with his flirting. Don't let it get to you. He's like that with every woman. It's just a bit of fun.'

Oh, sure! Great *fun*! For Harry Finn.

Elizabeth hated it.

However, she managed to paste a smile on her face. 'I'll keep that in mind,' she said. 'Must get to work now. And I'll book our table at The Mariners Bar.'

'Do that.' Another grin. 'We can discuss brothers and sisters over lunch.'

No way, Elizabeth thought as she walked briskly to her own office, firmly closing the door behind her to ensure that Michael didn't see Lucy when she dropped in. She didn't want her sister sparking any interest in his mind. Nor did she want Harry Finn intruding on any part of this special lunch date. This precious time together had to be about moving closer to each other on a really personal plane. All her hopes for a future with Michael Finn were pinned on it.

CHAPTER TWO

Ten thirty-seven.

Elizabeth frowned at the clock on her desk. The arrangement with the coffee shop on the ground floor was for coffee and muffins to be delivered at ten-thirty—black expresso and a chocolate muffin for Michael, cappuccino and a strawberry and white chocolate muffin for her. She skipped breakfast to have this treat and her empty stomach was rumbling for it. It was unusual for the delivery to be late. Michael hated unpunctuality and the shop tenants were well aware of his requirements.

A knock on her door had her scuttling out of her chair to open it, facilitating entry as fast as possible. 'You're late,' she said chidingly, before realising the tray of coffee and muffins was being carried by Harry Finn.

Vivid blue eyes twinkled at her. 'Short delay while they made coffee for me, too,' he said unapologetically.

'Fine! You can explain that to Michael,' she bit out, forcing her gritted teeth open to get the words out.

'Oh, I will, dear Elizabeth. Never would I leave a blemish on your sterling record of getting everything right for him,' he rolled out in the provocative tone that made her want to hit him. She was not given to violence but Harry Finn invariably stirred something explosive in her.

'And may I say you look stunning this morning. Absolutely stunning!' he rattled on as he stepped into her office, eyeing her up and down, his gaze pausing where the butterfly wings on her blouse framed her breasts, making her nipples stiffen into bullets. She wished they could be fired at him. His white T-shirt with tropical fish emblazoned on it wouldn't look so sexy on him if there were black holes through it to his all-too-manly chest.

'The hair is spectacular, not to mention—'

'I'd rather you didn't mention,' she cut him off, closing the door and waving him towards Michael's office. 'Your brother is waiting.'

He grinned his devil-may-care grin. 'Won't kill him to wait a bit longer.'

She crossed her arms in exasperated impatience with him as he strolled over to set the tray down on her desk, then hitched himself onto the edge of it, ignoring any reason for haste. The white shorts he wore emphasised his long, tanned, muscular legs. One of them he dangled at her, teasing her need for proper behaviour.

'A moth turning into a butterfly doesn't happen every day,' he happily remarked. 'I want to enjoy the glory of it.'

Elizabeth rolled her eyes. She was not going to stand for this. A moth! She had never been a moth! She had simply chosen to be on the conservative side with her appearance to exemplify a serious career person, not someone who could ever be considered flighty like her sister.

'The coffee will be getting cold,' she stated in her chilliest voice.

'Love the sea-green skirt,' he raved on. 'Matches the colour of the water near the reef. Fits you very neatly, too. Like a second skin. In fact, it's inspiring a fantasy of you as a mermaid.' He grinned. Evilly. 'I bet you'd swish your tail at me.'

'Only in dismissal,' she shot at him, pushing her feet to walk to the desk and deal with the coffee herself since Harry was not inclined to oblige. It meant she had to go close to him, which she usually avoided because the man was so overwhelmingly male, in-your-face male, that her female hormones seemed to get in a tizzy around him. It was extremely irritating.

He wasn't as classically handsome as Michael. He was more raffishly handsome—his longish black curly hair flopping around his face, crow's-feet at the corners of his eyes from being out in the weather, a slightly crooked nose from having it broken at some point in his probably misspent youth, and a mouth that was all-too-frequently quirked with amusement. At her. As it was now.

'Have you ever wondered why you're so uptight with me, Elizabeth?' he tossed out.

'No. I don't give you that much space in my mind,' she answered, deliberately ignoring him as she removed her coffee and muffin from the tray.

'Ouch!' he said as though she'd hurt him, then laughed to show she hadn't. 'If I ever get too big for my boots, I know where to come to be whipped back into shape.'

She gave him a quelling look. 'You've come to see Michael. Just follow me into his office.'

The devil danced in his eyes. 'Only if you swish your tail at me.'

She glared back. 'Stop playing with me. I'm not going there with you. Not ever,' she added emphatically.

He was totally unabashed. 'All work, no play—got to say you're safe with Mickey on that score.'

Safe? The word niggled at Elizabeth's mind as she carried the tray to Michael's door. Why was Harry so sure she was safe with his brother? She didn't want to be safe. She wanted to be desired so much, there would be no distance left between them.

Harry bounded past her, opened the door and commanded his brother's attention. 'Hi, Mickey! I held up the coffee train to have one made for myself. Have a few things to discuss with you. Here's Elizabeth with it now.'

'No problem,' Michael answered, smiling at her as she sailed in with the tray.

She hugged the smile to her heart. Michael was the man of true gold. Harry was all glitter. And she hated him calling his brother Mickey. It was rotten, schoolboy stuff—Mickey Finn—linking him to a spiked drink, and totally inappropriate for the position he now held. No dignity in it at all. No respect.

'Thanks, Elizabeth,' Michael said warmly as she unloaded the tray, setting out the two coffees and muffin on his desk. 'Table booked?'

'Yes.'

'What table?' Harry asked, instantly putting her on edge again.

'It's Elizabeth's birthday. I'm taking her out to lunch.'

'A...ha!'

Her spine crawled at the wealth of significance she heard in Harry's voice. If he was about to make fun of the situation... She picked up the emptied tray and swung around to shoot him a killing look.

He lifted his hand in a salute, pretending to plead for a truce between them but his eyes glittered with mocking amusement. 'Happy birthday, dear Elizabeth.'

'Thank you,' she grated out, and swiftly left the two men together for their discussions, closing the door to give them absolute privacy and herself protection from *that man*.

It was difficult to concentrate on work. She tried, but the clock kept ticking on—eleven o'clock, eleven-thirty, twelve. Lucy hadn't dropped in and Harry was still with Michael. Anything could have happened with Lucy. It frequently did. She might not make it into the office at all, which would be a relief, no chance of a meeting with Michael. Harry was the main problem. She wouldn't put it past him to invite himself to her birthday lunch. If he did, would Michael put him off?

He had to.

No way could a romantic mood develop between them if Harry was present. He would spoil everything.

A knock on her door cut off her inner angst. Elizabeth looked up to see the door opening and Lucy's head poking around it.

'Okay to come in?'

Her stomach cramped with nervous tension at the late visit but it was impossible to say anything but 'Yes.'

Lucy bounced in, exuding effervescence as she always did. Today she was dressed in a white broderie anglaise outfit: a little frilly skirt that barely reached midthigh, an off-the-shoulder peasant blouse, a wide tan belt slung around her hips, lots of wooden beads dangling from her neck, wooden bangles travelling up one forearm and tan sandals that were strapped up to mid-calf. Her long blond hair was piled up on top of her head with loose strands escaping everywhere. She looked like a trendy model who could put anything together and look good.

'Ooh...I *love* the hair, Ellie,' she cooed, hitching herself onto the edge of Elizabeth's desk, just as Harry had, which instantly provoked the thought they would make a good pair.

'It's very sexy,' Lucy raved on. 'Gives you that just-out-of-bed tumbled look and the colour really, really suits you. It complements the clothes I picked out for you brilliantly. I have to say you look absolutely marvellous.' Her lovely sherry-brown eyes twinkled with delight. 'Now tell me you *feel* marvellous, too.'

Lucy's smile was so infectious, she had to smile back. 'I'm glad I made the change. How was your weekend?'

'Oh, so-so.' She waved her hand airily then pulled a woeful grimace. 'But I've had the most terrible morning.'

Out of the corner of her eye Elizabeth caught the opening of the door to Michael's office. Tension whipped along her nerves. Was it Harry coming out or both men?

Lucy rattled out her list of woes, her hands making a host of dramatic gestures. 'A body was buried in the wrong plot and I had to deal with that. Then a call came in that someone was interfering with a grave. I had to go out to the cemetery and investigate, but that wasn't too bad. It was only a bereaved husband digging a hole on top of the grave to put in potting soil so he could plant his wife's favourite rose. Nice, really. The worst thing was a dog running amok in the memorial garden and knocking off some of the angels' heads. I had to collect them, load them into the van, and now I have to find someone who can stick them back on again. You wouldn't believe how heavy those angels' heads are.'

'Angels' heads…' It was Michael's voice, sounding totally stunned.

It jerked Lucy's attention to him. 'Oh, wow!' she said, looking Michael up and down, totally uninhibited about showing how impressed she was with him.

Elizabeth closed her eyes and sucked in a deep breath.

'Are you Ellie's boss?' The question popped out with barely a pause.

Elizabeth opened her eyes again to see Michael shaking his head as though bringing himself out of a daze, and Harry behind his shoulder, looking straight at her with a sharp intensity in his bedroom blue eyes she had never seen before. It gave her the weird feeling he was tunnelling into her mind. She quickly dropped her gaze.

'Yes. Yes, I am,' Michael finally answered. 'And you are?'

'Lucy Flippence. Ellie's sister. I work in cemetery administration so I often have to deal with angels.'

'I see,' he said, looking at Lucy as though she was a heavenly apparition.

She hopped off her perch on the desk and crossed the

floor to him with her hand extended. 'Pleased to meet you. Okay if I call you Michael?'

'Delighted,' he said, taking her hand and holding on to it as he slowly turned to make the last introduction. 'This is my brother, Harry.'

Elizabeth fiercely willed Lucy to find Harry more attractive. No such luck! Her hand was left in Michael's snug grasp. She raised her other in blithe greeting. 'Hi, Harry!' It was tossed at him in a kind of bubbly dismissal, which meant in Lucy's mind he didn't really count.

'Charmed,' Harry purred at her.

It floated right over her head, no impact at all.

Elizabeth's heart sank like a stone.

Lucy was intent on engaging Michael and he was obviously enthralled with her.

'I don't know if you know but it's Ellie's birthday today and I thought I'd treat her to a really nice lunch somewhere. You won't mind if I take her off and she's a bit late back, will you, Michael?' she said appealingly.

There was a terrible inevitability about what happened next.

'Actually, I'd decided to do the same myself. Lunch at The Mariners Bar.'

'Oh, wow! The Mariners Bar! What a lovely boss you are to take Ellie there!'

'Why don't you join us? It will be a better celebration of her birthday if you do.'

'I'll come, as well. Make a party of it,' Harry put in, instantly supporting the idea.

'I only booked a table for two,' Elizabeth couldn't help saying, even though knowing it was a futile attempt to change what wouldn't be changed now. Her secret dream was already down the drain.

'No problem. I'm sure the maître d' will make room for us,' Michael said, oozing confidence as he smiled at Lucy. 'We'd be delighted to have the pleasure of your company.'

'Well, a foursome should be more fun, don't you think, Ellie?'

The appealing glance over her shoulder forced Elizabeth to smile and say, 'Certainly no awkward silences with you, Lucy.'

She laughed. 'That's settled, then. Thank you for asking me, Michael. And it's good of you to join in the party, too, Harry.'

The death knell to a happy birthday, Elizabeth thought. Not only would she have to watch Michael being fascinated by her sister, she'd also have to put up with Harry getting under her skin all the time. She slid him a vexed look. His mouth quirked at her, seemingly with more irony than amusement, but that probably didn't mean anything. No doubt he was anticipating having heaps of *fun* at her expense.

This lunch was going to be the lunch from hell.

Elizabeth didn't know how she was going to get through it without throwing in the towel, having hysterics and drowning herself in the marina.

CHAPTER THREE

ELIZABETH knew she'd be paired with Harry for the stroll along the boardwalk to the marina, and she was. There was no point in trying to fight for Michael's company. His preference for Lucy to be at his side had been made so clear, pride dictated that the arrangement be accepted with as much dignified grace as she could muster.

The two of them walked ahead and it was sickening watching the connection between them flourishing. Lucy, of course, was never short of a word, and Michael was lapping up every one of them, enjoying her bubbly personality. It wouldn't last, Elizabeth told herself, but that was no consolation. The damage was done. Lucy had achieved in one minute flat what she had been unable to draw from Michael in two years. Even if he turned to her later on, she would never be able to forget that.

The boardwalk ran along the water's edge of the park adjoining The Esplanade, and she tried to distract herself with the people they passed; couples lounging under the shade of trees, children making use of the play areas set up for them, boys scaling the rock-climb. It was a relief that Harry was leaving her to her silence for a while. It was difficult to cope with him at the best of times, and this was the worst.

She could have chosen to tell Lucy about her secret passion for her boss. That would have warned her off although she wouldn't have understood it. It simply wasn't in Lucy to pine for a man who didn't respond to her as she wanted him to respond. She probably would have looked aghast and said, 'Throw him away, Ellie. He's not that into you if you've waited this long for him to make a move.'

That truth was staring her in the face right now.

And it hurt.

It hurt so badly, she had to keep blinking back the tears that threatened to well into her eyes. Her chest was so tight she could hardly breathe. She'd been a fool to hope, a fool to think today might be the day. It was never going to happen for her.

'Ellie...'

It was a jolt to her wounded heart, hearing Harry speak her childhood name in a low, caressing tone.

'I like it,' he went on. 'Much better than Elizabeth. It conjures up a more carefree person, softer, more accessible.'

Her spine stiffened. He was doing it again, digging at her. She shot him a hard, mocking look. 'Don't get carried away by it. Lucy simply couldn't say Elizabeth when she was little. She calls me Ellie out of habit.'

'And affection, I think.' There was a look of kindness in his eyes that screwed up her stomach as he added, 'She doesn't know she's hurting you, does she?'

Her mind jammed in disbelief over Harry's insightful comment. 'What do you mean?'

He grimaced at her prevarication. 'Give it up, Ellie. You're not Mickey's type. I could have told you so but you wouldn't have believed me.'

Humiliation burned through her. Her cheeks flamed with it. She tore her gaze from the certain knowledge in Harry Finn's and stared at his brother's back—the back Michael had turned on her to be with her sister. How had Harry known what she'd yearned for? Had Michael known, too? She couldn't bear this. She would have to resign from her job, find another.

'Don't worry,' Harry said soothingly. 'You can keep on working for him if you want to. Mickey doesn't have a clue. He's always had tunnel vision—sets his mind on something and nothing else exists.'

Relief reduced some of the heat. Nevertheless, it was still intensely disturbing that Harry was somehow reading her mind. Or was he guessing, picking up clues from her reactions? She hadn't admitted anything. He couldn't really *know*, could he?

'On the other hand, it would be much better if you did resign,' he went on. 'It's never good to keep being reminded of failure. And no need to go job-hunting. You can come and work for me.'

Work for him? Never in a million years! It spurred her into tackling him head-on, her eyes blazing with the fire of battle. 'Let me tell you, Harry Finn, I have never failed at any work Michael has given me and working for you has no appeal whatsoever.'

He grinned at her. 'Think of the pleasure of saying what you think of me at every turn instead of having to keep yourself bottled up around Mickey.'

'I am not bottled up,' she declared vehemently.

He sighed. 'Why not be honest instead of playing the pretend-game? Your fantasy of having Mickey fall at your feet is never going to come true. Face it. Give it up. Look at me as the best tonic for lovesickness you could have. Balls of fire come out of you the moment I'm around.'

'That's because you're so annoying!'

Her voice had risen to a passionate outburst, loud enough to attract Michael's and Lucy's attention, breaking their absorption in each other. They paused in their walk, turning around with eyebrows raised.

'It's okay,' Elizabeth quickly assured them. 'Harry was just being Harry.'

'Be nice to Elizabeth, Harry,' Michael chided. 'It's her birthday.'

'I *am* being nice,' he protested.

'Try harder,' Michael advised, dismissing the distraction to continue his tête-à-tête with Lucy.

'Right!' Harry muttered. 'We need some control here, Ellie, if you want to pretend there's nothing wrong in your world.'

'The only thing wrong in my world is you,' she muttered back fiercely. 'And don't call me Ellie.'

'Elizabeth reigns,' he said in mock resignation.

She bit her lips, determined not to rise to any more of his baits.

They walked on for a while before he started again.

'This won't do,' he said decisively. 'We'll be at the restaurant soon. If you sit there in glum silence, I'll get the blame for it and that's not fair. It's not my fault that Mickey's attracted to your sister. Your best move is to start flirting with me. Who knows? He might suddenly get jealous.'

This suggestion stirred a flicker of hope. Maybe…

The shared laughter from the couple in front of them dashed the hope before it could take wing. Nevertheless, Harry did have a valid point. If she didn't pretend to be having a good time, even Michael and Lucy would realise this birthday treat was no treat at all for her. She had to *look* happy even though she couldn't *be* happy.

She sighed and slid him a weighing look. 'You know it won't mean anything if I flirt with you.'

'Not a thing!' he readily agreed.

'It's just for the sake of making a cheerful party.'

'Of course.'

'It's obvious that you're a dyed-in-the-wool playboy, and normally I wouldn't have anything to do with you, Harry, but since I'm stuck with you on this occasion, I'll play along for once.'

'Good thinking! Though I take exception to the playboy tag. I do know how to play, which I consider an important part of living—something I suspect you do too little of—but that's not all I am.'

'Whatever…' She shrugged off any argument about his personality. Arguing would only get her all heated again and she needed to be calm, in control of herself. Harry was right about that.

They'd walked past the yacht club and were on the path to the cocktail bar adjoining the restaurant when Harry made his next move.

'Hey, Mickey!' he called out. 'I'll buy the girls cocktails while you see the maître d' about our table.'

'Okay' was tossed back at him, his attention reverting to Lucy with barely a pause.

'No doubt about it, he's besotted,' Harry dryly commented. 'How old are you today, Elizabeth?'

'Thirty,' she answered on a defeated sigh. No point in hiding it.

'Ah! The big three zero. Time to make a change.'

Precisely what she had thought. And still had to think now that Michael had proved his disinterest in her personally.

'Go with me on this,' Harry urged.

'Go with you on what?'

'Something I was discussing with Mickey this morning. I'll bring it up again after lunch. Just don't dismiss it out of hand. It would be the perfect change for you.'

'You couldn't possibly know what's perfect for me, Harry,' she said sceptically.

He cocked a teasing eyebrow. 'I might just be a better judge on that than you think I am.'

She shook her head, her eyes mocking this particular belief in himself.

He grinned. 'Wait and see.'

She wasn't about to push him on it. Harry enjoyed being tantalising. Elizabeth had found her best course was simply to show complete disinterest. In this case, she couldn't care less what he had in mind. All she cared about was getting through lunch without showing how miserable she was.

Michael left them at the cocktail bar, striding swiftly into the restaurant to speak to the maître d', obviously in a hurry to get back to Lucy. Harry led them to a set of two-seater lounges with a low table in between and saw them settled with her and Lucy facing each other.

'Now, let me select cocktails for you both,' he said, the vivid blue eyes twinkling confidence in his choices. 'A Margarita for you, Elizabeth.'

It surprised her that he'd actually picked her favourite. 'Why that one?' she asked, curious about his correct guessing.

He grinned. 'Because you're the salt of the earth and I revere you for it.'

She rolled her eyes. The day Harry Finn showed any reverence for her was yet to dawn. He was just making a link to the salt-encrusted rim of the glass that was always used for a Margarita cocktail.

'You're right on both counts,' Lucy happily volunteered. 'Ellie loves Margaritas and she *is* the salt of the earth. I don't know what I'd do without her. She's always been my anchor.'

'An anchor,' Harry repeated musingly. 'I think that's what's been missing from my life.'

'An anchor would only weigh you down, Harry,' Elizabeth put in dryly. 'It would feel like an albatross around your neck.'

'Some chains I wouldn't mind wearing.'

'Try gold.'

He laughed.

'Do you two always spar like this?' Lucy asked, eyeing them speculatively.

'Sparks invariably fly,' Harry claimed.

It was on the tip of her tongue to say she invariably hosed them down, remembering just in time that flirting was the order of this afternoon, so she gave him an arch look and said, 'I would have to admit that being with Harry is somewhat invigorating.'

Lucy laughed and clapped her hands. 'Oh, I love it! What a great lunch we'll all have together!' Her eyes sparkled at Harry. 'What cocktail will you choose for me?'

'For the sunshine girl... A Piña Colada.'

She clapped her hands again. 'Well done, Harry. That's *my* favourite.'

'At your service.' He twirled his hand in a salute to them both and headed off to the bar.

Lucy was beside herself with delight. 'He's just what you need, Ellie. Loads of fun. You've been carrying responsibility for so long, it's well past time you let loose and had a wild flutter for once. Be a butterfly instead of a worker bee.'

At least she didn't say *moth*, Elizabeth thought wryly.

'I might just do that,' she drawled, encouraging the idea there was a connection between her and Harry.

'Go for it,' Lucy urged, bouncing forward on her seat in excitement. 'I'm going for Michael. He's an absolute dreamboat. I'm so glad I wasn't held up any longer at the cemetery. I might have missed out on meeting him. Why didn't you tell me your boss was gorgeous?'

'I've always thought him a bit cold,' she said carefully.

Lucy threw up her hands in exasperation at her sister's lack of discernment. 'Believe me. The guy is hot! He makes me sizzle.'

Elizabeth shrugged. 'I guess it's a matter of chemistry. Harry is the hot one for me.' It wasn't entirely a lie. He frequently raised her temperature...with anger or annoyance.

Lucy heaved a happy sigh. 'Brothers and sisters... wouldn't it be great if we ended up together...all happy families.'

Elizabeth's mind reeled from even considering such a prospect. 'I think that's a huge leap into the future. Let's just take one day at a time.'

'Oh, you're always so sensible, Ellie.'

'Which is something I value very highly in your sister,' Michael declared, picking up on Lucy's words and smiling warmly at Elizabeth as he returned, but he seated himself beside Lucy, who instantly switched on a brilliant smile for him, fulsomely agreeing, 'Oh, I do, too. But I also want Ellie to have fun.'

'Which is where I come in,' Harry said, also catching Lucy's words as he came back. His eyes danced wicked mischief at Elizabeth. 'Starting with cocktails. The bartender will bring them over. Here are the peanuts and pretzels.'

He placed a bowl of them on the table and settled himself beside Elizabeth, too closely for her comfort. She wanted to shift away and somehow Harry knew it, instantly throwing her a challenging look that made her sit still and suffer his male animal impact. If she was really attracted to him, she would welcome it. Playing this pretend-game was not going to be easy, but she had to now in front of Lucy.

Her sister turned her smile to Harry. 'What cocktail did you order for Michael?'

'A Manhattan. Mickey is highly civilised. He actually forgets about sunshine until it sparkles over him.'

Lucy laughed. 'And yourself?'

'Ah, the open sea is my business. I'm a salty man so I share Elizabeth's taste for Margaritas.'

'The open sea?' Lucy queried.

'Harry looks after the tourist side of Finn's Fisheries,' Michael answered. 'I take care of buying in the stock for all our franchises.'

'Ah!' Lucy nodded, understanding why Harry was dressed the way he was and how very different the brothers were.

Why she was attracted to Michael and not Harry was beyond Elizabeth's understanding. Sunshine and sea should go together. They both had frivolous natures. It wasn't fair that sexual chemistry had struck in the wrong place. Why couldn't it strike sensibly?

The bartender arrived with their cocktails.

Harry handed her the Margarita and clicked his glass against hers. 'Happy Birthday, Elizabeth,' he said warmly, making her squirm inside even as she forced a smile and thanked him.

The others followed suit with their glasses and well-wishing.

Elizabeth settled back against the cushions and sipped her cocktail, silently brooding over the totally non-sensible ironies of life. Was there any reward for being *sensible*? The old saying that *good things come to those who wait* was not proving true for her.

She wondered how long was the life of a butterfly.

Probably very short.

But it might be sweet if she could bring herself to be a butterfly—just cut loose from all her safety nets and fly wild for a while, thinking of nothing but having a good time. She should take a vacation, get right away from whatever was developing between Michael and Lucy, try drowning her misery with mindless pleasures.

The Margarita was good. And it packed quite a punch. Maybe if she stopped being sensible and had two or three of them, her mind would get fuzzy enough to put this whole situation at an emotional distance, let her float through lunch...like a butterfly.

CHAPTER FOUR

ELIZABETH stared blankly at the luncheon menu. Food. She had to choose something. Her head was swimming from two Margaritas in quick succession. Bad idea, thinking alcohol could fix anything. It didn't help at all.

'I bet I know what you're going to order, Ellie,' Lucy said with a confident grin.

'What?' Any suggestion was welcome.

'The chilli mud crab.'

Chilli. Not today. Her stomach was in too fragile a state.

'Actually, I can't see that on the menu,' Michael said, glancing quizzically at Lucy.

'Oh, I didn't really look. I just assumed,' she quickly defended. No way would she admit that her dyslexia made reading menus difficult. 'What have you decided on, Michael?'

Lucy would undoubtedly choose the same. She was so adept at hiding her disability, hardly anyone ever guessed she had a problem.

'How about sharing a seafood platter for two with me, Elizabeth?' Harry said, leaning closer to point out the platter's contents on the menu. 'You get crab on it, as well as all the other goodies and we can nibble away on everything as we please.'

'Harry will eat the lion's share,' Michael warned.

Yes, Elizabeth thought, relieved to have such ready help, making it easier for her lack of appetite to go unnoticed.

Harry instantly raised a hand for solemn vowing. 'I swear I'll give you first choice of each titbit.'

'Okay, that's a done deal,' she said, closing the menu and slanting her food-rescuer a grateful smile.

'Sealed with a kiss,' he said, bright blue eyes twinkling wickedly as he leaned closer still and pecked her on the cheek.

Her teeth grated together as heat bloomed from the intimate skin contact. The *flirting* agreement flew right out of her mind. His ability to discomfort her on any spot whatsoever had her snapping, 'You can keep that mouth of yours for eating, Harry.'

He gave her his evil grin as he retorted, 'Elizabeth, I live for the day when I'll eat you all up.'

'That'll be doomsday,' she slung back.

'With the gates of heaven opening for me,' Harry retaliated, his grin widening.

Lucy's laughter reminded her just in time that flirting shouldn't have too sharp an edge, so she swallowed her *hell* comment, heaved a long-suffering sigh and shook her head at Harry. 'You are incorrigible.'

'A man has to do what a man has to do,' he archly declared, sending Lucy off into more peals of laughter.

Elizabeth declined asking what he meant.

Nevertheless, as the birthday luncheon progressed, she schooled herself to respond lightly to Harry's banter, pretending to be amused by it, making a show of enjoying his company. At least he was very persistent in claiming her attention, forcefully distracting her from Lucy's and Michael's stomach-curdling absorption in each other, and he did eat the lion's share of the seafood platter without trying to push her into trying more than she could manage.

It was weird finding herself grateful to have Harry at her side, but just this once she actually did. Without him she would feel wretchedly alone, facing the worst scenario of lost hopes. How she was going to cope, hiding her feelings from both Lucy and Michael in the days to come, she didn't know. She hoped they would go off somewhere together after this luncheon, give her some space, release her from the tension of keeping up a happy pretence that everything was fine.

A waiter cleared the table and offered them the sweets menu. Elizabeth decided on the selection of sorbets since they should just slide down her throat without any effort. As soon as the orders were given, Harry leaned an elbow on the table and pointed a finger at his brother, claiming his attention.

'Mickey, I have the solution to my problem with the resort.'

'You have to clear that guy out, Harry,' came the quick advice. 'Once you confront him you can't leave him there. The potential for damage…'

'I know, I know. But it's best to confront him with his replacement. We walk in and turf him out. No argument. A done deal.'

'Agreed, but you don't have a ready replacement yet and the longer he stays…'

'Elizabeth. She's the perfect person for the management job—completely trustworthy, meticulous at checking everything, capable of handling everything you've thrown at her, Mickey.'

Confusion over this brother-to-brother business conversation instantly cleared. *This* was what Harry had intended to bring up after lunch—the perfect change for her. Except it wasn't perfect. Working for him would drive her bats.

'Elizabeth is my PA,' Michael protested.

'I'm in more need of her than you are right now. Lend her to me for a month. That will give me time to interview other people.'

'A month...' Michael frowned over the inconvenience to himself.

A month...

That was a tempting time frame—manageable if Harry wasn't around her all the time. The resort wasn't his only area of interest and responsibility. A month away from Michael and Lucy was a very attractive proposition.

'On the other hand, once Elizabeth gets her teeth into the job, she might want to stay on,' Harry said provocatively.

No way—not with him getting under her skin at any given moment!

Michael glowered at him. 'You're not stealing my PA.'

'Her choice, Mickey.' Harry turned to her. 'What do you say, Elizabeth? Will you help me out for a month... stay on the island and get the resort running as it should be run? My about-to-be ex-manager has been cooking the books, skimming off a lot of stuff to line his own pockets. You'll need to do a complete inventory and change the suppliers who've been doing private deals with him. It would be a whole new challenge for you, one that...'

'Now hold on a moment,' Michael growled. 'It's up to me to ask Elizabeth if she'll do it, not you, Harry.'

'Okay. Ask her.'

Yes was screaming through her mind. It offered an immediate escape from the situation with Michael and Lucy; no need to explain why she wanted to go away; a whole month of freedom from having to see or talk to either of them; a job that demanded her complete attention, keeping miserable thoughts at bay. These critical benefits made the irritation of having to deal with Harry relatively insignificant. Her heart was not engaged with him. Her head could sort out his effect on her, one way or another.

Michael heaved an exasperated sigh, realising he'd been pushed into a corner by his brother. 'It's true. You would be helping us out if you'd agree to step in and do what needs to be done at the resort,' he conceded, giving Elizabeth an earnest look. 'I have every confidence in your ability to handle the situation. Every confidence in your integrity, too. I hate losing you for a month...'

You've just lost me forever, Elizabeth thought.

'...but I guess someone from the clerical staff can fill in for a while....'

'Andrew. Andrew Cook,' she suggested.

He frowned. 'Too stodgy. No initiative.'

'Absolutely reliable in doing whatever task he's set,' she argued, rather bitchily, liking the fact that Michael found him stodgy. He'd obviously found her stodgy, too, in the female stakes.

'I take it that's a yes to coming to the island with me,' Harry slid in, grinning from ear to ear.

She shot him a quelling look. 'I'm up for the challenge of fixing the management problems, nothing else, Harry.'

'Brilliant!'

He purred the word, making her skin prickle. It instantly gave her the unsettling feeling she might have bitten off more than she could chew with Harry Finn. But he wouldn't be at her side all the time on the island. Going was still better than staying at home.

'That's it, then,' Michael said with a resigned air.

'A whole month! I'll miss you, Ellie,' Lucy said wistfully.

'The time will pass quickly enough,' Elizabeth assured her—*particularly with Michael dancing attendance.*

The waiter arrived with the sweets they'd ordered.

'We need to get moving on this,' Harry muttered as he dug into his chocolate mud cake.

'As soon as possible,' Michael agreed.

'Today,' Harry decided, checking his Rolex watch. 'It's only three o'clock now. We could be over on the island by four-thirty. Have him helicoptered out by six. We leave here when we've finished our sweets, hop on the boat...'

'It is Elizabeth's birthday, Harry,' Michael reminded him. 'She might have other plans for today.'

'No, I'm good to go,' she said, recklessly seizing the

chance to be relieved of staying in Michael's and Lucy's company any longer.

'What about clothes and toiletries and stuff?' Lucy put in. 'You're going for a month, Ellie.'

'You can pack for her, Lucy,' Harry said decisively. 'Mickey can take you home, wait while you do it, take Elizabeth's bags and arrange their shipping to the island.'

'No problem,' Michael said, smiling at Lucy like a wolf invited into her home to gobble her up.

Lucy happily agreed with the plan, her eyes sizzling with sexual promises as she smiled back at her new lover-to-be.

Elizabeth shovelled the sorbet down her throat. The faster she got out of here, the better.

'Ready?' Harry asked the moment she put her spoon down.

'Ready,' she answered emphatically, grabbing her handbag and rising to her feet, wanting to run but knowing she had to discipline herself to suffer goodbyes.

Lucy wrapped her in a big hug, mischievously saying, 'Have a lovely time with Harry, Ellie.'

'I will,' she replied through gritted teeth. Denials of that idea would not only be a total waste of time, but also prolong this whole wretched togetherness.

Michael kissed her cheek, wryly murmuring, 'I'll miss you.'

I won't miss you, Elizabeth thought fiercely, barely managing to force a smile. 'Thank you for my birthday lunch, Michael.'

'Pleasure,' he replied, his gaze sliding to Lucy.

'We're off,' Harry said, seizing Elizabeth's hand and pulling her with him.

His hand was strong and hot, wrapping firmly around her fingers, shooting warmth up her arm, but she didn't care if heat travelled to her brain and fried it right now. He was acting fast, taking her to the freedom she needed, and she was grateful for that. Once they were outside, he led her straight to the long wharf where rows of million-dollar yachts were docked on either side.

'Where's your boat?' she asked.

'Right at the end. No shuffling around. A quick, easy getaway. Full throttle to the island.'

'Good!'

He slid her one of his devilish grins. 'I must say I admire your decisiveness.'

She gave him a baleful look. 'Save your chatting up for some other woman, Harry. I played your game in front of Michael and Lucy because it suited me to do it, and I accepted your job offer because that suited me, too. As far as I'm concerned, there's work to be done and I'll do it. I don't expect to have *a lovely time* with you.'

His eyes held hers with a blast of discomforting intensity. 'No, not right now,' he drawled. 'Having had your expectations comprehensively dashed, I daresay you'll be a sourpuss for some time to come. But the island is a lovely place and I hope it will work some magic on you.'

A sourpuss...

The shock of that description halted her feet. She stared back at the blazing blue eyes, hating the knowledge she saw in them, knowledge of her hopes and the humiliation of seeing Michael respond to her sister as he had never—would never—respond to her. She couldn't wipe away Harry's perception of the situation, couldn't deny the truth, but was that any reason to be sour on him? He'd been her saviour today.

'I'm sorry,' she blurted out. 'I haven't thanked you.'

His sexy mouth moved into an ironic tilt. 'No thanks necessary, Elizabeth.'

His voice was soft, deep, and somehow it made her heart turn over.

She shook her head. 'That's not true, Harry. You were very effective in covering up my…my difficulties with how things went down today. I am grateful to you for rescuing me every time I hit a brick wall.'

'You'll bounce back, Elizabeth. Look on tomorrow as the first day of a new life—a butterfly breaking free of its confining cocoon and finding a world of sunshine. Come on—' he started walking down the wharf again, tugging her along with him '—we're on our way there now.'

The first day of a new life…

Of course, that was how it had to be.

There was no point in looking back, mourning over foolish dreams that were never going to come true. She had to put Michael behind her. Lucy would still be there along the track, her episode with Michael gone and forgotten, flitting along in her usual ditzy way. Her sister would always be her sister. It was she who had to start a different journey and being sour about it was just going to hold her back from getting somewhere good.

Harry helped her onto a large, deep-sea fishing

yacht, which undoubtedly had powerful motors to get them to their destination fast. 'Do you get seasick, Elizabeth?' he asked as he released the mooring rope. 'There are pills in the cabin you can take for it.'

'No, I'll be fine,' she assured him.

'I need you to be in top form when we arrive.'

'What do you consider top form?' She needed to know, get it right.

He jumped on board, grinning at her as he stored the rope correctly. 'Your usual self. Totally in charge of everything around you and projecting that haughty confidence you do so well.'

'Haughty?' she queried, not liking that description of herself, either.

'You're brilliant at it. Subject me to it every time.'

Only because Harry was Harry. It was her defence against him.

'I want you to give our target a dose of it when we confront him. No chatter. Just freeze him off.'

'No problem,' she stated categorically.

He straightened up and headed for the ladder to the bridge, tapping her cheek in passing, his eyes twinkling as he said, 'That's my girl!'

She barely stopped her hand from clapping her cheek to rid it of his electric touch. She clenched it into a fist and swiftly decided there would have to be some rules made about this short-term job on the island—like no touching from Harry. No kissing on the cheek, either. He was altogether too cavalier about taking liberties with her.

She was his stand-in manager, *not his girl*!

She was never going to be *his girl*.

One Finn brother had taken a bite out of her life. She was not about to give Harry the chance to take another. A month was a month. That was it with the Finns. She was thirty years old. When she'd completed this escape phase, some serious steps would have to be planned to make the best of the rest of her life.

She needed to find herself a serious man to share all that could be shared.

There was no hope of that happening with a playboy like Harry.

'Think you can make us both a sobering coffee while I fire up the engines?' he tossed back at her from the ladder.

'Sure! Though I'm not the least bit intoxicated, Harry.' She'd sobered up over lunch.

He grinned at her. 'I am. A straight black would be good. Join me on the bridge when you've made it.'

'Okay.'

She wanted to be fully briefed on the situation she was walking into, and Harry certainly needed to be fully in command of himself before they reached the island. Not that she'd noticed any lack of command. In fact, he'd been quite masterful in manipulating Michael into complying with what he wanted. She would have to watch that particular skill of his and not fall victim to any manipulation that would end up with her in the playboy's bed!

CHAPTER FIVE

EXHILARATION bubbled through Harry's brain. Who would have thought when today had started out that he would be riding towards the end of it on this glorious high? Here he was on the open sea, carving through the waves, the problem with his thieving manager solved, and the deliciously challenging Elizabeth at his beck and call for at least a month.

Her brick wall against him was still in place, but that blind obsession of hers with Mickey was gone. Lovely, lovely Lucy had done the job, blitzing his brother right in front of her sister's eyes. And at the most opportune moment! So easy to step in and take advantage of Elizabeth's disillusioned state.

She'd found herself trapped in a situation where pride had forced her to side with him, undoubtedly kicking and screaming about it in her mind, but totally unable to disguise the fact that she reacted to him physically. Always had. She could deny it as much as she liked but sexual chemistry didn't lie, and now that Mickey was out of the picture, cultivating the instinctive attraction she couldn't quite control was going to be the most enjoyable task Harry had set himself for some time.

Ellie Flippence…

That's who she needed to be, not stiff-necked Elizabeth. Though she did have a lovely long neck. He'd often fantasised bending that swanlike column with a trail of hot kisses, melting the rest of her, too. She had beautiful lush breasts and the gorgeous butterfly wings on her blouse showed them off a treat.

This morning he'd wanted to reach out and touch them, cup them, kiss them. He'd find the right time and place for that now. The moment would come when she'd give in to good old healthy lust, and Harry intended to make it so good she'd forget all about her shattered Mickey dreams and revel in the pleasure he'd give her.

But business came first.

He definitely needed to sober up, not give away the game before Elizabeth was ready for it.

Just as well she'd worn sandals, Elizabeth thought as she moved around the galley, steadying herself to the sway of the yacht as it headed out to sea. High heels would have been disastrous in this environment. Clearly there were tricks to keeping everything safe on board. She found a drink holder attached to a sling which made transporting coffee to the bridge relatively easy, and mugs with lids like the takeaway variety used by coffee shops. There was no risk of slopping it onto her good clothes which had to last her until her luggage arrived.

A scene flashed into her mind of Lucy in their apartment, with Michael advising her on what to choose for her sister's island wear—an intimate little scene that made Elizabeth gnash her teeth. She had to stop thinking of *them* together, think about what was ahead of her instead.

Finn Island was at the high end of the tourist industry—exclusive to only twenty couples at a time, people who could pay thousands of dollars for a minimum three-day stay. She had never been there, since it was way beyond her pocket. However, the Cairns office did have a video of it, showing its attractions and facilities, so she had some idea of how it operated.

There were twenty luxury villas, a tennis court, a gym with a pampering centre offering all sorts of massages. The administration centre, boutique, restaurant and bar faced the main beach and were spread around a landscaped area with lush tropical plants and clusters of palm trees, plus a swimming pool and spa. Apart from this artfully designed section, most of the island was covered with rainforest. A creek running from the central hill provided delightful waterfalls and rock pools, and walking tracks had been made to these natural beauty spots.

Dive-boats for exploring the Great Barrier Reef were readily available, as were yachts for deep-sea fishing and small motorboats for reaching the other beaches at the various inlets around the shoreline. All in all, Finn Island provided the perfect tropical getaway…if you were rolling in money.

Guests who could afford it would obviously be demanding, expecting the best for what they were paying. Elizabeth hoped there would be no hiccups to the island's excellent reputation for providing it while she was in charge. She knew supply boats called regularly. However, how the staff operated was a mystery to her and the need for that information was foremost in her mind as she climbed the ladder to the bridge.

She sat down in the chair beside Harry's before handing him his coffee. 'Black, as requested,' she said, forcing a smile to disprove his *sourpuss* description and holding on to a fierce determination not to be prickly in his presence.

'Thanks.' He smiled back. 'We'll be there in about forty minutes.'

'I know the general layout of the resort, but I know nothing about the staff, Harry. Or how everything runs.'

'You'll learn fast enough,' he assured her. 'Basically you have three undermanagers. Sarah Pickard is the head housekeeper. She handles the cleaning staff. Her husband, Jack, is the head maintenance man, who has his own team of helpers. The head chef, Daniel Marven, runs everything to do with the restaurant. He also keeps a check on the bar and will tell you what needs to be ordered in.' He made a wry grimace. 'The guy you are going to replace was overordering and reselling elsewhere, not to mention a few other perks he was working.'

'His name?'

'Sean Cassidy. Not important for you to remember. He'll be gone within an hour of our arrival. I'll call up a helicopter to take him off.'

'Are you going to prosecute?'

He shook his head. 'Bad publicity. Besides, it wasn't major criminal stuff.'

'How did you find out he was crooked?'

'Our sommelier in Cairns remarked to me that our island guests drank an inordinate amount of wine and spirits. Surprisingly inordinate, despite the fact that we run an open bar. It rang warning bells. When Sean had his mainland leave this past weekend, I did a thorough check of all supplies and usage, and bingo! No doubt he was robbing us and has been doing it for some considerable time.'

'Will he know you were checking on him?'

'He knows I was there but I didn't tip my hand to anyone. Mickey and I still had to decide what to do about it. Any disruption is not good for business.' He flashed a grin at her. 'Which is where you come in. No disruption.'

She nodded. 'I'll do my best to make it appear a smooth transition, but I'll need some help to begin with.'

'No problem. I'll be your guide for the first few days, until you've familiarised yourself with how everything runs.'

A few days in close contact with Harry had to be tolerated. The groundwork for this management job had to be laid if she was to carry it through successfully. It was the measure of closeness she had to watch. If he started taking liberties with her person...somehow she had to deal with that if and when it happened.

'I'll get on top of it all as soon as I can,' she said with strong resolution.

Harry chuckled, his vivid blue eyes dancing with teasing knowledge as he slowly drawled, 'I'm sure you will, Elizabeth. Can't get rid of me fast enough, can you?'

She felt heat rushing up her neck and turned her face away, looking out to sea, hating how he could read her mind and provoke this reaction in her. 'I'm sure you have to keep a check on other things besides the resort,' she said flatly.

'True. Though I am aware that I'm throwing you into a position you haven't held before. I'll spend a few days with you, then drop in from time to time in case you have any problems that I can resolve.'

She wished she could say, *Don't. I'll call you if I need your help.* But he was her boss now and what he was laying out was reasonable. Problems could arise that she didn't even recognise because of her inexperience. 'Do you have accommodation kept especially for you on the island?' she asked, worrying about how *close* he was going to be to her.

'No. I'm happy sleeping aboard this yacht. The Pickards have their own private villa as they are the only ones on the staff, apart from the manager, who actually live on the island full-time. The rest work on a rotation basis—ten days here, four days on the mainland—and they're accommodated in a series of motel-like structures.'

'Is that where I'll be staying?'

He shook his head. 'You'll have your own private quarters in the administration building.'

Where Harry could make private visits.

Elizabeth grimaced at that thought. She was getting paranoid about the man. He could not get her into bed with him unless she allowed it. All she had to do was keep him at a sensible distance. It was only for a month and he wouldn't be there all the time.

'Don't be worrying about clothes for tomorrow,' he suddenly tossed at her. 'I'll get Sarah to issue you with the island uniform.'

'What's the island uniform?' she queried, not having seen that on the video.

'This...' He indicated his T-shirt and shorts and pointed to the emblem just below his left shoulder—a stitched line of waves in blue over which *Finn Island* was written in a small flowing multicoloured script to match the multicoloured fish across his chest.

She hadn't noticed the emblem before, distracted by the way the T-shirt clung to Harry's very male physique. 'I hadn't realised. Of course, you came from there this morning.'

So much had happened today, her state of hopeful eagerness this morning felt as though it had been wiped out a million years ago. Another life ago.

'Makes it easier for the guests to know who's staff and who's not,' Harry explained, adding with one of his devilish grins, 'That won't take care of your undies, though.'

He was probably having a fantasy of her naked beneath her outer clothes.

'I'll manage,' she said through gritted teeth.

He laughed. 'You can probably pick up a bikini from the boutique. Sarah can provide you with a hair-dryer and a toothbrush. Don't know about make-up.'

'I have some in my handbag.'

'No worries then.'

Only you, she thought.

Yet when they arrived on the island and confronted Sean Cassidy in his administration office, the playboy image Elizabeth had of Harry Finn in her mind was severely dented. Right in front of her eyes his easygoing attitude disappeared, replaced by a formidable air of authority. There was no semblance of light banter in his voice as he set about firing the crooked manager with ruthless efficiency.

Sean Cassidy had risen from the chair behind his office desk to greet his visitors, a smile on his face that didn't quite reach his eyes, which skated over Elizabeth and settled warily on Harry. He was a tall, lean man, dark-haired, dark-eyed, and the unheralded appearance of his boss clearly caused some tension in him.

'You're out, Sean,' Harry shot at him before the manager could say a word. 'Move away from the desk. Don't touch anything in this office. A helicopter will be arriving shortly to fly you to the mainland. Go and collect all your personal effects from your apartment. You won't be coming back.'

'What the hell…' the guy started to expostulate.

Harry cut him off. 'You know why. I have evidence of all your skimming activities. Providing you go quietly, I won't hand you over to the police at this time. If you know what's good for you, Sean, you'll stay quiet. Any bad-mouthing of the Finn family and its business operations will have consequences you won't like. Do you understand me?'

The threat had a steely edge to it that would have intimidated anyone. Sean Cassidy sucked in his breath, swallowed whatever defensive words he might have spoken and nodded. He looked shell-shocked.

'Let's go then.' Harry waved commandingly to a door in the rear wall of the office. 'I'll accompany you into the apartment to ensure you don't take anything that doesn't belong to you.'

As the man started to move as directed, Harry turned to Elizabeth, his blue eyes ice-hard, not a vestige of a twinkle in them. 'Take over the desk, Elizabeth. You're now in charge of this office.'

She nodded, her mouth too dry to speak. Her heart was beating faster than normal. The air felt charged with electricity. She was still stunned by the strike-anyone-dead energy that had emanated from Harry. In her two years of working for Michael, she had never witnessed anything like it coming from him, and she had always thought he was the stronger brother.

It wasn't until Harry had followed Sean into the apartment and closed the door that she could bring herself to actually move her feet. The desk was large and L-shaped with a computer workstation on one side. She sat in the chair that was now hers, grateful for its firm support. Witnessing the formidable side of Harry Finn had shaken her. The man was lethal, and she suddenly felt very vulnerable to whatever he might turn on her, now that she was locked into this situation with him.

That nerve-quivering blast of forcefulness... A shiver ran down her spine. Though surely he would never *force* a woman. *He wouldn't have to*, came the instant answer in her head. He was so innately sexy he could make her feel hot and bothered with just a teasing look. But he needed her here for business so maybe he would refrain from pushing anything sexual with her. Teasing was just teasing. Hopefully she could keep a level head with that.

Having cleared her mind enough to concentrate on business, Elizabeth took stock of the other office fur-nishings—filing cabinets, a couple of chairs for visi-tors, a coffee table with brochures fanned out on top of it, framed photographs of celebrities who had stayed here hanging on the walls.

On the larger section of the desk, which faced the entrance doors to administration, was a telephone attached to an intercom system with numbers for all the villas, the staff quarters and the restaurant. Beside it was a notepad and pen for writing notes or messages. On the top page were two reminders which had been ticked. *Chocs to 8. Gin to 14.* Obviously she had to deal with all requests from guests as well as handle bookings and coordinate the staff for whatever was needed.

Directly in front of her was a spreadsheet, detailing the occupancy of the villas this week—arrivals and departures. Three couples had left this morning. Their villas were vacant until another three couples arrived tomorrow. One of them was only staying three days, the other two for five. Most of the bookings were for five, only a few for a whole week. She would have to have her wits about her, coordinating the turnovers, personalising the welcomes and the farewells, memorising the names of all the guests. Wealthy people always expected that courtesy and respect.

She was matching names to the occupants of each villa when she heard the distinctive sound of a helicopter coming in. The door behind her opened and Harry led Sean, who was loaded up with luggage, out of the apartment, waving him to go ahead, pausing at the desk long enough to say, 'Hold the fort, Elizabeth. I'll be back in twenty minutes.'

He didn't wait for a reply, intent on escorting Sean to the helipad, wherever that was. The glass entrance doors to the office opened automatically for ease of access and Harry caught up with Sean as he made his exit. There was no verbal exchange between them. The ex-manager was going quietly.

Elizabeth watched Harry until he moved out of sight. Her heart was hammering again. Experiencing a completely different side of Harry Finn to the flirtatious tease she was used to was having a highly disturbing impact on her. It was impossible now to dismiss him as a lightweight playboy. The man had real substance, impressively strong substance, powerful substance, and it was playing havoc with her prejudice against him.

Michael had said this morning that Harry's mind was as sharp as a razor blade and he had his thumb on everything to do with his side of the business. That description could no longer be doubted. She'd had evidence enough today of how accurately he could read her thoughts—something she would have to guard against more carefully in the future—and she would never again underestimate how capable he was of being master of any situation.

His attraction was all the stronger for it. Dangerously so.

Nevertheless, that still didn't make him good relationship material.

He was a dyed-in-the-wool flirt with women.

And that wasn't just her judgment. Michael had said so.

Regardless of what Harry Finn made her feel, she was not going to have anything to do with him apart from the business of managing this resort for a month. He could flirt his head off with her but she would stand absolutely firm on that ground.

He was not what she wanted in her life.

She had to look for someone steady, solid, totally committed to her and the family they would have together.

Not like her father.

And not like Harry, who probably treated women as though they were a carousel of lollipops to be plucked out and tasted until another looked tastier.

CHAPTER SIX

WHEN Harry returned he was accompanied by a middle-aged woman with whom he appeared to be on very friendly terms. They were smiling at each other as they entered the office. She had short, curly dark hair, liberally streaked with grey, a very attractive face set in cheerful lines and merry hazel eyes that invited people to enjoy life with her. Of average height, her trim figure declared her fit to tackle anything, and she exuded positive vibes at Elizabeth as Harry introduced her.

'Sarah Pickard, Elizabeth.'

'Hi! Welcome to Finn Island,' the woman chimed in.

'Thank you.' Elizabeth smiled back as she rose from the desk to offer her hand at this first meeting. 'I'll have to learn a lot very fast and I'll appreciate any help and advice you can give me, Sarah.'

She laughed and gave Elizabeth's hand a quick squeeze. 'No problem. I'm only ever a call away. Harry tells me you've been Mickey's PA. I'm sure you'll fit in here very quickly.'

Mickey? The familiar use of Harry's name for his brother struck her as odd.

'Go into the apartment with Sarah, look around, see what you need,' Harry instructed. 'I'll man the desk.'

'Okay. Thank you,' Elizabeth replied, gesturing to Sarah to lead the way.

It was a basic one-bedroom apartment, spotlessly clean and pleasantly furnished with cane furniture, cushions brightly patterned in tropical designs. The floor was tiled and an airconditioner kept the rooms cool. The kitchenette was small, and its only equipment appeared to be an electric kettle, a toaster and a microwave oven.

'You won't need that for much,' Sarah explained. 'Meals will be brought to you from the restaurant. Just tick what you want on each menu. You'll find tea, coffee and sugar in the cupboard above the sink, milk and cold drinks in the bar fridge.'

Elizabeth nodded, thinking the gourmet meals provided here were a wonderful perk—no shopping for food, no cooking and no cleaning up afterwards.

'The bed linen was changed this morning so everything's fresh for you apart from these towels.' Which she'd collected from the bathroom as she'd showed Elizabeth the facilities. 'I'll send clean ones over for you. Plus a hair-dryer and toothbrush. Harry said he'd whipped you off Mickey with no time to pack anything.'

Again the familiar name usage. Elizabeth frowned quizzically. 'He's always been Michael to me. I've only heard Harry calling him Mickey. And now you.'

She laughed. 'I've known those two since they were teenagers. Jack and I looked after their parents' place in those days. I guess I was like a second mother to them. Never had kids of my own. Good boys, both of them. You couldn't be connected to better men, Elizabeth, as employers or people.'

It was a high recommendation, though probably a biased one, given Sarah's obvious fondness for them. 'They're very different,' she commented, wanting to hear more.

'Mickey's more like his dad, a seriously driven achiever. It's in his genes, I reckon. Harry's nature is more like his mum's. She had a very sunny disposition, radiating a joy in life that infected everyone around her. It was a wicked shame when...' She heaved a deep sigh. 'Well, I guess we never know the day or the hour, but I tell you, those boys are a credit to their parents. Losing them both when they did, they could have run off the rails, plenty of money to spend, but they took on the business and pushed forward. And they looked after everyone who could have been hurt by the loss. Like me and Jack.'

She paused, grimaced. 'Here I am running off at the mouth but you know Mickey. Harry said you've been working closely with him for two years.'

'Yes, I have.'

'You'll find Harry good to work for, too. Just a different nature, that's all.'

Sunny...like his mother...like Lucy. Was that why Michael was so attracted to Lucy? But why wasn't Harry? Why did he have to plague her with his endlessly provocative attention?

'I'll only be here for a month, Sarah. I'm the fill-in until Harry finds a replacement for Sean.'

'Whatever...' She waved airily. Obviously it was not something that weighed on her mind. 'I'll send over sets of the island uniform with the towels etc. Do you want short shorts, Bermuda length or three-quarters?'

'Bermuda length,' Elizabeth decided, thinking that would look more dignified for her position as manager.

'Harry thought a bikini…?'

'No. I'll wash my undies out tonight. I'll be fine, thanks, Sarah.'

She grinned. 'I love your butterfly blouse. It's just the kind of thing Harry's mum used to wear.'

Lucy's choice, Elizabeth thought. 'I'll gladly change it for tropical fish,' she said. The butterfly blouse represented failure with Michael and trouble with Harry, since he saw it as sexy. 'I'll be more comfortable here in the island uniform.'

'Well, it is easy. You don't have to think about what clothes to put on. I'll be off now. You might want to freshen up before rejoining Harry in the office.'

'Yes, I do. Thanks, Sarah.'

She was relieved to have such a good ally in the head housekeeper. It would surely make this job easier. Sarah's long association with the Finn family meant that she could be absolutely trusted, too.

What she'd said about *the two boys* lingered in Elizabeth's mind as she made use of the bathroom facilities. The plane crash that had taken the lives of Franklyn and Yvette Finn had been frontline news about ten years ago, soon after her own mother had died. She hadn't known the people so it had meant nothing personal to her at the time, yet it must have been a traumatic period for Michael and Harry, both young men, possibly still at university, having fun, believing there was plenty of time to work out what they wanted to do with their lives. It *was* admirable that they'd taken on their father's business empire instead of selling up and shedding all responsibility.

But it still didn't make Harry good relationship material. She could respect him for what he'd done. He might be very *solid* in that sense. However, that did not mean he had any staying power where women were concerned.

For the next hour she had to sit beside him at the computer workstation in the office while he went through the Finn Island website, showing her how bookings were made over the internet and their dates subsequently slotted into the island calendar. He explained how to work out all the schedules that had to be kept and Elizabeth had no trouble grasping what she had to do.

However, being so close to Harry—virtually shoulder to shoulder—did make concentration more difficult than it should have been. With their brief encounters in the Cairns office, she'd always managed to keep her distance from him, hating how he could exude a male sexiness that made her acutely conscious of being a woman whose needs weren't being answered. Now, having barely any space between them made her senses hyperalert to almost everything about him.

Her nose kept being invaded by his smell—a sharp tanginess like a sea breeze somehow mixed with an earthy animal scent. His strong, muscular forearms were a very masculine contrast to her more slender, softly rounded ones and she couldn't help noticing his long dexterous fingers as he worked the computer mouse—fingers that fascinated her into flights of erotic fantasy. He didn't touch her, not even accidentally, but she was wound up inside, expecting him to, silently schooling herself not to react as though his touch was like a hot iron scorching her skin.

She had to learn how to behave naturally around him. Whenever he glanced at her to check if she understood what he was explaining, the vivid blue eyes seemed to be tunnelling into her mind and she had to force herself to hold his gaze as she assured him everything was clear to her. Then he smiled approval which made her stupid stomach contract. He was an extremely disturbing man even when he wasn't teasing or flirting and she didn't want him to be. Hopefully his wretchedly unsettling effect on her would gradually fade away over the next few days.

People started strolling by on the path outside, heading towards the bar for predinner drinks. Harry named them as they passed. Of course he had been here over this past weekend, but it was impressive that he could identify every guest on the island and tell her where they came from, as well as how they'd come by their wealth. Elizabeth tried to commit most of what he said to memory but it was a struggle—too many of them, too quickly.

'You'll soon have them down pat,' Harry said confidently. 'I told Daniel we'd be eating in the restaurant tonight. I'll drill you on everyone at the other tables while we dine, then introduce you around before they leave.'

'That would help a lot,' she said gratefully.

'Hope you can find some more appetite than you had for lunch. Daniel will be miffed if you don't do justice to his gourmet creations.'

He knew she'd been too upset to eat much lunch but tonight she wouldn't have to watch Michael and Lucy gobbling up each other and she wanted to stop Harry from poking any further at the still-raw place in her heart. 'Actually I'm rather hungry. Must be the sea air,' she answered airily, resolving to eat everything put in front of her and show appreciation of it, regardless of how she *felt*.

His eyes glittered satisfaction. 'Remarkable what a sea change will do.'

Well, it won't extend to sharing your bed, she silently promised him as she rolled her chair back from the desk and stood up. 'Speaking of change, I'll go and swap these clothes for the island uniform before we go to the restaurant.'

Two young women on Sarah's staff—Maddie and Kate—had brought everything she needed while Harry had been teaching her the ins and outs of the website. The way they'd looked at Harry—telegraphing they thought he was *hot*—had made her wonder if he played musical beds on the island.

'Good idea!' He eyed her up and down in that lingering way that made her skin prickle. 'We wouldn't want our lady guests going pea-green with envy at how gorgeous you look in that outfit,' he drawled. 'Nor would we want their guys seeing you as more desirable than their partners.'

'Oh, really!' she huffed, crossing her arms defensively.

'Just telling you how it is, dear Elizabeth.'

'Don't *dear* me!' she snapped, still very much on edge from having to weather the sexual pitfalls of his proximity and wanting to cut off his flirting routine.

His eyebrows arched provocatively. 'What? I can't express how I feel about you?'

One of her hands sliced out in negative dismissal. 'I don't want to hear it.'

'Wrong time, wrong man, but that doesn't make it any less true.'

She rolled her eyes in disbelief. 'Let's keep to business, Harry.'

'Okay.' He gestured at the door to the apartment. 'Go and change. It will be a start to fitting in with me instead of Mickey.'

She felt purpose underlying those words, spine-crawling purpose as she turned her back on him and walked quickly from the office into the apartment, closing the door very firmly behind her.

It caused her to work up some steely purpose of her own. She would do her best to fit in on the island but fitting in with Harry on any personal basis had to stop. It had been a purely defensive move, going along with him today, using him as a shield to hide her distress. From now on she should take control of whatever happened between them. Her mind was very clear on that. She certainly didn't want to invite any sexual complications with him, which would only mess her around more than she was already messed up by the situation with Michael and Lucy.

It was a relief to shed the clothes that had fed her hopes this morning. She had a quick shower to wash away the misery of the day and give herself the sense of making a fresh start. It felt liberating donning the island uniform. This was the end of maintaining the professional image of an executive PA, at least for the next month. The casual, carefree look of shorts and T-shirt was suddenly very welcome to her.

It seemed she'd been carrying a heavy weight of responsibility for many years, ever since her mother had fallen ill with terminal cancer and her father had deserted them. The need to hold everything together for herself and Lucy had been driving her for a long time. Somehow it didn't matter so much anymore. She was on an island, away from the life she had known up until now, all by herself...except for Harry, who'd be gone as soon as she was on top of the job.

That was her main priority now—demonstrating to Harry that his guidance was no longer needed. Once she was free of his presence, this place might very well work some magic for her—time out of time to find herself again—no hanging on to what Michael thought or felt about her, no worrying about Lucy, just Elizabeth.

CHAPTER SEVEN

HARRY watched her come out of the apartment, all bright-eyed and bushy-tailed, determined to get on with the job and do it well. He admired her strength of character, her refusal to be utterly crushed by disillusionment. On the other hand, he had kept her mind very occupied these past few hours and would continue to do so until they parted for the night. That would be crunch time for her, when she was lying in bed, alone in the darkness. It would all be about Mickey and Lucy then.

He was strongly tempted to give her something else to think about—something she couldn't dismiss as easily as she had in the past, writing him off as of no account. He didn't like it. He never had liked it. Tonight might be too soon to pounce but…what the hell! She was never going to be *ready* for him. Her mind-set against getting personally involved with him was so fixed, perhaps physically shaking her out of it was the best way to go.

If he set the scene right…

An idea came to him. A private word to the chef before dinner, concentrate on business over the meal, wait until the guests had drifted off to their villas or the bar, then spring the surprise.

He grinned at her as he rose from the office chair. 'Time to see if the stars are burning bright tonight.'

She shook her head at him. 'It's not dark enough yet.' Her tone denied any interest in an activity which probably smacked of romance to her.

'Well, we can watch for them to appear from our table in the restaurant. You are allowed to enjoy the ambience of this island, Elizabeth.'

He could see her consciously relaxing, working up a smile. 'I will, Harry. I'm glad I have the opportunity to do so.'

'Good! I want you to be happy here.'

Happy...

Why not? Elizabeth thought. She should let everything else float out of her mind and embrace this experience—tropical night, stars burning bright, glorious food, lots of interesting people to meet. All she had to do was ignore Harry's insidious effect on her, and with the ready distraction of the guests around them, surely that could be kept at bay.

He led her out of the office, locked the doors and handed her the key, which made her feel secure about any unwanted attention coming from him later on in the evening. As soon as they entered the spacious, open-air restaurant, he was called over to a table where two couples were very happy with their day of diving near the reef, happy that Harry had arranged such a marvellous experience for them.

Elizabeth was introduced as the new manager. It was easy to smile at these people, easy to smile at all the other guests when other introductions were made throughout the evening. They were all having a great time and their mood was infectious, and however they'd filled in their day, the evening meal certainly topped it off.

Every course was superb. Elizabeth really enjoyed the food and complimented the chef on it, praising the attentiveness of the waiters, too. Daniel Marven definitely ran a high-class restaurant. Elizabeth couldn't see any problem arising on this front during her management month, and she was sure Sarah and Jack Pickard handled their roles just as efficiently. This could very well be a *happy* position for her.

'You have a great set-up here, Harry,' she complimented him over coffee. 'The guests are so clearly enjoying themselves.'

He leaned back in his chair, smiling at her. 'You've handled everything extremely well, Elizabeth.'

His voice was like a soft purr that somehow seemed to curl around her, adding more heat to the warmth of his smile. All evening it had been strictly business, with Harry coaching her in her managerial role, and she'd relaxed enough to actually feel comfortable with him. She was caught off guard by the switch to personal appreciation that felt as though he was physically caressing her.

Her pulse quickened. Her toes scrunched up in her sandals. He wasn't really *doing* anything, she fiercely told herself. It hadn't even been a flirtatious remark. Reacting like this was off the wall.

'Thank you,' she said quickly, fighting off the unwelcome feelings.

'No. Thank *you*,' he replied just as quickly, the smile gone, respect shining in his eyes. 'Coming in cold, taking over from Sean…you're picking up on everything much faster than I expected. This morning I had a problem. Tonight...' He spread his hands in an awed gesture. 'You're a wonder, Elizabeth.'

She floundered for a moment, his warmth and respect tearing at her heart—the heart she had given to Michael, who didn't want it. She made an ironic grimace. 'Your brother trained me to pick up on everything.'

He returned the grimace. 'Of course. Mickey would. But I'm glad you're here with me.'

And she was glad to have this getaway.

That was the bottom line.

She forced herself to relax again. Today was almost over. She'd made it through without falling apart.

As the last couple rose from their table to leave the restaurant they called out goodnights to Harry and Elizabeth, which, of course, they reciprocated. 'Colin and Jayne Melville from Goulburn,' Elizabeth murmured, shooting a triumphant grin at Harry. 'I've got them all sorted now.'

He laughed, the blue eyes twinkling pleasure in her. 'I knew you'd meet the challenge.'

Her heart did a flip-flop. The man was sinfully attractive, actually more so when he wasn't doing his playboy *flirting* stuff. Tonight he hadn't strayed into any irritating dalliance with her, focusing entirely on easing her into this new job. He'd been exceptionally good at it, too, charming the guests into talking about themselves, giving information for Elizabeth to memorise. They enjoyed chatting with him. Of course, in their eyes Harry Finn was an equal. He had the money, the looks and the self-assurance that came with both those assets.

'One more thing to do before we part for the night,' he said, standing up and moving to draw back her chair.

'What's that?' she asked, pushing herself up from the table, feeling it had been a very long day already.

'A little ceremony from the staff to welcome you,' he answered. 'It's been set up down on the deck.' He nodded towards the bar where many of the guests had gathered for a nightcap. It was directly across from the restaurant, the walkway down to the pool deck dividing the two entertainment areas. 'More private than here.'

Elizabeth had no qualms about accompanying Harry to wherever the welcome ceremony was going to be held. It was a nice gesture from the staff and gave her the opportunity to meet more of them.

There were actually two decks. The first one surrounded the swimming pool. It was strewn with sun-lounges, tables with folded-up umbrellas, and a couple of day beds flanking it. Steps led down to a lower deck, which had a large spa to one side.

A table for two was set up just in front of more steps that led straight onto the beach; white tablecloth, an ice bucket containing a bottle of champagne, two flute glasses, two bread plates with cake forks beside them. *A table for two*, in what was so obviously a romantic setting, close to the sound of waves lapping on the beach and under a sky full of stars.

Elizabeth jolted to a halt. Her pulse jumped into an erratic beat. This looked too much like a playboy setting. Was Harry about to turn into a wolf now that business was over for the day? She shot him a hard, suspicious look.

'I don't see any staff.'

'Waiting for me to get you settled,' he said, moving ahead to hold out one of the chairs for her.

Was it true? Surely he wouldn't lie when the lie could be so quickly disproved. It was okay, she told herself, taking a deep breath and letting it out slowly as she forced her feet forward and sat where Harry had directed. He lifted the bottle of champagne out of the ice bucket, popped the cork and filled the flute glasses before sitting down himself.

'A celebratory drink,' he said, smiling at her as he raised his glass, expecting her to do the same.

She did, though his smile did nothing to calm her down. Quite the opposite.

'To a new start,' he added, clicking her glass with his.

'A new start,' she echoed, hoping the staff would hurry up and appear. Her nerves were twitching. Her heart was thumping. There was too much intimacy about being alone with Harry out here, and the control she was trying to hold on to was frayed by having had to deal with too many difficult situations.

Harry's eyes caressed her with admiration as he complimented her again. 'You've been brilliant today, Elizabeth.'

For some stupid reason, tears pricked her eyes. She managed a half smile of acknowledgment and quickly sipped the champagne, needing it to loosen up the sudden lump in her throat. The day had been overloaded with tensions but it was almost over. All she had to do was hold herself together a little bit longer.

'Ah! Here it comes!' Harry said happily, looking up towards the restaurant.

Elizabeth blinked hard, set her glass down, mentally gathered herself to deal with the welcome ceremony, then turned her head to see…

Not a group of staff members.

Only one person walking down the steps.

It was Daniel Marven, carrying a cake on a platter.

She looked for others to come streaming down behind him but no one did. He proceeded to the table alone, placing the platter in front of her.

'Enjoy,' he said, smiling at her.

Happy Birthday Elizabeth was written across the chocolate icing on top of the cake. She stared at it, barely finding voice enough to say, 'Thank you.'

'Good work, Daniel,' Harry said, and the chef took off, leaving the two of them together.

A dam of tightly held emotion burst inside Elizabeth. Her birthday. Her thirtieth birthday. She'd so much wanted it to be…not how it had turned out. Tears spurted into her eyes, welling over and streaming down her cheeks. Impossible to stop them. Her heart was not strong enough to absorb any more stress. It felt as though it was breaking.

Strong hands lifted her out of her chair. Strong arms engulfed her, clamping her to a strong chest. Her head was gently pressed onto a strong shoulder. There was no resistance in her. None at all. She was as weak as a baby—a baby who had been born thirty years ago and didn't know what life had in store for her. Still didn't. And she was too much at sea to think about it…think about anything.

CHAPTER EIGHT

HARRY had not anticipated having a weeping Elizabeth in his arms. The birthday cake surprise had been planned to give her pleasure and undermine her resistance to a friendly goodnight kiss, which could have easily escalated into something more, sparking up the chemistry that she'd always been so determined to deny. He didn't feel right about taking advantage of *this* situation.

What had caused such deep distress? Was it the reminder that she had turned thirty today? Single women could be rather touchy about reaching that age goalpost, particularly if they weren't in a relationship and wanted to be. Was it the lost chance with Mickey catching up with her at the end of the day?

It was so damnably frustrating. He'd finally got her to himself. She felt good in his arms—all woman— soft, warm and curvy. Smelled good, too. He rubbed his cheek over her hair, breathing in the scent of her—a fruity shampoo and an enticing trace of exotic perfume. He patted her back, trying to impart comfort, and felt relieved when the weeping started trailing off, interrupted by deep, heaving breaths that made him very aware of the lush fullness of her breasts. He wanted to pick her up, carry her over to the nearest day bed and blow her mind with wild, passionate sex.

The emotional storm eventually came to a shuddering halt but she remained leaning on him, her head resting on his shoulder, her body still, limp, spent of all energy. His hands wanted to wander, travelling down the very female curve of her spine to her even more female bottom—the bottom that swished provocatively every time she'd turned away from him. His fingers itched to curl around it, press her body into a more intimate fit with his, stir the same desire in her that was heating up his blood, arousing the beast.

He couldn't stop himself from hardening, didn't want to anyway. Let her feel what she did to him. Let her know she was desirable even as a limp, tear-soaked rag doll. It might jolt her out of whatever sea of misery she was swimming in. Life was for living, not wallowing in a trough of depression.

Elizabeth didn't care that it was Harry holding her. It was simply nice to be held in such a secure comforting way, propping her up when she was down, not asking anything of her, just being another body emanating warmth that took the chill of loneliness from her bones.

She wished she had someone who would always be there for her like this, someone strong who would never let her down. She'd wanted to believe it would be Michael, but it wasn't. And Harry...oh hell! She could feel him getting hard! No matter that she'd been weeping all over him. He still had sex on his mind.

A flood of embarrassment poured heat into her face as she jerked her head up from his shoulder. She'd been hanging on to him like a limpet. It took a moment to unglue her hands from his back and try shoving them up his chest to make some space between them.

'Sorry…sorry,' she gabbled, frantically looking up to beg his understanding that she hadn't been passively inviting *anything*!

'Sorry for what?' he mocked, his eyes glittering a hard challenge at her.

'I didn't mean to…to use you like that.'

'You needed to…just like I need to do this.'

He whipped up a hand to hold her chin. Elizabeth didn't have time to protest, nor time to take any action to stop his mouth from swooping on hers. The impact shocked her. It was not a gentle seductive kiss. It was a full-on sensual assault, his lips working over hers, forcing them open with the strong thrust of his tongue that instantly swept over her palate, causing her whole mouth to tingle as though it had been charged with electricity.

Instinctively she used her own tongue to fight the invasion of his, angry at his bold aggression. Whether he took this as encouragement or not, she didn't know, but his hand moved to the back of her head, fingers thrusting into her hair, holding her so there was no escape from his marauding mouth. His tongue was teasing, goading, enticing hers to tangle erotically with it, resulting in an explosion of sensation that tore any sensible thoughts out of her mind.

The whole physicality of the moment was totally overwhelming. She didn't care that he pressed her lower body so closely to his that his erection furrowed her stomach. Some primitive part of her revelled in it, revelled in the hot hard wall of his chest squashing her breasts. She was swamped by a tidal wave of chaotic need to feel everything more and more intensely. Her own hands raked down his beautifully muscled back and curled around his taut male butt, exulting in the sense of taking this incredibly sexy man as hers.

It was wildly exciting, intoxicating—one avid kiss merging into another and another, inciting a fever of passion that possessed her with such power she completely lost herself in it, craving the fierce climactic union they were driving towards, the desire for it sweeping through her like a firestorm, all-consuming.

The mouth engaging hers suddenly broke the primal connection. 'Yes…' hissed into her ear—a sound of exultant triumph. Then the intimate body contact was shifted. Her legs were hoisted up and she was being carried with heart-pounding speed, cool air wafting over her hot face, reducing the fever of urgently demanding desire.

She was tumbled onto a bed and Harry—Harry!—was leaping onto it to join her there. Her eyes were wide-open now. Her mind crashed into working gear. This was one of the day beds on the deck. She'd wanted the sex that Harry was intent on having with her. Her body was still quivering at a peak of need for it. But it was madness to go on with it—madness to muddy up what should be a clean break away from everything, starting what would inevitably be a messy affair going nowhere and interfering with carrying through this management job.

He flung one strongly muscled thigh over hers and started lifting her T-shirt as he lowered his head to start kissing her again. She'd lain inert with shock at finding herself so complicit in stirring this situation. It had to be stopped. Now! Already his hand was on her breast, fingers moving under the cup of her bra, tweaking her nipple, and for a moment she was paralysed by a rebellious wish to feel more of his touch. She stared at his mouth coming closer and closer, her mind screaming that another kiss would tip her over into Harry's world.

Did she want that?

Did she?

Losing control of everything?

A flash of fear whipped her hand up to Harry's mouth, covering it just before it made contact with hers. His eyebrows beetled down in a puzzled frown.

'Stop!' she croaked.

He jerked his head back from her halting hand, his frown deepening as he shot a disbelieving 'What?' at her.

She swallowed hard to give her voice more strength. 'I don't want you to take this any further, Harry.'

'Why not?' he demanded. 'You want it as much as I do.'

She wrenched his hand away from her breast and pulled the T-shirt down. 'A momentary madness,' she excused.

'Rubbish! It's been simmering between us for years,' he insisted vehemently. 'It just came to a head and it's damned dishonest of you to back off now.'

Anger stirred. She hadn't really consented to this. He'd started it when she was at her weakest, taking advantage of her vulnerable state. 'I don't care what you call it, I don't choose to go on with it,' she said fiercely and attempted to roll away from him.

He scooped her back to face him, his eyes blazing furious frustration. 'What is the matter with you? We want each other. It's only natural to…'

'Let me go, Harry. This isn't right for me.'

'Not right?' he repeated incredulously. 'It sure as hell felt right until you suddenly decided it wasn't, but I'm not into forcing any woman to have sex with me.' He threw up the arm that had halted her rejection of any more togetherness. 'If you hadn't responded as you did…'

'I didn't mean to,' she yelled at him, her face flaming at the truth he was flinging at her.

'Oh, yes you did! Just for once you let that steel-trap mind of yours open enough for your instincts to take over and it was dynamite between us. Is that what scares you, Elizabeth?'

She hated how he could always hit the nail on the head with her. Yes, it scared her but she wasn't going to admit it. She glared resentment at him. 'I figure you're dynamite to a lot of women, Harry, and I don't care to be left in little pieces when you move on to your next piece of fluff.'

His hand sliced the air in savage dismissal of her argument. 'I don't think of you as *fluff*! Do you imagine I'd give this management job to someone I thought of as *fluff*?'

'I'm not saying you didn't believe I could do the work. But having a bit of sex on the side was on the plate, too, wasn't it?' she hurled back at him. 'And now you're peeved because I've decided not to cooperate.'

He rolled his head in exasperation. 'Peeved does not describe what I feel right now, Elizabeth.'

There was a mountain of feeling brooding behind those words and Elizabeth instantly felt threatened by it. She scrambled off the day bed, swinging around on her feet to face down any follow-up from Harry. He hadn't moved. He lay sprawled across the bed with his head propped up on his hand, his eyes searing hers with blistering accusation.

'You're shutting the gate on living life to the full,' he said bitingly. 'I don't want your cooperation, Elizabeth. I want your surrender to what we could have together.'

'That's not the life I want,' she retorted decisively.

'You're chasing dreams instead of taking on what's real.'

'*My* choice.'

'One I can't respect,' he mocked.

'I won't stay here unless you do, Harry.'

'Oh, I will on the surface, Elizabeth. You need have no fear of any unwelcomed advances from me. It will be strictly business tomorrow and any other day I'm here.'

She should have felt relieved, but there was an aching heaviness in her stomach, a drag of physical disappointment that was not about to be easily shifted. 'In that case I'll stay,' she said flatly. Where else could she go and not be faced with Michael and Lucy? One thing she could certainly say for Harry—he had the knack of blotting them out for a while.

'Your call.' His mouth took on an ironic twist as he added, 'And do feel free to call on me if you decide to change your mind and explore a different kind of life to the one you've planned so rigidly.'

She took a deep breath to ease the tightness in her chest and said, 'Well, I'm glad we have that sorted.'

'Yes, you're a regular sorting machine, Elizabeth, everything slotted into its proper place,' he drawled as he rolled off the other side of the day bed and faced her across it. 'One day you might find there's pleasure in improper activities.'

'Not today,' she said through gritted teeth, determined not to be taunted into doing anything reckless and stupid.

'No, not today,' he agreed mockingly. 'I take it you're about to say goodnight?'

'Yes.'

'I'll fetch your cake. I wouldn't want you to go without comfort food in the lonely darkness of the night.'

The cake.

She had completely forgotten it.

Wanted to forget it now but she couldn't, not with the chef having made it especially for her. She would have to eat some of it, too, show appreciation.

Harry strode down the steps to the table that had been set for them. At his orders. She was sure of that. Hoping to sweeten her up to the point where he would slide into making a move on her. Her stomach curdled at how easy she had made it for him, and how quickly she had been caught up in the dynamic sexuality he could put out at will.

Her thighs were aquiver from having been in such intimate contact with him and her breasts were still in a state of arousal. He had excited her—almost to the point of no return—and he could probably do it again if she let him. Would he keep his word—strictly business from now on unless she gave him the green light?

He picked up the cake platter. Elizabeth realised she hadn't even moved from where she'd scrambled off the day bed. If Harry saw her still standing beside it he might think she regretted her decision. She jerked into walking, rounding the bed and heading up towards the administration office.

Harry had given her the door key after he had locked up before dinner. She dug it out of her shorts pocket, anxious to have the door open and be standing right there, ready to receive the cake from him so he had no reason to come in with it. Being alone with him in any enclosed space right now would severely stretch nerves that were already wildly agitated at having to be face to face with him, just for a few moments.

It surprised her to see guests laughing and chatting in the open bar lounge as she passed by. It had seemed so *private* on the lower decks. What if any of these people had strolled down to the beach while she and Harry... It didn't bear thinking about. Reckless, shameless...her face flamed at how very nearly she had succumbed to almost a *public* sex act.

Anger simmered as she unlocked the door, opened it and turned to take the cake platter from Harry, who had virtually caught up with her. 'Did you realise there were still people up and about when you swept me off to that bed?' she demanded accusingly.

'So what?' He arched his eyebrows at her as though she was mad.

'Oh, you don't care about anything, do you?' she

cried in exasperation and tried to snatch the platter from him.

He held on to it, forcing her to meet his gaze, a blast of hot resentment burning over her own. 'On the contrary, I care about a lot of things, Elizabeth. As to your quite unnecessary embarrassment at the thought of being observed in flagrante, this happens to be a tropical island where people drop their inhibitions and feel free to have sex wherever and whenever they want it. Using that bed under the stars for some natural pleasure in the privacy of the night would not offend anyone.'

'I'm not a guest. I'm staff,' she argued furiously.

His chin jutted with arrogant authority. 'This island is mine. I can make any rules I like for whomever I like.'

'I live by my own rules, Harry,' she flared at him. 'Now let me have the cake and let's say goodnight.'

He released the platter and stepped back, nodding mockingly as he said, 'Goodnight, Elizabeth.'

Then he strode away, back towards the beach, not giving her the chance to say another word.

She was so wound up it took several seconds for her to realise the threat of him was gone—not that he'd been threatening her. It was just how she felt with him, as though in constant danger of having her *rules* undermined or blown apart.

She quickly took the platter to the office desk, set it down and returned to lock the door, telling herself she was now safe for the night. Tomorrow…well, she would deal with tomorrow when it came.

She carried the untouched cake into the apartment, shutting herself into her own private domain. In a violent reaction to the whole stressful day, she found a knife and cut the *Happy Birthday* writing off the icing. It had been a rotten birthday. No happiness at all. She'd suffered a devastating let-down from Michael, as well as what felt like a betrayal from Lucy and persecution from Harry.

Tomorrow had to be better.

She only had to put up with Harry tomorrow.

And while that might not be a piece of cake, she would stomach it somehow.

No way was she going to break up again anywhere near Harry Finn!

CHAPTER NINE

HARRY clenched his hands into fists as he strode back down to the lower deck. The urge to fight was still coursing through him. He'd barely reined it in to bid Elizabeth a fairly civilised goodnight. He certainly didn't *feel* civilised.

Okay, he'd jumped the gun with her but she'd been right there with him. Not one other woman he'd been with had ever pulled back when both of them were fired up to have sex. Being rejected like that was an absolute first, though he probably should have been prepared for it. Elizabeth Flippence had made an art form of rejecting him over the past two years.

What were her damned rules? No mixing business with pleasure? She would have mixed it with Mickey so that didn't wash. Did she have to have a wedding ring on her finger before she'd have sex? Where was she coming from to have that kind of attitude in this day and age? A thirty-year-old virgin? Harry didn't believe it. Not with her looks.

Clearly he needed to know more about her, form another plan of attack because she was *not* going to get away from him. He didn't understand why she dug so deeply under his skin, what made her so compellingly desirable, but the buzz was there and he couldn't get rid of it. What caused him even more frustration was *knowing* she felt the same buzz around him.

It was a maddening situation.

He lifted the bottle of champagne out of the ice bucket, stepped over to the edge of the deck and poured the remaining contents onto the sand. The only thing worse than flat champagne was the flat aftermath of flattened desire. He popped the emptied bottle back in the bucket and started the long walk down the beach to the wharf where his yacht was docked.

He thought of his own birthday—thirty-three last month. Mickey had thrown him a party. They always did that for each other because their parents had and neither of them could quite let go of that golden past, though they had sold the marvellous family property on the hill overlooking Cairns because it wasn't the same—couldn't be—without their mother and father there.

He remembered the great tennis parties and pool parties his mother had organised. His and Mickey's school friends had loved coming to their place—always so much fun to be had. The fishing trips with his father had been great, too. He'd had the best childhood, best teen years, a really happy life until that black day when his father's plane went down.

This resort had still been on the drawing board then. His father had been excited about building it, showing him and Mickey the plans, talking about how he would market it. After the funeral Harry had wanted this project, wanted to be physically busy, creating something, bringing his father's vision to reality. He'd lived here, worked here until it was done, organising everything for it to be a successful enterprise.

Mickey had thrown himself into managing the franchises, needing to be busy, too, both of them wanting to feel their parents would be proud of them. It had seemed the best way to handle their grief, filling the huge hole of loss with hard absorbing work. Neither of them had been interested in managing girlfriends during that dark period, not wanting any emotional demands on them from people who had no understanding of what was driving them. The occasional night out, some casual sex...that had been enough.

Over the years neither he nor Mickey had fallen into any deep and meaningful relationships. Somehow there was always something missing, something that didn't gel, something that put them off. Occasionally they chatted about their various failures to really connect with one woman or another. It always came back to how happy their parents had been together, complementing each other, and ultimately that was what they wanted in a life partner. In the meantime they floated, docking for a while with whatever woman they felt attracted to.

Harry wondered if Lucy would last with Mickey, then chewed over his own problem of even getting a start with Elizabeth.

Why was giving in to a perfectly natural attraction such a problem to her? Why not pursue it, find out if it could lead to a really satisfying relationship? Was she so hung up on her unrequited love for Mickey that she didn't want to admit that something else could be better?

Whatever...he'd get to the bottom of her resistance and smash it, one way or another.

By the next morning Harry had cooled down enough to realise he should give Elizabeth more time to come to terms with the changes in her life. He had rushed her last night. Today he would be very *civilised*. Though not necessarily according to *her* rules.

He had breakfast on the yacht, suspecting that Elizabeth would avoid having breakfast with him in the restaurant. Undoubtedly Miss Efficiency had set her bedside alarm clock for an early hour to be up and about before any of the guests, opening the office and at her desk, ready to deal with anything that came her way. She would certainly have used the convenience of a call to the restaurant to have her breakfast delivered.

As expected, she was at her desk when Harry strolled into the administration office. He beamed a warmly approving smile at her and put a bright lilt in his voice. 'Good morning, Elizabeth.'

It forced her attention away from the computer. She pasted a tight smile on her face and returned his greeting. Her big brown eyes had no shine. They were guarded, watchful. Harry knew her brick wall was up and there would be no easy door through it. The urge to at least put a chink in her defensive armour was irresistible.

He hitched himself onto the corner of the desk, viewing her with curious interest. 'Are you a virgin, Elizabeth?'

That livened up her face, her eyes widening in incredulity and shooting sparks of outrage as she completely lost control of her voice, shrilling, 'What?' at him.

'It's a simple question,' Harry said reasonably. 'Are you a virgin, yes or no?'

'You have no right to ask me that!' she spluttered.

He shrugged. 'Why is it a problem?'

Anger shot to the surface. 'It's none of your business!'

'I guess the answer is yes since you're so sensitive about it,' he tossed at her affably.

'I am *not* sensitive about it!'

'Looks that way to me.'

She glared at him, and if her eyes had been knives they would have stabbed him in a million painful places. Harry found it wonderfully exhilarating. He'd definitely got under her skin again, regardless of how firmly she had decided to keep him out.

Her jaw tightened and he knew she was gritting her teeth as she struggled to bring herself under control. Finally she gnashed out the words 'It's just none of your business, Harry. It is totally irrelevant to this job and I'll thank you to remember that.'

'Bravo!' he said admiringly.

It confused her. 'Bravo what?'

He grinned at her. 'The rule book rules. Almost forgot it there for a moment, didn't you?'

She huffed to release some of the tension he'd raised, viewing him balefully. 'I'd appreciate it if *you* didn't forget it.'

'I do apologise for the transgression.' He made a wry grimace. 'Curiosity slipped through my usual sense of discretion. However, it does give me a better understanding of you now that I know you're a virgin. Head stuffed with romantic dreams…'

'I am *not* a virgin!' tripped out of her mouth before she could stop the wave of exasperation he'd whipped up.

He arched his eyebrows in surprise. 'You're not?'

She closed her eyes. Her mouth shut into a tight thin line. Quite clearly she hated herself for biting at his bait. Harry revelled in her discomfort. Serve her right for the discomfort she'd given him last night. And it was great to have that problem box ticked off. No virginity barrier.

Another big huff. Her eyes opened into hard, piercing slits. Shards of ice came off her tongue. 'Can we please get down to work now?'

'Jumping to it,' he said obligingly, hitching himself off the desk and rounding it to view the computer screen. 'Any bookings come in this morning?'

'Yes.' She swung her chair around to face the computer and started working the mouse. 'I think I've dealt with them correctly. If you'll check what I've done...?'

For the next half hour Harry kept strictly to business, giving Elizabeth no reason to complain about his behaviour. She had a good understanding of what was required of administration. Supply issues still had to be addressed but that could wait until later. She was so uptight he decided to give her a break, let her relax for a while.

'Before the heat of the day sets in, I'm going to call Jack Pickard to take you around the resort, show you the practical aspects of how it runs. You need to be familiar with all of it,' he said, reaching for the telephone. 'I'll stand in for you here.'

'Okay,' she answered levelly, but the relief he sensed coming from her told him exactly what she was thinking.

Escape.

Escape from the pressure of having to keep denying what was undeniable…the constant sizzle of sexual chemistry between them.

Harry told himself he could wait.

Sooner or later it would come to a head and boil over.

Then he would have her.

Elizabeth took an instant liking to Jack Pickard. She probably would have liked anyone who took her away from Harry this morning but Sarah's husband was a chirpy kind of guy, nattering cheerfully about the island and his maintenance job—easy, relaxing company. He was short and wiry and his weather-beaten face had deep crow's-feet at the corners of his eyes from smiling a lot. His hair looked wiry, too, a mass of unruly curls going an iron-grey.

'Show you one of the vacant villas first.' He grinned at her. 'Before the new guests fly in this morning.'

'Do they all come by helicopter?' Elizabeth asked.

'Uh-uh. Most come by motor launch. We meet them at the jetty and drive them around to administration. Those that fly in land on the back beach and take the wooden walkway that leads here.'

Wooden walkways led everywhere, with flights of steps wherever they were needed. The one they took to the vacant villa ran through rainforest, the lovely green canopy of foliage above it shading them from the direct heat of the sun. On either side of them were masses of tropical vegetation—palms, vines, bamboo, hibiscus, native flowers.

The villa was situated on a hillside overlooking the

bay leading into the main beach. Its front porch had a lovely view and the breeze wafting in from the sea made it a very inviting place to sit in the deckchairs provided. Jack opened a sliding glass door and gestured for her to step inside.

The structure was split-level. Elizabeth entered a spacious living room—a comfortable lounge setting with coffee table facing a television set and CD player, a writing desk and chair, a counter along one wall containing a sink and a bar fridge. Above the counter were cupboards containing a selection of glasses for every kind of drink, bottles of spirits, plus tea and coffee-making facilities, a jar of home-made cookies and a selection of crackers to go with the cheese platter in the fridge, which also held a box of Belgian chocolates, fruit juice, beer, champagne, wine and plenty of drink mixers.

Up a few steps from the living area was a mezzanine bedroom containing a huge king-size bed, lots of pillows, plenty of cupboard space, bedside tables with lamps in the shape of dolphins. All the decor had a sea-and-beach theme, most of the furnishings in white and turquoise, knick-knacky things constructed from driftwood and coral and shells. White walls and polished floorboards completed the clean, airy look.

'There's an extensive library of books, CDs and games in the bar-lounge adjacent to the restaurant,' Jack told her. 'Guests can help themselves to whatever they like. You, too, Elizabeth.'

She smiled at him. 'That's good to know.'

Should fill in some lonely hours, she thought, once Harry was gone and she could get him out of her mind.

That *virgin* question still had her seething, as though *that* was the only possible reason for not getting her pants off for him. In hindsight, she probably should have said she was, put him right off his game. On the other hand, he might have fancied himself as teacher, giving her a first experience in sex. It was impossible to pin down anything with Harry. He could slide this way or that way at the blink of an eye. Which made him so infuriating and frustrating and...

Elizabeth clamped down on those feelings, forcing herself to focus on what she was seeing here. The bathroom was positively decadent, a shower for two, a spa bath, the walls tiled in a wavy white with turquoise feature tiles and turquoise towels. The long vanity bench held two wash basins and a pretty collection of shells. Everything in the villa was clearly designed to give guests pleasure.

'This is all fantastic,' she commented to Jack.

He nodded agreement. 'Sarah and I reckon Harry did a great job of it.'

'Harry? Surely he had an interior decorator fitting out the villas.'

'Oh, he had a professional finding the stuff he wanted, but how the villas are all decked out was his idea. His dad had an architect design how they're built. It was his vision in the first place, but after he died, Harry took on the whole project and saw it through to completion. Did a great job of marketing it, too.'

This information did not fit her view of Harry Finn as a playboy. It was disconcerting until she remembered that admirable work and talent had no relevance to how he dealt with women.

She and Jack moved on. He showed her the gym, which contained most of the popular work-out equipment, introducing her to staff she hadn't met yet. A large shed near the beach where the helicopter landed contained a desalination plant that ultimately provided fresh water for the resort. The power generator was also housed there.

'This beach faces west,' Jack said, pointing to the hill above it. 'Up there are the two pavilion villas, both of them occupied today so I can't show them to you. Their porches lead out to infinity pools that catch the sunset. Feels like there's just you and the water and the sky. They weren't on the original plan. Harry's idea to build them, make them really special.'

Elizabeth nodded. 'I noticed it cost more to stay in them.'

Jack grinned. 'Honeymoon paradise.'

As they continued the tour, chatting as they went along, Elizabeth realised her escort was extremely well skilled—electrician, plumber, carpenter, gardener—capable of turning his hand to any maintenance work.

She couldn't help remarking, 'How come you never started a business of your own, Jack? You're so well qualified.'

He grinned. 'Hated all the paperwork the government expects you to do. Reckon I got a plum job with Harry's dad, maintaining the property he had overlooking Cairns. Free cottage, good pay, all the fun of creating and being in a beautiful environment. Got the same deal here on the island with Harry. We've got a good life, Sarah and me. Can't think of anything better.'

'Then you're very lucky,' she said warmly.

'That we are.'

A contented man, Elizabeth thought, wondering if she would ever reach the same state of contentment. Not today. And not here with Harry waiting for her back at the office. It was awful to think of how tempted she had been last night to just let herself be swept up in physical sensation. It had been a long time—almost three years since her last semiserious relationship ended—but that was no reason to engage in casual sex.

She'd never been into bed-hopping. Trying guys out on a purely physical basis did not appeal to her. She needed to feel really connected to the person before taking the next step to absolute intimacy. If Harry considered that attitude a headful of romantic dreams it was because it didn't suit his playboy mentality. Bending her principles for him was not on, though she had to admit he was the sexiest man she had ever met, which made everything wretchedly difficult when she was alone with him.

Just one hour in the office this morning had been exhausting, having to use so much energy blocking out his physical impact on her. Of course, last night's wild interlude had made her even more sexually aware of him. She'd been out of her mind to let him go so far with her. Now she had to cope with that memory in his eyes as well as the memories he'd stamped on her consciousness.

On the walk back to administration, Jack started talking about Harry again, how good he had been at all sports in his teens—that was easy to imagine—and what a pity it was that the untimely death of his parents had caused him to drop them. 'Could have been a champion on any playing field,' was Jack's opinion.

Elizabeth could think of one sport Harry hadn't given up.

He was a champion flirt.

She hoped he wouldn't exercise that particular skill while she had to be with him for the rest of the day. So long as he kept to business, she should be reasonably okay. Nevertheless, it was impossible to stop her nerves twitching in agitation when Jack left her at the office door and Harry swung his chair around from the computer and smiled at her.

'Enjoy the tour?'

She smiled back, deciding to show appreciation of all he'd done here. 'You have created quite an extraordinary resort, Harry. I can't think of anything that could make it better.'

'If you do, let me know. I aim for perfection.'

Would he be the perfect lover?

Elizabeth was shocked at how that thought had slid right past her guard against *the playboy*. She hurled it out of her mind as she hitched herself onto the corner of the desk just as he had this morning, casually asking, 'Anything come in that I should know about?'

'Mickey called. He's putting the suitcase your sister packed for you on the helicopter bringing the guests today.' He gave her a quirky smile. 'Should save you from having to wash out your undies tonight.'

'That's good,' she said equably, determined not to be baited into being prickly.

'Lucy says if she's missed anything you need, send

her an email,' Harry went on. 'She'll bring it with her when she comes here with Mickey this weekend.'

Elizabeth sat in frozen suspension.

Her heart stopped.

Her lungs seized up.

Her mind stayed plugged on one horribly chilling thought.

Lucy…coming with Michael…to her island escape from them.

No escape at all!

CHAPTER TEN

HARRY saw her eyes glaze. She sat completely still. He knew this was a crunch moment. He waited, silently speculating on how she would react to the bombshell when she snapped out of the shock wave.

Would pride dictate that she welcome Mickey and her sister onto the island, keeping up the pretence that seeing them together did not hurt her?

Mickey was totally unaware that Elizabeth was hung up on him. So was Lucy. Neither of them would be looking for signs of hurt. It was quite possible to get through this visit, leaving them none the wiser, especially if Elizabeth was willing to let him be the man *she* was interested in. Which had to bring them several steps closer, Harry thought, willing her to choose that path.

Alternatively, since her escape from Mickey and Lucy had just been scuttled, the island no longer represented a safe refuge for her. And Harry knew he'd gone too far too fast last night, which was certainly ruffling her feathers. She might throw in this job, walk down to the back beach, wait for the helicopter to come in and fly out on it, take a trip somewhere else, not caring what anyone thought—wipe her hands of all of them.

Except she couldn't quite.

Lucy was her sister.

Lucy depended on her to be her anchor and Elizabeth took responsibility seriously. She wasn't the type to cut free. Not completely. But she might want to for a while.

Harry needed to stop her from walking out on him. Having her here on the island was his best chance with her. It gave him time to keep challenging her, wear down her resistance, make her realise they could have something good together.

Elizabeth felt totally numb. It had been such a struggle, holding herself together in front of Michael and Lucy yesterday, a struggle coping with what Harry made her feel, a struggle learning how to manage this resort as fast as she could. Now the whole reason for so much effort, the whole reason for being here was slipping away from her.

She couldn't bear to play out yesterday's scenario with Michael and Lucy again this weekend. It was too much pretence, too much pressure, too much everything with Harry hanging around, ready to take advantage of any weak moment, and she'd be tempted to use him again as a buffer. It was all horribly wrong and the worst part was she was trapped here—trapped by her own deceit.

If she walked out on the job after pretending to like being with Harry, how could she ever explain that to Lucy? It wouldn't make sense. Telling her the truth wasn't fair. It would cut into whatever happiness she was finding with Michael, tarnish it because it was causing her sister unhappiness, which Elizabeth knew

Lucy would never knowingly do. Underneath all her ditziness was a very caring heart.

Having taken a deep breath and slowly released it to get her lungs working again and feed some much-needed oxygen into the hopeless morass in her brain, she squared her shoulders and looked directly at Harry Finn—her rescuer and tormentor. There was no devilish twinkle in the blue eyes. They were observing her with sharp attention, alert to any give-away signs of what she was thinking and feeling.

He had demonstrated yesterday how perceptive he was, and remembering how accurately he had read the situation, Elizabeth felt a strong stab of resentment that he hadn't acted to protect her this time.

'You could have dissuaded your brother from coming, Harry,' she said accusingly.

'How?' he challenged. 'By saying you don't want him here? Mickey wants to see if you're managing okay. Both of them do.' His mouth lifted in an ironic tilt. 'I did spring the job on you, Elizabeth.'

'You could have said all the villas were taken—no ready accommodation for them,' she argued.

He shrugged. 'I'm not in the habit of telling lies. Besides, Mickey has a motor-cruiser. They'll be arriving in it and could just as easily sleep in it. A head count of guests at dinner would have told him we have two villas vacant this weekend and he might have confronted me about it, raising questions. Would you have liked to answer them?'

She grimaced, accepting there was no way out of this and there was no point in protesting the arrangements already made. 'Which villa did you put them in?' she asked flatly.

'Mickey requested a pavilion villa if available. Since one of them is vacant from Friday afternoon to Sunday afternoon, I've obliged him.'

A pavilion villa…honeymoon paradise!

She turned her head away, evading Harry's watchful gaze. Flashing through her mind were images of Michael and Lucy enjoying an intimate weekend—making love on the king-size bed, cooling off in the infinity pool, drinking champagne as they watched the sunset. It was sickening. She couldn't help thinking, *It should have been me with Michael. Me, not Lucy.*

For two years she had been dreaming of having just such a romantic weekend with him. Why couldn't he have found her as wildly attractive as he obviously found Lucy? Harry had no problem in seeing her as sexy. He would have whizzed her off to bed in no time flat. Almost had last night.

'They're not coming in until Saturday morning,' Harry said quietly. 'It will only be for one night, Elizabeth.'

As though that made it better, she thought savagely. Lucy would be parading her happiness with Michael from the moment she landed to the moment she waved goodbye, and during that two-day span it was going to be one hell of an uphill battle to keep pretending happiness with Harry.

Unless…

A wicked idea slid into her mind.

It grew, sprouting a whole range of seductive thoughts,

becoming a plan that promised a way to get through this weekend reasonably intact.

Harry would view it as a night of fun and games, the playboy triumphant. He wouldn't care about what she was using him for since he'd get what he wanted. And *she* wouldn't be hurt by it because she was the one directing the play, the one in control of what was to happen.

She could set aside her principles, be a butterfly flying free for one night. Maybe it was what she needed to do, use it as a catharsis, releasing all the emotional mess in her mind and heart and wallowing in purely physical sensation. Harry had proved last night he could drive up her excitement meter. Why not experience how far he could take it?

If it was good…if it was great…she could face Lucy and Michael without the horribly hollow sense of missing out on everything, especially since she would have already had what they were going to have and where they were going to have it. That part of it should kill off any sense of jealousy and envy, which were horribly negative feelings that she didn't want to have towards her sister. Lucy was Lucy. It wasn't her fault that Michael was totally smitten by her, and Elizabeth was not going to let *their* connection affect the close relationship she'd always had with her sister.

But she needed help from Harry to make all this stick.

His expert playboy help, smashing her mind with so much pleasure it took away the pain.

If he didn't cooperate with her plan… But he would,

wouldn't he? He wanted her to *surrender* herself to him and that was what she'd be doing.

She threw a quick glance at him. He was leaning back in the chair, apparently relaxed as he waited for her to respond to the situation. However, his gaze instantly caught hers, sharply searching for what was in her mind. There was no point in taking any evasive action. She had decided on what she wanted from him. Her own eyes watched his very keenly as she put the question which would start a new situation rolling.

'Do you still want to have sex with me, Harry?'

His eyebrows shot up in surprise. There was no instant *yes*. Elizabeth's heart pounded nervously as she waited for his reply, watching his eyes narrow speculatively. He was obviously digesting what this change from her meant.

'That's been a constant for me over quite a long time, Elizabeth,' he said slowly. 'I think the more pertinent question is do you finally realise that you want to have sex with me?'

'Yes, I do,' she answered unequivocally. 'But only if certain conditions are met.'

It had to be her plan or nothing.

His head tilted to one side. He was not rushing to accommodate her. His eyes watched her with an even higher level of intensity. Elizabeth held his gaze defiantly, determined not to budge from this stance. After a long nerve-racking silence, he casually waved a hand in an invitational gesture.

'Spell out the conditions.'

Elizabeth took a deep breath, fiercely willing him to fall in with what she wanted. 'The pavilion villa is empty on Friday night. I want it to be there. And then. The rest of this week we just keep to business.'

It took every ounce of Harry's control not to react violently, to absorb this slug to his guts and remain seated, appearing to be considering what all his instincts were savagely railing against. This wasn't about him and the chemistry between them. It was about Mickey and Lucy. In some dark twisted place in her mind, she probably wanted to pretend he was his brother, having it off in the same romantic setting where Mickey was about to take her sister.

No way would he be used as a freaking substitute!

It was a bitter blow to his ego that she should ask it of him. It showed how little she cared about what he thought, what he felt. He had encouraged her to use him as a blind to hide her angst over Mickey yesterday but to use him this far…it was brutal and he hated her for corrupting what they could have had together.

Hate…

He'd never felt that towards anyone. Why did she get to him so strongly? It was crazy. He should wipe her off his slate right now, find some other woman who thought he was worth having, who'd be sweetly giving, at least for a while.

Except…damn it! He still wanted the ungettable Elizabeth Flippence!

Have her and be done with it, he thought savagely.

He could use her scenario his way, add his own conditions, make her so hyped up with sexual awareness, Mickey would be blotted right out of her mind and he'd be *the man*—the only man she'd be conscious of all through the night.

She was patiently waiting for his agreement, her eyes boring into his, boldly challenging his desire for her. He sensed that some essential part of her had clicked off. She'd moved beyond caring what he said or did. The equation was simple. He either went with her plan or that was the end of anything personal ever happening between them.

'Okay,' he said calmly. 'I'll make arrangements for us to occupy the pavilion villa on Friday night.'

She nodded, the expression in her eyes changing to a knowing mockery. She had labelled him a playboy on quite a few occasions so he knew what she was thinking—a night of sex would always be amenable to him, regardless of why it was offered.

He decided to live up to her idea of him.

'As long as you'll fit in with some conditions I have in mind,' he said with a quirky little smile.

That shot some tension through her. 'Like what?' she asked sharply.

'Like not saying no to anything I want to do.'

She frowned. 'I won't do kinky stuff, Harry.'

'I'm not into sado-masochism, domination or bondage,' he assured her. 'But I don't particularly care for clinical intimacy, either. A bit of sexy fun is more to my liking.'

'What do you consider sexy fun?' she asked suspiciously.

He grinned. 'How about you wear that butterfly blouse again, without a bra underneath? Be *wicked* for me.'

Hot colour raced up her neck and scorched her

cheeks. Harry didn't care if she connected the butterfly blouse to her Mickey fantasy. He'd had a few fantasies about it himself.

'And team it with a bikini bottom with side strings
that I can undo with a flick of the fingers,' he added.
'Some bright colour that goes with your butterfly. I'm
sure you'll be able to find one in the boutique.'

She rolled her eyes. 'I didn't realise you needed provocative clothes to turn you on, Harry.'

He shrugged. 'I don't. I'd simply like you to look
and be accessible for once. I've been hitting a brick
wall with you for two years. *Accessible* has a lot of appeal to me.'

Her cheeks heated up again, making her eyes look
glittery. 'Do you have anything else in mind?' she
clipped out.

He waved an airy hand. 'Let me think about it. You
have rather sprung this on me. If I'm only to ever get
one night with Elizabeth Flippence...' He cocked an
eyebrow at her. 'That is the plan, isn't it?'

'Yes' hissed out between her teeth.

'Then I want it to be a night to remember. Something
extra special. The most sensual trip of a lifetime. I need
to let my imagination work on it for a while.'

'Fine!' she snapped, and hopped off the desk, adopt-
ing a brisk and businesslike air. 'You have three and
a half days for your imagination to flourish. Since we
have the essentials settled, let's get on with resort management.'

He could almost hear the steel click in her mind. In
his experience of women, Elizabeth Flippence was defi-

nitely something else. But she would soften for him on Friday night. He'd make damned sure she did!

He rose from the chair. 'I've brought up the file on all our suppliers on the computer. Go through it. Write down any questions you have and I'll be back later to answer them. Okay?'

'Okay.'

Her relief that he was leaving her to work alone was palpable.

He strode quickly out of the office, needing time apart from her, too. He was still churned up inside. A work-out in the gym should rid him of the violent energy that was currently coursing through him.

Three and a half days...

He wondered if he'd feel free of this mad obsession with Elizabeth Flippence after Friday night. He really was beginning to hate how much she got to him. Probably she hated how he got to her, too.

Was having sex the answer to settling everything?

Impossible to know beforehand.

Afterwards...

That should tell him whether to persist with trying to form a relationship with this infuriating woman or let her go. It all hung on one night and—by God!—he was going to make the most of it!

CHAPTER ELEVEN

ELIZABETH found herself rebelling against any regret over her decision to take Harry Finn as her lover for one night. It might be stupidly reckless of her to have sex with him. There would probably be consequences she wouldn't like but she refused to care about what could happen next. Just for once she would be totally irresponsible, except for the important issue of birth control, which was impossible to ignore.

She tackled Harry on that point as soon as he returned to the office. 'I'm not on the pill,' she stated bluntly. 'Will you take care of contraception on Friday night?'

'No problem,' he blithely replied. 'And incidentally, I've thought of another condition.'

Elizabeth tensed. If it was too outlandish...

'When we're in the villa, I want to call you Ellie.'

She was startled into asking, 'Why?'

He shrugged. 'A childhood name, conjuring up the age of innocence. I like that idea.'

'I'm not innocent, Harry.' Surely he couldn't still be thinking she was a virgin.

'Nevertheless, it's what I want. Okay?'

She shook her head over his whimsy but…what did it matter? 'If it pleases you,' she said carelessly.

'It *will* please me,' he asserted, then smiled at her. 'I also want to please you. If you think of anything you'd particularly enjoy on the night, let me know. Your wish is my command.'

'I prefer to leave everything in your very capable hands, Harry,' she said dryly, not wanting to think too much about it.

But she did over the next couple of days. And nights. It was weird how completely distracted she was from thinking about Michael and Lucy. The now-certain prospect of having sex with Harry made her more physically aware of him than ever, and the anticipation of it was zinging through her almost continually.

He didn't come up with any more conditions, didn't raise the subject at all, keeping their time together on a strictly business basis, as she had requested. Somehow that contributed to a sense of secretive intimacy, knowing what they were going to do when Friday night came but not mentioning it.

She found a red string bikini in the boutique and bought it, deciding it suited the occasion since she was acting like a scarlet woman, taking a lover she didn't love. Oddly enough she felt no guilt about doing it. Somehow it represented the kind of freedom she probably wouldn't feel with someone she did love. There were no dreams to be smashed, no expectations of sharing a life together. It was just a night of sexy fun with Harry Finn.

On Friday morning, Harry announced he had business in Port Douglas and would be gone for most of the day. He printed a notice that the office would be closed at 6:00 p.m. today and stuck it on the door. 'Go on up to the villa then,' he instructed. 'I'll be there. Don't want to miss the sunset,' he added with a smile that sparkled with anticipation.

'I'll bring a bottle of champagne from the bar,' she said, remembering how she had envisaged the scene with Michael and Lucy.

'No need. I'll have one ready to open.'

'What about food? Shall I order...?'

He shook his head. 'I have that organised, as well. You only have to bring yourself, Elizabeth.' He raised his hand in a farewell salute. 'Bye for now. Have a nice day.'

'You, too,' she replied, smiling back at him.

It was a genuine smile, not the slightest bit forced. Not having to keep her guard up against him all the time had made her more relaxed in his company. She had nothing to guard against since she was giving in to what he wanted from her. And if she was completely honest with herself, she wanted it, too.

He was a sexy man.

He made her feel sexy.

She was looking forward to having this experience with Harry tonight. She probably would have hated herself if she'd been seduced into it, but the sense of empowerment that came with having decided on it herself made all the difference.

Nevertheless, when six o'clock came and she was on her way to the pavilion villa, her nerves started getting very jumpy. She had never had an assignation like this before. It was totally out of character for her. But there was no turning back from it, she told herself fiercely. Everything was in place to take this step, and take it she would.

Harry was standing by the infinity pool, looking out to sea. He wore only a pair of board shorts, printed with white sailing ships on a blue background. She paused on the last step leading to the open deck, her heart skittering at the sight of so much naked masculinity—broad shoulders tapering to lean hips, bronze skin gleaming over taut, well-defined muscles. He had the perfect male physique and it tugged on some deeply primitive female chord in Elizabeth.

It was okay to feel attracted to him, she told herself.

It was natural.

On the physical level.

As though sensing her presence he swung around, his gaze instantly targeting her, piercing blue eyes raking her from head to toe, making her hotly conscious that she was still in the island uniform. She quickly held up the carry bag holding the clothes he'd requested and gabbled an explanation.

'I've just finished at the office, Harry. I thought I'd take a shower here.'

He nodded. 'Make it fast. The sun is already low in the sky.'

The glass doors to the villa were open. The layout inside was similar to the one Jack had shown her. She headed straight for the bathroom, anxious not to be found wanting in keeping to her side of their deal. One minute to turn on the shower taps and strip off her clothes, two minutes under the refreshing beat of the water, one minute to towel herself dry, one minute to pull on the red bikini bottom and put on the butterfly blouse, fastening only one button to keep it more or less together.

Accessible was what he'd asked for. He couldn't say she wasn't delivering it. The shape of her braless breasts and the darker colour of her areolae were certainly visible through the sheer fabric, and her nipples were already stiffening, poking at the butterfly wings. She hoped he had the champagne ready. Carrying this much accessibility off with any air of confidence required some alcoholic fortification.

It was only on her exit from the bathroom that Elizabeth caught a waft of nose-teasing scent coming from the mezzanine level. She looked up to where the king-size bed was waiting for intimate activity. Candles—from small to large—lit a path to it. A long sniff identified their fragrance as frangipani, the flower most reminiscent of tropical nights.

Harry must have set them up. Had he bought them in Port Douglas today? Why go to the trouble? This was not a night of romance. Did he want her to imagine it was? And why should he want that? She didn't understand. But it was…nice of him to do it.

She was smiling over what she had decided was playboy fun as she walked out onto the deck. 'Do you treat all your women to scented candles?' she asked.

He was about to pop the cork of a bottle of champagne. He paused to give her a very long, all-encompassing look that made her extremely conscious of every female part of her body. 'No. I simply associate the scent of flowers with butterflies, Ellie. An innocent pleasure,' he said softly.

His use of her childhood name instantly reminded her of how he'd linked it to an age of innocence. She wished she knew what was going on in his mind. It seemed to be off on some quirky journey tonight.

He popped the cork and reached for one of the flute glasses sitting on the low table that served the sun-lounges. A plate of lush fresh strawberries was placed beside the ice bucket that awaited the opened bottle. As he poured the champagne, Elizabeth saw that a couple of crushed strawberries lay in the bottom of the glass, making it a very sensual drink.

'Enjoy,' he said as he passed it to her, his smile inviting her to share all sorts of pleasure with him.

'Thank you, Harry,' she said appreciatively, grateful that he wasn't grabbing at her *accessibility* or doing anything off-putting.

He waved her to one of the sun-lounges. 'Relax. Looks like being a spectacular sunset.'

She sat on the lounge, not quite ready to put herself on display by stretching out on it. Harry poured champagne for himself, then clicked her glass with his. 'To our first night together,' he said, smiling as he dropped onto the adjacent lounge, propped himself against the backrest, lifted his long legs onto the cushioned base and gazed out to a sea that was shimmering like polished crystal.

It released Elizabeth's inhibitions about doing the same. This villa certainly had a prime position for viewing the sunset. The subtle colour changes in the sky would challenge any artist—impossible to capture on canvas, she thought. It truly was lovely, just watching it and sipping strawberry-flavoured champagne.

'Have you ever been to Broome?' Harry asked.

'No.' Broome was right across the country on the coast of Western Australia. She knew it was world famous for its pearls but she'd never had any reason to go there. 'Why do you ask?'

'Sunset there is amazing. People drive down on the beach, set up their barbecues, bring eskies loaded with cold drinks, play music, sit back and enjoy Mother Nature's display for them. They completely tune out from news of the world and just live in the moment.'

He rolled the words out in a low, almost spellbinding tone that was soothing, like a physical caress that eased the last threads of tension in Elizabeth's body.

'We don't do enough of it...living in the moment,' he went on in the same seductive murmur. 'Let's try to do that tonight, Ellie. No yesterdays...no tomorrows... just each moment as it comes.'

'Yes,' she agreed, happy with the idea.

They sipped their champagne in silence for a while, watching the sun slowly disappear below the horizon.

'My parents used to do this...have a sundowner together at the end of the day,' Harry said, slanting her a reminiscent little smile. 'What about yours, Ellie? Do they have a special time to themselves?'

She shook her head. 'My mother died of cancer when I was nineteen. I haven't seen my father since the funeral. He's a miner and living with some other woman in Mt Isa. It was never much of a marriage. Mum more or less brought Lucy and me up by herself.'

Harry frowned at her. 'Your father doesn't care about you?'

She grimaced. 'I think we were responsibilities he

didn't really want. Mostly when he came home on leave from the mine, he'd get drunk and we'd stay out of his way.'

'What about when your mother became ill?'

'He came home less. Didn't want to be faced with what was happening to Mum. He said it was up to me and Lucy to take care of her.'

'That must have been hard,' Harry said sympathetically.

'Yes. Though it was a special time, too. Like you said…living in the moment…because the last moment could come at any time so every good moment was precious.'

'At least you knew that,' he murmured, nodding understandingly before throwing her a wry little smile. 'Mickey and I…we didn't realise how precious those good moments were until after our parents were gone.'

'I guess that kind of sudden death is harder to come to terms with,' she said thoughtfully.

'I don't know. We didn't have to see them suffer.' He shook his head. 'You were only nineteen. How did you manage?'

'I was at business college so I could be home quite a lot. Lucy dropped out of school to look after Mum when I couldn't be there.'

'Did she pick up her education again at a later date?'

'No.' Impossible to explain that school had never been easy for Lucy. She didn't like people knowing about her dyslexia. 'She didn't want to, didn't need it to get work.'

'But without qualifications…'

'Lucy is adept at winning her way into jobs.'

'While you're the one with the steady career. That's why she calls you her anchor.'

Elizabeth heaved a sigh. 'This is a weird conversation to be having when we're supposed to be enjoying a night of sexy fun, Harry.'

'Oh, I don't know. I'd call this an intimate conversation. We have all night to get to physical intimacy. We've been on the fringes of each other's worlds for two years. I think I know Elizabeth fairly well—' he rolled his head towards her, giving her his quirky smile '—but I want to get to know Ellie tonight.'

'That's yesterday, Harry. My childhood,' she pointed out. 'It's not living in the moment.'

The blue eyes gathered the piercing intensity that always gave her discomfort. 'Ellie is inside you right now,' he said softly. 'She's the foundation of the woman you are. She directs your life.'

'That's ridiculous!' she protested.

'Is it? You're the older child, the one who helped your mother, the one who protected your sister, the one who carried the responsibility of arranging everything when your mother was ill, when she died, the one who wants a man in her life who will never do to her what her father did to her mother, to his children.'

He was digging at her again—digging, digging, digging! In a burst of frustration, Elizabeth swung her legs off the lounge, sat up straight and glared at him. 'I did not come up here to be psychoanalysed, Harry.'

He swung his legs down to the deck in a more leisurely fashion, his eyes holding hers in glittering challenge. 'No, you didn't. Ellie wanted to break out of the Elizabeth cocoon and fly free for once, didn't she?'

She hated how he could connect everything up and be so damned right about everything! It made her feel naked in far more than the physical sense. In a purely defensive action, she snatched the bottle of champagne from the ice bucket, intending to refill her glass.

Harry took it from her. 'Allow me.'

She did, letting him pour the champagne, though it made her feel he was taking control away from her, which wasn't how she'd planned to have this encounter with Harry. 'Do you probe into the lives of all your one-night stands?' she asked waspishly.

He cocked an eyebrow at her. 'What makes you think my life consists of a series of one-night stands?'

'The way you flirt. Michael said you flirt with every woman. It isn't just me.'

'Flirting can be fun. It can be enjoyable to both parties. In a way it's a search for that magic click which will lead to bed, but that doesn't happen very often. When it has, I can't recall one instance when it only lasted for one night. You've assumed something about me that isn't true, Ellie.'

'Well, this is only going to be for one night,' she insisted, needing to regain the control that seemed to be sliding out of her grip.

'Why?'

'Because…' She floundered, not wanting to say the whole idea had erupted from the fact his brother was going to be here with her sister and she hadn't really looked beyond that painful circumstance. 'I just don't want to get heavily involved with you, Harry,' she said evasively, wishing he would simply accept what she'd offered him.

'Why not? You think I'll let you down?'

Yes was on the tip of her tongue but he didn't give her time to say it.

'Did I let you down when you needed to cover up your distress over Mickey attaching himself to your sister? Did I let you down when you needed an escape from them? Have I let you down in fulfilling your requests this week, meeting what you wanted? Haven't I shown I care about how you feel, Ellie?'

She couldn't deny any of that, yet... 'It...it fitted into your own agenda,' she blurted out.

'Which is?' He bored in.

Her head was spinning from the pressure he was subjecting her to with all his questions. She had to seize on the one point she was certain of, drive it home. She set her glass on the table, stood up, challenging him to get on with what he'd been aiming for all along.

'Having me like this! *Accessible!*' She threw the words at him. 'So why don't you stop talking and take what you want with me?'

Anger burned through Harry. He'd tried to reach out to her, tried find a special meeting ground with her. She just kept closing her mind, shutting the door on him, keeping him out. He set his glass down, rose to his feet and hurled her confrontation right back in her face.

'You want to be treated like a piece of meat instead of a woman I care about? Fine! Just stand there and let me oblige!'

CHAPTER TWELVE

HARRY saw her eyes dilate with shock.

He didn't care.

She'd invited him to take her without caring and his level of frustration with her was so high, turning away from following through on her invitation was beyond him. His hands lifted and cupped the breasts they'd wanted to cup in Mickey's office days ago. He fanned her rock-hard nipples with his thumbs. The soft sheer fabric of the butterfly blouse gave a sensual sexiness to feeling her like this, causing a rush of hot blood to his loins.

He wanted her.

He'd been burning up for her all week.

Her eyes refocused on his, still slightly glazed but clearing as she sucked in a deep breath.

Yes, look at me! he thought savagely. *Know it's me and not Mickey!*

He undid the button holding her blouse together and spread the edges apart, wanting to feel the naked lushness of her breasts against his chest. His arms slid around her waist, scooping her into firm contact with him. It felt good. It felt great.

'Harry...' It was a husky gasp.

He didn't want to hear anything she had to say. His name on her lips shot a soaring wave of triumph through him—*his* name, not Mickey's—and he was hell-bent on keeping it stamped on her consciousness. His mouth crashed onto hers, intent on a blitzkrieg invasion that would blast any possible thought of his brother from entering her head.

To his surprise her tongue started duelling with his and a wild elation burst through his brain when her hands clutched his head, not to tear them apart but to hold them together, her fingers kneading his scalp, her mouth working to meet and escalate the passion surging through him.

He pressed one hand into the sexy pit of her back, forcing her body into contact with his erection as he pulled the bikini string at her hip apart, changed hands to do the same with the other, whipped the scrap of fabric from between her legs. The lovely female curves of her naked bottom were sensual dynamite, igniting his need for her to the brink of explosion.

He tore his hands off them to sweep the blouse from her shoulders and pull it off her arms. It broke her hold on his head, broke the marauding madness of their kissing, but it had to be done. She was fully naked now, totally *accessible* to anything he wanted with her.

He bent and scooped her off her feet, holding her crushed to his chest as he strode from the deck, into the villa, up the steps to the mezzanine level. He tumbled her onto the king-size bed, snatched up the contraceptive sheath he'd laid ready on the bedside table, discarded his board shorts in double-quick time, pulled on the sheath and leapt onto the bed, rolling her straight into his embrace, not allowing any sense of separation to strike any doubts about what they were doing in her mind.

Their mouths locked again, driving passion to fever pitch. Her body was arching into his, explicitly needful. He barely controlled the urge to zero in to the ultimate intimacy with her. Only the bitter recollection of her *one night* insistence forced him to a different course of action. If this was all there was to be between them he'd satisfy every desire she'd ever stirred in him—eat her all up so he could spit her out afterwards, not be left fantasising over what he could have done.

He wrenched his mouth from hers, trailed hotly possessive kisses down her lovely long neck, tasted the tantalising hollow at the base of her throat, slid lower to feast on her sensational breasts, swirling his tongue around her provocative nipples, sucking on them, devouring them, taking his fill of her luscious femininity, revelling in the little moans vibrating from her throat, the twist of her fingers tangling with his hair.

He reached down to part the soft folds of her sex, his own fingers sliding, searching, finding the excited wetness that gave him easy entry to stroke the excitement to a much-higher level. She cried out, her body arching again, her need growing in intensity. He moved lower, determined on driving her crazy for him.

He spread the folds apart to expose the tight bud of her clitoris and licked it, slowly teasing at first, then faster, faster until she was writhing, screaming for him, begging, her legs encircling him, feet beating a drum of wild wanting. He surged up to take the ultimate plunge, but the savage need inside him demanded a last absolute surrender from her.

Her head was thrashing from side to side. He held it still. 'Look at me!' he commanded.

She blinked and looked but there was no real focus in her eyes.

'Say my name!'

'What?' It was a gasp of confusion.

'Say my name!'

'Har...ry...' It was a weak waver of sound.

'Say it again!'

'Harry, Harry, Harry...' she cried hysterically. 'Please...'

'You want me?'

'Ye-s-s-s.' She beat at his shoulders with tightly clenched fists. 'I'll kill you if you don't...'

He silenced her with a deep, thrusting kiss as he propelled his flesh into hers. When he lifted his head, the animal groan of satisfaction from her throat rang jubilant bells in his ears. She clutched his buttocks, trying to goad him into a fast rhythm, but he wanted the excitement to build and build, not explode all at once. He started slowly, revelling in her eagerness for him, the convulsive little spasms that told him she was totally engaged in feeling him—*him*, not Mickey.

He felt her creaming around him and couldn't keep controlling the rampantly growing need of his own body. It overtook his mind, oblivious to everything but the physical scream to reach climax, releasing the fierce tension raging through every muscle of his body. It pumped from him in a glorious burst of ecstatic satisfaction, and with all tension draining away, he rolled onto his side, pulling her with him, wanting to hang on to the sense of intimate togetherness as long as he could.

She didn't attempt any move away from him. Maybe she was drained of all energy, too. Whatever…she left her legs entwined with his, their bodies pressed close, her head tucked under his chin. He stroked her hair, enjoying the soft silky texture of it, thinking he still had the freedom to touch. He wondered how she was going to act for the rest of the night. Would Ellie emerge and see him for the man he was, or would Elizabeth stick to her guns?

He couldn't call it.

He told himself he didn't care.

At least he had the satisfaction of making her want him with every fibre of her being, if only for one night.

Elizabeth didn't want to move. It felt unbelievably good, cuddled up with Harry, having her hair stroked. Her mind drifted to her childhood, sitting on her mother's lap, head resting just like this while her hair was stroked lovingly. No one else had ever done it. She'd always been the one to comfort Lucy, not the other way around. It was weird, feeling comforted by Harry but…she didn't want to move.

She liked being naked with him, too, the warm flesh contact, the sense of his male strength holding her safe. It was so nice and peaceful after the storm of incredible sensation. Having sex with Harry…her mind was still blown by it…just totally unimaginable before experiencing it. She'd never tipped so utterly out of control, never been taken to such peaks of exquisite pleasure-pain, and the sheer ecstasy of floating in the aftermath of one climax after another...well, that had certainly set the bar for how fantastic sex with the right man could be.

Though she hadn't thought Harry was the right man in any other respect...or...might he be?

Maybe she had been a bit too quick to judge, misreading his character. Or maybe she was just being influenced by how *right* he was in bed for her. Most probably he was the best action man on that front for every woman he took to bed. Just because this had been special to her didn't make it special to him. But she was still glad she'd had this with Harry.

'Are you okay?' he murmured caringly.

She sighed contentedly. 'Very okay, thank you.'

'Then let's go take a shower. Once we're done there we can get in the pool and cool off.'

She *was* hot and sticky. 'Good idea,' she said.

The shower was more than big enough for two and Elizabeth was in no hurry using it this time. She enjoyed soaping Harry's great body, touching him intimately, letting him do the same to her.

'Having fun?'

The wry note in his voice made her look up. There was no amusement twinkling in the vivid blue eyes. The mocking glint in them dried up the pleasure she had been feeling, sending a chill through her as she remembered her taunt about having a night of sexy fun, rejecting having any deeper involvement with him, virtually dismissing him as a person of no account in her life. He'd been so angry—*shockingly* angry. She'd forgotten that, her mind swamped by so much else.

Instinctively she reached up to touch his cheek in an

apologetic appeal. 'I was taking pleasure in you, Harry. I thought you were taking pleasure in me.'

For a moment his mouth took on an ironic twist. Then he bent his head and kissed her, a long sensual kiss that swallowed up any worry about him still being angry with her.

Finishing off in the infinity pool was another sensual pleasure, the water like cool silk caressing her skin. 'Just stay there,' Harry instructed as he heaved himself out. 'I'll light the torches to keep the insects away and bring out the oysters with some chilled wine.'

'Oysters!' She laughed. 'I don't think I need an aphrodisiac, Harry.'

He stopped. His shoulders squared and she saw his back muscles tense. He half turned to face her, a cutting look in his eyes that ripped through the amusement in hers. 'I'm not into playboy tricks, Elizabeth. I simply remembered you liked them at your birthday lunch.'

That coldly spoken *Elizabeth* slapped her with the realisation that she was offending him every time she painted him as a playboy. Perhaps even insulting him. He'd told her straight out that the label was wrong in his eyes. Had she been doing him an injustice all this time? What hard evidence did she actually have that he used women lightly? None!

There was a sitting shelf at one end of the pool, and she settled on it, still enjoying the soft ripple of the water around her dangling legs as she thought back over the two years Harry had been dipping into her life while she'd been working for his brother. When he'd first walked into her office he'd emanated a megawatt attraction that had put her in such a tizzy physically she had instantly mistrusted and disliked his power to do that to her.

She'd reasoned that a man with so much personal magnetism was very likely to stray from any relationship since other women would always be eyeing him over, wanting a chance with him, especially when he was both wealthy and sexy. Determined not to go anywhere near that playing field, she had kept a rigid guard against his insidious assaults on her armour.

Now it felt as though she had prejudiced herself against a man who might well be worth knowing in a deeper sense than she had ever believed possible. Could he actually fulfil everything she had been looking for? His brother had definitely been more the type of character that appealed to her—solid, responsible—not dangerous like Harry. Yet Michael had not seen what he wanted in her. And was Harry really dangerous, or was that a false perception on her part?

She watched him emerge from the villa and stroll across the deck towards her, carrying a platter of oysters, a bottle of wine and two fresh glasses. He'd tucked a white towel around his waist. The sky had darkened and the flickering light of the torches he'd lit at the corners of the deck was not bright enough for her to see the expression in his eyes. Was he still angry with her?

'Shall I get out?' she asked.

'Not if you don't want to,' he answered with a careless shrug. 'I can serve you just as easily there.'

'The water's lovely.'

'Then stay.'

He set the platter on the deck, sat on the edge of the

pool and proceeded to open the bottle of wine and fill the glasses.

'I do like oysters, Harry. Thank you for remembering,' she said, hoping to erase the *aphrodisiac* remark.

He handed her the glass of white wine with a droll little smile. 'I remembered your sister saying you loved chilli mud crab, too. I know a restaurant in Port Douglas that specialises in that dish so I had it cooked for you and it's waiting in the microwave to be heated up when you want it.'

She stared at him, horribly shamed by his caring and generosity when she had treated him so meanly, using him as a distraction, even to going to bed with him in this villa because of Michael bringing Lucy here.

'I'm sorry,' she blurted out.

He frowned. 'Sorry about what?'

'My whole attitude towards you. It's been uncaring and bitchy and…and soured by things that you weren't even a part of. I haven't been fair to you, Harry. I've never been fair to you and I don't know why you're being so nice to me because I don't deserve it.' Tears suddenly welled into her eyes and she quickly tried to smear them away with the back of her hand. 'I'm sorry. I'm all messed up and I can't help myself.'

'It's okay,' he said soothingly. 'Just take a few deep breaths and let it all go. Life is a bitch sometimes. The trick is to get past the bad bits. I've been trying to help you do that, Ellie.'

Ellie… The soft caring way her childhood name rolled off his tongue brought another spurt of tears to her eyes and screwed her up inside, stirring up the craven wish for someone to take care of her. She'd been taking care of herself and Lucy for so long, she needed someone to simply be there for her. But she couldn't expect Harry to keep doing that. She didn't know how far his kindness would stretch. What she could do was bask in it for a little while.

It took quite a few deep breaths to bring herself under control enough to manage a smile at him. 'Thank you for helping me.'

'You do deserve to have nice things done for you,' he said seriously. 'Everyone does. It makes the world a happier place. My mother taught me that. She was brilliant at it.'

She sipped the wine he had poured for her, remembering Sarah Pickard's description of Yvette Finn—*a sunny nature, radiating a joy in life that infected everyone around her.* 'Sarah said you're like your mother,' she remarked, starting to reappraise the man in a completely different light to how she had previously perceived him.

He gave a wry shake of his head. 'A hard act to follow, but I try.'

'Tell me about her,' she said impulsively, wanting to understand where Harry was coming from.

He made an indecisive gesture. 'Where to start?'

'Start with how your father met her,' she encouraged.

He laughed. 'In hospital. He'd broken his leg and Mum was the only nurse who wouldn't let him be grumpy.'

'She was an ordinary common nurse?' It surprised her, having imagined that Franklyn Finn would have married some beautiful accomplished socialite.

Harry shook his head. 'I don't think anyone would

have said she was ordinary. All the patients loved her, my father included. He always considered himself extremely privileged that she learned to love him back. It took him quite some time to win her.'

'She didn't like him at first?'

'It wasn't that. She wasn't sure about how she would fit into his life. Dad was a seriously driven guy. In the end, she made up a set of rules for how their marriage could work and he had to promise to keep to them.'

'Did he?'

'Never wavered from them. She was the light of his life and he was never going to let that light go out.' He grimaced. 'In a way, I guess it was a kind fate that they died together. They were so tied to each other.'

It must have been a wonderful marriage, Elizabeth thought, wishing she could have one like it. Her own mother hadn't known much happiness in hers and the end of her life had certainly not been kind, though she and Lucy had done their best to ease the pain of it. 'I always thought Lucy could have made a great nurse,' she murmured, remembering how good she had been at cheering up their mother.

'She could have become one if she'd wanted to,' Harry remarked.

'No' slipped out before she could stop it.

'Why not? She could have gone back to school....'

'Lucy was never good at exams,' she prevaricated. Her dyslexia made it impossible for her to pass them. She was smart enough to pick up anything as an apprentice and she had a great memory, but examinations that required reading and writing within a set time simply couldn't be done. 'I don't think she had the head for study after Mum died,' she added to put him off pursuing the point. 'She was only seventeen and she took it hard, Harry.'

'Understandable,' he said sympathetically.

She sipped some more of the wine and eyed the platter of oysters. 'I think I'm ready to eat now.'

He laughed. 'Help yourself.'

'I'll get out first.'

Harry quickly rose to his feet, grabbing a towel to dry her off and wrap around her. She didn't try to take it from him and didn't protest his action when he finished up tucking it around her waist, leaving her breasts bare. 'They're too beautiful to cover up,' he said with a smile.

'I'm glad you think so,' she said a little shyly.

Exhilaration zinged through Harry. She'd dropped all the barriers. There was no rejection in her eyes, no guard up against him. And it remained like that for the rest of the evening, no bitchy barbs slung at him, no hiding what she thought or felt about anything, no shutting him out.

She might not have forgotten all about Mickey but she had definitely put his brother aside and was actively taking pleasure in finding connections with him—connections beyond the purely physical. The sexual chemistry was still there, of course, simmering between them, heightened by their newly intimate knowledge of each other, but Harry was encouraged to believe this could actually be the beginning of a relationship that might become very special.

He wasn't driven to carry her off to bed in a fury of frustration a second time. She happily walked with him and they both indulged in slow, sensual lovemaking—a sweet pleasuring of each other that was intensely satisfying to Harry. No way was this going to be a one-night stand. He wouldn't accept that. Elizabeth Flippence had opened up to him and he liked it too much to let her slip away from him.

Tomorrow he would see if her attachment to Mickey had been broken.

He wanted it broken.

It had to be broken.

CHAPTER THIRTEEN

A WOMAN I care about...

Those words spoken last night kept running through Elizabeth's mind all morning, keeping any anxiety over coming face to face with Michael and Lucy again at bay. She added up all the caring from Harry and realised no other man in her life had done as much for her—helping, comforting, pleasuring, answering her needs.

It couldn't be just about having sex with her.

There had been genuine concern in his eyes when he'd asked, 'Are you going to be okay today?' before leaving her at the office door after their night at the pavilion villa.

She'd assured him that she would be and he'd added, 'I'll be on hand.'

Ready to run interference if she needed it, as he had last Monday.

It felt really good to have him caring about her—someone she could depend on to get her through this weekend without too much heartache. Oddly enough, she wasn't feeling any heartache at all over Michael wanting Lucy, although seeing them together again might strain her current sense of being able to set them at an emotional distance.

Harry was to meet them at the jetty and transport them to the administration centre. Elizabeth felt reasonably confident about handling their queries about how well she was coping with management responsibilities. Lucy, of course, would angle for a private conversation with her, but she didn't think that would trouble her too much. She no longer felt so shattered over her lost dreams.

A few guests dropped into the office to check on arrangements they'd made for diving expeditions. There were inquiries about bookings to be answered. A couple of beach picnics had to be sorted out with the chef. Sarah Pickard came by, ostensibly to put in an order for new towels, but her eyes shone with lively curiosity about this new development between Harry and his stand-in manager.

Probably all the staff on the island knew about it by now since the villa had to be cleaned this morning, ready for Michael and Lucy. Elizabeth had decided it didn't matter but she certainly wasn't going to talk about her private life to anyone.

'Harry said it's your sister coming with Mickey today,' Sarah remarked.

'Yes,' Elizabeth answered briefly.

'That's nice.'

Elizabeth smiled. 'Yes, it is.'

'When did they meet?'

'Lucy came into the Cairns office to see me and they clicked. Simple as that,' she said airily.

'And Harry, of course, met you when he went to see Mickey.'

'Yes.'

Realising that Elizabeth was not about to be chatty, Sarah backed off, only tossing out the comment, 'Well, it's all very interesting,' as she left the office.

It wasn't interesting so much as complicated, Elizabeth thought. She didn't know if these connections were likely to lead anywhere good for either Lucy or herself. Two brothers who were close, two sisters who were close, the work situation—if things started going wrong, there could be a nasty ripple effect.

She remembered Lucy's blithe comment when Harry had been ordering their cocktails last Monday—*wouldn't it be great if we ended up together...all happy families!* Possibly it could be great if it worked out like that but Elizabeth wasn't counting on it. It was far too early to think the possibility was high.

Lucy slid out of relationships almost as fast as she started them.

As for herself and Harry, she couldn't even call it a relationship yet. All she could really say for certain was that her stance against him had been substantially shifted. And he was fantastic in bed!

It was almost midday when he called from the jetty to say Mickey's motor-launch was about to dock. Her nerves instantly started jangling, mocking any idea that she could breeze through this meeting with no angst at all. She fiercely told herself the important thing was to keep her composure, regardless of what she was feeling.

Lucy was hugging Michael's arm when Harry led them into the office—the woman in possession and obviously loving having this man in tow. Her skin was glowing, her eyes were shining and the smile on her face beamed brilliant happiness. Elizabeth's heart contracted at this evidence that her sister was over-the-moon in love.

'This island is fabulous, Ellie,' she cried. 'What a great place to work!'

'Tropical paradise,' Elizabeth responded, pasting a smile on her face and moving from behind the desk to greet them appropriately.

Lucy released Michael's arm to rush forward and give her a hug. 'Are you loving it?' she asked, her eyes bright with curiosity about the situation, which, of course, included Harry.

'Not too much, I hope,' Michael semigrowled in the background.

'It's been quite a change,' she said dryly, flicking him a sharply assessing look.

Somehow he was more handsome than ever, his face relaxed in a friendly way, his very male physique shown off in casual clothes—smartly tailored shorts in a blue-and-grey check teamed with a royal blue sports shirt. He still had the impact of an alpha man scoring ten out of ten, but she wasn't feeling it so personally anymore. He belonged to her sister now.

'A good one, I hope,' Harry slid in, drawing her attention to him.

Another alpha man—no doubt about it now—and the memory of last night's intimacy caused a wave of warm pleasure to roll through her. The piercing blue eyes were digging at her again, but she didn't resent it this time. He *cared* about what she was feeling.

'Yes,' she answered with a smile, wanting to allay his concern for her.

'Now, Harry, poaching my PA is not on,' Michael shot at him.

'Like I said before, Mickey—*her choice*,' he replied with an affable shrug.

'Okay, while you two guys argue over my brilliant sister, I want her to show me her living quarters,' Lucy put in quickly. 'You can mind the office, can't you, Harry?'

'Go right ahead,' he said agreeably.

'Come on, Ellie,' she urged, nodding to the door at the back of the office. 'Michael said your apartment was right here. I want to see everything. And while I'm at it, may I say you look great in the island uniform?'

Elizabeth laughed. 'Not as spectacular as you this morning.'

Lucy wore cheeky little navy denim shorts with a red-and-purple halter top, big red hoop earrings, red trainers on her feet and a purple scrunchie holding up her long blond hair in a ponytail.

'Am I over-the-top?' she asked.

Elizabeth shook her head. 'You can carry off anything, Lucy.'

'I wish...' she replied with a wry grimace as Elizabeth ushered her into the apartment and closed the door on the two men in the office.

Elizabeth eyed her quizzically, sensing something was weighing on her sister's mind. 'Is that a general wish or...?'

'Oh, nothing really,' came the airy reply, her hands gesturing dismissively as her gaze swung around the living room. 'This is lovely, Ellie. Show me the bedroom and bathroom.'

She stopped at the queen-size bed, her sherry-brown eyes twinkling mischief at Elizabeth. 'Have you shared this with Harry yet?'

'Actually, no.' Wanting to divert any further personal probing, she retaliated with, 'Do you want to tell me what's going on with Michael?'

She threw up her hands. 'Everything is happening! I swear to you, Ellie, I've never been this mad about a guy. I'm in love like you wouldn't believe, and while it's incredibly wonderful, it's also scary, you know?'

'In what way scary?'

She flopped onto the bed, put her hands behind her head and stared at the ceiling. 'Michael is smart. I mean *really* smart, isn't he?'

'Yes.'

'So what happens when he finds out that my brain wasn't wired right and I'm a dummy when it comes to reading and writing? So far I've been winging it as I usually do, but this is far more intense than it's been with other guys, and he's bound to start noticing I'm a bit weird about some things.' She rolled her head to look straight at Elizabeth, a yearning appeal in her eyes. 'You've worked for him for two years. Will it put him off me if I tell him I'm dyslexic?'

Having experienced how exacting he was about everything to do with work, Elizabeth could only answer, 'I honestly don't know, Lucy. Does it feel as though he's in love with you?'

'Well, definitely in lust.' Her forehead puckered. 'I can't be sure that's love, but I really want it to be, Ellie. More than I've wanted anything. I want him to care so much about having me, it won't matter that I'm flawed.'

Elizabeth sat on the bed beside her and smoothed the worried furrows from her brow. 'It shouldn't matter if he loves you. And stop thinking of yourself as a dummy, Lucy. You're very smart, and you have so many talents…any man would be lucky to have you in his life.'

She heaved a rueful sigh. 'Well, I don't want him to know yet. I couldn't bear it if…' Her eyes shot a pleading look at Elizabeth. 'You haven't told Harry, have you?'

'No. And I won't.'

'I need more time. To give it a chance, you know?'

'Yes, I know.'

'I've been running off at the mouth about me. What about you and Harry?'

Elizabeth shrugged. 'Same thing. More time needed.'

'But you do like him.'

'Yes.' The hostility towards him had completely dissipated last night, as had the steaming vexation and resentment he had so frequently stirred. As it was now, there was nothing not to like.

Lucy propped herself on her elbow, an earnest expression on her face. 'Promise me you won't go off him if things don't work out between me and Michael.'

She hadn't expected Lucy, who had always seemed to be a live-in-the-moment person, to look ahead and see complications arising from the situation. It took her by surprise. Before she could consider the promise, Lucy rattled on.

'Harry could be the right guy for you. Let's face it… he's gorgeous and sexy and wealthy and obviously keen to have you in his corner. You could be great together and I don't want *me* to be the reason for you not having a future with him. I'd be happy to see you happy with him, Ellie, regardless of what happens between me and Michael.'

Deeply touched by her sister's caring, she couldn't help replying, 'But being so madly in love with Michael, you'll be hurt if he walks away from you.' Just as *she* had been on Monday—totally shattered and never wanting to see him again.

'Oh, I'll muddle along like I always do,' Lucy retorted with a wry grimace. 'I'm good at putting things behind me. I've had a lot of practice at it.' She reached out, took Elizabeth's hand and squeezed it reassuringly. 'You mustn't worry about me. Go for what you want. You deserve a good life, Ellie.'

'So do you.'

'Well, maybe we'll both achieve it. Who knows? I just want to clear the deck for you and Harry. Now tell me you're okay with that.'

Elizabeth heaved a sigh to relieve the heavy emotional fullness in her chest and finally said, 'I'm okay if you're okay.' She squeezed her sister's hand back. 'Whatever happens with either of us, we'll always have each other, Lucy.'

'Absolutely!' she agreed, the earnestness breaking into a wide grin. 'Now let's go get our men!' She bounced off the bed and twirled around in a happy dance. 'Let's have a fabulous weekend, following our hearts' desire and not thinking about tomorrow.' She paused in the doorway to the living room to give Elizabeth a wise look. 'You never know when something might strike us dead so we do what we want to do. Right?'

'Right!' Elizabeth echoed, suddenly wondering how much of Lucy's attitudes and behaviour stemmed from their mother's early death and the suffering that had preceded it. She'd only been seventeen. Would Michael wrap her in the loving security blanket she needed? It was simply impossible to know at this point.

When she and Lucy emerged from the apartment, the two men were still standing where they'd left them in the office. Michael's attention instantly swivelled away from Harry, his face lighting up with pleasure at seeing her sister again. He held out his arms in a welcome-back gesture and Lucy waltzed straight into them, laughing up at him as she curled her arms around his neck.

'All done here?' he asked indulgently.

'Yes. But I want all four of us to lunch together in the restaurant.'

He threw a quick appeal to his brother. 'That can be arranged?'

'Leave it with me,' Harry said, not exactly committing to the idea. 'Why don't you take Lucy across to the restaurant, order a bottle of wine, and we'll join you when we've cleared the way?'

'See you soon,' Lucy tossed at Elizabeth as Michael scooped her away with him.

Which left her alone with Harry.

She'd been watching Michael very intently, wishing she could see into his mind and heart, knowing now that he could hurt Lucy very badly if lust didn't turn into love. This wasn't another flash-in-the-pan attraction for her—easy come, easy go.

Was he *the right man* for her sister?

A little while ago she had believed he was the perfect

match for herself. It was hard to get her head around transferring that sense of *rightness* to the connection between Michael and Lucy, but at least it didn't hurt anymore. She felt no jealousy. No envy. Just a rather horrid sense that fate was playing a capricious trick in seeding attractions with the potential to mess up their lives.

Harry clenched his hands in instinctive fighting mode. Throughout the whole encounter with Mickey and Lucy, Elizabeth's attention had been trained on them. She hadn't looked to him for any help. Even now with them gone, her focus was inward, probably measuring her feelings and unwilling to reveal them.

Was she still obsessed with Mickey?

He needed to know.

'Elizabeth...' he said more tersely than he'd meant to.

Her gaze flicked up to his. He saw no pain in her eyes. It was more a look of curious assessment. *Of him.* Was she comparing what she'd felt for Mickey with how she now felt about him? Last night's intimacy had to have had some impact on her. She'd responded to him very positively.

'If you'd rather not have lunch with them...' he started, willing to make up some excuse for her to avoid spending more time in their company if she found it intolerable.

'No, it's fine,' she cut in. 'If it's okay with you for me to vacate the office for the lunch hour.'

'You're sure?' he asked, wanting absolute confirmation that she was free of any angst over her sister's connection with his brother.

A whimsical smile softened her expression as she

walked towards him. To his surprise and delight, when she reached him she slid her hands up his chest and linked them around the back of his neck. 'Lucy said to go get our men and right now you're my man, Harry. I hope you're happy about that,' she said in a soft seductive lilt.

Was it true?

He fiercely didn't want it to be on the rebound.

He wrapped his arms around her and pulled her into full body contact with him. No resistance. In fact, she rubbed herself teasingly against him, stirring an instant erection. Her eyes blazed with a boldness he'd never seen in them and he sensed a determination in her to take life by the scruff of the neck and give it a good shake.

Whatever... Her dream about Mickey was gone and she was choosing to have him. He kissed her and she kissed him right back, no hesitation, no inhibitions—a full-blooded response that made it extremely difficult to rein in the desire she'd fired up. It was the wrong time to race her off to bed. Mickey and Lucy were waiting for them in the restaurant and he wouldn't put it past Lucy to come looking for them if they didn't appear within a reasonable time.

Besides, the promise was certainly there that last night was not going to be the one-night stand Elizabeth had dictated.

He could wait.

He was satisfied that he'd won.

Elizabeth Flippence was now *his* woman.

CHAPTER FOURTEEN

ELIZABETH woke up on Sunday morning and was instantly aware of the man lying in the bed he hadn't shared with her before last night—the sound of his breathing, the warmth emanating from his naked body, the memories of intense pleasure in their lovemaking. Harry Finn...

She rolled onto her back to look at him, a smile twitching at her lips. He was still asleep. Her gaze wandered over every part of him that was not covered by the bed sheet—the strongly muscled shoulders and arms, the ruggedly masculine face with its slightly crooked nose, the black curls flopping over his forehead, the five o'clock shadow on his jaw. *Her man*, she thought, at least for the time being.

It felt slightly weird but definitely liberating to have thrown out her rule book on how life should be led, diving straight into the deep end with Harry and not caring if it was a big mistake. Lucy's comment yesterday—*you never know when something might strike us dead so we do what we want to do*—had made it seem stupid to deny herself what Harry could give her out of fear that she'd made a rash choice and this lovely time with him probably wouldn't last.

So what if it didn't!

She was thirty years old. Why not experience all the pleasure she could with this man? When—*if*—it ended, at least she would have had the most marvellous sex any woman could have.

She wondered if Lucy was feeling the same about Michael. Was he as good a lover as his brother? Did being *in love* make it better? It was far too soon to say she was in love with Harry but he was much—*nicer*—than she had ever thought he could be, not like a superficial playboy at all. He really did care about her feelings.

His eyes suddenly flicked open, instantly catching her looking at him. 'Hi!' he said, his mouth curving into a happy smile.

She smiled back. 'Hi to you, too!'

'How long have you been awake?'

She reached out and ran a finger down his nose. 'Long enough to wonder how this got broken.'

He laughed and rolled onto his side, propping himself up on his elbow, answering her good-humouredly. 'Rugby tackle. It made a bloody mess of my nose but I stopped the other guy from scoring a try and we won the game.'

'Sport,' she said, mentally correcting her former prejudice that had decided the injury had come out of a misspent youth. 'Jack Pickard told me you'd been good at all sports in your teens. He reckoned you could have been a champion on any playing field.'

He cocked an eyebrow at her. 'You were asking him about me?'

'No. I was being told about you. But I am asking

now. Tell me about those years, Harry. What were your proudest moments in sport?'

He was happy to talk about them, basking in her interest. For two years she had rejected knowing more about him, always projecting the attitude that he wasn't worth knowing. That glacier of disinterest had definitely thawed over the past two days.

'Did you ever dream of competing in the Olympic Games? Or representing Australia in rugby or cricket?' she asked.

He shook his head. 'I simply enjoyed sport. I never aimed to make a career out of it. Mickey and I wanted to join Dad in the business. He used to talk to us about what he was doing, what he was planning. It was creative, challenging, exciting....' He grinned. 'And you made your own rules, no toeing a line drawn for you by sport officialdom.'

'You were lucky to have a father like that, Harry.'

Not like hers.

He saw it in her eyes, heard it in the tinge of sad envy in her voice. He remembered what she had told him about her own father and realised how cautious she would be about her relationships with men, judging them on character before allowing them into her life. Playboy—womaniser—that would be a firm no-no regardless of physical attraction. No doubt she would instantly back off from anyone showing a bent towards drinking too much alcohol, as well.

A very strong-minded woman.

Her sister's anchor.

She'd been a challenge to him and he hadn't looked

any further than winning her over, having her like this, but he found himself wanting to prove she was safe with him. He was not one of the bad guys.

'I'm going to be the same kind of father to my children,' he said firmly.

It raised her eyebrows. 'You see a future with a family in it?'

'Yes, I do. Don't you?'

She looked uncertain. 'I don't know anymore. I feel a bit adrift at the moment, Harry.'

She had probably dreamed of it with Mickey and that dream was gone. He understood her sense of being adrift. He didn't know how deep it went until much later in the day.

Lunch with Lucy and Michael again before they headed back to the mainland. Elizabeth felt no stress about joining them. She wanted to observe how well they were responding to each other, watch for any pricks in their bubble of happiness. It troubled her that Lucy saw her dyslexia as a possible breaking point. She wished she could have given her sister an assurance that it wouldn't be.

It was a problem, no denying it. She suspected it played a big part in Lucy's flightiness, why relationships and jobs never lasted long. It wasn't a happy position—being thought defective. If Michael ever did think it and rejected her sister on that basis, Elizabeth knew she would hate him for it.

As soon as they were all seated in the restaurant and handed menus with the limited list of four starters, four mains and four sweets, Elizabeth mused over all of them out loud so Lucy could make her choice without having to say she'd have the same as someone else. Often in restaurants a waiter listed Specials which made a selection easy, but that wasn't the case here.

Lucy grinned at her, eyes sparkling gratitude, and it was obvious that nothing had changed between her and Michael. They still looked besotted with each other, and the meal progressed in a very congenial atmosphere.

Until they were sitting over coffee at the end of it.

'Any prospects for the position of manager here, Harry?' Michael asked.

He shrugged. 'A few résumés have come in. I haven't called for any interviews yet. Elizabeth may want to stay on now that she's on top of the job.'

'Elizabeth is mine!' Michael shot at him with a vexed look.

'No!' tripped straight out of her mouth.

The vexed look was instantly transferred to her. 'Don't tell me Harry has seduced you into staying here.'

'No, I won't be staying here beyond the month he needs to find someone suitable.'

As beautiful as the island was, it was a getaway, too isolated from a normal social life for her to stay on indefinitely, too far away from Lucy, too. Besides, if the affair with Harry ran cold, she'd feel trapped here.

'So you come back to me,' Michael insisted.

She shook her head. 'I'm sorry, Michael, but I don't want to do that, either.'

Being his PA wasn't a straightforward work situation anymore. The personal connections that had started this week—him and Lucy, herself and Harry—made it too emotionally complicated for her to feel comfortable about working closely with him.

'Why not?' he persisted.

She was acutely aware of Lucy listening and needed to dissuade her sister from thinking it was because of her. 'Being here this week made me realise I want a change. Try something different. I'd appreciate it if you'd take this as my notice, Michael.'

He wasn't happy. He glared at his brother. 'God-dammit, Harry! If it wasn't for you...'

'Hey!' Harry held up his hands defensively. 'I'm not getting her, either.'

'Please...' Elizabeth quickly broke in, feeling the rise of tension around the table. 'I don't want to cause trouble. I just want to take a different direction with my life.'

'But you're brilliant as my PA,' Michael argued, still annoyed at being put out.

'I'm sorry. You'll just have to find someone else.'

She wasn't about to budge from this stance. It felt right to divorce herself from both the Finn men as far as work was concerned. Whatever developed in a personal sense had to be something apart from professional ties, not tangled up with how she earned her income.

'Why not try out Lucy as your PA?' Harry suggested to Michael with an airy wave of his hand. 'She's probably as brilliant as her sister.'

Lucy looked aghast, panic in her eyes.

'It's not her kind of thing,' Elizabeth said firmly.

Michael frowned and turned to her sister. 'You do work in administration, Lucy,' he remarked quizzically.

'I'm the front person who deals with people, Michael,' she rushed out. 'I don't do the desk work. I'm good at helping people, understanding what they want, helping them to decide...there's quite a bit of that in cemetery administration. And I like it,' she added for good measure, pleading for him to drop the issue.

He grimaced, accepting that Lucy was no easy solution to his problem.

She reached out and touched his hand, desperate to restore his good humour with her. 'I'm sorry I can't fill Ellie's place.'

The grimace tilted up into a soothing smile. 'I shouldn't have expected it. You are a people person and I like that, Lucy. I wouldn't want to change it.'

Elizabeth saw relief pouring through the smile beamed back at him. Another hurdle safely jumped, she thought. Yet hiding the dyslexia from Michael couldn't go on forever and there was one thing she needed from him before the situation could get horribly messed up.

'I hope you'll give me a good reference, Michael.'

He sighed and turned a rueful smile to her. 'It will be in the mail tomorrow. I hate losing you but I wish you well, Elizabeth.'

'Thank you.'

Harry didn't like Elizabeth's decision any more than Mickey did. She was cutting ties with them, closing doors, and he didn't know her reasons for it. This morning he could have sworn she was over her emotional fixation on his brother but if that was true, why give up her job with him? It was a top-line position and on the salary front Harry doubted she could better it.

He had offered her an alternative but she wasn't taking up that option. It was understandable that staying on the island long-term would not suit her. She and her sister lived together and were obviously close—family who really counted as family, like him and Mickey. Apart from that, if she wanted to rejoin the social swing, Cairns was the place to do it.

He didn't like this thought, either. It meant she didn't see much of a future with him, which raised the question in his mind—how much of a future did he want with her?

She touched places in him that no other woman had, but did he do the same to her? More time together should sort that out, but there was one thing he needed to know right now because it was twisting up his gut.

Was she still using him to fight off her feelings for Mickey?

Elizabeth silently fretted over whether she had spoken her mind too soon, aware that her announcements had upset the happy mood around the table. Although Michael had accepted her decision on the surface, it was obvious from the stony glances he threw at Harry that he blamed his brother for it and was barely holding in his frustration over the situation. Her nerves picked up tension emanating from Harry. Lucy kept looking anxiously at her. No one chose to eat any of the petit fours that accompanied coffee.

As soon as Elizabeth had finished her cappuccino, Lucy pushed back her chair and rose to her feet. 'I'm off to the ladies' room. Will you come with me, Ellie?' Her eyes begged agreement.

'Of course,' she said, immediately rising to join her sister.

The barrage started the moment they were closeted in the ladies' room. 'Why are you leaving your great job with Michael? He's not happy about it.'

Elizabeth shook her head. 'It's not my mission in life to keep Michael happy,' she said dryly.

'But you always said you loved that job.'

'I did, but it's high pressure, Lucy. I didn't realise how much it demanded of me until I came out here. I don't want to be constantly on my toes anymore. I want to look for something else—more relaxed, less stressful.'

'Then it's not because of me and him?' she said worriedly.

'No,' Elizabeth lied. 'I'm sorry Michael is unhappy about it but I don't think he'll take it out on you, Lucy. If he does, he's not the man for you.'

She heaved a sigh. 'You're right. Okay. It's completely fair for you to look for something else. He's just got to lump being put out by it.'

'You can play nurse and soothe his frustration,' Elizabeth said with a smile.

Lucy laughed.

It eased the tension on that front.

However, Michael's displeasure with her decision made the farewells after lunch somewhat strained. Elizabeth hoped that Lucy's company would be bright enough to move his annoyance aside. She hadn't meant to spoil their day.

Harry followed her into the administration office, obviously intent on pursuing the issue of her leaving his

employ, as well, although he shouldn't have any griev-
ance with her. She had only ever agreed to the month
needed for him to find another manager.

Wanting to clear that deck, she swung around to face
him, quickly saying, 'I won't stay on, Harry. I didn't
promise to.'

His grim expression surprised her. The laser-blue
eyes were so hard and piercing, her heart jumped into
a gallop. The air between them seemed to gather an intensity that played havoc with her nerves.

'Why did you throw in your job with Mickey?' he
shot at her.

'I explained why,' she said defensively.

'You waffled to whitewash the true reason,' he accused. 'Tell me, Elizabeth.'

He had no right to delve into her private reading of
a highly personal situation for herself and her sister. It
was not his business. It was the involvement with his
brother that was the problem and she was not about to
spell that out.

'I'm sorry you thought it was waffle.' She shrugged.
'I don't know what else to say.'

His mouth thinned in frustration. He shook his head
at her refusal to open up to him. 'I knew you were using
me on Friday night,' he stated bitingly. 'That whole
scenario at the pavilion villa was more about Michael
and Lucy than being with me. I want to know if what
you've done with me since then and what you decided
today was also driven by your feelings for my brother.'

Her face flamed with shame at how she had used him
and her mind jammed with shock that he could believe
she was still doing it. 'No!' she cried, forcing her feet

forward to go to him, her eyes pleading forgiveness for her brutal lack of caring for *his* feelings. 'I don't even think of Michael anymore, not with any wanting in my mind or heart,' she said vehemently. 'I haven't been using you, Harry. Even on Friday night I was confused about why I was doing what I did with you.'

She reached him and laid her hands on his chest, meeting his scouring gaze with open honesty. 'Since then, I swear I've enjoyed every minute with you, wanting to know the person you are, liking what I'm learning about you. Please don't think any of it was related to your brother.'

He frowned, not yet appeased by her outcry. 'Then why not work for Mickey?'

She grimaced at his persistence. 'Maybe I just don't want to be reminded of how silly I was. A break is better, Harry.' She slid her hands up around his neck and pressed her body to his, craving the wild warmth and excitement of his desire again. 'Can we forget about Michael now? Please?'

His eyes still scoured hers for the truth. His hands gripped her waist hard as though he was in two minds whether to pull her closer or push her away. 'He's my brother,' he said gruffly.

And Lucy was her sister, whom Michael could hurt very badly.

'Does that mean I *have* to work for him or I'll lose any interest you have in me, Harry?'

Again his brow beetled down. 'That's not the point.'

'Good! Because as much as I want what you and I are having together, I won't let any man dictate how I lead my life.'

That was a core truth.

She wanted a partner in life, not a lord and master.

Harry believed her. There was a strength in this woman that had always challenged him. As much as it had frustrated him in the past, he admired the way she made a decision and stuck to it. A warrior woman, he thought wryly, one who would fight tooth and nail for what she believed was right.

Yet she was vulnerable to the womanly needs that he'd tapped into. The wanting for him was in the soft giving of her body appealing to his, the hand-lock at the back of his neck, the slight pouting of her mouth waiting for a kiss that would blow everything else away. The challenge in her eyes burned into his brain. She was his for the taking, not Mickey's, and the compulsion to take her forced him to set all reservations aside.

He kissed her.

She kissed him back.

And Harry revelled in the sense that this was a true beginning of a relationship that promised to be more *right* than any he had known.

CHAPTER FIFTEEN

ELIZABETH managed the administration office on her own throughout her second week on Finn Island. She didn't feel lonely. There were daily meetings with Sarah and Jack Pickard and Daniel Marven. Apart from them, many of the guests dropped by to chat about what they'd done or what they planned to do while they were here. Quite a few were much-travelled tourists from other countries, who couldn't resist comparing this place to other getaways they had enjoyed, always favourably, which Elizabeth thought was a feather in Harry's cap.

He'd carried through his vision for this resort with an attention to detail that was every bit as meticulous as Michael's in his side of the business. In that respect he was just as solid as his brother. In fact, he really had none of the characteristics of a playboy who cared little for anything except indulging himself with passing pleasures.

He called her each day to check on how she was doing and they had quite long conversations that always left her smiling. Contact with him didn't make her tense anymore. They discussed many things with an ease that she thoroughly enjoyed. Even the flirtatious remarks that she'd once hated, once left her steaming with anger, now made her laugh and spread a delicious warmth through her body.

It continually amazed her how much her life had changed in such a short amount of time. Giving up the Michael dream that had been gnawing at her for so long and giving in to the attraction Harry had always exerted on her...it was as though a whole lot of inner conflict had been lifted from her. She had set aside worries about the future, letting herself be a happy butterfly. When serious issues had to be faced, she would face them. But that wasn't yet.

Emails from Lucy were full of dizzy pleasure with her love affair with Michael. According to her sister, he was everything wonderful. Still early days, Elizabeth thought, but hoped the relationship would become what both of them were looking for to complement their lives. And who knew...maybe Harry might turn out to be the right partner for her?

He returned to the island on Saturday morning, strolling into the office, a wide grin on his face, eyes sparkling with pleasure at seeing her again. Her heart jumped. Her feet jumped. She was out of her chair, wanting to skip around the desk and hurl herself at him, driven by a wild eagerness to revel in all the sexual excitement his physical presence instantly aroused in her. Only a sense of decorum held her back. Or rather a very basic female instinct to have him demonstrate his desire for her first.

Her smile, however, was an open invitation to take up where he'd left off last weekend. 'Hi!' she said in a breathy rush.

He strode forward, dumped the attaché case he was

carrying on the desk and swept her into his embrace. 'Can't wait another minute,' he said and kissed her with a hunger that ignited the same hunger in her.

It was great to feel so wanted.

What made the physical sizzle between them even better was the respect he subsequently showed for her opinion. He'd brought the résumés of the most likely prospects for the position of manager with him and wanted her input on them before deciding on interviews. This sharing on a business level made Elizabeth feel like a real partner, not just for sharing a bed.

They talked about the possibilities for most of the day, weighing up the pros and cons, deciding on who would best deal with the situation. There seemed to be a wonderful, vibrant harmony flowing between them, making their lovemaking that night extra special. It wasn't until Harry chose to query her choices that the pleasurable flow was broken.

They were lying face to face, their legs still intimately locked together. Harry softly stroked the feathery bangs off her forehead, looking deeply into her eyes. 'I'd really like you to stay on here, Ellie,' he said. 'It's not too late to change your mind.'

Her chest instantly grew tight. It was difficult to resist the seductive pressure of his words when she wanted to cling onto the sweet sense of everything being perfect. 'I can't, Harry,' she blurted out.

He frowned at her quick reply. 'You've been happy here this past week. I've heard it in your voice every time I've called. And today you've been so relaxed, confident. Why not reconsider?'

'It's better that you get someone else,' she argued.

'But I like feeling you're part of my world, Ellie. It's been great this week, sharing it with you.'

She sucked in a deep breath, needing to hold firm against the persuasive pull of a future that might mean sharing his world forever. It was too soon to know, her mind screamed, too soon to commit to the possibility. She reached up and stroked his cheek, her eyes pleading for understanding.

'I'm not rejecting you, Harry. I just need to be where Lucy is. Being on this island in a permanent position is too far away.'

He heaved a sigh, his mouth turning into a wry grimace. 'You have to be there for her.'

'Yes.'

'Well, I guess I'll just have to invade your world in Cairns.'

She relaxed at his acceptance of her decision, smiling as she said, 'I hope you do.'

Harry told himself to be content with her apparent willingness to continue their relationship once she was back in Cairns. Separating herself from both Mickey and himself professionally had niggled at him. She'd been so elusive in the past, he wasn't absolutely confident that he'd won her over into moving forward with him.

They'd certainly gone beyond a one-night stand and he no longer thought this was a rebound situation. The connection between them was too good to doubt it. Still, the fact that she was severing the work connection... Harry shook it out of his mind. There was no point in letting it throw a cold shadow over the warmth of their intimacy tonight.

He had her where he wanted her.

It was enough for now.

The call-tune on his mobile phone woke him to the dim light of dawn.

Elizabeth stirred, as well, asking, 'Who'd be wanting to contact you at this hour?'

'Don't know,' he muttered, hoping it wasn't bad trouble of some sort as he rolled out of bed and retrieved the mobile from his shorts pocket. He quickly flipped it open, held it up to his ear and spoke a terse, 'Yes?'

'Harry Finn?' asked a male voice he didn't recognise.

'Yes. Who's speaking?'

'This is Constable Colin Parker. I'm calling from the Cairns Base Hospital. I'm sorry to say your brother, Michael Finn, was involved in a serious car accident earlier this morning....'

Harry's heart stopped. Shock and fear jammed his mind for a moment, fear spearing through to force out the words, 'How serious?'

'Your brother and two teenagers are in intensive care. I can't say exactly what injuries were sustained but I'm told they are extensive. Two other teenagers...'

'He's not dead.' Relief poured through Harry. Although there was no guarantee Mickey would pull through, at least he had a chance, not like their parents.

'Who?' Elizabeth cried, alarmed by what she'd heard.

It instantly recalled the high probability that Lucy had been with Mickey—a Saturday night—out on the town. 'Was my brother alone in his car?'

Elizabeth clapped her hands to her face, her eyes wide with horror, a gasp of shock leaving her mouth open.

'Yes, he was. No passengers.'

'Lucy wasn't with him,' he swiftly assured her. 'Thank you for letting me know, Constable. I'll get to the hospital as soon as I can.'

He grabbed his clothes and headed straight for the bathroom, his mind racing over which would be the fastest way to the mainland. Calling for a helicopter, getting the pilot out of bed and to the airfield—no, he couldn't bear waiting around. Best to take the yacht back to Cairns at full throttle, be on the move. He could easily summon a car to meet him at the marina, drive him straight to the hospital, no time wasted.

You hang on, Mickey, he fiercely willed his brother.

Elizabeth had wrapped a robe around her and was pacing the bedroom floor when he emerged from the bathroom. 'How bad is it?' she shot at him, anguish in her eyes.

It made Harry think she still cared a hell of a lot for his brother, which put another savage twist in his heart.

Her hands lifted in urgent plea. 'Lucy will want to know.'

Anguish for her sister or herself? He shook his head. He didn't have time to sort this out. 'He's in intensive care. That's all the cop could tell me,' he answered. 'I have to go now, Elizabeth. Will you hold on here until… until…' He couldn't bring himself to voice whatever was going to happen.

'Of course I will,' she cried. 'I'll do anything you want me to do. Just call me. I'll stand by as long as you need me.'

Yes, Harry thought. *The one who had always carried the load. Always would. The anchor.*

He walked over to her, scooped her into a tight embrace, needing a brief blast of warmth to take some of the chill out of his bones. He rubbed his cheek over her silky hair and kissed the top of her head. 'Thank you. I'll be in touch,' he murmured, then set her aside to go to his brother.

Elizabeth was not going to leave him any day soon. Mickey might.

Elizabeth's heart bled for him as she watched him make a fast exit from her apartment. To have his parents killed in an accident and now to have his brother on the danger list from another accident…it was a wickedly unkind twist of fate.

When she had thought Lucy could be involved, too… The huge relief at hearing she wasn't made her feel guilty for being spared what Harry was going through—totally gutted with fear and anxiety. It was no empty promise that she would do anything to help. If she had the power to make everything better for him, she would. He was a good man.

So was Michael.

And Lucy would want to know that the man she loved was in hospital, possibly fighting for his life.

Where was her sister? Why hadn't she been with Michael? Had there been a bust-up between them? Questions fired through Elizabeth's mind as she used her mobile phone to make contact with her. The call tone went on for a long nerve-tearing time before it was finally cut off by Lucy's voice, sounding groggy with sleep.

Of course, it was still very early in the morning—

Sunday morning—but time didn't matter. 'Wake up, Lucy!' she said sharply. 'There's been an accident.'

'What? Is that you, Ellie?'

'Yes. Michael was injured in a car accident early this morning. He was badly hurt.'

'Michael…oh, no…no…' It was a wail of anguished protest. 'Oh, God! It's my fault!'

'How is it your fault?'

'I ate something at dinner last night that upset me. He brought me home. I was vomiting and had dreadful diarrhoea. He left me to find an all-night pharmacy, get me some medicine. I was so drained I must have drifted off to sleep. He should have come back but he's not here and… Oh, God! He went out for me, Ellie!'

'Stop that, Lucy! You didn't cause the accident and getting hysterical won't help Michael,' she said vehemently, needing to cut off the futile guilt trip. 'I take it everything was still good between you last night?'

'Yes…yes…he was so caring when I was sick. Oh, Ellie! I'll die if I lose him.'

'Then you'd better do whatever you can to make him want to live. Are you still sick? Can you get to the hospital? He's in an intensive care unit.'

'I'll get there.' Gritty determination was in her voice, hysteria gone.

'Harry was with me on the island. He's on his way. Be kind to him, Lucy. Remember he and Michael lost their parents in an accident. I have to stay here. Harry's counting on me to take care of business but I think he'll need someone there, too.'

'I understand. You love him but you can't be with him.'

Love? That was typical Lucy. Elizabeth cared about

the man and she certainly loved aspects of him, but she mentally shied from putting a boots-and-all love tag on her feelings for Harry. However, right at this moment it was easier to just let her sister think what she wanted to think.

'I need to know what's happening, Lucy. Please... will you keep me informed?'

'Sure! I'll call you with news as soon as I have it. Moving now. Over and out. Okay?'

'Okay.'

Elizabeth took a long deep breath, trying to settle some of her inner agitation. There was no more she could do about the situation, yet the need for some kind of action was twitching through her nerves. The office didn't have to be opened for hours yet. It was too early for anyone on the island to require her for anything.

She showered and dressed, then walked down to the beach, dropping onto a deckchair to simply sit and watch the sunrise, wanting to feel some peace with a world that had just changed again. Nature kept rolling on, regardless of what happened to human beings. While it could be ugly, too—cyclones, floods, droughts—this morning it had a beautiful tranquillity that soothed the turmoil in her soul.

The sea was a glittering expanse of shimmering wavelets. The sky slowly turned into a pastel panorama of pinks and lemons. The sun crept up over the horizon, shooting beams of light into the tinted clouds. It was a lovely dawning of a new day—another day that she was *alive*.

Life was precious.

More than ever Elizabeth felt a pressing need to make the most of it.

This past week with Harry had been good.

She'd felt happy with him.

Love was a big step from there but her mind and heart were opening up to the chance that Harry Finn might be the man who could and would share her life in all the ways she'd dreamed of.

CHAPTER SIXTEEN

ELIZABETH was on tenterhooks all morning waiting for news of Michael. She thought it would be Lucy who called, but it was Harry, instantly assuring her that his brother's injuries were not life-threatening as they had feared.

'He was hit on the driver's side, right arm and hip fractured, broken ribs, lacerations to the face, a lot of bruising, concussion. The doctors were worried that a broken rib had punctured his liver but that's been cleared and bones will mend.' His sigh transmitted a mountain of relief. 'He's going to be incapacitated for quite a while, but there should be no lasting damage.'

'That's good news, Harry,' Elizabeth said, her own relief pouring into her voice.

'Lucy's here. I've left her sitting beside Mickey, holding his left hand. She's certainly a surprise, your sister.'

'What do you mean?'

'He's not a pretty picture—face cut, bruised and swollen. I didn't think it was a good idea, her going in to see him. Thought she'd have hysterics or faint at the sight of him. She gave me an earbashing on how much she cared about Mickey and she was no wimp when it came to facing anyone who was suffering anything.'

Elizabeth smiled, imagining the scene. 'I told you she was good with Mum.'

'Looks like she'll be good with Mickey, too. Like Mum was with Dad. He'll need cheering up in the days to come, that's for sure. He's sedated right now. Haven't spoken to him, only to the doctors, who assure me he's out of the woods.'

'That's the important thing, Harry. Whatever the future brings, he does have a future.'

'Thank God!'

'How did the accident happen? Lucy said he'd left her to find an all-night pharmacy...'

'Drunken teenagers in a stolen car running a red light. They just slammed into him. All four of them are here in the hospital, undoubtedly ruing their stupid joy ride. I can't say I'm feeling any sympathy for them.'

Harsh words, but justified, Elizabeth thought. Nevertheless, concern for him made her ask, 'Are you okay, Harry? I know shock can hit hard and have lingering after-effects.'

He heaved another big sigh, releasing tension this time. 'I'll be fine. Got to step in for Mickey. I'll have to run the Cairns office until he can pick up the reins again. I can delegate the running of the tourist side for a while, but Mickey has always kept a very personal control of the franchises. There's no one I can hand it to.'

'I know,' she murmured understandingly, realising that his mind was racing, trying to foresee problems he had to deal with.

'I'll set up interviews with the two people we selected for the management position on the island, hopefully this week, then send the one I think is most appropriate out to you. If you'll train whomever I choose...'

'No problem,' she assured him. 'I'll get Sarah and Jack and Daniel to come on board for that, as well. We'll handle it for you, Harry. Don't worry about it. You'll have enough on your plate taking over from Michael. Just keep me informed on what's happening.'

'Will do. And thanks for...' He paused a moment, his voice gathering a husky note as he added, 'for being you, Elizabeth.'

The emotional comment brought a lump to her throat. It had been a stressful morning and she teetered on the edge of weeping now that the practicalities of the situation had been sorted out. She knew intuitively that Harry was close to breaking up, too, having held himself together to face the worst.

Having swallowed hard to clear her throat, she softly said, 'Don't be too alone in this, Harry. Anything you need to share...you can talk to me any time. Okay?'

Another pause, longer this time, making her wonder if she had stepped too far, assuming an intimacy he didn't feel with her when they weren't in bed together.

'Though I'm not into phone sex,' she blurted out.

He cracked up. Peal after peal of laughter sent her brain into a tizzy. She had no idea what it meant— a release from tension, amusement at her prudish restriction?

'Oh, Ellie! I love you,' he bubbled forth. 'I really, truly do.'

She was stunned into silence. Was this a genuine declaration or was he funning her?

'And it will kill me if you don't love me back,' he went on, slightly more soberly.

How was she to reply to that? 'Umm... Well, don't die any time soon, Harry.'

'I won't. I have too much to live for. And so do you, Ellie,' he said with conviction. 'Bye for now.'

Elizabeth didn't know what to think. In the end she decided Harry's *loving* her was simply an impulsive re-action to her helping him at a time of crisis. It was more comfortable putting it in that box than believing he was serious, because she didn't want to feel pressured about loving him back. As much as she liked him—maybe loved him—she wasn't ready to lay her heart completely on the line. It was too...*hasty.*

Harry knew he'd jumped the gun with the *love* words. They'd spilled out of him before he realised what he was saying, no consideration given to how they'd be received or interpreted and, worst of all, he couldn't *see* Elizabeth's reaction to them.

He'd spoken the truth. He knew that without any doubt now. The instinctive attraction had always been there and he'd never been able to give up on it, despite her constantly blocking it, preferring to see his brother as the more desirable man. But they were *right* together, *right* for each other. He felt it in his bones. Though he suspected she wasn't quite ready to hear or accept it.

Having given her word, she would still stand by him during this crisis. But until he was actually with her again, he'd steer clear of pouring out personal feelings. He wasn't absolutely sure that her emotions had been detached from his brother. Having sex with him—liking it, wanting it—that was certainly answering a need in her, but whether he'd won through to her heart was not certain at this point.

Patience, Harry, he cautioned himself.

Elizabeth Flippence was the woman worth keeping.

He had to convince her he was the man worth keeping.

Every day following Michael's accident, Elizabeth found herself literally hanging on calls from Cairns. She cared about Michael's progress—of course, she did—yet she grew impatient when Lucy went on endlessly about every little detail and her sympathy was sorely stretched at times. She really wanted to hear from Harry, not her sister.

Her heart always jumped when his voice came over the line and her body flooded with warm pleasure. Not once did he mention *loving* her, and despite thinking she didn't want to hear it, weirdly enough she actually did, although she was happy to simply chat with him and it felt really good to help him with problems he was encountering in Michael's office.

His confidence in her, his respect for her opinion, his desire for her input on everything, did touch her heart. Very deeply. None of her previous relationships with men had reached this level of sharing. She loved it. When he told her he was bringing his chosen candidate for manager over to the island himself at the weekend, she was thrilled at the prospect of being with him again, if only for a few hours.

He instructed her to hold a villa aside for herself from Saturday to the following Friday as the new manager would be taking over the apartment and she would probably need a week to ensure he was on top of the job. His name was David Markey and he was only twenty-eight, but he'd had experience as assistant manager at a resort on Kangaroo Island, which was down below Adelaide off the coast of South Australia. According to his résumé, he was keen to take up a position in a more tropical climate. Elizabeth had thought him a good possibility and she was glad he had interviewed well, leading Harry to choose him.

They were to arrive by helicopter on Saturday morning and the moment Elizabeth heard the distinctive noise of the rotors, her pulse started racing. She'd barely slept the night before, thinking of Harry and how it might be with him this time. It was difficult to contain the nervous excitement buzzing through her but somehow she had to keep it in check while she handled the business side of this visit.

Professionalism insisted that she couldn't run down to the back beach, waving madly like a child as the helicopter landed and flinging herself at Harry the moment he stepped out of it. Waiting in the office for the men to enter it was the right and sensible thing to do—the Elizabeth thing, she thought wryly, not the Lucy thing. But Harry was counting on her to be sensible and helpful. This was not *butterfly* time.

She'd asked Jack to meet the helicopter, introducing himself to David Markey as well as giving any help needed with luggage. While she waited, she forced herself to check through items laid out on her desk in preparation for making the job transition as easy as possible for David—a list of the current guests and the villas they occupied with a notation of activities some of them had booked today, contact numbers for the chef and the Pickards, a list of staff names under headings of housekeeping, maintenance and restaurant. It was all there waiting...waiting....

Harry led the others into the office. His vivid blue eyes connected with hers with such riveting intensity, Elizabeth was pinned to her chair while her heart rocketed around her chest. She stared back, feeling as though he was wrapping a magnetic field around her entire being, claiming her as his, tugging her towards him.

She stood. Her thighs were quivering, but her legs moved as though drawn by strings, drawn by the power of an attraction that had become totally irresistible. His smile bathed her in tingling pleasure. She was so consumed by sheer awe at the strength of feelings shooting through her, the man moving in beside Harry didn't register on her radar until her attention was directed to him.

Harry lifted his hand in an introductory wave, inclining his head towards the slightly shorter man. 'David Markey, Elizabeth.'

'Good to meet you,' the newcomer promptly said, stepping forward and extending his hand.

Elizabeth met it with her own hand, belatedly smiling a welcome. 'Likewise, David. I hope you'll be very happy working here on Finn Island.'

He was a clean-cut, good-looking young man—short brown hair, bright brown eyes with a ready smile to charm, a typical front man in the hospitality industry. 'I'm very glad to have the chance,' he said enthusiastically.

Jack had manoeuvred around the two men, wheeling two suitcases towards the door into the manager's apartment. Harry gestured towards him as he spoke to David. 'If you'll just follow Jack, he'll show you your living quarters and answer any questions you might have about them. I want a private word with Elizabeth.'

'Of course. Thank you,' was the ready reply, and taking the privacy hint, he closed the apartment door after himself.

The brief business with David had given Elizabeth enough distraction to recover from the initial impact of Harry's presence. Having regained some control of herself, she turned to him with a sympathetic smile. 'Tough week?'

'Mmm...' His eyes twinkled teasingly as he spread his arms in appeal. 'I think I need a hug.'

Her heart started racing again as she laughed and moved straight into his embrace, eager for the physical contact she had craved all week.

He hugged her tightly to him, rubbing his cheek against her hair, breathing in deeply and releasing a long, shuddering sigh before murmuring, 'There is nothing like a warm living body to make you feel better. I have so much wanted you with me this week, Ellie.'

'I wished I could have been there for you, too, Harry.'

'Can't be in two places at once,' he said wryly, tugging her head back so they were face to face. 'I'll stay here overnight if that's okay with you.'

'I was hoping you would,' she answered, openly showing that she welcomed every intimacy with him.

Desire blazed into his eyes. He lifted a hand and ran a feather-light finger over her lips. 'If I start kissing you I won't want to stop and there's no time for it now.

When Jack comes out I'll leave you with David. Sarah wants me to lunch with them, hear all the news about Mickey firsthand. You should lunch with David in the restaurant, introduce him to the guests. I'll catch up with the two of you afterwards, find out how he's doing and hopefully get you to myself for a while.'

Assured they would be together later in the afternoon, Elizabeth didn't mind seeing Harry go off with Jack, happy with the plan of action he'd laid out. She knew how fond Sarah was of both the Finn brothers, and it was nice of Harry to answer the housekeeper's concern about Michael. It was also appropriate for her to introduce David to the guests since she was known to them, having been the resident manager all week.

Over lunch, David proved to have a very pleasant manner with the guests and the restaurant staff. Elizabeth quite enjoyed his company herself. He readily answered her questions about his experience on Kangaroo Island and was keen to question her experience at this resort, garnering as much knowledge as he could as quickly as he could.

It occurred to her that it might not take a week to fill him in on everything and make sure he understood the whole working process of the island. He wasn't coming in cold to the job as she had. He was already a professional in this field. It might only take a few days and then she could get back to Cairns.

To Lucy...

To Harry...

To real life again...

Although the island *getaway* hadn't really been a getaway for her. She'd been well and truly faced with real life here—forced to accept the reality of Michael's connection with Lucy, having her misconceptions about Harry ripped apart, learning that an attraction based on sexual chemistry could gather many more levels, given the chance.

Her time here had been one of intense emotional turmoil, yet coming now to the end of it, she was ready to move forward, wanting to move forward, hopefully with Harry, who had become a very vital part of her world. No denying that. Though she was not going to spin rosy dreams about him, as she had with Michael. She would do the realistic thing and live in the moment with Harry.

The moment could not come fast enough today.

She accompanied David back to the office after lunch and they settled in front of the computer workstation to go through the booking system. It took an act of will for Elizabeth to concentrate on it. Anticipation was like a fever in her blood. She kept glancing at the wall clock, wondering how long Harry would stay with Jack and Sarah, aching for him to leave them and come for her.

It had just turned two o'clock when he entered the office, filling it with an electric energy that zapped through every nerve in Elizabeth's body.

'How's it going?' he asked.

'Fine!' Elizabeth managed to clip out.

'Fine!' echoed David.

'Well, I need to have a meeting with Elizabeth now,' Harry said, exuding the alpha male authority that had so surprised her when he'd sacked Sean Cassidy. 'After we leave, you can close the office, David. It doesn't need to be reopened until five o'clock. Take the time to settle in or stroll around, familiarising yourself with the island's attractions. We'll have dinner together this evening.' His arm beckoned commandingly. 'Elizabeth...'

'See you later, David,' she threw at him as she rose from her chair, her heart pounding with excitement at the prospect of spending at least three hours with Harry.

That gave her a lot of moments to live in...to the full.

CHAPTER SEVENTEEN

As soon as they left the office, Harry caught her hand, his long fingers intertwining with hers, gripping possessively, shooting an instant wave of tingling heat up her arm. 'Which villa is yours?' he asked.

'Number one. It's the closest to the office in case I'm needed.'

He smiled at her, his eyes twinkling admiration and approval. 'Standing by,' he said warmly.

'I don't think I'll have to stand by for long, Harry. David's very quick on the uptake.'

He nodded. 'A case of been there, done that. Do you like him?'

'Yes. I think he'll manage very well. He's at ease with the guests, too, eager to please.'

'Good!'

'I doubt he'll need me for more than a few days. When I'm satisfied he's on top of everything I'll come back to Cairns and help you in the office.' She threw him an anxious look, suddenly thinking she might have assumed too much. 'If you want me to.'

He grinned happily. 'I was going to ask if you would. Just to tide us over until Mickey can take control again. Andrew—the guy you suggested could fill in for you—

is floundering like a fish out of water under the pressure of too much responsibility. Not his bag at all. Mickey had already directed an agency to find a better replacement for you, but had yet to set up interviews.'

'I'll stay until that can be sorted out,' she promised.

'You wouldn't walk out on anyone at a bad time, would you, Ellie?'

His eyes caressed her as though she was someone very special and her heart fluttered with happiness. 'Not if I could help,' she answered, knowing intuitively that Harry wouldn't, either. He was a caring man who had looked after the people who could have been hurt by Franklyn Finn's sudden death. He hadn't walked away. Not like her father, she thought.

She didn't mind him calling her Ellie anymore. Every time he used that name she heard affection in it, and Harry's affection had become very addictive.

They mounted the steps to the villa's deck. He paused by the railing, his gaze sweeping around the bay below. 'I don't know how Mickey can stand being closed up in an office day after day.'

'He likes running the franchises,' Elizabeth pointed out. 'And since you say he has tunnel vision, I guess that's all he sees when he's there.'

'Mmm...lucky for me! I don't think I could have handled it. I'll be glad when he's back in the driving seat.' His gaze swung to target hers, the blue eyes gathering the intensity that always made her feel he was digging into her mind. 'What about you, Ellie? Have you thought of what you want to do when everything's on course again?'

She shook her head. 'I'm just taking one day at a time.'

'May I make a suggestion?'

'I'm not going to work full-time for you, Harry,' she said quickly, hoping he wouldn't try to persuade her to take up that option again. She had fallen in love with him, and while working together might be great for a while, if he lost his desire for her...

'I wasn't about to ask you to,' he said, drawing her into his embrace.

'What then?' she asked, relieved by this assurance and sliding her hands up his chest, over his shoulders and around his neck, inviting a kiss, wanting him to make love to her, craving intimate contact.

His mouth quirked teasingly. He lifted a hand and gently stroked her cheek, looking deeply into her eyes. 'I don't want you working for me, Ellie. I want you living with me. I'm suggesting that you think about marrying me. We could start a family, make a home together and hopefully live happily ever after. How does that sound?'

She was totally stunned. No way had she anticipated a marriage proposal! Her heart slammed around her chest. She stared at Harry, utterly speechless, barely able to believe what he'd just said.

The shock dilating her eyes told Harry he'd jumped the gun again. This time he didn't care. He wanted her thinking about it, wanted her knowing that he was serious about sharing his future with her. She was *the one* he'd been looking for, *the one* who would complement his life in all the ways that mattered to him. He couldn't bear her having any doubts about where she stood with him.

He had no doubts. This past week had clinched it for him. His brother was no longer a gut-tearing factor in their relationship. That had become clear in all the conversations they'd had. Caring for Mickey had not been at the heart of them. Her focus had been on him—his thoughts, his concerns, his feelings.

He wanted to banish her sense of being adrift, wanted to become *her* anchor, just as she had become his. She might not yet be ready to commit herself to marriage but he saw no harm in laying it on the line. Her mind was clearly rocked at the moment but he didn't sense any negative vibrations coming from her.

'Think about it, Ellie,' he softly commanded, then kissed her.

Elizabeth didn't want to think. She wanted to feel all that Harry made her feel. She threw herself into the kiss, hungry for the wild rush of passion between them—the passion that swept away everything else but the fierce need for each other. It surged through her bloodstream. Her body ached for him, yearned for him, silently but intensely communicating more than she could say.

Harry didn't push for any verbal answer from her. He swept her into the villa and they tore off their clothes, reaching for each other, desire at fever pitch, falling onto the bed, moving urgently to come together. She grasped him with her hands, her legs. He kissed her as the strong shaft of his flesh slid into the pulsating passage that exultantly welcomed their joining. The sheer bliss of it spread through her entire body.

Her mind sang his name...Harry, Harry, Harry....

They rode the waves of pleasure together, driving up the intensity of feeling, instinctively intent on making it more sensational than it had ever been because it was more than physical this time. Much more. Her heart was beating with love for this man, bursting with it as they both climaxed, tipping them over into a world that was uniquely theirs, an intimate sharing that Elizabeth now knew with absolute certainty she would never find with any other man.

It was only a few weeks since she had dreamed of having this with Michael. It seemed weird that in such a short time Harry had so completely supplanted his brother in every sense, but he had. And this was *real*, not a fantasy. She hugged him to her, wanting this *reality* to go on forever.

She thought of Lucy.

Did her sister feel as deeply as this with Michael?

She heaved a sigh, knowing that whatever happened in that relationship was beyond her control.

Harry planted a warm kiss on her forehead. 'Is that a sigh of satisfaction?' he murmured.

'I do love you, Harry,' she said, opening up to him. 'It may seem like an incredible turnaround, but it's true.'

He eased away enough to prop himself up on his elbow and look into her eyes. A smile slowly curved his mouth. 'I love you, too. We're right for each other, Ellie. I know you'll stand by me in all the years to come and I hope you know I'll stand by you.'

'Yes...yes, I do,' she said with certainty.

'So...will you marry me?'

She wanted to.

Lucy would want her to, regardless of what happened with her and Michael. She'd told her so, saying quite vehemently that she didn't want to be the reason for Elizabeth not to have a future with Harry.

Her long hesitation prompted him to ask, 'What reservation do you have in your mind?'

'Will you be kind to Lucy if she and Michael break up?'

It was important to her. She couldn't brush that possibility aside as though it wouldn't count in the future.

He frowned, obviously puzzled that she should be concerned about this. 'Of course I will, Ellie. She's your sister.'

'And Michael's your brother,' she reminded him. 'We could have divided loyalties, Harry.'

'We'll work it out,' he said without hesitation. 'I know Mickey would never interfere with what makes me happy and I bet Lucy would hate feeling she was any kind of block to your having a happy life with me. Am I right about that?'

'Yes,' she conceded, remembering how accurately Harry could read people.

'Then we don't have a problem,' he argued. 'They might not end up together but that won't break our family ties, Ellie. They will both wish us well.'

Yes, she could believe that. It shouldn't be too much of a problem.

'Ellie, we only have one life to live,' Harry pressed on, the intensity back in his eyes. 'We've found each other. Let's not waste time we could have together. You never know when it will be taken away from us.'

Like it had been with his parents.

Like what had almost happened to Michael.

'You're right,' she said, all doubts blown away. 'We should get married. Start having a family. I'm thirty, you know.'

His face broke into a wide grin. 'Yes, I know. And it was the best birthday of all because it brought you to me.'

She laughed, her eyes happily teasing. 'Not very willingly.'

'It was only a matter of time,' he said with arrogant smugness.

She heaved a contented sigh before challenging him one last time, her eyes dancing flirtatiously. 'Well, you're not going to waste any of it, are you? I have to be back at the office…'

His mouth silenced hers.

Her body revelled in having this man.

Her mind was at peace.

She loved Harry Finn and he loved her.

Whatever future they had together they would make the most of it, always being there for each other. That was how it should be and it was going to happen. She and Harry would make it happen because they both wanted it. Everything felt right.

It *was* right.

* * * * *

THE CEO'S
BABY SURPRISE

HELEN LACEY

For my mother, Evelyn.

Who believes in me no matter what.

Prologue

Mary-Jayne Preston yawned, opened her eyes and blinked a few times. The ceiling spun fractionally, and she drew in a soft breath.

I'm not hungover.

She closed her eyes again. The two glasses of champagne she'd drunk the night before weren't responsible for the way she felt. This was something else. An unusual lethargy crept into her limbs and spread across her skin. Her lids fluttered, and she glimpsed a sliver of light from between heavy drapes.

An unfamiliar room.

Her memory kicked in. The Sandwhisper Resort. Port Douglas.

But this isn't my bedroom.

This was a villa suite. And a top-end one, judging by the plush feel of the giant king-size bed and lavish damask drapes. Extravagance personified. Her eyelids drooped before opening again as she stretched her spine—and then nearly jumped out of her skin when she realized she wasn't alone in the big bed.

A man lay beside her. She twisted her head and saw a long, perfectly proportioned back. Smooth skin, like the sheerest satin stretched over pressed steel, broad shoulders, strong arms and dark hair. He lay on his stomach, one arm flung above his head, the other curved by his side. And he was asleep. The soft rhythm of his breathing was oddly hypnotic, and she stared at him, suddenly mesmerized by his bronzed skin and lean, muscular frame.

And then, in stunning Technicolor, it came rushing back.

The party.

The kiss.

The one-night stand.

Her first. Her *last*.

She needed to get up. To *think*. She shimmied sideways but quickly stopped moving when he stirred. She wasn't quite ready for any kind of face-to-face, morning-after awkwardness. Not with *him*. She took a deep breath and tried again, inching her hips across the cool sheet so slowly it was agonizing. Finally one leg found the edge of the mattress and she pushed the cover back. He moved again and she stilled instantly. He made a sound, half groan, half moan, and flipped around, the sheet draping haphazardly over his hips as he came to face her.

But still asleep.

Mary-Jayne's breath shuddered out as she caught sight of his profile. He was ridiculously handsome. No wonder she'd lost her head. The straight nose, chiseled cheeks and square jaw was a riveting combination. And she quickly recalled those silver-gray eyes of his…just too sexy for words. As her gaze traveled lower her fingertips tingled.

His body was incredibly well cut, and she fought the urge to touch him just one more time. She spotted a faint mark on his shoulder. Like a love bite.

Did I do that?

Heat surged through her blood when she remembered what they'd done the night before, and again in the small hours of the morning. No sweet wonder her muscles ached and her skin seemed ultrasensitive. She'd never had a night like it before, never felt such intense desire or experienced such acute and mindboggling pleasure.

It was like a dream. A fantasy.

And she needed to wake up from this particular dream. Quickly.

She managed to ease off the bed and quickly looked around for her clothes. Her underwear was by the bed, and she snatched it up with guilty fingers and then quickly dressed into the thong and bra. The shoes were easily spotted—one was by the window, the other under a chair in the corner of the room. But the black dress was nowhere to be seen. The smooth fabric had clung to her curves, and the man in the bed had told her how beautiful and desirable she'd looked. No one had ever said those words quite that way to her before. She found her purse on the chair and continued looking for the dress, keeping a mindful eye on him.

Please don't wake up...

He didn't, thankfully, and a few moments later she found the dress, scrunched in a ball and hidden beneath the quilt that had fallen to the foot of the bed. She stepped into it and slipped it up and over her hips, settling her arms through the bodice before she twisted herself into a pretzel to do up the zipper. Breathless, she cast another look toward the sleeping man.

I'm such a fool...

For weeks she'd stayed resolute, determined to avoid crashing into bed with him. But the moment he'd touched her, the moment he'd made his move she'd melted like an ice cube in hell.

Mary-Jayne pushed her feet into her patent pumps, grabbed her purse and ran.

Chapter One

*P**regnant.*

Not a bout of food poisoning as she'd wanted to believe.

Mary-Jayne walked from the doctor's office and headed for her car. Her head hurt. Her feet hurt. Everything hurt. The snap on her jeans felt tight around her waist. Now she knew why.

She was three months and three weeks pregnant.

She opened the door of the borrowed Honda Civic and got inside. Then she placed a hand over her belly and let out a long, heavy breath.

Twenty-seven. Single. Pregnant.

Right.

Not exactly the end of the world…but not what she'd been expecting, either.

One day she'd imagined she'd have a baby. When she was married and settled, not while she was trying to carve out a career as a jewelry designer and wasn't exactly financially stable.

She thought about calling her older sisters, Evie and Grace, but quickly shrugged off the idea. She needed time to think. Plan. Sort out what she was going to do, before she told anyone. Especially her sisters, who'd want to know *everything*.

She'd have to tell them about that night.

She gripped the steering wheel and let out a long, weary sigh. She'd tried to put the memory from her mind countless times. And failed. Every time she walked around the grounds of the Sandwhisper Resort she was reminded. And every time she fielded a telephone call from *him* she was thrust back to that crazy night.

Mary-Jayne drove through the gates of the resort and took a left down the road that led to the employees' residences. Her villa was small but well appointed and opened onto the deck and to the huge heated pool and spa area. The Sandwhisper Resort was one of the largest in Port Douglas, and certainly one of the most luxurious. The town of Port Douglas was about forty miles north of Cairns, and its population of over three thousand often doubled during peak vacation times. Living and working at the luxurious resort for the past four and half months hadn't exactly been a hardship. Running her friend Audrey's boutique was mostly enjoyable and gave her the opportunity to create and showcase her own jewelry. Life was a breeze.

Correction.

Life *had* been a breeze.

Until she'd had an uncharacteristic one-night stand with Daniel Anderson.

CEO of Anderson Holdings and heir apparent to the huge fortune that had been made by his grandfather from ore and copper mining years earlier, he owned the Sandwhisper Resort with his two brothers. There were four other resorts around the globe—one in Phuket, another along the Amalfi coast in Italy, another in the Maldives and the flagship resort in the San Francisco Bay Area.

He was rich, successful, uptight and absurdly arrogant. Everything she'd always abhorred in a man.

He was also reported to be kind, generous and honest. Well…according to his grandmother.

Eighty-year-old Solana Anderson adored her grandsons and spent her retirement flying between the east and west coasts of Australia and America, living at the resorts during the spring and summer months in alternating time zones. Mary-Jayne liked the older woman very much. They'd met the first day she'd arrived at the resort after the desperate emergency call from her old school friend Audrey had sent her flying up to Port Douglas with barely a packed suitcase. Audrey had moved into Mary-Jayne's small house in Crystal Point so she could be close to her ill mother while Mary-Jayne moved into Audrey's condo at the resort. Once she was in residence, she read the scribbled note with instructions her friend had left and opened the boutique at an unrespectable eleven o'clock. It was meant to be a temporary gig—but Audrey insisted her mother needed her. So her planned three weeks ended up being for six months.

And Solana, straight backed and still vibrant at nearly eighty years of age, had come into the store looking for an outfit to wear to her upcoming birthday party, and within the hour they were chatting and laughing over herbal tea and several outfit changes. It was then she learned that Solana's American-born husband had died a decade earlier and how she'd borne him a son and daughter. Mary-Jayne had listened while Solana talked about her much-loved grandsons, Daniel, Blake and Caleb and granddaughter Renee. One hour ticked over into two, and by three o'clock the older woman had finally decided upon an outfit and persuaded Mary-Jayne to let her see some of her hand-crafted jewelry pieces. Solana had since bought three items and had recommended Mary-Jayne's work to several of her friends.

Yes, she liked Solana. But wasn't about to tell the other woman she was carrying her great-grandchild. Not until she figured out what she was going to do. She was nearly four months along, and her pregnancy would be showing itself very soon. She couldn't hide her growing stomach behind baggy clothes forever.

He has a right to know...

The notion niggled at her over and over.

She could have the baby alone. Women did it all the time. And it was not as if she and Daniel had any kind of relationship. If she wanted, she could leave the resort and go home and never see him again. He lived mostly in San Francisco. She lived in Crystal Point, a small seaside town that sat at the southernmost point of the Great Barrier Reef. They had different lives. Different worlds.

And she didn't even like him.

She'd met him three times before the night of Solana's birthday. The first time she'd been in the store window, bent over and struggling to remove a garment from the mannequin. When she was done she'd straightened, turned to avoid knocking the mannequin over and came face-to-face with him on the other side of the glass. He'd been watching her, arms crossed.

Of course she'd known immediately who he was. There were several pictures of him and his brothers in Solana's villa, and she'd visited the older woman many times. Plus, he looked enough like his younger brother Caleb for her to recognize the family resemblance. Caleb ran the resorts in Port Douglas and Phuket while his twin Blake looked after Amalfi, Maldives and San Francisco. And according to staff gossip Daniel lorded over the resorts, his brothers and the staff from his private jet.

Still, it was hard not to be impressed by his ridiculous good looks, and despite the fact he was not her type, Mary-Jayne was as susceptible as the next woman. The impeccably cut suit, creaseless white shirt and dark tie were a riveting combination on his broad, tall frame, and for a second she'd been rooted to the spot, unable to move, unable to do anything other than stare back, held captive by the look in his gray eyes. For a moment, at least. Until he'd raised one brow and a tiny smile whispered along the edges of his mouth. He'd then looked her over with a kind of leisurely conceit that had quickly sent alarm bells clanging in her head.

There'd been interest in his expression and if he'd been anyone else she might have made some kind of encouraging gesture. Like a smile. Or nod. But Daniel Anderson was out of her league. A rich and successful corporate shark with a reputation for having no tolerance for fools in business, and no proclivity for commitment in his private life. He was the kind of man she'd always planned to avoid like the plague. The kind of man that had never interested her before.

But something had passed between them in that first moment. A look... Recognition.

Awareness...

Heat...

Attraction...

When her good sense had returned she'd darted from the window and got back to the customer waiting in the changing room. By the time she'd moved back to the front of the store and began ringing up the sale he was gone.

Mary-Jayne saw him a day later, striding across the resort foyer with his brother at his side. She'd been coming from the day spa, arms loaded with jewelry trays, when Caleb had said her name. She'd met the younger Anderson many times over the previous weeks. He was rich, charming and handsome and didn't do a solitary thing to her libido. Not so his older brother. She'd fumbled with the trays and stayed rooted to the spot as they approached and then managed to nod her way through an introduction. He was unsmiling, but his eyes regarded her with blistering intensity. Caleb's attention had quickly been diverted by the day-shift concierge and she'd been left alone with him, silent and nervous beneath his unfaltering gaze.

Then he'd spoken, and his deep voice, a smooth mix of his American upbringing and Australian roots, wound up her spine like liquid silk. "My grandmother tells me you're here for six months rather than the few weeks you'd originally planned on?"

He'd talked about her with Solana? "Ah, that's right," she'd croaked.

"And are you enjoying your time here?"

She'd nodded, feeling stupid and awkward and not in the least bit like her usual self. Normally she was confident and opinionated and more than comfortable in her own skin. But two seconds around Daniel Anderson and she was a speechless fool. Übergood looks had never interested her before. But he stirred her senses big time.

"Yes, very much."

"And I trust your friend's parent's health is improving?"

He knew about Audrey's mother? Solana *had* been busy sharing information.

"A little...yes."

A small smile had crinkled the corner of his mouth and Mary-Jayne's gaze had instantly been drawn to his lips. He had seen her reaction and his smile had increased fractionally. There was something extraordinarily hypnotic about him, something she couldn't quite fathom. Something she'd known she had to extricate herself from...and fast.

She'd hastily excused herself and taken off as fast as she could.

And hadn't seen him again for two days.

She'd left the resort for a run along the beach and had come upon him jogging in the other direction. He'd slowed when he was about twenty feet from her and come to a halt right next to her. And the look between them had been electric. Out of this world and all-consuming. She'd never experienced such blatant and blistering physical attraction for anyone before. And it shocked her to the core. He wasn't her usual type. In fact, Daniel Anderson was the epitome of everything she *didn't* want in a man. Money, power, arrogance... They were attributes her small-town, middle-class self had decided long ago were not for her. She dated musicians and out-of-work artists. Not corporate sharks.

His expression had been unwavering and contained hot sexual appreciation. He wanted her. No doubt about it. And the look in his eyes had made it clear he thought he'd get her.

"You know," he'd said with a kind of arrogant confidence that made her tremble. "My villa is only minutes away."

She knew that. The family's quarters were secluded and luxurious and away from the main part of the resort and had a spectacular view of the beach.

"And?" she'd managed to say, despite the way her heart had thundered behind her ribs and her knees wobbled.

He'd half smiled. "And we both know that's where we're going to end up at some point."

Mortified, she'd quickly taken off like a bullet. But her body was thrumming with a kind of intoxicating aware-

ness that stayed with her for hours. For days. Until she'd
seen him again two days later at Solana's birthday party.
The older woman had insisted she attend the celebration
and Mary-Jayne respected Solana too much to refuse the
invitation. She'd ditched her usual multicolored skirts and
long tops and rummaged through Audrey's wardrobe for
a party dress. And she'd found one—a slip of silky black
jersey that clung to her like a second skin. The huge ball-
room was easy to get lost in...or so she'd thought. But it
had only taken ten minutes until she'd felt him watching
her from across the room. He'd approached and asked if
she wanted a drink. Within half an hour they had been out
on the balcony, talking intimately. Seconds later they'd
been kissing madly. Minutes later they'd been in his villa
tearing each other's clothes off.

But Mary-Jayne wasn't under any illusions.

She knew enough about Daniel Anderson to realize she
was simply another notch on his bedpost. He was handsome, successful and wealthy and played the field merci-
lessly. Something he had done without compunction since
the death of his wife and unborn child four years earlier.
He certainly wouldn't be interested in her for anything
other than a one-night stand. She wasn't his type. Oh, he'd
knocked on the door of her villa the day after Solana's
party and asked her out. But she'd shut him down. She'd
piqued his interest for a moment and that was all. Thankfully, he'd left the resort the following day and returned
to San Francisco, exactly as she'd hoped. But she hadn't
expected that he'd call the store two weeks later and an-
nounce that he wanted to see her again when he returned
from California.

See her?

Yeah...right. The only thing he wanted to see was her
naked body between the sheets. And she knew that for a

man like Daniel Anderson, the chase was all that mattered.
She'd refused him, and that was like pouring oil onto a fire.

When he'd called her again two weeks later she'd been
in South Dakota for a friend's wedding. Annoyed that he
wouldn't take the hint and all out of patience, she'd lost
her temper and told him to go to hell. Then she'd returned
to the Sandwhisper Resort and waited. Waited for another
call. Waited for him to arrive at the resort and confuse and
seduce her with his steely-eyed gaze and uncompromis-
ing intensity. But he hadn't called. And hadn't returned.
As one week slipped into another, Mary-Jayne had slowly
relaxed and convinced herself he'd lost interest.

Which was exactly what she wanted.

Only now, the tables had turned. She was having his
baby. Which meant one thing—she'd have to see him and
tell him she was having his baby. And soon.

Daniel had struggled with the remnants of a headache
for two days. The three other suits in the conference room
were grating on his nerves. Some days he wanted nothing
more than to throw off the shackles of his name, his legacy
and everything else and live a simple, quiet life.

Like today.

Because it was his birthday. He was turning thirty-four
years old. He had money and power and a successful business at his command. He had apartments in San Francisco,
another in London and then there was the family-owned
hilltop chateau in France that he hadn't been near for over
four years. He also had any number of women willing to
warm his bed with minimal notice and who understood
he didn't want commitment or anything resembling a serious relationship. He traveled the world but rarely saw
anything other than the walls of boardrooms and offices

at the resorts he'd helped build into some of the most successful around the globe. Nothing and no one touched him.

Well…except for Mary-Jayne Preston.

She was a thorn in his side. A stone in his shoe. A pain in his neck.

Months after that one crazy night in Port Douglas and he was still thinking about her. She was incredibly beautiful. Her green eyes were luminous; her lips were full and endlessly kissable. But it was her hair that had first captured his attention that day in the store window. She had masses of dark curls that hung down past her shoulders. And of course there were her lovely curves, which she possessed in all the right places.

He'd checked out her history and discovered she came from a middle-class family in Crystal Point, had studied at a local technical college and had an online business selling her handcrafted jewelry. She rented her home, owned a dog, volunteered at a number of animal shelters, had strong opinions about the environment and politics and liked to dress in colorful skirts or jeans with holes in the knees. She had piercings in her ears and navel and a butterfly tattoo on one shoulder.

She wasn't his type. Not by a long shot.

Which didn't make one ounce of difference to the relentless effect she had on him whenever she was within a twenty-foot radius. And the night of his grandmother's birthday party he'd almost tripped over his own feet when he'd caught a glimpse of her across the room. She'd looked incredible in a dress that highlighted every dip and curve of her body. And with her dark hair cascading down her back in a wave he just about had to cleave his tongue from the roof of his mouth. She looked hot. Gorgeous. Desirable.

And he knew then he wanted to get her in his bed.

It took half an hour to get her alone. Then he'd kissed her. And she'd kissed him back.

And before either of them had a chance to come up for air they were in his villa suite, tearing off clothes with little finesse and more eagerness than he'd felt in years. It had been a hot, wild night, compounded by months of abstinence and the fact he'd had Mary-Jayne Preston very much on his mind since the first time he'd seen her.

"Are you listening?"

Daniel shook off his thoughts and glanced to his left. Blake was staring at him, one brow cocked. "Always."

Blake didn't look convinced and quickly turned his attention to the other suits in the room. After a few more minutes, he dismissed the two other men, and once they were alone his brother moved to the bar and grabbed two imported beers from the fridge.

Daniel frowned. "A little early, don't you think?"

Blake flicked the tops off the bottles and shrugged. "It's after three. And you look as if you need it."

He didn't disagree, and stretched back in his leather chair. "Maybe I do."

Blake passed him a beer and grabbed a seat. "Happy birthday," his brother said, and clinked the bottle necks.

"Thanks," he said but didn't take a drink. The last thing he wanted to do was add alcohol to the remainders of a blinding headache.

His brother, who was probably the most intuitive person he'd ever known, looked at him as if he knew exactly what he was thinking. "You know, you should go home."

"I live *here*, remember?"

Blake shook his head. "I meant *home*...not here. Port Douglas."

Except Port Douglas didn't feel any more like home than San Francisco, Phuket or Amalfi.

Nowhere did. Not since Simone had died. The bay-side condo they'd bought still sat empty, and he lived in a villa at the San Francisco resort when he wasn't at any of the other four locations. He'd been born in Australia and moved to California when he was two years old. The San Francisco resort was the first, which made it home, even though he'd spent most of his adult life shifting between the two countries.

He scowled. "I can't do that right now."

"Why not?" Blake shot back. "Caleb's got the Phuket renovation under control. Things are sweet here in San Francisco." His brother grinned. "You're not really needed. CEOs are kind of superfluous to the running of a company anyhow. We all knew that when Gramps was at the helm."

"Superfluous?"

Blake's grin widened. "Yeah…like the foam on the top of an espresso to go… You know, there but not really nec-essary."

"You're an ass."

His brother's grin turned into a chuckle. "All I'm say-ing is that you haven't taken a real break from this gig for years. Not even when…"

Not even when Simone died.

Four years, four months and three weeks ago. Give or take a day. She'd been driving back from a doctor's ap-pointment and had stopped at the mall for some shopping. The brakes on a car traveling in the opposite direction had failed. Simone had suffered terrible injuries and died an hour later in hospital. So had the baby she carried. He'd lost his wife and unborn daughter because of a broken brake line. "I'm fine," he said, and tasted the lie on his tongue.

"I'm pretty sure you're not," Blake said, more serious. "And something's been bugging you the past few months."

Something. Someone. *Green eyes... Black curling hair... Red lips...*

Daniel drank some beer. "You're imagining things. And stop fretting. You're turning into your mother."

His brother laughed loudly. They both knew that Blake was more like their father, Miles, than any of them. Daniel's mother had died of a massive brain hemorrhage barely hours after his birth, and their father had married Bernadette two years later. Within six months the twins, Blake and Caleb, were born. Bernie was a nice woman and had always treated him like her own, and wasn't as vague and hopeless as their father. Business acumen and ambition had skipped a generation, and now Miles spent his time painting and sculpting and living on their small hobby farm an hour west of Port Douglas.

Daniel finished the beer and placed the bottle on the table. "I don't need a vacation."

"Sure you do," Blake replied. "If you don't want to go to Australia, take a break somewhere else. Maybe Fiji? Or what about using that damned mausoleum that sits on that hill just outside Paris? Take some time off, relax, get laid," his brother said, and grinned again. "Recharge like us regular folk have to do every now and then."

"You're as tied to this business as I am."

"Yeah," his brother agreed. "But I know when to quit. I've got my cabin in the woods, remember?"

Blake's *cabin* was a sprawling Western red cedar house nestled on forty hectares he'd bought in small town Colorado a few years back. Daniel had visited once, hated the cold and being snowbound for days on end and decided that a warm climate was more his thing.

"I don't need a—"

"Then, how about you think about what the rest of us need?" Blake said firmly. "Or what Caleb and I need, which isn't you breathing down our necks looking for things we're doing wrong because you're so damned bored and frustrated that you can't get out your own way. Basically, *I* need a break. So go home and get whatever's bugging you out of your system and spend some time with Solana. You know you've always been her favorite."

Daniel looked at his brother. Had he done that? Had he become an overzealous, critical jerk looking for fault in everything and everyone? And bored? Was that what he was? He did miss Solana. He hadn't seen his grandmother since her birthday weekend. And it was excuse enough to see Mary-Jayne again—and get her out of his system once and for all.

He half smiled. "Okay."

Chapter Two

"Everything all right?"

Mary-Jayne nodded and looked up from the plate of food she'd been pretending to give way too much attention. "Fine."

"Are you still feeling unwell?" Solana asked. "You never did tell me what the doctor said."

"Just a twenty-four-hour bug," she replied vaguely. "And I feel fine now."

Solana didn't look convinced. "You're still pale. Is that ex-boyfriend of yours giving you grief?"

The *ex-boyfriend*. The one she'd made up to avoid any nosy questions about what was becoming her rapidly expanding middle. The ex-boyfriend she'd say was the father of her baby until she summoned the nerve to tell Solana she was carrying her grandson's child. Raised to have a solid moral compass, she was torn between believing the father of her baby had a right to know, and the fear that telling him would change everything. She was carrying Solana's great-grandchild. An Anderson heir. Nothing would be the same.

Of course, she had no illusions. Daniel Anderson was not a man looking for commitment or a family. Solana had told her enough about him, from his closed-off heart to his rumored no-strings relationships. He'd lost the love of his life and unborn child and had no interest in replacing, either.

Not that she was interested in him in *that* way. She didn't like him at all. He was arrogant and opinionated and as cold as a Popsicle. Oh, she'd certainly been swept away that one night. But one night of hot and heavy sex didn't make them *anything*.

Still…they'd made a baby together, and as prepared as she was to raise her child alone, common courtesy made it very clear to her that she had to tell him. And soon. Before Solana or anyone else worked out that she was pregnant.

She had another two weeks at the store before Audrey returned, and once that was done, Mary-Jayne intended returning to Crystal Point to regroup and figure out how to tell Daniel he was about to become a father.

"I'm going to miss you when you leave," Solana said and smiled. "I've grown very fond of our talks."

So had Mary-Jayne. She'd become increasingly attached to the other woman over the past few months, and they lunched together at least twice a week. And Solana had been incredibly supportive of her jewelry designing and had even offered to finance her work and help expand the range into several well-known stores around the country. Of course Mary-Jayne had declined the offer. Solana was a generous woman, but she'd never take advantage of their friendship in such a way…good business or not.

"We'll keep in touch," Mary-Jayne assured her and ignored the nausea scratching at her throat. Her appetite had been out of whack for weeks and the sick feeling still hadn't abated even though she was into her second trimester. Her doctor told her not to worry about it and assured her that her appetite would return, and had put her on a series of vitamins. But most days the idea of food before three in the afternoon was unimaginable.

"Yes, we must," Solana said warmly. "Knowing you has made me not miss Renee quite so much," she said of her granddaughter, who resided in London. "Of course, I get to see Caleb while I'm here and Blake when I'm in San Francisco. And Daniel when he's done looking after things and flying in between resorts. But sometimes I wish for those days when they were kids and not spread all over the world." The older woman put down her cutlery and sighed. "Listen to me, babbling on, when you must miss your own family very much."

"I do," she admitted. "I'm really close to my sisters and brother and I miss my parents a lot."

"Naturally." Solana's eyed sparkled. "Family is everything."

Mary-Jayne swallowed the lump of emotion in her throat, like she'd done countless times over the past few months. Her hormones were running riot, and with her body behaving erratically, it was getting harder to keep her feelings under wraps. One thing she did know—she wanted her baby. As unplanned as it was, as challenging as it might be being a single mother, she had developed a strong and soul-reaching love for the child in her womb.

Family is everything...

It was. She knew that. She'd been raised by wonderful parents and loved her siblings dearly. Her baby would be enveloped in that love. She *could* go home, and Daniel need never know about her pregnancy. She'd considered it. Dreamed of it.

Except...

It would be wrong. Dishonest. And wholly unfair.

"I should very much like to visit your little town one day," Solana said cheerfully.

Crystal Point. It was a tiny seaside community of eight hundred people. From the pristine beaches to the rich soil of the surrounding farmlands, it would always be home, no matter where life took her.

"I'd like that, too," she said, and pushed her plate aside.

"Not hungry?" Solana asked, her keen light gray eyes watching everything she did.

Mary-Jayne shrugged. "Not really. But it is delicious," she said of the warm mango salad on her plate. "I'm not much use in the kitchen, so our lunches are always a nice change from the grilled-cheese sandwich I'd usually have."

Solana grinned. "Didn't your mother teach you to cook?"

"She tried, but I was something of a tomboy when I was young and more interested in helping my dad in his workshop," she explained.

"Well, those skills can come in handy, too."

Mary-Jayne nodded. "For sure. I can fix a leaking tap and build a bookcase...but a cheese toastie is about my limit in the kitchen."

"Well, you'll just have to find yourself a husband who can cook," Solana suggested, smiling broadly.

"I'm not really in the market for a husband." *Not since I got knocked up by your grandson...*

Solana smiled. "Nonsense. Everyone is looking for a soul mate...even a girl as independent and free-spirited as you."

Mary-Jayne nodded vaguely. Independent and free-spirited? It was exactly how she appeared to the world. And exactly how she liked it. But for the most part, it was a charade. A facade to fool everyone into thinking she had it all together—that she was strong and self-sufficient and happy-go-lucky. She'd left home at seventeen determined to prove she could make it on her own, and had spent ten years treading water in the hope no one noticed she was just getting by—both financially and emotionally. Her family loved her, no doubt about it. As the youngest child she was indulged and allowed to do whatever she liked, mostly without consequence. Her role as the lovable but unreliable flake in the Preston family had been set from a young age. While her older brother, Noah, took over the family business, perennial earth-mother Evie married young and pursued her art, and übersmart Grace headed for a career in New York before she returned to Australia to marry the man she loved.

But for Mary-Jayne there were no such expectations, and no traditional career. She'd gotten her first piercing at fourteen and had a tattoo by the time she was fifteen. When school was over she'd found a job as a cashier in a supermarket and a month later moved out of her parents' home and into a partly furnished cottage three streets away. She'd packed whatever she could fit into her battered Volkswagen and began her adult life away from the low expectations of her family. She never doubted their love... but sometimes she wished they expected more of her. Then perhaps she would have had more ambition, more focus.

Mary-Jayne pushed back her chair and stood up. "I'll take the dishes to the kitchen."

"Thank you. You're a sweet girl, Mary-Jayne," Solana said, and collected up the cutlery. "You know, I was just telling Caleb that very thing yesterday."

It was another not-so-subtle attempt to play match-maker.

Solana had somehow got it in her head that her younger grandson would be a good match for her. And the irony wasn't lost on Mary-Jayne. She liked Caleb. He was friendly and charming and came into the store every couple of days and asked how things were going, and always politely inquired after Audrey. The resort staff all respected him, and he clearly ran a tight ship.

But he didn't so much as cause a blip on her radar.

Unlike Daniel. He was the blip of the century.

Mary-Jayne ignored Solana's words, collected the dishes and headed for the kitchen. Once there she took a deep breath and settled her hips against the countertop. Her stomach was still queasy, and she took a few deep breaths before she turned toward the sink and decided to make a start on the dishes. She filled the sink and was about to plunge her hands into the water when she heard a decisive knock on the front door, and then seconds later the low sound of voices. Solana had a visitor. Mary-Jayne finished the washing up, dried her hands and headed for the door.

And then stopped in her tracks.

Even though his back was to her she recognized Daniel Anderson immediately. The dark chinos and white shirt fitted him as though they'd been specifically tailored for his broad, well-cut frame. She knew those shoulders and every other part of him because the memory of the night they'd spent together was etched into her brain, and the result was the child growing inside her.

Perhaps he'd tracked her down to confront her? Maybe he knew?

Impossible.

No one knew she was pregnant. It was a coincidence. He'd forgotten all about her. He hadn't called since she'd told him to go to hell. He'd returned to see his grand-mother. Mary-Jayne's hand moved to her belly, and she puffed out the smock-style shirt she wore. If she kept her arms to her sides and kept her clothing as loose as possible it was unlikely he'd notice her little baby bump. She lingered by the doorway, her mind racing at a trillion miles an hour.

Solana was clearly delighted to see him and hugged him twice in succession. "What a wonderful surprise," his grandmother said. "Why didn't you tell me you were coming?"

"Then it's not a surprise," he replied. "Is it?"

As they chatted Mary-Jayne moved back behind the architrave and considered her options. Come clean? Act nonchalant? Make a run for it? Running for it appealed most. This wasn't the time or place to make any kind of announcement about being pregnant, not with Solana in the room. She needed time to think. Prepare.

I have to get out of here.

The back door was through the kitchen and off the dining room. But if she sneaked out through the back Solana would want to know why. There would be questions. From Solana. And then from Daniel.

"Show some backbone," she muttered to herself.

She'd always had gumption. Now wasn't the time to ditch her usual resolve and act like a frightened little girl. Mary-Jayne was about to push back her shoulders and face the music when an unwelcome and unexpected wave of nausea rose up and made her suddenly forget everything else. She put a hand to her chest, heaved and swallowed hard, fighting the awful feeling with every ounce of will-power she possessed.

And failed.

She rushed forward to the closest exit, racing past Solana and *him* and headed across the room and out to the patio, just making it to the garden in time.

Where she threw up in spectacular and humiliating fashion.

Daniel remained where he was and watched as his grandmother hurried through the doorway and quickly attended to the still-vomiting woman who was bent over in the garden. If he thought he was needed Daniel would have helped, but he was pretty sure she would much prefer his grandmother coming to her aid.

After several minutes both women came back through the door. Mary-Jayne didn't look at him. Didn't even acknowledge he was there as she walked to the front door and let herself out, head bowed, arms rigid at her sides. But he was rattled seeing her. And silently cursed himself for having so little control over the effect she had on him.

"The poor thing," his grandmother said, hovering in the doorway before she finally closed the door. "She's been unwell for weeks. Ex-boyfriend trouble, too, I think. Not that she's said much to me about it...but I think there's been someone in the picture."

Boyfriend?

His gut twinged. "Does she need a doctor?" he asked, matter-of-fact.

"I don't think so," his grandmother replied. "Probably just a twenty-four-hour bug."

Daniel ignored the twitch of concern. Mary-Jayne had a way of making him feel a whole lot of things he didn't want or need. Attraction aside, she invaded his thoughts when he least expected it. She needled his subconscious. Like she had when he'd been on a date a couple of weeks back. He'd gone out with the tall leggy blonde he'd met at a business dinner, thinking she'd be a distraction. And spent the evening wishing he'd been with someone who would at least occasionally disagree and not be totally compliant to his whims. Someone like Mary-Jayne Preston. He'd ended up saying good-night to his date by nine o'clock, barely kissing her hand when he dropped her home. Sure, he didn't want a serious relationship, but he didn't want boring conversation and shallow sex, either.

And since there had been nothing boring or shallow about the night he'd spent with the bewitching brunette, Daniel still wanted her in his bed. Despite his good sense telling him otherwise.

"So," Solana said, and raised her hands. "Why have you come home?"

"To see you. Why else?"

She tutted. "Always a question with a question. Even as a toddler you were inquisitive. Always questioning everything, always asking *why* to your grandfather. Your brothers were never as curious about things as you were. Do you remember when you were eight and persuaded your grandfather to let you ride that mad, one-eyed pony your dad saved from the animal rescue center?" She shook her head and grinned. "Everyone wanted to know why you'd want to get on such a crazy animal. And all you said was, *why not*?"

Daniel shrugged. "As I recall I dislocated my collarbone."

"And scared Bernie and me half to death," Solana said and chuckled. "You were a handful, you know. Always getting into scraps. Always pushing the envelope. Amazing you turned out so sensible."

"Who say's I'm sensible?" he inquired lightly.

Solana's smile widened. "Me. Your brothers. Your grandfather if he was still alive."

"And Miles?"

His grandmother raised a silvery brow. "I think your dad would like you to be a little *less* sensible."

"I think my father would like me to eat tofu and drive a car that runs on doughnut grease."

"My son is who he is," Solana said affectionately. "Your grandfather never understood Miles and his alternative ways. But your dad knows who he is and what he wants from life. *And* he knows how to relax and enjoy the simple things."

Daniel didn't miss the dig. It wasn't the first time he'd been accused of being an uptight killjoy by his family. "I can relax."

His grandmother looked skeptical. "Well, perhaps you can learn to while you're here."

Daniel crossed his arms. Something about her tone made him suspicious. "You knew I was coming?"

Solana nodded, clearly unapologetic. "Blake called me. And of course it was my idea." She sat down at the table. "Did you know your grandfather had his first heart attack at thirty-nine?"

Daniel sighed. He'd heard it before. Mike Anderson died at sixty-nine from a massive coronary. His fourth. After two previous bypass surgeries the final heart attack had been swift and fatal, killing him before he'd had a chance to get up from his desk. "Gran, I—"

"Don't fob me off with some vague assurance that it won't happen to you," she said, cutting him off. "You work too hard. You don't take time off. You've become as defined by Anderson Holdings as your grandfather was... and all it got him was an early grave. There's more to life than business."

He would have dismissed the criticism from anyone else...but not Solana. He loved and respected his grandmother, and her opinion was one of the few that mattered to him.

"I know that. But I'm not ready to—"

"It's been over four years," Solana reminded him gently. "And time you got back to the land of the living. Simone wouldn't want you to—"

"Gran," Daniel said, hanging on to his patience. "I know you're trying to help. And I promise I'll relax and unwind while I'm here. I'm back for a week so I'll—"

"You'll need more than a week to unwind," she said, cutting him off again. "But if that's all you can manage then so be it. And your parents are expecting you to visit, in case you were thinking you'd fly under the radar while you're here."

Guilt spiked between his shoulder blades. Solana had a way of doing that. And he hadn't considered *not* seeing his father and stepmother. Not really. True, he had little in common with Miles and Bernadette...but they *were* his parents, and he knew they'd be genuinely pleased that he'd come home for a visit.

From a young age he'd known where his path lay. He was who his grandfather looked to as his protégé. At eighteen he'd been drafted into Anderson's, studying economics at night school so he could learn the business firsthand from his grandfather. At twenty-three, following Mike Anderson's death, he'd taken over the reins and since then he'd lived and breathed Anderson's. Blake and Caleb had followed him a few years later, while Daniel remained at the helm.

He worked and had little time for anything resembling a personal life. Simone had understood that. She was a corporate lawyer and worked seventy-hour weeks. Marrying her had made sense. They were a good match...alike in many ways, and they'd been happy together. And would still be together if fate and a faulty brake line hadn't intervened. She'd still be a lawyer and he would still spend his waking hours living and breathing Anderson Holdings. And they would be parents to their daughter. Just as they'd planned.

Daniel stretched his shoulders and stifled a yawn. He was tired. Jet-lagged. But if he crashed in the afternoon he'd feel worse. The trick to staying on top of the jet lag was keeping normal sleep patterns. Besides, there were two things he wanted to do—take a shower, and see Mary-Jayne Preston.

Mary-Jayne knew that the knock on her door would be Daniel. She'd been waiting for the sound for the past hour. But the sharp rap still startled her and she jumped up from the sofa, where she'd been sitting, hands twisted and stomach churning.

She walked across the living room and down the short hallway, grappling with the emotions running riot throughout her. She ruffled out her baggy shirt and hoped it disguised her belly enough to give her some time to work out how she was going to tell the man at her door he was going to become a father. She took a deep breath, steadied her knees, grabbed the handle and opened the door.

His gray eyes immediately looked her over with unconcealed interest. "How are you feeling?"

His lovely accent wound up her spine. "Fine."

"My grandmother is worried about you."

"I'm fine, like I said."

He tilted his head slightly. "You sure about that?"

Her chin came up. "Positive. Not that I have to explain myself to you."

"No," he mused. "I guess you don't."

"Is there something else you wanted?"

A tiny smile creased one corner of his mouth. "Can I come in?"

"I'd rather you didn't," she said, and stepped back, shielding herself behind the door. "But since you own this resort I guess you can do whatever the hell you want."

There was laughter in his eyes, and she realized the more hostile she got, the more amused he appeared. Mary-Jayne took a deep breath and turned on her heels, quickly finding solace behind the single recliner chair just a few feet away. She watched as he closed the door and took a few easy strides into the room.

"I hear you've been taking my grandmother to see fortune-tellers?"

Solana had told him about that? The older woman had sworn her to secrecy, saying her grandsons would think her crazy for visiting a clairvoyant. "It was *one* fortune-teller," she informed him. "And a reputable one, I might add."

His brows came up. "Really? You believe in all that nonsense?"

She glared at him. "Well, she did say I'd meet a man who was a real jerk...so I'd say she was pretty accurate, wouldn't you agree?"

"Is that a question?" he shot back. "Because I'm probably not the best judge of my own character. Other people's characters, on the other hand, I can usually peg."

"Don't start with—"

"Why did you hang up on me when I called you?"

She was genuinely surprised by his question. And didn't respond.

"You were in South Dakota at your friend's wedding," he reminded her. "I was in San Francisco. I would have flown you to the city."

Into the city. And into his bed. Mary-Jayne knew the score. She might have been a fool the night of Solana's birthday party, but she certainly wasn't about to repeat that monumental mistake.

"I wasn't in the market for another meaningless one-night stand."

His mouth twitched. "Really? More to the point, I guess your boyfriend wouldn't have approved?"

She frowned. "My what?"

"My grandmother can be indiscreet," he said and looked her over. "Unintentionally of course, since she has no idea we had that *meaningless one-night stand.*"

Color rose and spotted her cheeks. And for several long seconds she felt a kind of riveting connection to him. It was illogical. It was relentless. It made it impossible to ignore him. Or forget the night they'd spent together. Or the way they'd made love. The silence stretched between them, and Mary-Jayne was drawn deep into his smoky gray eyes.

"I don't have a boyfriend or lover," she said quietly. "I made that up to stop Solana from asking questions about…" Her words trailed off and she moved back, putting distance between them.

"About what?"

She shook her head. "Nothing. I really can't… I can't do this."

"Do what?" he asked.

"I can't do this with you."

"We're not doing anything," he said. "Just talking."

"That's just it," she said, her voice coming out a little strangled. "I'm not ready for this. Not here. Not today. I feel unwell and I—"

"I thought you said you were feeling better?" he asked, cutting her off.

"Well, I'm not, okay? I'm not better. And seeing you here only makes me feel worse."

"Such brutal honesty. I don't know whether to be flattered or offended."

She let out an agonized moan. "That's just it. I am honest. *Always*. And seeing you now makes it impossible for me to be anything else. And I'm not ready for it... I can't do this today. I simply can't—"

"What are you talking about?" he asked impatiently and cut her off again.

"I'm talking about... I mean... I can't..."

"Mary-Jayne," he said, saying her name like he had that night, when he'd said it over and over, against her skin, against her breath. "I'm not sure what's going on with you, but you're not making much sense."

The truth screamed to be told. There was no other way. She couldn't stop being who she was. She was an honest, forthright person who wore her heart on her sleeve. Mary-Jayne stepped out from behind the chair and spread her hands across her stomach, tightening the baggy shirt over her middle. Highlighting the small bump that hadn't been there four months ago.

"I'm talking about *this*."

Daniel quickly refocused his gaze onto her middle and frowned. "You're pregnant?"

She nodded and swallowed hard. "Yes."

"And?"

She shrugged and her hair flipped around her shoulders. Now or never.

"And isn't it obvious? You're the father."

Chapter Three

He hadn't moved. Mary-Jayne looked at him and took a long breath. "This isn't how I wanted you to find out. I was going to call and tell you and—"

"You're not serious?" he asked, cutting through her words with icy precision.

She nodded. "I'm perfectly serious. I'm pregnant."

He raised a dark brow. "We used protection," he said quietly and held up a few fingers. "Three times, three lots of birth control. So your math doesn't quite work out."

"My math?" She stared at him. "What exactly are you accusing me of?"

"Nothing," he replied evenly. "Simply stating an irrefutable fact."

A fact?

Right. There was no possible way of misunderstanding his meaning. "I'm not lying to you. This baby is—"

"Yours," he corrected coldly. "And probably the ex-boyfriend who my grandmother said is giving you grief at the moment."

She fought the urge to rush across the room and slug him. "I don't have a *boyfriend*. Ex or otherwise."

"You do according to my grandmother," he stated. "Who I trust more than anyone else."

No punches pulled. He didn't believe her. *Okay.* She could handle it. She didn't care what he thought. "I only told Solana that to stop her from asking questions about why I've been unwell."

He crossed his arms, accentuating his broad shoulders, and stood as still as a statue. He really was absurdly good-looking, she thought, disliking him with every fiber in her body. His gray eyes had darkened to a deep slate color and his almost black hair was short and shiny, and she remembered how soft it had been between her fingertips. His face was perfectly proportioned and he had a small cleft in his chin that was ridiculously sexy. Yes, Daniel Anderson was as handsome as sin. He was also an arrogant, overbearing, condescending so-and-so, and if it weren't for the fact he was the biological father of her child, she'd happily *never* see him again.

"Do I really appear so gullible, Miss Preston?"

Miss Preston?

"Gullible? I don't know what you—"

"If you think naming me in a paternity claim will fatten your bank balance, think again. My lawyers will be all over you in a microsecond."

His pompous arrogance was unbelievable. "I'm not after your money."

"Then, what?" he asked. "A wedding ring?"

Fury surged through her. "I wouldn't marry you if you were the last man left on the planet."

Her words seemed to amuse him and he looked at her

in such a haughty, condescending way that her palms actually itched with the urge to slap his face. In every way she'd played the scene out in her head, and not once had she imagined he wouldn't believe that her baby was his. Naive perhaps, but Mary-Jayne had been raised to take someone at their word.

"That's quite a relief, since I won't be proposing anytime soon."

"Go to hell," she said quietly as emotion tightened her chest, and she drew in a shuddering breath. He pushed her buttons effortlessly. He really was a hateful jerk.

"Not until we've sorted out this little mix-up."

"Mix-up?" She glared at him. "I'm pregnant and you're the father. This is not a mix-up. This is just how it is."

"Then, I demand a paternity test."

Daniel hadn't meant to sound like such a cold, unfeeling bastard. But he wasn't about to be taken for a ride. He knew the score. A few months back his brother Caleb had been put through the ringer in a paternity suit that had eventually proved the kid he'd believed was his wasn't. And Daniel wasn't about to get pulled into that same kind of circus.

Mary-Jayne Preston's baby couldn't possibly be his... could it? He'd never played roulette with birth control. Besides, now that he could well and truly see her baby bump she looked further along than four months. Simone hadn't started showing so obviously until she was five months' pregnant.

"I'd like you to leave."

Daniel didn't move. "Won't that defeat the purpose of your revelation?"

She scowled, and he couldn't help thinking how she still looked beautiful even with an infuriated expression.

"You know about the baby, so whatever you decide to do with the information is up to you."

"Until I get served with child-support demands, you mean?"

She placed her hands on her hips and Daniel's gaze was immediately drawn to her belly. She was rounder than he remembered, kind of voluptuous, and a swift niggle of attraction wound its way through his blood and across his skin. Her curves had appealed to him from the moment they'd first met, and watching her now only amplified that desire.

Which was damned inconvenient, since she was obviously trying to scam him.

"I don't want your money," she said stiffly. "And I certainly don't want a wedding ring. When I get married it will be to someone I actually like. I intend to raise this baby alone. Believe me, or don't believe me. Frankly, I don't care either way."

There was such blatant contempt in her voice that he was tempted to smile. One thing about the woman in front of him—she wasn't afraid to speak her mind. And even though he knew it was crazy thinking, it was an interesting change from the usual lengths some women went to in order to get his attention. How sincere she was, he couldn't tell.

"We spent the night together a little over four months ago," he reminded her. "You look more than four months pregnant."

Her glare intensified. "So it's clearly a big baby. All I know is that the only possible way I got pregnant was from that night I spent with you. I hadn't been with anyone for a long time before that night. Despite what you think of me, I'm not easy. And I don't lie. I have no reason to want this child to be yours. I don't like you. I'm not interested in you or your money or anything else. But I am telling you the truth."

He still wasn't convinced. "So the ex-boyfriend?"

"A figment of my imagination," she replied. "Like I said, Solana was asking questions and I needed a little camouflage for a while."

He kept his head. "Even if there is no boyfriend and you are indeed carrying a supersize baby…we used contraception. So it doesn't add up."

"And since condoms are only ninety-eight percent effective, we obviously managed to slip into the two percent bracket."

Ninety-eight percent effective?

Since when?

Daniel struggled with the unease clawing up his spine. "You cannot expect me to simply accept this news at face value."

She shrugged, as if she couldn't care either way. "Do, or don't. If you want a paternity test to confirm it, then fine, that's what we'll do."

He relaxed a little. Finally, some good sense. "Thank you."

"But it won't be done until the baby is born," she said evenly and took a long breath. "There are risks associated with tests after the fifteen-week mark, and I won't put my baby in jeopardy. Not for you. Not for anyone."

There was such unequivocal resolve in her voice, and it surprised him. She was a flake. Unreliable. Unpredictable. Nothing like Simone. "Of course," he said, and did his best to ignore the stabbing pain in his temple. His shoulders ached, and he could feel the effects of no sleep and hours flying across the globe begin to creep into his limbs. "I wouldn't expect you to put your child at risk."

Her child.

Her baby.

This wasn't what he'd expected to face when he'd decided to come home. But if she was telling the truth? What then? To share a child with a woman he barely knew. It was a train wreck waiting to happen.

And he hated waiting. In business. In his personal life.

He'd waited at the hospital when Simone was brought in with critical injuries. He waited while the doctors had tried to save her and their unborn daughter. He'd waited, and then received the worst possible news. And afterward he'd experienced a heartbreaking despair. After that night he became hollow inside. He'd loved his wife and daughter. Losing them had been unbearable. And he'd never wanted to feel that kind of soul-destroying anguish again.

But if Mary-Jayne *was* carrying his child, how could he turn his back?

He couldn't. He'd be trapped.

Held ransom by the very feelings he'd sworn he never wanted to feel again.

"So what do you want from me until then?"

"Want? Nothing," she replied quietly. "I'll call you when the baby is born and the paternity test is done. Goodbye."

He sighed. "Is this how you usually handle problems? By ignoring them?"

Her cheeks quickly heated. "I don't consider this baby a problem," she shot back. "And the only thing I plan to ignore is you."

He stared at her for a moment, and then when he laughed Mary-Jayne realized she liked the sound way too much. She didn't want to like *anything* about him. Not ever. He had become enemy number one. For the next five months all she wanted to do was concentrate on growing a healthy baby. Wasting time thinking about Daniel and his sexy laugh and gray eyes was off her agenda.

"You don't really think that's going to happen, do you?" he asked, watching her with such hot intensity she couldn't look away. "You've dropped this bombshell, and you know enough about me to realize I won't simply fade away for the next five months."

"I can live in hope."

"I think you live in a fantasyland, Mary-Jayne."

The way he said her name caused her skin to prickle. No one called her that except her parents and her older brother, Noah. Even her sisters and closest friends mostly called her M.J. To the rest of the world she was M. J. Preston—the youngest and much loved sibling in a close-knit middle-class family. But Daniel had always used her full name.

Mary-Jayne took a deep breath. "A fantasyland?" She repeated his words as a question.

"What else would you call it?" he shot back as he looked her over. "You're what, twenty-seven? Never married or engaged. No real career to speak of. And a barely solvent online business. You've rented the same house for nearly ten years. You drive a car that's good for little else but scrap metal. You have less than a thousand dollars in the bank at any given time and a not-so-stellar credit rating thanks to a certain dubious ex-boyfriend who ran up a debt on your behalf over five years ago. It looks very much like you do—"

"How do you know that?" she demanded hotly, hands on hips. "How do you know all that about me? I've not told Solana any of…" She trailed off as realization hit. And then she seethed. "You had me investigated?"

"Of course," he replied, unmoving and clearly unapologetic.

"You had no right to do that," she spat. "No right at all. You invaded my privacy."

He shrugged his magnificent shoulders. "You are working at this resort and have befriended my grandmother—it was prudent to make sure you weren't a fortune hunter."

"Fortune hunter?" Mary-Jayne's eyes bulged wide and she said a rude word.

He tilted his head a fraction. "Well, the jury's still out on that one."

"Jury?" She echoed the word in disbelief. "And what does that make you? The judge? Can you actually hear yourself? Of all the pompous, arrogant and self-important things I've ever heard in my life, you take the cake. And you really do take yourself and the significance of your opinions way too seriously."

He didn't like that. Not one bit. She watched, fascinated as his eyes darkened and a tiny pulse in his cheek beat rapidly. His hands were clenched and suddenly his body looked as if it had been carved from granite. And as much as she tried to fight it, attraction reared up, and heat swirled around the small room as their gazes clashed.

Memories of that night four months ago banged around in her head. Kissing, touching, stroking. Possession and desire unlike any she had known before. There had been a quiet intensity in him that night, and she'd been swept away into another world, another universe where only pleasure and a deeply intimate connection existed. That night, he hadn't been the rigid, unyielding and disagreeable man who was now in her living room. He'd been tender and passionate. He'd whispered her name against her skin. He'd kissed her and made love to her with such profound eagerness Mary-Jayne's entire mind and body had awakened and responded in kind. She'd never been driven to please and be pleasured like that before.

But right now she had to get back to hating him. "I'm going to get changed and go for a walk to clear my head. You know the way out."

He didn't move. And he looked a little pale, she thought. Perhaps the shock that he was going to be a father was finally hitting home. But then she remembered that he didn't believe he actually was her baby's father, so that probably wasn't it.

"We still have things to discuss."

"Not for another..." Her words trailed off and she tapped off five of her fingers in her palm. "Five months. Until then, how about you treat me with the disdain that you've clearly mastered, and I'll simply pretend that you don't exist. That will work out nicely for us both, don't you think?"

Of course, she knew saying something so provocative was like waving a red cape at a bull. But she couldn't help herself. He deserved it in spades. And it was only the truth. She didn't want to see him or spend any more time in his company.

"I don't treat you with disdain."

And there it was again—his resolute belief in the sound of his own voice.

"No?" She bit down on her lip for a moment. "You've admitted you had me investigated and just accused me of being a fortune hunter. Oh, and what about what you said to me on the phone when I was in South Dakota?" She took a strengthening breath. "That I was a flake who dressed like a hippie."

His eyes flashed. "And before you told me to go to hell you called me an uptight, overachieving, supercilious snob, if I remember correctly." He uncrossed his arms and took a step toward her.

"Well, it's the truth. You are an uptight snob."

"And you dress like a hippie."

"I like to be comfortable," she said, and touched her head self-consciously. "And I can't help the way my hair gets all curly in the humidity."

His gaze flicked to her hair and she saw his mouth twitch fractionally. "I didn't say a word about your hair. In fact it's quite...it's...it's..."

"It's what?" she asked.

"Nothing," he said, and shrugged. "I would like to know your plans."

Mary-Jayne stared at him. "I don't have any plans other than to have a healthy baby in five months' time."

He looked around the room. "When are you leaving here?"

"Audrey's back in two weeks. I'll go home then."

"Have you told your family?"

She shook her head. "Not yet."

"Have you told anyone?"

She met his gaze. "You."

His expression narrowed. "And since she didn't mention it while you were throwing up in her garden, I'm guessing you haven't told my grandmother, either?"

"Just you," she replied, fighting the resentment fueling her blood. "Like I said. Incidentally, Daniel, if you're going to disbelieve everything that comes out of my mouth, it's going to be a long five months."

He grinned unexpectedly. "So you do know my name? I don't think you've ever used it before. Well, except for that night we spent together."

Her skin heated. She remembered exactly how she'd said his name that night. Over and over, whispered and moaned, as though it was the only word she'd known.

"Like I said, you know the way out."

He didn't budge. "We still need to talk."

"We've talked enough," she said tensely. "You don't believe me and you need a paternity test. *And* you think I'm after your money. Believe me, I've got your message loud and clear."

"You're angry because I want proof of paternity?"

He actually sounded surprised. Mary-Jayne almost laughed at his absurd sense of entitlement. "I'm angry because you think I'm lying to you. I don't know what kind of world you live in where you have this compulsion to question someone's integrity without cause, but I don't live in that world, Daniel. And I would never want to."

She spun on her heel and left the room, barely taking a breath until she reached the sanctuary of the main bedroom. She leaned against the closed door and shuddered.

It's done now. He knows. I can get on with things.

She pulled herself together, changed into sweats and sneakers and loitered in the room for more than ten minutes to ensure he'd be gone.

She strode into the living room and then stopped in her tracks. The room was empty. He'd left. As if he'd never been there.

A strange hollowness fluttered behind her ribs. She was glad he was gone—arrogant and disbelieving jerk that he was. She was well rid of him. With any luck she'd never have to see him again. Or speak to him. Or have to stare into those smoky gray eyes of his.

She could go home and have her baby.

Simple.

But in her heart she knew she was dreaming to believe he'd just disappear from her life. She was having his baby—and that made it about as complicated as it got.

When Daniel woke up he had a crick in his neck and his left leg was numb. It was dark out. He checked his watch: six-forty. He sat up and stretched. When he'd left her condo, he'd walked around the grounds for a few minutes before heading back to his own villa. Once he'd sat down, the jet lag had hit him with a thud. Now he needed coffee and a clear head.

He got to his feet and rounded out his shoulders. The condo was quiet, and he walked from the living room and headed for the kitchen. He had to refocus and figure what the hell he was supposed to do for the next five months until the baby came into the world.

The baby.

His baby...

I'm going to be a father.

Maybe?

Daniel still wasn't entirely convinced. Mary-Jayne potentially had a lot to gain by saying he'd fathered her child. He wasn't naive and knew some people were mercenary enough to try to take advantage of others. He remembered how devastated Caleb had been when he'd discovered the boy he'd thought was his son turned out to belong to his *then* girlfriend's ex-husband. And Daniel didn't want to form a bond with a child only to have it snatched away. Not again. Losing Simone and their unborn daughter had been soul destroying. He wasn't going to put himself in a position to get another serving of that kind of loss.

He made coffee and drank it. Damn...he felt as if his head was going to explode. He'd had it all planned out... come back to Port Douglas, reconnect with Mary-Jayne for a week and get her out of his system once and for all.

Not going to happen.

Daniel rounded out his shoulders and sucked in a long breath. He needed a plan. And fast. He swilled the cup in the sink, grabbed his keys and left the villa.

By the time he reached her condo his hands were sweating. No one had ever had such an intense physical effect on him. And he wasn't sure how to feel about it. The crazy thing was, he couldn't ignore it. And now that had amplified a hundredfold.

They needed to talk. There was no way around it. Daniel took another breath and knocked on the door.

When she answered the door she looked almost as though she'd been expecting him to return. He didn't like the idea that he was so transparent to her.

"I'm working," she said, and left him standing in the doorway. "So you'll need to amuse yourself for ten minutes before we get into round two."

The way she dismissed him so effortlessly *should* have made him madder than hell. But it didn't. He liked her spirit, and it was one of the things he found so attractive about her.

He followed her down the hall, and when he reached the dining room she was already standing by a small workbench tucked against the wall in one corner. She was bent over the narrow table, one elbow resting, using a small soldering iron. There was enough light from the lamp positioned to one side for him to see her profile, and despite the protective glasses perched on her nose he couldn't miss the intense concentration she gave her craft. There were several boards fashioned on easels that displayed her jewelry pieces, and although he was no expert, there was certainly style and creativity in her work.

She must have sensed him watching her because she turned and switched off the soldering iron. "So you're back?"

He nodded. "I'm back."

"Did you call your lawyer?"

"What?"

She shrugged a little. "Seems like something you'd do."

Daniel ignored the irritation clawing at his spine. "No, Mary-Jayne, I didn't call my lawyer. Actually, I fell asleep."

She looked surprised and then frowned a little. "Jet lag?"

He nodded again. "Once I sat down it hit me."

"I had the same reaction when I returned from Thailand last year. It took me three days to recover. The trick is to stay awake until bedtime."

There was something husky and incredibly sexy about Mary-Jayne's voice that reached him deep down. After they'd slept together, he'd pursued her and she'd turned him down flat. Even from across an ocean she'd managed to throw a bucket of cold water on his attempts to ask her out. And get her back in his bed. Because he still wanted her. As foolish as it was, as different and unsuitable for one another as they were—he couldn't stop thinking about her.

She knew that. She knew they were from different worlds. She'd accused him of thinking she was an easy mark and that was why he wanted her. But it wasn't that. He wanted her because she stirred him like no other woman ever had. From her crazy beautiful hair to her curvy body and her sassy mouth, Daniel had never known a woman like her. He might not like her...but he wanted her. And it was as inconvenient as hell.

"So what do you want, then?"

Daniel's back straightened. She didn't hold back. She clearly didn't think she had anything to gain by being friendly or even civil. It wasn't a tactic he was used to. She'd called him a spoiled, pampered and arrogant snob, and although he didn't agree with that assumption, it was exactly how she treated him.

"To talk," he replied. "Seems we've got plenty to talk about."

"Do you think?" she shot back. "Since you don't believe

that this baby is yours, I can't see what's so important that you felt compelled to come back so soon."

Daniel took a breath. "I guess I deserve that."

"Yeah," she said and plucked the glasses off her nose. "I guess you do."

He managed a tight smile. "I would like to talk with you. Would coffee be too much trouble?"

She placed the soldering iron on the bench. "I guess not."

As she walked past him and through the door to the kitchen it occurred to Daniel that she swayed when she moved. The kitchen seemed small with both of them in it, and he stayed on the outside of the counter.

"That's quite a collection your friend has up there," he remarked and pointed to the cooking pots hanging from an old window shutter frame that was suspended from the ceiling.

"Audrey likes pans," she said without looking at him. "I don't know why."

"She doesn't need a reason," he said and pulled out a chair. "I collect old books."

She glanced up. "Old books?"

"First editions," he explained. "Poetry and classic literature."

One of her eyebrows rose subtly. "I didn't peg you as a reader. Except perhaps the *Financial Times*."

Daniel grinned a little. "I didn't say I read them."

"Then why collect them?"

He half shrugged. "They're often unique. You know, rare."

"Valuable?" she asked, saying the word almost as an insult. "Does everything in your life have a dollar sign attached to it?"

As digs went between them, it was pretty mild, but it still irked him. "Everything? No."

"Good," she said, and held up a small sugar pot. When he shook his head, she continued speaking. "Because I have no intention of allowing my baby to become caught up in your old family money or your sense of self-entitlement."

Daniel stilled. "What does that mean?"

"It means that people like you have a kind of overconfident belief that money fixes everything."

"People like me?" Daniel walked across the small room and moved around the countertop. "Like me?" he asked again, trying to hold on to the annoyance sneaking across his skin. "Like me, how...exactly?"

She stepped back. "You're rich and successful. You can snap your fingers and have any number of minions willing to do whatever you need done."

He laughed humorlessly. "Really? I must try that next time I want someone to bring me my slippers."

Her green eyes glittered brilliantly. "Did you just make a joke? I didn't realize you had it in you."

Daniel's shoulders twitched. "Perhaps I'm not quite the *uptight, overachieving, supercilious snob* you think I am."

"Oh, I wouldn't go that far," she said and pushed the mug along the countertop. "There's milk in the fridge."

"This is fine." Daniel took the mug and leaned a hip against the counter. "Thank you."

"No problem. And you *are* uptight, Daniel. Everything about you screams order and control."

"Because I don't live in chaos?" he asked, deliberately waving a hand around the untidy room. "That doesn't necessarily equate to being a control freak."

She crossed her arms. "Chaos? So now you think I'm a slob?"

He drank some coffee and placed the mug on the

counter. "What I think is that it's interesting that you express every opinion you have without considering the consequences."

"Oh, have I offended your sensibilities?"

"Have I offended yours?"

She shrugged. "I'd have to care what you thought, wouldn't I?"

In all his life he'd never met anyone who tried so hard to antagonize him. Or anyone with whom he'd been compelled to do the same. Mary-Jayne got under his skin in ways he could barely rationalize. They were all wrong for one another and they both knew it.

And now there was a baby coming…

His baby.

Daniel glanced at her belly and then met her gaze.

"Mary-Jayne." He said her name quietly, and the mood between them changed almost immediately. "Are you… are you sure?"

She nodded slowly. "Am I sure the baby is yours? Yes, I'm certain."

Resistance lingered in his blood. "But we—"

"I may be a lot of things, Daniel…but I'm not a liar." She drew in a long breath. "The contraception we used obviously failed. Despite what you think of me, I've been single for over twelve months and I haven't slept with anyone since…except you."

A stupid, egotistical part of him was glad to hear it. One part wanted to believe her. And the other…the other could only think about what it meant for them both if what she said was true.

"I need to be sure," he said.

"I understand," she replied. "You can have your proof when he or she is born."

Guilt niggled its way through his blood. "I appreciate you agreeing to a paternity test."

She shrugged lightly. "There's little point in being at odds over this. Be assured that I don't want anything from you, and once you have your proof of paternity you can decide how much or how little time you invest in this."

As she spoke she certainly didn't come across as flighty as she appeared. She sounded like a woman who knew exactly what she wanted. Which was her child...and no interference from him.

Which of course wasn't going to happen.

If the baby *was* his, then he would be very involved. He'd have no choice. The child would be an Anderson and have the right to claim the legacy that went with the name. Only, he wasn't sure how he'd get Mary-Jayne to see it that way.

"If this child is mine, then I won't dodge my responsibility."

She looked less than impressed by the idea. "If you're talking about money, I think I've made it pretty clear I'm not interested."

"You can't raise a child on good intentions, Mary-Jayne. Be sensible."

Her mouth thinned and she looked ready for an argument, but she seemed to change her mind. Some battles, he figured, were about defense, not attack...and she knew that as well as he did.

"We'll see what happens," she said casually as she crossed the small kitchen and stood in front of the refrigerator. She waited for him to stand aside and then opened the door. "I'm heating up lasagna. Are you staying for dinner?"

Daniel raised a brow. "Am I invited?"

She shrugged, as if she couldn't care either way. But

he knew she probably wanted to tell him to take a hike in some of her more colorful language.

"Sure," he said, and grabbed the coffee mug as he stepped out of her way. "That would be good."

He caught a tiny smile on her mouth and watched as she removed several items from the refrigerator and began preparing food on the countertop. She placed a casserole dish in the microwave and began making a salad. And Daniel couldn't take his eyes off her. She was fascinating to watch. Her glorious hair shone like ebony beneath the kitchen light, and she chewed her bottom lip as she completed the task. And of course thinking about her lips made him remember their night together. And kissing her. And making love to her. She had a remarkable effect on his libido, and he wondered if it was because they *were* so different that he was so achingly attracted to her. She was all challenge. All resistance. And since very little challenged him these days, Daniel knew her very determination to avoid him had a magnetic pull all of its own.

And he had no idea what he was going to do about it.

Or if he could do actually do anything at all.

Chapter Four

Mary-Jayne finished preparing dinner, uncomfortably conscious of the gorgeous man standing by the kitchen table. There was such blistering intensity in his gaze she could barely concentrate on what she was doing. She hated that he could do that to her. If she had her way she'd never see him again.

But the baby she carried bound them together.

He wouldn't, she was certain, simply disappear from her life.

She had five months until the baby came, and she had to figure out how to get through those months with Daniel in the background. Or worse. He wasn't the kind of man who'd simply go away until the baby came…regardless of how much she might wish for things to go that way.

"How long are you staying at the resort?" she asked, hoping he'd say not too long at all. Best he leave quickly.

"I'd planned to only be here a week to visit with my

grandmother," he replied, and shrugged slightly. "But now I'm not sure."

She frowned. "Don't you have a company to run or something?"

"Yes."

"Isn't it hard to do that from here? You live mostly in San Francisco, right?"

He placed the mug on the dining table and crossed his arms. "Most of the time. Anderson's corporate offices are there. And the Bay Area resort is the largest."

"Well, I'm sure they need you back."

His mouth twitched. "Eager to see me gone, Mary-Jayne?"

"If I said no I'd be lying," she replied, and brought plates and cutlery to the table. "And as I've repeatedly said, I don't lie. So if you're thinking of extending your stay on my account, there's really no need. The birth is five months away and there's nothing you can do until then."

Mary-Jayne brought the food to the table and gestured for him to take a seat. When he was sitting she did the same and took the lids off the salad and lasagna. She didn't bother to ask what he wanted and quickly piled a scoop of pasta on his plate. Once she'd filled her own plate she picked up the utensils and speared some lettuce and cucumber with a fork.

"What…is…that?"

She looked up and smirked when she saw how Daniel was staring at his food. "Lasagna. With mushroom, spinach, shredded zucchini flowers and goat cheese."

He looked as if she'd asked him to chew broken glass. He took a breath and met her gaze. "You're a vegetarian?"

"Of course."

Mary-Jayne knew his parents were strict vegans. She

also knew he and his brothers had made a point from his early teens of *not* following in their footsteps.

"Of course," he repeated with more than a touch of irony. "Looks...delicious."

"I'm not much of a cook," she said frankly. "So don't hold your breath."

"Thanks for the warning."

She smiled to herself as they began to eat. He was being good-humored about her attempts to wind him up and it surprised her. Maybe he wasn't quite as straitlaced and up-tight as she'd believed. Which didn't mean anything. He could be nice. He could be the most charming and agree-able man on the planet and it wouldn't change the one sig-nificant fact—they were like oil and water and would never mix. Despite the fact that they'd made a baby together and were now bound by parenthood. They were in different leagues, and she had to remember that every time she was tempted to think about his sexy voice and broad shoulders.

"I have an ultrasound appointment on Tuesday at ten-thirty," she said, and speared some pasta. "My doctor gave me a referral to a medical center in Cairns."

The regional city was forty miles south of Port Douglas. "And?"

"And you're welcome to come along if you want to," she replied flatly.

He didn't really look as though he wanted to. But he did nod. "I'll pick you up."

"I can drive myself."

He raised a brow. "I'll pick you up."

She was about to argue, but stopped herself. Battling with Daniel over the small stuff was pointless. "Okay," she said, and didn't miss the flash of surprise in his eyes.

For a while the only sound in the room was the clicking of cutlery. He seemed happy not to talk and Mary-Jayne was content to eat her food and not think about how intimate the situation was. Once dinner was done he offered to help wash up, and before she had a chance to refuse his assistance he was out of the chair and in the kitchen, rinsing the plates with one hand while he opened the dishwasher with the other.

"You know your way around a kitchen," she said, surprised.

He shrugged. "Bernie made sure my brothers and I knew how to cook and clean up."

"That's your mother?"

"Stepmother," he replied, and began stacking the dishwasher. "She married my dad when I was two."

Her insides contracted. "Solana told me your mother passed away just after you were born."

"That's right."

Mary-Jayne moved into the kitchen. "You were born in Australia, weren't you?"

"That's right. My dad moved to California when he married Bernie and the twins were born there. They moved back here about ten years ago."

"I like your dad."

He glanced sideways. "I didn't realize you were acquainted."

"He came here to visit your grandmother and Caleb a few weeks ago. I was with Solana at the time and she introduced me to him. He had a very relaxed sense of self, if that makes sense. He was very charismatic and friendly," she said, and smiled a little.

"Not like me, you mean?"

Mary-Jayne grabbed a tea towel. "I'm sure you could be the same if you put your mind to it."

He turned and faced her. "And ruin my image of being an uptight bore?"

She laughed softly. "One thing you're not, Daniel, is boring."

"Just uptight?" he asked.

Mary-Jayne shrugged lightly. "I guess it goes with the territory. Solana told me how you took over the business when you were in your early twenties. That must have been quite a responsibility to shoulder. Duty above all else, right?"

He didn't move. "My grandfather was dead. My father had tried his hand at the business and bailed when he realized he was happier growing organic vegetables and pursuing his art. So yes, being drafted into the business that young had its challenges. But I wasn't about to let my family down. Or the people who rely on Anderson's for their livelihood. I did what I had to do… If that made me an uptight bore in the process, then I guess I'll simply have to live with it."

She took a deep breath. There was something so seductive about his deep voice it was impossible to move. She could have easily moved closer to him. The heat that had been between them from the start was as vibrant and scorching as it had ever been.

It's just sex…

Of course she knew that. Sex and lust and some kind of manic chemical reaction that had her hormones running riot. She had to get them under control. And fast.

"So I'll see you Tuesday. Around nine o'clock."

His gaze darkened. "Are you kicking me out?"

Mary-Jayne took a tentative step backward. "I guess so."

He laughed. "You know, I've never met anyone quite like you. There are no punches pulled with you, Mary-Jayne— you say exactly what you think."

"Blame it on my middle-class upbringing."

"I'm not criticizing you," he said, and folded his arms. "On the contrary, I find it intriguing. And incredibly sexy."

She stepped back again. "If you're flirting with me, stop right now. Your *charm* has got us into enough trouble already."

He laughed again. "Good night, Mary-Jayne."

"Good night," she whispered as she followed him up the hall, and she didn't take a breath until she closed the front door behind him.

After a restless night spent staring mostly at the ceiling, Daniel went for a long run along the beach around ten o'clock on Sunday morning. He stayed out for over an hour, and when he returned to his villa, took a shower and dressed and was about to head for his grandmother's when there was a tap on his door.

It was Caleb.

His brother walked across the threshold and dropped a set of keys onto the narrow hall table. "The keys to my Jeep," Caleb said and grinned. "In case you want to visit the folks."

Caleb never failed to remind him or Blake about the importance of family.

"Thanks," he said, and walked down the hallway.

His brother followed, and they each dropped into one of the two leather sofas in the living room. "Have you heard from Audrey?" Daniel asked the one question he knew his brother wouldn't want to answer.

Caleb shook his head. "I screwed up, and she's not about to forgive me anytime soon."

"You did what you thought was right."

"I moved my ex-girlfriend and her child into my house without thinking about what it would mean to my *current* girlfriend. I mean, I know Audrey and I had only been together a couple of months…but still…" The regretful look on his brother's face spoke volumes. "I should have done things differently. I shouldn't have taken Nikki's word that he was my kid without getting tested. I should have known Audrey was going to end up bailing. Hell, I probably would have done the same thing had the situation been reversed. When her mother got sick she had just the out she needed to get away from the resort for a while…and from me."

Which had been the catalyst for Mary-Jayne coming to the resort. Daniel was certain that his brother was in love with Mary-Jayne's friend Audrey. But when his ex-girlfriend had arrived on his doorstep, holding a baby she'd claimed was his, Caleb had reacted instinctively and moved them into his home.

"She's coming back in two weeks."

"Audrey?" Caleb's gaze narrowed. "How do you know that?"

He shrugged. "Gran must have mentioned it."

"Gran did?" His brother raised both brows. "You sure about that?"

"I don't know what—"

"Less than twenty-four hours, hey?" Caleb laughed. "I take it you've seen her?"

Her.

He'd told Caleb about spending the night with Mary-Jayne. He hadn't been able to avoid it since his brother had spotted her leaving his villa early that morning. "Yes, I've seen her."

"You still hung up on her?"

Daniel shrugged one shoulder. Caleb knew him well enough to sniff out a lie. "Things are a little more complicated."

"Complicated?"

He didn't flinch. "She's pregnant."

His brother's eyes bulged. "Hell! And it's yours?"

"So she says."

Caleb let out a long breath. "Do you believe her?"

"Do I have doubts?" He shrugged again. "Of course. But Mary-Jayne isn't like—"

"Like Nikki?" Caleb suggested, cutting him off. "Yeah, you're right. She seems like a real straight shooter. I know Audrey trusted her to run the store in her absence without hesitation. You gonna marry her?"

Daniel's back straightened. "Don't be stupid. I hardly know her."

Caleb grinned. "Well, you'll have plenty of opportunity to get to know her once you start raising a child together."

Raising a child together...

Daniel knew it wouldn't be that simple. She lived in Crystal Point. He lived in San Francisco. There was a hell of a lot of geography separating them. Which would make him what? A once-a-year father? Summer-vacation time or less? He was looking down the barrel at an impossible situation.

"We'll see what happens."

His brother's expression turned serious. "Tell me you're getting a paternity test?"

"Once the child is born," he said, and explained about the risks of doing the test during the second trimester.

Caleb nodded slowly. "And what do you plan to do until then?"

He shrugged a little. "It's not really up to me."

His brother made a disagreeable sound. "I can see that attitude lasting about two days," he said, and smiled. "Until the shock really hits you."

Caleb knew him well. The idea of doing nothing until the baby came sat like a lead weight in his gut. But what choice did he have? Mary-Jayne wasn't the kind of woman to take easily to being watched or hovered over. She was obviously fiercely independent and made it clear she didn't need him for anything.

Which should have put him it at ease.

Instead his insides churned. He was torn between wanting to believe her child was his and knowing it would be much better for them both if it wasn't true. But he had no real reason to disbelieve her. Sure, he thought she was a bit of a flake. But according to Solana she was honest and forthright and exactly as she seemed—a free, independent spirit who answered to no one but herself. Not the kind of woman to claim paternity when she wanted nothing in return.

"I thought I'd visit Gran," Daniel said, and sprang from the sofa. "Feel like joining me?"

Caleb shook his head and grinned as he stood. "I'm not on vacation like you. I have a business to run. And don't forget to go and see the folks this week."

"I won't," Daniel promised, and walked his brother down the hall.

Once Caleb left he locked up the villa, grabbed the keys on the hall stand and headed out. He walked around the grounds for a few minutes, and instead of going directly to Solana's villa made his way to the western side of the resort where the condos were smaller and home to many of the employees. He tapped on Mary-Jayne's door and ignored the interested looks from a few people in corporate shirts who passed him on the pathway that separated the apartments.

The door swung back and she stood in front of him. "Oh...hi."

She sounded breathless, and he was immediately concerned. "Are you okay?"

"Fine," she replied and took a deep breath. "I've been doing Pilates."

Daniel looked her over. Her hair was tied up in a haphazard ponytail and she wore black leggings and a hot pink racer-back tank top that clung to her curves. Her belly looked like it had popped out a little more overnight and he fought the unexpected urge to place his hand on her stomach. Her cheeks were flushed and her lips looked plump and red. There was something wholly healthy and attractive about her that warmed his blood.

"Pilates?" he echoed, and curled his fingers into his palms to stop himself from reaching out to touch her.

"It's good for the baby," she replied. "And me. So did you want something?"

"Only to see how you are feeling today."

"I'm fine," she said, her hand positioned on the door like she couldn't wait to close it. "How are you?"

"Okay," he said.

"Well, thanks for stopping by."

Daniel shifted on his feet. "I thought… I wondered if you would like to have lunch."

Her brows arched. "Lunch? With you? Where?"

He shrugged a little. "There are four restaurants at this resort…take your pick."

Her brows stayed high. "Beneath the prying eyes of wait staff and various employees? Isn't that a little risky? People might start thinking you've been consorting with the help."

Daniel's jaw clenched. She was an argumentative and provocative pain in the neck. And he wanted her anyway.

"First, I don't care what anyone thinks. And second, you are not *the help*, Mary-Jayne. Are you going to be difficult and refuse every request I make? Or accept that you need to eat and since you're a lousy cook anyway, it would—"

"I'm not a *lousy* cook," she retorted and a tiny smile

curved her mouth. "Just not a good cook. And while I appreciate your invitation, I'm hardly dressed for anything other than a cheese sandwich in front of the TV."

He looked her over again and his libido twitched. "I'll come back in half an hour. Unless you need help getting out of your clothes?"

For a second he thought she might slam the door in his face. But to his surprise she laughed softly. "I'm sure I can manage. Okay, see you in thirty minutes."

Then she did close the door and Daniel turned on his heels. And as he walked back down the path he realized he was grinning foolishly.

Lunch.
Great idea.
Not...

As she slipped into a knee-length white denim sundress, Mary-Jayne cursed herself repeatedly for being so agreeable and for finding Daniel Anderson charming and attractive and so darn sexy he could ask her to jet to the moon and she probably would.

She had to get a handle on the chemistry between them. There was no other option.

He tapped on her door exactly thirty minutes later and Mary-Jayne scowled as she moved down the short hallway. He was the punctual type. It figured. Everything about him screamed order and control.

She opened the door and faced him. "I'm ready."

"So I see," he said, and stood aside to let her pass.

Mary-Jayne closed the door and dropped the key into the tote draped over her left shoulder. "Where are we going?" she asked.

"Your choice," he replied. "Like I said."

Mary-Jayne took a deep breath. There were four restaurants at the resort: two bistros designed for families, a trendy Japanese teppanyaki bar and an exclusive à la carte restaurant named after his grandmother that Mary-Jayne had never been in because the menu was way out of her price range, even though Solana had offered to take her there several times.

She smiled sweetly. "Solana's. Think you'll be able to get a table at such short notice?"

His mouth turned up a little. "I'm sure they will be able to accommodate us."

Mary-Jayne looked up at him. "No one would dare defy you, would they?"

"Oh, I could think of someone who would."

He was smiling now and it made her smile back. *Keep your head*. The warning voice at the back of her mind told her to ignore the way her insides fluttered. She didn't want to *flutter* around him. She didn't want to have any kind of reaction. He was her baby's father—that was all. Besides, he didn't actually believe he had fathered her baby, so she should keep being madder than hell and resentful that he thought her so deceptive.

"Well, there's no point in going through life thinking you can have everything your own way, is there?" she replied, and started walking down the path.

He caught up with her in a few strides. "Or thinking you can say whatever you like."

Mary-Jayne stopped in her tracks. "Is that a nice way of saying I have a big mouth?"

"Actually," he said as he came to a halt beside her, "you have a very…lovely mouth."

There was something so flagrantly suggestive about his words that heat quickly travelled up her legs, belly and chest and then hit her directly in her cheeks. Memories banged around in her head. Memories of his touch.

His kiss. His possession. It was too easy to recall the crazy chemistry they shared and the night they'd spent together.

"I wish you wouldn't…"

Her words trailed off as she met his steely gaze. He had a hypnotic power that was uniquely his and it was something she'd never experienced before. She didn't *like* him. She didn't *want* him in her life. But Daniel had a way of invading her thoughts and plaguing her dreams.

"You wish I wouldn't…what?"

She sucked in a shallow breath and stepped sideways. "Stand so close," she said and crossed her arms.

A grin tugged at his mouth. As if he knew just how profoundly he affected her. And as if it pleased him no end.

"Not everything has to be a battle, Mary-Jayne."

And she wished he'd stop saying her name like that… kind of silky and smooth and sexy and impossible to ignore.

He was wrong. Everything did have to be a battle. It was the only way she'd remain unscathed. "Sure," she said and started walking again.

He stopped to make a phone call and was by the main entrance when he caught up with her. Without saying another word she followed him inside, across the foyer and then toward the elevator. The looks and stares from staff as they passed didn't go unnoticed, and Mary-Jayne suspected she'd quickly be the subject of whispers and conjecture. Since she'd arrived at the resort she'd kept to herself. She hadn't socialized with the staff or other store owners. She managed Audrey's store during the day and worked on her jewelry in the evenings. After Solana's birthday party she'd kept her head down and minded her own business, figuring others would do the same in regard to her. And mostly the staff did. Of course everyone knew about Audrey's disastrous affair with Caleb and speculation was rife that her friend had bailed simply to get away from the resort and him and avoid further humiliation. Only Mary-Jayne knew the truth. Sure, Audrey's mother was unwell…but it *was* exactly the excuse Audrey had needed to salvage her pride and put serious miles between herself and the man who'd hurt her so badly.

Mary-Jayne certainly didn't want to trade one scandal for another.

And she certainly didn't want anyone thinking she was sleeping with the boss!

"Everything all right?"

She glanced sideways and pulled her tote close to her belly. "Peachy."

"Worried what people might think?"

Her mouth tightened. He was too intuitive for her liking. "Couldn't care less."

She stepped into the elevator and he moved in behind her. He stared at her for a second before raising one dark brow. "Perhaps you're not as free-spirited as I thought."

She shrugged. "Maybe not."

The door opened, and Mary-Jayne was about to step out when she realized they weren't on the restaurant level. They were one floor up on the conference suites and boardroom level.

He touched her back and gently urged her forward. "Come on."

"Why are we here? I thought we were—"

"This way," he replied, and kept her moving down the short corridor.

A door opened at the end of the hall and a young man in white chef's gear greeted them. Mary-Jayne had seen him around the resort a few times. Daniel greeted him by name and they were shown directly into a private dining area. It was luxury personified. There were half a dozen

tables covered in crisp white linen and the finest dinner-
ware and crystal. A long panel of windows overlooked the
pool area and also offered an incredible view of the ocean.

A waiter emerged from another door and pulled out a
seat at a table by the window.

Mary-Jayne rocked back on her heels and looked at
Daniel. "Nice view."

"Shall we sit?"

His words were more request than question, and she
fought the urge to turn around and leave. Instead she
smiled a little and sat down. The waiter offered her some
sparkling water, and she gave a grateful nod and only
spoke again when the young man and the chef left the
room.

She dropped her tote to her feet, stared out the window
for a moment before resting her elbows on the table and
turning her gaze toward the man sitting opposite. "Clearly
I'm not the only one concerned about what people think."

He stilled. "What?"

She waved a hand vaguely. "Up the back elevator and
into a secret room?"

"Private," he clarified. "Not secret. I thought you might
prefer it. Personally I couldn't care less what people think."

She wondered if that were true. Daniel possessed a kind
of confidence she suspected was born from arrogance. He
was used to getting his own way. Used to telling people
what to do. He called the shots...and she couldn't imagine him tolerating speculation from anyone in his employ.

"Well, they'll be *thinking* plenty once my belly really
pops out."

His mouth curled at the edges. "They can think what
they like. I should have realized you were pregnant when
I first saw you yesterday," he said quietly. "It suits you."

She smirked a little. "Am I glowing?"

He nodded. "Yes."

It was a nice compliment, and her skin warmed. "I'll probably end up the size of a house, though," she said and laughed. "All the women in my family have looked like they've swallowed an elephant when they were pregnant."

His mouth curled at the sides, and it was incredibly sexy. "Tell me about them."

"My family?" She shrugged. "There's not much to tell. We all live in Crystal Point. My parents are both retired. My older brother, Noah, is married to Callie and they have four kids. He builds boats and she's a horse-riding instructor. Then there's my sister Evie, who's an artist and runs a bed-and-breakfast. She's married to Scott—who's actually Callie's brother. He's a firefighter and they have two kids. Then there's Grace, who is married to Noah's best friend Cameron. He's a cop, she's a finance broker and they had their first baby two months ago. And then there's little-old-knocked-up me."

He smiled at her words. "No...not much to tell at all."

Mary-Jayne laughed again. It occurred to her that despite how much he aggravated her, she smiled a lot around Daniel. "They're good people."

"I don't doubt it. I imagine you had a very happy childhood."

"Mostly," she admitted. "Of course it was fraught with the usual teenage-girl angst and rebellion, I suppose. I'm the youngest and therefore it's expected that I would be the most troublesome."

He grinned a little. "What kind of trouble?"

"Oh...crushes on inappropriate boys, late nights, the wrong company...and I got my tattoo at fourteen."

He grimaced. "Brave girl."

"Getting a tattoo? Brave or foolish, you mean, because basically I'm marked for life."

"I mean the pain thing."

"Pain?"

"They use needles...right?"

Mary-Jayne tilted her head. "Well...yes."

"I don't like needles."

She laughed loudly. "Chicken."

"You're mocking me," he said, his mouth twisting a little. "That's something of a habit of yours."

The waiter returned with their drinks and placed a menu on the table. Once the young man left, she returned her attention to Daniel.

"I imagine your ego is healthy enough to take it."

He grinned again. "You're probably right. So..." he said and pushed the glass around the table. "Is there any chance your father is going to come after me with a shotgun?"

She laughed loudly. "Not one. My brother, Noah, on the other hand, is very protective of his sisters." She took a long breath. "Seriously...my family let me live my own life. I'm fully prepared to raise this baby alone, Daniel. Be involved or don't. It's that simple."

His brows rose fractionally. "With me in San Francisco and you in Crystal Point? That's not simple. That's about as complicated as it gets, Mary-Jayne. Because I'm not about to avoid my legal and moral responsibility...no matter how much it seems you would like me to."

She frowned and touched her belly. "If I wanted that I would never have told you I was pregnant. Frankly, I just don't want you to get hung up on what you think you *have* to do. Sure, I'd like my baby to have a father who's involved in his or her life, but I don't want this to turn into some kind of parenting battleground with you on one side and me on the other and our child stuck in the middle."

"Nice speech. Is it meant to put me in my place?"

She shrugged. "Take it how you want. It's all rather

moot, anyhow…isn't it? Since you don't actually believe this baby is yours."

His eyes darkened and she was quickly drawn into them. Something passed between them, a kind of relentless energy that warmed her blood.

"It's not that…it's…"

"It's what?" Mary-Jayne asked, and met his gaze and asked the question hovering on her lips. "Is it because of your wife?"

Chapter Five

Daniel stilled. It was the first time the subject had been mentioned since Mary-Jayne had told him she was pregnant. Had he spared Simone more than a fleeting thought in the past twelve hours? The past twenty-four? He'd become so consumed by Mary-Jayne and the idea she was carrying his baby that he could barely think of anything else.

"I gather my grandmother told you what happened?"

She shrugged lightly. "Solana told me she was killed in a car wreck a few years ago."

"Four years," he corrected. "Four years, four months and three weeks."

Her eyes shone. "She was pregnant, wasn't she?"

He nodded slowly as his throat tightened. "Yes. Five months."

"I'm so sorry." Her hand moved across the table and connected with his for a moment before she quickly pulled it back. "It must have been devastating."

"It was the single worst day of my life."

She gathered her hands together in her lap and opened her mouth to speak when the waiter returned. Daniel watched as she studied the menu for a few seconds and then ordered one of the three vegetarian options he'd insisted be included. When she was done he ordered the swordfish, and when the waiter left he grabbed his glass and took a drink.

He put the glass down and spoke. "If you want to ask me about it, go ahead."

Her eyes widened. "You don't mind?"

He shrugged one shoulder.

"How did it happen?"

Daniel closed his eyes for a second as memories banged around in his head. He'd gone over that day countless times in his mind and the pain never lessened. "Simone was driving home from a doctor's appointment and stopped off at the mall to get a birthday gift. She pulled out of the parking lot and into the flow of traffic and a vehicle coming in the opposite direction slammed into her car. The brake line had snapped on the other car and the inexperienced driver panicked, hit the accelerator and crossed over the road."

"Was she killed instantly?"

He shook his head, almost admiring Mary-Jayne's blunt questioning. There was no false pity in her expression. Only curiosity and genuine concern.

"She died in hospital. The doctors tried to save her but her injuries were too severe."

"And the baby?"

"Our daughter died within minutes of Simone passing away."

"That's so sad. Did you have a name picked out for her?"

Daniel pushed down the heat clawing up his throat.

"We'd planned on naming her Lana, after my grand-mother."

She was quiet for a moment, her gaze lowered, clearly absorbing what he'd said. When she looked up her eyes were bright, almost glistening. He watched as she bit down on her bottom lip as moisture quickly filled her eyes. He'd observed many emotions cross her face in the time they'd known one another—anger, dislike, humor, passion—but this was something else. Sadness. Acute and heartfelt. He didn't like how it made him feel. Dealing with the combative, argumentative Mary-Jayne was easy compared to seeing her in tears.

"I'm sorry," she said, and grabbed the napkin to dab at her eyes. "I didn't mean to..." Her words trailed and she swallowed hard. "It's the baby hormones. They get me at the most unexpected times. Anyway," she said, her voice a little stronger, "thank you for telling me."

"It's not a secret. I'm sure my grandmother or Caleb would have told you the same thing had you asked them. It was an accident...and like all accidents, it was simply a series of events that merged into one terrible outcome."

She looked at him with silent intensity. "You mean, if she'd lingered at the mall a little longer, or if she had taken another exit from the parking lot, or the other driver had gotten out of bed ten minutes later that morning things would have turned out differently?"

"Exactly."

"You said she was buying a birthday gift. Who was it for?"

Daniel hesitated for a moment. "My grandmother."

It took a moment, but her eyes widened as realization dawned. "So...that night...the night of Solana's birthday party...it was the...the..."

"The anniversary of their deaths? Yes, it was."

The waiter returned with their meals before she had a chance to respond, and Daniel watched with keen interest as she took a long breath and stared into her plate. Once the waiter left them she looked up.

"Is that why you…why you…"

"Why I what?" he asked.

"The party, you know…and how we…" Her words trailed and she shrugged lightly.

"We had sex, you mean?"

Sex. He wasn't going to call it anything else. He wasn't going to suggest they'd made love because it would have been a lie. He used to make love to his wife. There was love and heart and passion between them. They'd been friends since college and started dating when Simone had finished law school. What he felt for Mary-Jayne wasn't grounded in that kind of friendship or any measure of deep emotion. It was base and instinctual and fuelled by attraction and sexual desire. And he intended for it to stay that way. She might be under his skin, but he wasn't about to let her get into his heart.

"I thought there might be a connection," she said and arched one brow. "Like you were wanting…to forget about…"

"I could never forget my wife," he said quietly.

She flinched a little. "I didn't mean that. I was thinking perhaps you needed a distraction that night and that's why you were interested in me."

"I was *interested* in you from the moment I saw you in the store window."

He knew she wouldn't be surprised by his admission. There had been heat between them from that first glance. Daniel wasn't conceited, but he knew the attraction he felt for Mary-Jayne was very much reciprocated.

"Oh…okay."

"The fact it was my grandmother's birthday was a co-incidence," he said, stretching the truth to avoid her questions or her censure. He wasn't about to admit that the hollow feeling that had haunted him since Simone's death had been amplified that night. Or that for a few incredible hours he'd found solace in the arms of a woman he barely knew. "So have you been well other than the nausea?" he asked, shifting the subject.

"Mostly," she replied. "Both my sisters suffered from gestational diabetes when they were pregnant, so my doctor is keeping watch on my sugar levels. But I feel fine at the moment."

Concern tightened his chest. "Does that mean this pregnancy holds risks for you? Is there something we should talk to your doctor about? Perhaps a second opinion is needed to ensure you get the best possible care. I can arrange an appointment with a specialist if—"

"I'm fine," she said sharply, interrupting him as she picked up the cutlery. "The nausea and appetite issues are a normal part of being pregnant. And I like my current doctor just fine, thank you. Stop interfering."

He bit back a grin at her impatience. "Don't mistake concern for control, Mary-Jayne."

She flashed him an annoyed look. "I don't."

"Oh, I think you do. I think you're so desperate to stay in control here that anything I say will be like waving a red flag at a bull."

She looked as if she wanted to jab him in the forehead with her fork. "You really do love to hear the sound of your own voice."

He laughed. "Hit a nerve, did I?"

"By implying that I value my independence?" she shot back. "Not a nerve…a fact. I'm not about to be lorded over like some spineless minion."

"That's a favorite insult of yours," he said and watched her. "Despite what you've conjured in your colorful imagination, I don't live in a house filled with servants. I cook my own meals, launder my own clothes and even tie my own shoes."

Her green eyes flashed. "Doesn't stop you from being a condescending horse's ass, does it?"

He laughed again. They had a way of pushing each other's buttons, and watching her fiery expression quickly stirred his blood and libido. "We have five months to get through until the baby comes, and I'd prefer it if we could manage that time without constantly goading one another, wouldn't you?"

She shrugged as if she couldn't have cared less. But Daniel wasn't fooled. She was as wound up as he was. "Since you'll be in San Francisco and I'll be in Crystal Point, what difference does it make?"

An ocean. Thousands of miles. A different life. There would be so many things between them. Between him and the child she carried. The child she said was his. Most of the shock had worn off overnight. Sure, he wanted a paternity test, but there were months ahead where he either had to accept the child was his, or not. And, despite everything between them, he realized that he believed Mary-Jayne. His grandmother knew her, trusted her... and although some old cynical instincts banged around in his head, Daniel realized he trusted her, too.

"You could come to San Francisco."

She looked up and made a scoffing sound. "Yeah... right."

Maybe not. "What about here?"

Her gaze sharpened. "Here? At the resort?"

"Yes."

"I can't do that, either," she said, and put down her fork.

"Why not?" he shot back. "Your jewelry business is mostly done online, so you could do that anywhere...San Francisco or here."

"This isn't my home, that's why not. I live in Crystal Point... I've lived there all my life. It's where I was born and it's where my baby will be born."

"Our baby."

Her jaw dropped slightly. "You believe me?"

He took a breath and nodded. "I believe you."

She looked wary. "Why the sudden change of heart?"

"Because *not* believing you essentially means I forfeit any rights to be part of this experience."

Mary-Jayne stilled. Rights? What did he mean by that? He wanted rights? He believed her? It should have put her at ease. Instead her entire body was suddenly on red alert. What had she expected? That once she told him about her pregnancy then he would quietly go away and leave her to raise her child alone?

Naive idiot.

The urge to get up and leave suddenly overwhelmed her, and it took all her strength to remain in her seat. She slowly met his unwavering gaze. "I'll be leaving in less than two weeks," she said. "As soon as Audrey returns I'm going home. My home," she reiterated. "Where I belong."

"Then I'll go with you," he said, so casually that her blood simmered. "We need to tell your folks, anyhow."

"*I'll* tell *my* family when *I* choose," she said, and pushed back her chair a fraction. "Stop bossing me about."

"Stop acting like a child."

It was the kind of verbal gridlock she expected when she was near him. They didn't like one another. They never would. They had sexual chemistry and nothing more. Fatigue and a sudden surge of queasiness shortened her patience and she pushed the seat back.

"Thanks for lunch," she said, and stood. "I'll see my own way out."

"My case in point," he said as he got up. "Run when you don't like what you hear. That's a child's way out, Mary-Jayne."

Her rage sought release. "Go to hell."

His mouth quirked fractionally. "I'll see you Tuesday morning, at nine, for the ultrasound appointment."

"I'd rather—"

"At nine," he insisted, cutting her off.

She didn't respond. Instead she grabbed her tote, thrust back her shoulders and left the room with a pounding heart, more determined than ever to keep him at arm's length.

Back in her condo she calmed down a little, took a shower and called Audrey. Her friend didn't answer her phone so she left a brief message. She spent the remainder of the day staring at her phone, hoping Audrey would call and watching an old movie on the television. By the time she dropped into bed her head was thumping and her rage was festering.

How dare he call her childish? He was an arrogant, pompous jerk! The sooner she was away from him, the better.

On Monday Mary-Jayne lay low. She opened the store and kept away from the front window as much as possible, in case *he* walked by. Or watched her. Or stalked her. But thankfully he didn't show up at the store and didn't call. And since Caleb didn't do his usual midmorning drop in either, Mary-Jayne knew Daniel had told his brother to steer clear.

Puppet master...

Controlling everything and everyone around him.

It made her mad, and got her blood boiling.

On Tuesday morning she set her alarm an hour early, showered and forced herself to eat breakfast. She dressed in a knee-length button-up blue floral dress and tied her hair up in a ponytail. Then she waited on the sofa for him to arrive, hands clasped together. He tapped on the door at nine o'clock with his usual annoying promptness.

He looked so good in jeans and a collared black T-shirt she could barely croak out a greeting when her level gaze met the broad expanse of his chest. She stupidly wished she were taller, more slender, more elegant...and able to meet his eyes without having to look up.

"Good morning."

Mary-Jayne forced out a smile. "Are you always on time for everything?"

"Always."

"It's an annoying trait of yours."

He grinned and motioned for her to pass. Once he pulled the door shut he placed a hand into the small of her back and ushered her forward. "Well, I guess it's one of those things you'll have to get used to."

Not when there's an ocean between us I won't...

By the time they were in his car she was so worked up her teeth chattered. He asked for the address and she replied quietly, staying silent as he punched the information into his GPS. Once they were on their way she dropped her tote to her feet and stared out the side window. But his nearness still rattled her. He was so close and had a kind of hypnotic power she'd never experienced before. Any man she'd ever known paled beside him. Any attraction she'd had in the past seemed lukewarm compared to the heat that simmered between them. The arguments didn't mask anything. It only amplified the undercurrent of desire and made her remember the passion and pleasure they'd shared that night four months ago.

She turned her head to glance at his profile. "Have you ever done that before?"

"Done what?"

"Sleep with someone you hardly know."

His mouth curved, but he looked straight ahead. "I don't recall either of us getting a whole lot of sleep that night."

Her cheeks heated. "You know what I mean." She swallowed hard. "I… It's just that I… Despite how I *seem*… I'm not like that…usually."

"Usually?"

She let out a heavy breath. "I don't sleep around…okay. I might come across as free-spirited and all that…but when it comes to sex I'm not easy. I've had three serious relationships including my high school boyfriend and I've never had a one-night stand before."

"Are you asking how many relationships I've had? Or one-night stands?" He glanced at her for a moment. "Does it really matter?"

His reticence irritated her and she frowned. "Is the subject off-limits for some reason?"

His jaw tightened. "My wife died over four years ago. Have I remained celibate since then? No. Have I had a committed relationship since then? No. Is that enough of an answer, Mary-Jayne?"

She got the message. She was one in a long line of meaningless one-night stands.

Just as well she didn't like him in the least, or she might have been offended by his admission. "I don't have any kind of ulterior motive for asking," she said and stared directly ahead. "I was curious, that's all."

"Well, if your curiosity has you imagining I have a

different woman in my bed every night, you'll be disappointed."

She didn't want to think about any woman in his bed, different or otherwise. "I'd have to care to feel disappointment, wouldn't I?"

"I guess you would," he said quietly. "But in case you've been having sleepless nights over it—my bed has been empty since you left it so quickly in the small hours of the morning all those months ago."

It was a dig. She'd snuck out of his villa, all right, and he clearly didn't appreciate her efforts to avoid any uncomfortable morning-after postmortems. Obviously he'd been stung by her disappearing act. And it took her a moment to realize what he'd said about his empty bed.

"No one since? Have you already nailed every woman in San Francisco? Is that the problem?"

He laughed humorlessly. "You're the problem."

"Me?" She almost squeaked the word out. "I can't imagine why."

"One night didn't really do us justice, did it? Not with that kind of instant attraction."

She knew what he meant. The store window. The resort foyer. The beach. Solana's party. Every time they'd met the heat had ramped up a notch. Until it had become so explosive the outcome was unavoidable.

"So you want...you still want..."

He chuckled. "You know, you really are a fascinating contradiction. For such a *free-spirited* woman, you can be equally shy and self-conscious."

"Because I think sex should mean something? Because I think one-night stands are empty and pointless and of little importance?"

His profile was unmoving. "Since our night together

resulted in this pregnancy, I'd say it's about as important as it gets, wouldn't you?"

She frowned. "You're twisting my words. I meant the sex wasn't important...not the baby."

There was insult in her words, and she was surprised that he stayed silent.

Silent and seething.

He was mad. Perhaps his ego wasn't as rock solid as she thought?

"That's not a complaint, by the way," she said, and pushed the tote around with her feet. "The sex was very... nice."

"It wasn't *nice*, Mary-Jayne. It was hot and incredibly erotic and about as good as it gets."

He was right. They both knew it.

"That, too," she admitted. "And the reason I left," she said, and figured she may as well tell him the truth, "is I didn't want any morning-after awkwardness. I thought it would be easier to bail and forget the whole thing. I mean, it was never going to be any more than one night. I think we both knew that."

"If I believed that I wouldn't have repeatedly asked you out."

It was true. He *had* pursued her. And she'd refused him every time. Because they were too different. As clichéd as oil and water. He wanted her in his bed and he got what he wanted. Only a fool would imagine he was looking for anything more.

"To get me into bed again, right? Which means we would have been back to square one. The point I'm making is men and women generally think about sex differently. I'm not saying I'm after a picket fence quite yet, but I'm not foolish enough to waste time on something or someone where it wouldn't be on the table ever."

"That's quite a judgment."

"Can you deny it?" she asked. "Let's face it, Daniel, you and I are polar opposites in every way. Sure, we have chemistry, but that's all. Most of the time we barely seem to tolerate one another. That's not a recipe for romance. It's a recipe for disaster."

She turned back to look out the side window with a heavy sigh, and they didn't say another word to one another until they'd reached Cairns. With a population of over one hundred thousand, the bustling regional city was a popular tourist spot and served as a starting point for people wanting to visit the Great Barrier Reef.

Within minutes they were pulling into the car park in front of the medical center. She got out of the Jeep, grabbed her tote and waited for him to come around to the passenger side.

"If you like, we can look around town when we're done," he suggested and locked the vehicle. "Maybe have lunch."

"The way you keep trying to feed me, anyone would think I need fattening up."

His brows narrowed. "Well, I have noticed you don't eat enough."

Mary-Jayne put her hands on her thickening waist. "I eat plenty. Have you seen my ever-expanding middle? I told you how the women in my family look when they're pregnant."

"You hardly touched your food the other day."

Mary-Jayne looked up at him. "I was too mad to eat."

"Too hot headed, you mean."

"You were being a bossy, arrogant jerk. It annoyed me."

"Everything I do appears to annoy you," he said and ushered her toward the steps that led into the building. "Perhaps you should consider why that is."

"I know why," she said, and moved up the steps. "Because you're a bossy, arrogant jerk."

He laughed softly and grasped her hand, stopping her before they reached the door. Mary-Jayne looked up and met his gaze. His gray eyes were dark and intense, and for a second she couldn't do anything but stare at him. The pulse in his cheek throbbed and she fought the urge to touch the spot.

He threaded their fingers and drew her closer. "How about you let me off the hook for a little while, hmm?"

Don't do it...

"I can't..."

"Sure you can," he said, and rubbed his thumb inside her palm. "I'm not your enemy, Mary-Jayne...except perhaps in your lively imagination."

"Daniel..."

"Come on," he said, and gently led her inside. "Let's go and meet this baby."

It took about twenty minutes to find the correct office, see reception and be shown to a small room when she was instructed to lie on the bed and wait for the doctor. A nurse appeared and wheeled the imaging machine close to the bed and told them the doctor would be in soon.

"Are you okay?" he asked from the chair he sat on from across the room.

Mary-Jayne lay back on the table and wiggled. "Fine. Peachy. Never better."

"You look nervous."

She shrugged. "Well, I've never done this before, so of course I'm a little nervous."

As she said the words it occurred to her that Daniel probably *had* done this before. With Simone. With the wife he'd loved and the baby they'd lost. It must have been hard for him to come into the room with her, a woman he hardly knew, and potentially have the same experience he'd shared with his wife.

Shame hit her square between the shoulders.

All morning she'd been thinking of herself and hadn't spared a thought for his feelings. *What's happened to me? When did I become so self-absorbed?*

"I'm sorry."

He looked at her. "For what?"

"For not considering how difficult it must be for you to do this."

His gaze didn't waver. "It's not difficult. Just…different. Simone and I had planned everything, from conception to her due date. She'd had endometriosis for several years and had trouble getting pregnant. Eventually we used IVF and she got pregnant after three attempts. It was all rather clinical and organized and more about the treatments and processes rather than the baby…at least in the beginning. So, yes, this is different."

There was heat in her throat. "Okay," she said, and smiled a little. "You're off the hook."

The doctor came into the room then and Daniel got to his feet. Mary-Jayne lay back and tried to relax. He moved beside her and touched her shoulder.

"So," Doctor Stewart said once she'd introduced herself and perched on a stool at the side of the bed. "Would you like to know your baby's sex?"

Mary-Jayne looked at Daniel.

He shrugged lightly. "It's up to you."

She swallowed hard. "I think… Yes…I'd like to know."

She glanced at him again and thought he looked relieved.

The doctor got her to unbutton her dress, and Mary-Jayne tried not to be self-conscious of Daniel's presence in the chair at her side as her belly was bared. A cool gel was placed on her stomach and she shivered a little. Daniel took hold of her hand and squeezed gently.

Once the ultrasound started she was riveted to the image on the small screen. It didn't look like anything at first, until the doctor pointed out an arm and the baby's head. Emotion welled inside her and she bit back a sob.

Hi there, peanut... I'm your mother...and I love you more than I thought possible.

"And there's your baby," the doctor said, and rolled the device lower. "You have a perfectly lovely boy."

She looked at Daniel and noticed he stared directly at the screen, clearly absorbed by what they saw. He'd never looked more attractive to her, and in that moment an unexpected surge of longing rushed through her entire body.

Longing and desire and something else...something she couldn't quite fathom.

Something she didn't want to think about.

"Oh…"

The doctor's voice quickly cut through her thoughts.

"What is it?"

Daniel's voice now. Deep and smooth and quicker than usual. It gave her comfort. If something was wrong, he was there, holding her hand, giving her strength. He glanced at her and squeezed her fingers.

Doctor Stewart looked at them both. "Well…I see."

"What?" he asked again, firmer this time. "Is something wrong?" It was the question she was too afraid to ask.

"Nothing's wrong," the doctor said, and smiled broadly. "It's just…there are two of them."

Mary-Jayne stared at the screen. "What do you mean?"

The doctor smiled. "Congratulations to you both… you're having twin boys."

Chapter Six

Someone could have told him that he was going to live on the moon for the next fifty years and he wouldn't have been more shocked.

Twin boys...

"You're sure?" he asked the doctor, and noticed how Mary-Jayne hadn't moved. He squeezed her hand reassuringly. "And they're fine?"

The doctor nodded. "Fine. Big, strong and healthy. Would you like to listen to their heartbeats?"

Daniel didn't recall saying yes. But within seconds he had small earphones on and heard the incredible sound of his sons' hearts. Emotion rose up and hit him directly in the solar plexus, polarizing him for a moment. He swallowed hard, fighting the heat in his eyes and throat. Nothing he ever heard again would match the sound of the two tiny heartbeats pounding almost in unison. Longing, absolute and raw, filled his chest with such force he grabbed the side of the chair for support.

The doctor said something about having a picture done for them, but he barely heard. He took off the earphones and gently placed them over Mary-Jayne's head. Watching her expression shift from shock to wonderment was incredible. Her face radiated with a joy so acute it was blinding in its intensity. She'd never looked more beautiful.

The doctor stood. "I'll arrange for a picture and come back in a little while," she said, and quickly left the room.

Daniel tightened his grip on Mary-Jayne's hand. "Are you okay?"

She dropped the earphones onto the bed. "Um…I think so."

"Not what you were expecting, huh?"

She sighed. "Not exactly. But…" Her words trailed off for a moment. "I'm happy." She glanced at the now-blank screen. "I can't quite believe it."

"Are there many twins in your family?" he asked, and rubbed her fingertips. She shrugged. "Not really. I know there are in yours, though."

He nodded and grinned. "Yes. My brothers are twins. My grandfather was a twin, and I have two sets of cousins who are twins. It's like an epidemic in my family."

"This is all your doing, then?" she said and smiled.

"I don't think there's actually a genetic link on the father's side, but I'll happily take the credit if you want," he said softly. "Are you okay with this?"

"I'm happy, like I said. And a little scared. I wasn't expecting two." She looked down at her naked stomach. "I wonder if the nurse will come back to get this goo off my belly."

Daniel released her hand and got up. He found a box of tissues on the counter and came back to her side. "This should do it," he said as he sat down and began wiping the gel off her skin.

It was the most intimate thing they'd done in months, and even though he acted as perfunctory as he could, it didn't stop a surge of desire from climbing up his spine. She lay still, perfectly composed. Until he met her gaze and saw that she was watching him with scorching intensity. When he was done her hand came up and she grabbed his fingertips and then gently laid his palm against her belly. She placed her hand on top of his, connecting them in a way that was mesmerizing. Feeling her, feeling their babies, Daniel had no answer for the sensation banging around in his head.

He'd never wanted to feel this again. Not after Simone.

But it was inevitable. They were his children. His sons. They were part of him. How could he not get drawn into feeling such acute and blinding love for them? He couldn't. And he wanted them. He wanted to be part of their lives. Full-time. A real parent.

A real father.

He looked at Mary-Jayne. Her eyes were bright. Luminous. She chewed on her bottom lip and his gaze immediately went to her mouth. He touched her forehead with his other hand and felt the connection down deep. Soul-deep.

In that moment he could nothing else but kiss her.

And her lips, as new as they were familiar, softened beneath his instantly. Daniel's pulse quickened as the kiss quickly deepened. Her breath was warm, her tongue accepting when he sought it with his own. She sighed deep in her throat, and a powerful surge of desire wound through his blood. He touched her hair, twirling the glorious strands between his fingertips. Her hand came up to his chest and he felt the connection through to his bones. And he kissed her again. And again. With each kiss his need for her grew. As did the knowledge he had one option. One way to make things right.

"Mary-Jayne," he said against her lips, trailing his mouth down her cheek to the sensitive spot by her earlobe. A spot he knew made her quiver. "We should get married."

She stilled instantly. Her mouth drew in a tight line and she pushed his hand off her belly. "What?"

Daniel pulled back and stared into her face. "Married," he said again. "We should get married."

She put a hand on his shoulder and gave him a shove. "Don't be ridiculous."

He straightened and got to his feet. "It's the only solution."

"To what?" she said, and pulled her dress closed over her stomach as she swung her legs off the bed. "Since there's no problem, we don't need a solution." She swiftly buttoned up her dress.

He crossed his arms. "There *is* a problem. We're having two children together and we live on opposite sides of the world."

"I said you can see the baby…I mean, babies, as much as you want. But I'm not interested in a loveless marriage, Daniel. Not with you or anyone else."

The doctor returned before he had an opportunity to say anything more. She gave them the photo of the twins and advised Mary-Jayne to make another appointment with her obstetrician in the next few weeks. Daniel listened while she briefly explained how she was returning home to Crystal Point in the next fortnight and how she would see her family doctor once she was back home.

Home…

He almost envied the way she spoke about the tiny town where she'd lived all her life. Nowhere felt like home to Daniel. Not Port Douglas. Not San Francisco.

They left a few minutes later and Mary-Jayne didn't

say a word as they made their way out of the building toward their vehicle.

"Are you hungry?" he asked as he opened the passenger door. "We could stop somewhere for—"

"I'd prefer to just go back to the resort," she said, cutting him off. "I'm a little tired."

Daniel didn't argue. He nodded and closed the door once she was inside. They were soon back on the road, and he made a quick stop to refuel and grab a couple of bottles of water. She took the water with a nod and tucked it by the seat. Fifteen minutes into their return trip he'd had enough of her unusual silence and spoke.

"Avoiding the subject isn't going to make it go away, Mary-Jayne."

"What subject?"

"My proposal."

She glanced sideways. "I thought you must have been joking."

"I'm perfectly serious. Once you calm down you'll realize it's the only thing we can do."

She huffed. "I'm perfectly calm. And marrying you is the *last* thing I want to do."

"Why not?" he asked, ignoring how much disdain she had in her voice.

"Because I'm not in the market for someone like you."

"Like me?" He smiled at her relentless insults. "Straight, healthy and financially secure?"

"Arrogant, judgmental and a pain in the—"

"Don't you think our children deserve two parents?"

"Our children *will* have two parents," she said, her knuckles white where she clasped her hands together. "Two parents who live in different countries. Two parents who have too much good sense to marry because it's expected they should." She turned her head. "Be honest, Daniel. You don't want to marry me, you just think you *have* to. But you don't. You're off the hook here. So please, don't mention it again."

He pushed down his irritation. She wound him up like no one else ever had. "I take it you're not opposed to marriage entirely...just marriage to me?"

"I'm opposed to marrying someone I don't love," she said bluntly. "And someone who doesn't love me. The thing is, I believe in love...and I want it. I want to be with someone who wants *me* above all others. Who wants only me and sees only me and who carries only me close to his heart."

It was foolish and romantic nonsense. "How can that matter when there are children involved?"

"Because it does," she insisted. "You've had some attack of conscience since you saw them on that screen and think marriage will somehow uncomplicate this...but it won't. We're too different to be tied to one another for life. And I'm not criticizing your motives, I'm simply trying to do what's best for everyone involved...including you."

Daniel wasn't convinced. His father and stepmother had married because Bernie was pregnant, and their marriage had turned out fine. They'd scraped a family together despite their differences. And if he was going to have any chance of being a hands-on father to his sons, Daniel knew he had to do the same.

But he knew Mary-Jayne well enough to recognize she wasn't prepared to discuss it any further. At least for now.

"We'll talk about it later."

"No, we won't," she reaffirmed. "And what was with that kiss?"

"It was a kiss. People kiss, Mary-Jayne."

She pointed to him and then herself. "Well, not *these* people. Don't do it again."

Had he lost his mind?

Marriage? As if she'd ever agree to that? Couldn't he see it was madness? He'd married for love once...how could he be prepared to settle for anything less? He could still be a father to their children. Sure, it would be challenging, considering the miles between them. But they could make it work. Plenty of people did the same. He was simply being bullheaded about it. Wanting his own way. Trying to control her.

Well, she wasn't about to be maneuvered into a loveless marriage.

She didn't care how much chemistry they had.

And he better not try to kiss her again, either!

"I'd like to stop and see my parents and tell them the news, if that's okay with you?"

Mary-Jayne turned her head. "Sure. Whatever."

It was a small detour, but she didn't mind. She liked Miles and figured they had to start telling people about the babies at some point. It took about half an hour to reach their small hobby farm, and Mary-Jayne sat up straight as he turned off into a narrow driveway and drove half a mile down the bumpy road until they reached the house. She saw the lovely timber home with wide verandas and noticed a small structure built in replica.

"My dad's studio," Daniel explained.

She turned her head. He watched her with such intensity for a moment her breath stuck in her throat. There was something riveting about his gaze, and she turned hot all over. She foolishly thought about the kiss again. It had been sweet and hot and had stirred her libido.

People kiss...

His words fluttered around in her head. Of course she knew it had been a spur-of-the-moment thing—they were looking at their babies for the first time, he'd helped remove the gel from her belly... No wonder she'd kissed him back so eagerly. She was only human. But he had an agenda. He'd decided what he wanted and would use whatever method he could to achieve that goal—which included seducing her!

She stared at him. "Please, Daniel...don't..."

"Don't what?" A smile creased the corners of his mouth. "What have I done now?"

"You know what," she said, pretty sure she sounded like a petulant child but not caring. "You kissed me."

"You kissed me back."

Color spotted her cheeks. "Well, I'm not going to be swept up in a whole lot of sex stuff...if that's what you're thinking."

He laughed as though he thought her hilarious. "I guess time will tell."

She seethed. "Just because you got me into bed once doesn't mean you will again. That night was out of character for me. I don't even *like* you."

Daniel sat back and turned the engine off. "Is this your usual mode of defense, Mary-Jayne? Attack first?"

She made a scoffing sound. "That's rich, coming from you. You're the corporate shark, not me."

"What is it exactly that you think I do for a living—steamroll over whoever gets in my way? I hate to disappoint you, but I'm not that mercenary. I'm the CEO of a large business that employs several thousand people around the globe. I'm not sure what it is you find so disagreeable about that or me."

"Everything," she replied. "Your arrogance for one...

like right now when you think I'm loopy because I dare to admit that I don't like you."

"I think you're scared," he said quietly. "Not loopy. And I think your emotions are heightened because you're pregnant."

Logically, she knew he was right. But he wound her up in a way that fueled every rebellious streak she possessed. And she was fairly certain he knew it.

"It's not baby brain," she shot back. "This is *me*. Emotional and loopy."

He made an exasperated sound. "Can we put a hold on this conversation? My dad is on his way over."

Sure enough, Miles Anderson was walking toward them from his studio, one strap of his shabby overalls flapping in the breeze. At sixty, he was still handsome and fit, and Mary-Jayne got a snapshot of what Daniel would be like in thirty years. The notion made her insides flutter. *Stupid*. She had to concentrate on now, not some time in the unknown future.

Daniel got out of the vehicle and Mary-Jayne remained where she was for the moment, watching as the two men greeted one another and shook hands. No embrace. No obvious display of affection. It saddened her a little. Would Daniel be like that with his own sons? He spoke to his father for a moment and then turned back toward the Jeep. Mary-Jayne was half out by the time he met her at the door. Miles wasn't far behind, and he watched as his son helped her out of the car.

"Lovely to see you again M.J.," Miles said cheerfully.

"Mary-Jayne," Daniel corrected, as though his father had committed the crime of the century.

She grabbed her tote and looked up at him. "No one really calls me that," she said quietly as he closed the door. "Except my folks...and you."

His mouth twitched. "It's your name."

"It's an old-fashioned mouthful."

"I think it's very pretty," Miles said, and took her arm. "Let's get up to the house. Bernie will be delighted you're here."

She could feel Daniel behind her as they walked toward the house. Mary-Jayne made a comment about how lovely the gardens were and Miles began chatting about the vegetable patch, the chickens and the new milking goat he'd recently bought who kept getting into the yard and eating the zucchini flowers.

Once they reached the veranda Miles spoke again. "My wife has a client in half an hour, but we have time for coffee and some of her pecan cookies."

Mary-Jayne noticed a door to the left of the main door and the shingle that hung to one side—Homeopath, Masseuse and Acupuncturist. Daniel's stepmother came through the open doorway, wearing a blue-and-gold tunic over white trousers, her blond hair flowing. She rushed toward him with a happy squeal and gave him a long hug.

"I'm so glad to see you," she said, all breathless energy, as they pulled apart. "Your brother told us you were back. Four months in between visits is too long."

He is loved.

It was all Mary-Jayne could think of. And then she realized how lucky her babies would be to have two such lovely people as grandparents. Her hand moved instinctively to her belly, and she noticed how Bernie's gaze immediately shifted toward the movement. She looked as though she was about to say something when Daniel stepped back and introduced them.

"It's lovely to meet you," Bernie said, smiling broadly. "Solana has told me all about you, of course. You've made quite an impression on my mother-in-law, and she's the best judge of character I know."

Mary-Jayne returned the smile. "Thank you."

Bernie tapped her husband's shoulder. "Why don't you take Daniel to the studio and show him the piece you're working on for the Phuket renovation, and Mary-Jayne and I will make coffee," she suggested, and then looked back toward Mary-Jayne. "My talented husband is sculpting an incredible bronze for the resort's foyer," she explained animatedly. "It's a dolphin pod diving through a wave." She sighed and smiled. "Just breathtaking."

Mary-Jayne grinned at the other woman's enthusiasm. She liked her immensely. "How lovely," she said, and noticed Miles looked faintly embarrassed by the praise. Daniel stood beside her, unmoving. She tapped his shoulder lightly, trying not to think about how her fingertips tingled at the connection. "You go, I'll be fine."

"Of course she will be," Bernie said, and linked their arms.

They headed inside and into the huge red cedar kitchen in the center of the house. Mary-Jayne noticed the dream catchers in nearly every window and smiled. A large pebbled water feature took up almost an entire wall, and the sound of the water slipping gently over the rocks created a charming ambience and feeling throughout the house.

"You have a lovely home," she said and perched onto a stool behind the wide kitchen counter.

"Thank you. We've been here for nearly ten years. We wanted somewhere where Miles could work without disturbing the neighbors," she said and grinned as she fiddled with the coffee machine. "Sometimes the soldering and battering goes on for hours. But we love it here and we wanted a place where our boys could call home. You know, for when they get married and have families of their own."

The innuendo wasn't missed and she dropped her gaze, took a breath and then met the other woman's inquisitive look head-on. "Yes, I'm pregnant. And yes, Daniel is the father. And we just learned we're having twin boys."

Bernie's beaming smile was infectious, and she came around the counter and hugged her close for a few seconds. "I'm so delighted. He deserves some happiness in his life after what he's been through."

Mary-Jayne was pretty sure Daniel wouldn't consider her a tonic for unhappiness.

"He loved his wife a lot, didn't he?" she asked quietly when the other woman moved back around the bench.

Bernie shrugged a little. "Simone? Well, she was easy to love. She was a nice woman, very kind and good-hearted. She was a lawyer, you know, very successful one, too, from all accounts."

As the other woman made coffee for the men and tea for them, Mary-Jayne fiddled with the silver ring on her right hand. She wasn't sure how she felt knowing Daniel had loved his wife so much. Not jealous—that would be plain stupid. Because it would mean she had feelings invested in him. Which she didn't. But displaced. As though she didn't quite belong. She wasn't someone whom Daniel would *choose* to bring home to meet his parents. Or choose to marry. She was there because she was carrying his babies. If she hadn't gotten pregnant that night they spent together then they probably would never have seen one another again.

"I'm sure she was lovely," she said and smiled.

"Daniel doesn't talk much about her," Bernie remarked, and grabbed four mugs. "He's always been a little closed off from his feelings. When Simone and their unborn baby died he kind of turned inward. The only person he really opens up to is Solana—they're very close. He never knew his real mother," she said and sighed. "I've always treated him like my own, of course. He was just a toddler when the twins were born. But I think losing his mother had a profound impact on him. And Miles grieved for a long time," she said candidly. "Even after we married and had our sons he was still mourning her death. I tried not to take it personally. I still don't on those times when he mentions her."

Mary-Jayne didn't miss the message in the other woman's words. But the situations weren't the same. She was sure Miles Anderson loved Bernadette, even if he had still grieved the wife he lost. Whereas Daniel didn't even *like* her. He might want her in his bed, but that was all it was.

"Thanks for the talk," Mary-Jayne said and smiled. "And the support."

"Anytime," Bernie said just as the men walked in through the back door.

Mary-Jayne swiveled on the stool and looked at Daniel. "How's the sculpture look?"

"Good."

Miles clapped a hand onto his son's shoulder. "Why don't you take her to the studio and show her?" he suggested, then winked at Mary-Jayne. "I should've guessed a brilliantly creative girl like you might want to critique my work. Go easy on this old man, though. My fragile artistic ego can't take too much criticism."

Mary-Jayne laughed. She genuinely liked Miles and understood his self-effacing humor. "Of course," she said and slid off the stool.

Daniel watched the interaction in silence and only moved when she took a few steps toward the door. "Coming?" she asked.

She was through the door and down the back steps quickly and didn't wait for him to catch up as she headed across the yard toward the studio. She was already inside and staring at the huge bronze sculpture when he came up behind her.

"Wow," she said as she stepped around the piece and admired the effort and imagination that had gone into its creation. "This is incredible."

Daniel came beside her. "He'll be delighted you approve."

She looked up and raised a brow. "I suppose you told him, then."

"About the babies?" He nodded. "Yes. He's delighted about that, too. Told me it was about time I settled down and raised a family."

"I hope you set him straight?"

"You mean did I tell him you've turned down my proposal? No, I thought I'd try my luck again before I admitted that."

Mary-Jayne offered a wry smile. "One marriage proposal in a day is enough, thanks very much."

"Even if I get down on my knee this time?" he asked, his eyes glittering. "Or get you a ring?"

"You're too uptight to get your kneecap dirty," she shot back, saccharine sweet. "And I want to design my own ring when I *eventually* get married."

He laughed, and she liked the sound way too much. "So, how'd Bernie take the news?"

"Very well. Tell me something, why do you call her Bernie? She's the only mother you've known, right?"

"I call her Mom sometimes," he said, looking just a little uncomfortable. "And stop cross-examining me."

"Gotta take the chance when I can. They're very nice," she said and moved around the sculpture some more. "And they love you."

"I know that," he said, and came closer again. "We just live different lives."

"But you had a happy childhood?"

He shrugged loosely. "I guess. Although there were times when I wished they'd stop moving the furniture around the house to accommodate their feng shui beliefs or eat a steak and fries instead of tofu burgers. Or have an aspirin for a headache instead of Bernie's acupuncture jabs to the temple."

Mary-Jayne stilled and looked up at him. "Is that why you don't like needles?"

"Well, I—"

She was mortified when she realized what it meant. "They stuck needles into their child?"

"They thought they were doing the right thing," he said and moved around behind her.

She turned to face him and looked up. "But that's why you don't like needles?"

"I guess," he said and shrugged again. "Seems foolish to make that kind of connection, though. It was a long time ago and it wasn't as if it was some kind of deliberate torture. Bernie's well qualified in her field and she thought she was helping. They were good parents."

"I know. And we'll be good, too," she assured him. "We've had good role models."

"Good parents who live in two different countries?" He reached out and touched a lock of her hair, twirling it between his fingertips. "I want to be their father, Mary-Jayne. All I'm asking for is a chance to do that."

Her heart tugged, and she pushed back a sudden swell of emotion "I can't. It wouldn't work," she implored. "Look, I'm not saying it's going to be easy doing this with the situation being what it is. We both know there will be challenges, especially as the children get older. But I can't and won't commit to a loveless marriage. I want what my parents have, and I want to raise my children in the town I've lived in all my life." She moved back fractionally and his hand dropped. "And I know you think that's all a load of overly romantic hogwash, but I can't change who I am and what I believe any more than you can. I've never really been in love. But I want to be."

"Yeah," he said, and shook his head. "And you want some romantic sap to carry you next to his heart... I heard all that the other day."

"But did you listen? Love isn't an illusion, Daniel. You loved your wife, right? Bernie said she was smart and beautiful and how everyone adored her. So if love was good enough for you back then, why do you think I'm so foolish for wanting the same thing?"

"Because it doesn't last."

"It does," she refuted. "Our parents are testament to that."

"So maybe sometimes it does last. But when it doesn't... When it's gone it's about as bad as it gets."

There was real pain in his voice, and she unconsciously reached out and grasped his upper arm. The muscles were tight and bunched with tension, and she met his gaze head on.

"You're still hurting," she whispered, fighting the need to comfort him.

He looked down into her face, his expression unmoving. The pulse in his cheek throbbed, and his gray eyes were as dark as polished slate. Her fingers tingled where she touched him, and when he reached up and cupped her cheek Mary-Jayne's knees wobbled.

"Most days...most days I'm just...numb."

Every compassionate and caring instinct she possessed was quickly on red alert. "It was an accident, Daniel. A terrible accident. And she wouldn't want you to feel this way, would she?"

"No," he said and traced her cheek with his thumb. "She'd want me to marry you and raise our sons together. And that's what we're going to do, Mary-Jayne. We have to get married. For the sake of our sons. All you need to do is say yes."

Chapter Seven

She didn't say yes. She didn't say anything. Instead she pulled away from him and headed back inside. They stayed for another twenty minutes, and when Bernie's client showed up they said their goodbyes and Daniel promised to return to see them in a couple of days. Being around his family made her long for her own, and Mary-Jayne stayed quiet on the trip back to the resort.

All you need to do is say yes...

As if it was so easy.

She almost admired his perseverance. Almost. He was relentless when he wanted something. No wonder he was so successful professionally. Solana had told her that he'd pretty much singlehandedly turned the chain of Sandwhisper Resorts into a flourishing enterprise around the globe. When his grandfather had been at the helm, Anderson's had only recently ventured into the new direction after spending years in copper and ore mining. Most of that was sold off now and the business focused on the resorts. While other empires had failed, Daniel had kept Anderson's afloat by using natural business acumen and innate tenacity. She remembered how he'd told her how so many people relied on the company for their livelihood and that was what made him determined to keep the organization growing.

Once they got back to the resort, he walked her to her door and lingered for a moment. "Can I see you tonight?"

Mary-Jayne shook her head. "I don't think so."

His eyes flashed. "You can't avoid me. I'm not going away, and neither is this situation."

"I'm tired, that's all. It's been a long day. And eventful," she said, and waved the envelope that held the picture of their babies.

He nodded. "All right, Mary-Jayne, I'll back off for tonight. But we have to get this sorted out."

"Yes," she said, and sighed heavily. "And we will. Just not today."

He left her reluctantly, and once he was gone she moved into the living room and slumped into the sofa. She was more confused than ever. *Daniel* confused her. Confounded her. He was relentless about the marriage thing. But she wouldn't change her mind. She couldn't. It would be a complete disaster.

She wanted love...not duty. Maybe he wasn't quite the closed-off corporate shark she'd first thought him to be; maybe there were moments when she enjoyed his company and liked the way they verbally sparred. And maybe there *was* a constant undercurrent of attraction and desire between them that made her head spin. But it still wasn't enough. And it never would be. Attraction alone wasn't enough. And those few unexpected moments where she relaxed around him were unreliable.

She hung around the condo for the remainder of the afternoon and at five o'clock was about to call Audrey again when there was a knock on her door. She groaned, loathing the thought of going another round with Daniel when all she wanted to do was talk to her friend and then curl into bed.

But it wasn't Daniel at her door. It was his grandmother.

"Can I come in?" Solana asked.

Mary-Jayne stepped back and opened the door wider. "Of course."

Once they were both settled in the living room, Solana spoke again.

"My grandson came to see me," she said and smiled. "He told me you were expecting twin boys."

Mary-Jayne wasn't surprised. It was the last thing he'd said to her when he'd walked her to her door earlier that day. He'd announced how he planned telling his grandmother about her pregnancy.

She nodded. "Yes, I am."

"And are you happy about it?"

"Very," she admitted. "I'm sorry I haven't told you earlier. Things were a little complicated and I—"

"You don't need to explain yourself. Daniel told me what happened."

She was relieved Solana understood. "Thank you. I know it must be something of a shock."

The older woman smiled. "Well, I was lining you up for Caleb...but now I think about it, you are definitely much better suited to Daniel. He needs someone who won't let him rule the roost. Caleb is way too easygoing. Whereas Daniel," Solana grinned widely, "is as wound up as a spring. You'll be good for him, I'm sure of it."

Mary-Jayne perched on the edge of the sofa. "Oh, it's not like that. We're not together or anything," she explained, coloring hotly. "I mean, we were *together*…just that once…but not now."

Solana's brows raised. "He said you've refused his marriage proposal."

"I did," she replied. "I had to. Please try to understand."

"I do," Solana said gently. "You want to fall in love and be swept off your feet. You want roses and moonlight and real romance."

"Yes," she admitted. "Exactly."

"And my grandson is too sensible and pragmatic for all that, right?"

Mary-Jayne shrugged. "We're not in love. We never would be. It would be a catastrophe."

Solana got up and moved to sit beside her on the sofa. "My son Miles married his first wife after dating her for two years. They were more in love than I'd ever seen two people in love. When she died so soon after Daniel was born Miles was heartbroken. And then along came Bernie and a few months later she was pregnant. It wasn't a love match at first…but they've made a good marriage together and raised three boys into the finest men I know."

She ignored the heavy thump behind her ribs. It was a nice story. But it's wasn't hers and Daniel's. "I know you want to see your grandson happy, but believe me, I could never be the person to do that. We don't even *like* one another."

Solana's hand came out and she briefly touched her stomach. "Oh, I'd say you liked one another well enough."

"That's not love…that's…"

"It's a place to start, that's all," Solana said. "Don't make a rash decision because you're scared of the future. Work on the present and let the future take care of itself."

It was a nice idea. But Mary-Jayne wasn't convinced.

Once the other woman left, she returned to her pacing.

She wasn't about to marry a man she didn't love. She might want him. She might even like him a little bit. Maybe more than a little bit. Maybe she liked him a lot. But it wasn't enough. It would never be enough. And she wasn't about to be railroaded into something she didn't want.

The phone rang and she snatched it up. It was Audrey.

"Thank God," she said, and quickly explained what was happening to her concerned friend.

Fourteen hours later Mary-Jayne was on a flight home.

She was gone.

Gone...

Again.

Daniel's mood shifted between concern and rage and in varying degrees.

How could she leave without a word?

Damn it, they were his children, too. His flesh. His blood.

He'd knocked on her door on Wednesday afternoon after Caleb had called and told him the store was closed again. He knocked and waited, and when she didn't respond he called her cell. It went to message and he hung up. On Thursday morning Audrey Cooper answered the door. And he knew instantly that she'd bailed. Her friend was of little help and regarded him with barely concealed contempt. The pretty redhead stood in the doorway, arms crossed, defiant and clearly willing to go into battle for her friend.

"Is she back in Crystal Point with her family?" he asked, his rage simmering, his patience frayed.

Audrey pushed back her hair, clearly unimpressed. "I'm not saying. But wherever she is, there's no point in going after her. I think it's fairly clear she doesn't want to see or hear from you."

"She said that?"

Audrey, who evidently had as much contempt for him as she did for Caleb, nodded slowly. "If you go after her she'll spook and disappear."

It sounded a little melodramatic. Mary-Jayne wouldn't do that. She wouldn't put their babies at risk. Not for anything. He knew her well enough to realize that. "That doesn't make sense."

Audrey's brows rose sharply. "I know M.J. way better than you do. She doesn't like to be hemmed in, and if you push her she'll react and run. She's got friends all over the place and they and her family would do anything for her...and that includes helping her avoid you at all costs. Just leave her alone."

Run? Jesus...she wouldn't... Would she?

Audrey grabbed the door and closed it a little. "Since you own this place, I should tell you I'm looking for someone to take over the lease on the store. If I can't find anyone in a week I'm closing up and leaving. So if you want to sue me for breach of contract, go right ahead. And tell that lousy brother of yours to stay out of my way."

Then she closed the door in his face.

Daniel was furious by the time he reached Caleb's office. His brother was sitting at his desk, punching numbers into the computer.

"Your redhead is back," he said when the door was shut.

Caleb almost jumped out of his chair. "Audrey?"

"Yeah."

"Is she still..."

"Angry?" Daniel nodded. "She hates you as much as ever and me by association, which is why she wouldn't confirm that Mary-Jayne has gone home."

His brother grabbed his jacket off the back of the chair. "I'm going to see her. Is she at the—"

Daniel pulled the jacket from his brother's hands and tossed it on the desk. "You'd better not. She's leaving the resort, closing up the store if she can't find someone to take on her lease."

Clearly agitated, Caleb grabbed the jacket again. "She can't do that. She signed a contract. We'll get the lawyers to make sure she—"

"Stop being such a hothead," Daniel said, and took the jacket, throwing it onto the sofa by the door. "And leave the lawyers out of it. She's angry and hurt and has every reason to hate you, so if she wants to leave and break the lease agreement then she can do just that...without any interference from you, understand?"

Caleb glared at him. "When did you get so sentimental?"

"When I realized that Audrey has probably already contacted Mary-Jayne and told her I'm looking for her."

His brother's temper calmed a little. "Okay, I get the point. You're concerned Mary-Jayne might do something rash."

"Actually," he said, calmer now, "I think she'll do whatever is best for the babies. Which in her eyes is going home to be around her family."

"And that's where you're going?"

He shrugged. "I have to make this right."

Caleb raised an eyebrow. "You sure you want to make a commitment to a woman you don't love? Hell, you don't even know for sure if those babies are yours."

"I do know," he said. He wound back the irritation he felt toward his brother and tapped his hand to his chest. "I feel it...in here."

And that, he figured, was all that mattered.

Mary-Jayne had been holed up in her small house for four days. Her family knew she was back, but she'd insisted she had a bad head cold and said she needed some time to recover. Her mother had tutted and pleaded to bring her some soup and parental comfort, but Mary-Jayne wasn't prepared for them quite yet. Her sisters called every day and her friend Lauren did the same. Her dog, Pricilla, and parrot, Elvis, were happy she was home and gave her all the company she needed. While she waited for Daniel to turn up. Which she knew he would.

He wasn't the kind of man to give up when he wanted something.

Mary-Jayne had no illusions... His proposal was only about their children. He didn't want to marry *her*. And she didn't want to marry him. He was single-minded in his intent... He wanted the babies. He'd take her, too, if it meant getting full-time custody of their sons.

She wondered what his next move would be. And made herself sick to the stomach thinking about the possibilities. Since she'd refused his outrageous proposal, would he try another tack? Was he thinking about sole custody? Would he fight her in court to get what he wanted? He had money and power, and that equated to influence. He could afford the finest lawyers in the country and they'd certainly be out to prove she was less capable of giving their children the best possible life. Maybe the courts would see it that way, too.

By Sunday morning she was so wound up she wanted to scream. And cry. And run.

But she wouldn't do any of those things. She needed to stay strong and focus on growing two healthy babies. She'd fight the fight she needed to when she faced it head on. Until then, her sons were all that mattered.

When Evie and Grace arrived at her door late on Sunday afternoon she was almost relieved. She hated lying to her sisters, even if it was only by omission.

One look at her and Evie squealed. "Oh, my God, you're pregnant!"

"Well, don't tell the whole neighborhood," she said, and ushered them both inside.

Grace, who was easily the most beautiful woman Mary-Jayne had ever known, was a little less animated. She'd also had her first child two months earlier. But Evie, ever the nurturer, who had a seventeen-year-old son and a toddler daughter, was still chattering as Mary-Jayne closed the door and ushered them down the hallway.

"Tell us everything," Evie insisted as the trio dropped onto the big chintz sofa. "And first the part about how you've managed to keep from spilling the beans about this."

"Forget that," Grace said and smiled. "First, tell us who the baby's father is?"

"Babies," Mary-Jayne said and waited a microsecond before her sisters realized what she meant.

There were more shrieks and laughter and a load of questions before Mary-Jayne had an opportunity to explain. It took several minutes, and when she was done each of her sisters had a hold of her hands.

"And he wants to marry you?" Grace asked.

She shrugged. "That's what he says."

Evie squeezed her fingers. "But you don't want to marry him, M.J.?"

She screwed up her face. "Definitely not."

"Is he that awful?"

She opened her mouth to respond, but quickly stopped herself. She couldn't, in good conscience, make out as if he was some kind of ogre. Once he'd settled into the idea that he was the father he'd been incredibly supportive. And she couldn't forget his caring behavior when she'd had the ultrasound.

And then there was that kiss.

Don't forget the kiss...

Of course she needed to forget the kiss. It shouldn't have happened. It had only confused her. "He's not awful," she said and sat back in the chair. "Most of the time he's quite...nice."

Grace frowned. "Most?"

"Well, he can also be an arrogant jerk," she replied. "You know, all that old money and entitlement."

"Is he tall, dark and handsome to go along with all that old money?" Evie asked and grinned.

"Oh, yeah. He's all that. And more."

"And you *still* don't want to marry him?"

"I want to marry for love," she said and sighed. "Like you both did. I don't want to settle for a man who looks at me as some kind of incubator. We might have a whole lot of chemistry now, but when that goes what's left? An empty shell disguised as a marriage? No, thanks."

"That's a fairly pessimistic view of things," Grace remarked. "And not like you at all."

"I'm tired of being the eternal optimist," she said, feeling stronger. "Being pregnant has changed my thinking. I want to build a good life for my babies—one that's honest and authentic. And if I married Daniel I would be living a lie. Despite how much I..." She stopped and let her words trail.

"Despite how much you *like* him, you mean?" Evie prompted.

She shrugged again. "Sure, I like him. But I dislike him, too, and that's where it gets complicated."

"Maybe you're making it more complicated than it needs to be," Grace suggested. "I mean, you don't really know him very well. Perhaps over time you will change your mind."

"I doubt it," she said. "I live here and he lives in San Francisco. There's a whole lot of ocean in between. Look, I'm happy for him to see his sons and have a relationship with them. I *want* them to have a father. But when I get married I want it to be with someone who wants *me*…and not just because I'm the mother of his children."

She was about to get to her feet when the doorbell rang.

"That's probably the folks," Evie said and smiled. "They've been worried about you. Which might have something to do with the fake head cold you said you had to keep us all at bay."

"Not that it did any good," Mary-Jayne said and grinned.

"Want me to get it?" Grace asked.

"Nah," she said and pulled herself out of the soft sofa. "I got it."

She walked down the hall and opened the front door, half expecting her mother to be standing there with a big pot of chicken soup. But it wasn't either of her parents.

It was Daniel.

He looked so good. So familiar. In jeans and a blue shirt, everything about him screamed sexy and wholly masculine. She wished she was immune. She wished he didn't set her blood and skin on fire. His steely gaze traveled over her slowly until he finally met her eyes with his own and spoke.

"So you didn't run too far after all?"

"Run?"

Daniel had expected her to slam the door. But she didn't look all that surprised to see him on her doorstep.

"Your friend said you might be tempted to run to get away from me."

"Audrey did?" She laughed loudly. "I'm afraid she's got a vivid imagination and a flair for the dramatic."

"Speaking of which," Daniel said pointedly, "taking off without a word was a little theatrical, don't you think?"

She shrugged and her T-shirt slipped off her shoulder. "I needed some breathing space."

"I wasn't exactly smothering you."

"Maybe not to you," she flipped back.

He grinned a little, even though his insides churned. She had a way of doing that—a way of mixing up his emotions. He was as mad as hell with her for taking off without a word, but he wouldn't show her that. Daniel turned to briefly look at the two cars in her driveway. "You have company?"

She nodded. "My sisters."

His gaze dropped to her belly. "You told them?"

"They told me," she said, and pulled the T-shirt over her middle a fraction. "Hard to hide this from the world now."

"You shouldn't," he said quietly. "You look good."

She shrugged. "So...I guess I'll see you around."

Daniel laughed lightly. "Oh, no, Mary-Jayne, you don't get out of it that easy."

Her gaze narrowed. "You plan on camping on my doorstep?"

"If I have to," he replied. "Or you could invite me in."

His eyes widened. "You want to meet my sisters, is that it?"

"Absolutely."

She exhaled heavily and stepped back. "Okay. Best you come inside."

Daniel crossed the threshold of her small cottage and followed her down the hall. Her house was filled with old furniture and bric-a-brac and was as muddled as he'd expected. The Preston sisters regarded him curiously when he entered the living room and as Mary-Jayne introduced him. They were similar, all with the same dark curling hair and wide green eyes. Evie was down to earth and friendly, while Grace had a kind of ethereal beauty that made her look as though she'd stepped off the set of a Hollywood movie.

The eldest, Evie, asked him if he'd had a good trip and began chatting about flying and vacations, which he figured she was doing to break the ice a little. The other sister was more serious and content to stand back and watch Mary-Jayne and him interact. It didn't bother him. All he cared about was Mary-Jayne.

He cared...

Damn.

He didn't want to think about that. But he couldn't get the vision of her staring up at him in his dad's studio, her hand gently rubbing his arm, all wide-eyed and lovely. In that moment he realized she was kind and considerate, despite the bouts of exuberant bravado.

Her siblings were nice women who were clearly curious about him but were too polite to say too much. They stayed for a few minutes, and he asked about Evie's art and mentioned how his father was an artist, and she said she knew his work. Both women talked about Crystal Point and how much they loved the small town. Daniel hadn't taken much notice as he'd driven along the waterfront. His mind was set on seeing Mary-Jayne, not the beach. Evie suggested he drop by her bed-and-breakfast, and he noticed how Mary-Jayne scowled at her sister. Maybe he had an ally in the Preston sisters? Maybe they agreed that she should marry him? He wasn't averse to using whatever leverage he could if it meant he'd have the chance to be a full-time father to his sons.

Once they left, Mary-Jayne propped her hands on her hips and glared at him.

"I suppose you'd like coffee?"

He smiled. "If it's not too much trouble."

She tossed her incredible hair. "Oh, it is...not that it would make one damn bit of difference to you. And by the way," she said as she walked down the hall, "don't think you can sway me by charming my family. I've already told my sisters what a jerk you are."

He laughed and walked after her. "I don't think they quite believed you, Mary-Jayne."

When he reached the kitchen he stood by the counter for a moment, looking around at the crowded room with its cluttered cabinets, colorful drapes and assortment of pots hanging from hooks above the stove top. But as untidy and overdone as it was, there was something oddly welcoming about the room. With its mismatched table and chairs and the wrought iron stand in the corner jammed with an array of ceramic vases containing a variety of overgrown herbs, it was far removed from the huge ultramodern kitchen in his San Francisco apartment. He never used it these days. Even when he was married, Simone had worked long hours like he did and they preferred to dine out most evenings. But Mary-Jayne's kitchen suited her. It was easy to imagine her sitting at the round scrubbed table, sipping tea from one of the patterned china cups from the collection on the dresser.

"Yes," she said, still scowling. "I'm a slob, remember?"

"Did I say that?"

"Words to the effect. One of my many flaws."

He chuckled and watched her pull a pair of ceramic mugs from the cupboard. She looked so beautiful with her scowl, all fired up and ready to do battle with him. One thing was for sure, life with Mary-Jayne Preston sure wasn't dull!

Daniel came around the counter and stood beside her.

She turned and rested her hip against the bench, arms crossed.

"Yes?"

"Nothing," he said and reached for her, curling his hand gently around her neck.

"Don't you dare," she said, but didn't move.

"What are you so afraid of?" he asked, urging her closer. "That I'm going to kiss you? Or that you'll like it?"

"Neither," she said on a shallow breath. "Both."

"You never have to be afraid of me, Mary-Jayne," he said quietly, bringing her against him. The feel of her belly and breasts instantly spiked his libido. "I'd never hurt you. Or make you to do something you didn't want to do."

"Then, stop asking me to marry you," she said, still breathless as she looked up into his face.

"I can't. When I want something I'm—"

"Relentless," she said, cutting off his words. "Yeah, I know. I'm not used to someone like you," she admitted, her mouth trembling a little. "My last boyfriend was—"

"An unemployed musician," he finished for her, not in the mood to hear about the man she'd once dated. "Yes, I had you investigated, remember?"

She frowned and wriggled against him. "Jerk."

Daniel moved his other arm around her waist and gently held her. "Me or him?"

"You."

He chuckled. "You know, I don't think you really mean that."

"Sure I do," she said, and wriggled some more. "And kissing me isn't going to get me to change my mind."

"Maybe not," he said and dipped his head. "But it sure beats arguing about it."

Her lips were soft when he claimed them. Soft and sweet and familiar. Her hands crept up his chest and reached his shoulders and she clung on to him. Daniel pressed closer and she moaned softly. The sweet vanilla scent that was uniquely hers assailed his senses, and he tilted her head a fraction. Their tongues met and danced. And he was pretty sure she knew exactly the effect she had on him and his libido. His hand moved down to her hip, and he urged her closer. Heat flared between them, and suddenly kissing wasn't enough. Her fingertips dug into his shoulders and she arched her back, drawing them closer together.

"Mary-Jayne," he whispered against her mouth and trailed his lips down her cheek and throat. "Let me stay with you tonight."

She shivered in his arms. "I can't," she said on a shallow breath. "Tomorrow..."

"Forget tomorrow," he said, and pushed the T-shirt off her shoulder. Her creamy skin was like tonic for the desire that churned through his blood. "Forget everything but right now."

It was what he wanted. What he needed. Her skin, her mouth, her tender touch. He'd shut off from truly feeling anything for so long, but Mary-Jayne made him feel in ways he could barely understand. They fought; they battled with words and with ideals. But underneath the conflict simmered an attraction and a pull that was the most powerful of his life.

And it also had the power to undo him.

Chapter Eight

She didn't let him stay. She couldn't. If he'd stayed and they'd made love she wasn't sure she would have had the strength to refuse his marriage proposal. He'd use sex to confuse and manipulate her, even if that wasn't his intention. She was like putty in his arms. One kiss, one touch and being with him was all she could think about.

Idiot...

Mary-Jayne garnered all her strength and sent him packing. And tried to convince herself she couldn't care less where he went. There were plenty of quality hotels in the nearby town of Bellandale. It was barely a twenty-minute drive from Crystal Point. He had a GPS. He'd be fine. She didn't feel bad at all.

She had a shower, made soup and toast and curled up on the sofa to watch TV with Pricilla and pretended she'd put Daniel out of her mind once and for all.

Her dreams, however, were something else altogether.

He invaded them. She couldn't keep him out. His touch was like a brand against her skin, and she could still feel the heat of his body pressed against her for hours later. And his kiss... It was like no other. She remembered his comment about her ex-boyfriend. *An unemployed musician?* Toby had been exactly that. He wasn't even much of a musician. They'd dated off and on for two years and she often wondered if she'd brought home a tattooed, frequently pierced, dreadlocked boyfriend simply because that was what everyone expected of her. Her teenage willfulness made her rebel against what she'd considered the average or mundane. After she'd left home she'd saved her money and quickly headed overseas. She'd returned feeling even more independent and more determined to live her own life.

And Toby was the end result. A deadbeat, she realized now. Someone who took advantage of her generous nature and swindled her out of her money and her pride. She'd been left with a debt for a car he crashed and a guitar he'd taken with him when he walked out the door. He had no goals, no ambition and no integrity. She'd had one serious relationship since with a man who ended up complaining about her spending too much time worrying about her career. He'd had no ambition, either—except the desire to sit in front of his computer all day playing games. She'd foolishly believed she chose men who were free-spirited and artistic. Now they simply seemed lazy and immature.

She tossed and turned all night and woke up feeling nauseated and unable to stomach the dry crackers and green tea that usually helped most when morning sickness came upon her.

She changed into her favorite overalls and grinned when she discovered she had to leave two of the three side buttons undone to accommodate her rapidly expanding middle. Her workshop needed a cleanup before she got to work on the few back orders she had, so she headed outside and began decluttering the counters. It was midmorning before she took a break and snacked on some apple slices and a cup of tea.

At eleven Daniel rocked up.

In dark jeans and a navy polo shirt he looked effortlessly handsome, and her stomach flipped with familiar awareness. He looked her over and smiled.

"Cute outfit."

Her overalls were paint splattered and had holes in each knee. But they were comfy, and she could care less what he thought about her clothes. "Thanks. Did you want something?" she asked, pushing the memory of his kisses from her mind.

"We're going out."

Bossy, as usual. "Are we? Am I allowed to ask where we're going?"

"To see your parents," he said swiftly. "It's about time they were told they're about to become grandparents again."

"I'd rather tell them myself."

"*We'll* tell them," he said, firmer this time. "Stop being stubborn."

Mary-Jayne turned and sashayed down the hall. "I'd really prefer to do it some other time. Please try to understand."

"Well, I don't. We're in this together," he said, and followed her into the house. "We told my parents together… and now we'll tell yours…together. That's how things are going to be, Mary-Jayne. They have a right to know, don't you think?"

When she reached the living room she turned and

propped her hands on her hips. "Of course. I just don't want you to meet them right now."

His brows shot up. "Why the hell not?"

"Because," she said, and dragged out a long breath, "you don't know them. One look at you and they'll get all...thingy."

He stilled. *"Thingy?"*

Her patience frayed. "Excited, okay? Thrilled. Happy. They'll feel as though they've won the lottery in the potential son-in-law department."

He laughed. "They want you to nab a rich husband?"

"No," she corrected. "That's not it. It's just that you're different from anyone I've ever...you know...dated. You're not an *unemployed musician*," she explained, coloring hotly. "Or a beach bum or a lazy good-for-nothing, as my dad would say. You're...*normal*... You're successful and hardworking and come from a nice family. Once they know that, they'll get all worked up and start pressuring me to...to..."

"Marry me?"

"Well, yeah," she admitted. "Probably."

"I thought you said they let you lead your own life?"

"They do," she replied. "But they're still my parents. They still want what's best for me. Once they clap eyes on you, I'll be done for."

His mouth twitched at the edges. "Best you get changed so we can get going."

Mary-Jayne frowned. "Didn't you hear what I said?"

"Every word," he said, and dropped into the sofa. "Hurry up, *dear.*"

Impatience snaked up her spine. "You are the most infuriating and—"

"Want me to kiss you again?" he asked as he grabbed a

magazine from the coffee table and opened it at a random page. "If not, go and get changed."

Irritated, she turned on her heels and stomped to her bedroom. He was an ass. He didn't give a hoot what she wanted. Or care about how she felt. By the time she'd dressed, Mary-Jayne was so mad she could have slugged his smug face.

Once they were out of the house she pointed to her car. "I'll drive," she said and rattled her keys. "I know the way."

Daniel stopped midstride and looked at the battered VW in the driveway. "In that hunk of junk? I don't think so." He gestured to the top-of-the-range Ford sedan parked alongside the curb. "We'll take my rental car."

"Snob."

He laughed and gently grasped her elbow. "Come on."

"Sometimes I really don't like you much at all."

He laughed again. "And other times?"

She quickstepped it to the car and waited by the passenger door. It was hard to stay mad at him when he was being so nice to her. "No comment."

Once they were in the car she gave him the address. The trip took only minutes, and by the time they pulled into the driveway her temper had lost its momentum.

"You're something of a hothead, aren't you?" he asked as he unclipped his seat belt.

"Around you?" She raised a brow and smiled a little. "Yeah."

He seemed to find that idea amusing and was still chuckling by the time he was out of the car and had come around to her side. "It's one of the things I find captivating about you, Mary-Jayne."

Captivating? That was quite an admission. He usually didn't admit to anything, not when it came to feelings. Oh, sure, she knew he wanted her in his bed, but anything else seemed off his agenda. He'd said he felt numb. The very idea pained her deep down. He'd lost the woman he'd loved and didn't want to love again... That was clear enough.

"What are you thinking about?" he asked as he took her hand.

I'm thinking about how it must feel to be loved by you...

Mary-Jayne's fingers tingled at the connection with his. She didn't want to be so vulnerable to his touch, but her attraction for him had a will of its own. She simply couldn't help herself. That was why she'd become so caught up in the heat and passion between them the night of Solana's birthday party. It was heady and powerful and drove her beyond coherent thought. It was more than attraction. More than anything she'd felt before.

And the very idea scared her senseless.

Her parents, as expected, were delighted, if not a little shocked at their news. Once the shock settled, her mother had countless questions for Daniel and he answered every one without faltering. He was as resilient as the devil when under intense scrutiny. Barbara Preston skirted around the question about marriage and Mary-Jayne was relieved that Daniel didn't mention that she'd refused his proposal. There was time for that revelation later. Her father, she realized, looked as pleased as she'd ever seen him. Bill Preston approved. Daniel was a hit. Her parents were clearly delighted, even with her out-of-wedlock pregnancy. Her mother was all hugs and tears when they explained she was expecting twins.

Over a jug of iced tea her father spoke. "What do you think of our little town, son?"

Son?

Her dad was already calling Daniel "son"?

Great.

"I haven't had a chance to see much of it yet," Daniel

replied. "But I'm hoping Mary-Jayne will show me around sometime today."

She smiled sweetly and nodded, and then noticed how her mother seemed to approve wholeheartedly about the way Daniel used her full name. He could clearly do no wrong.

I'm doomed.

They stayed for two hours, and Daniel answered every probing question her parents asked. He talked about his career, his family and even his wife and the baby they had lost. Before they left her father ushered him off to his garage to inspect the Chevrolet Impala that he was restoring, and Mary-Jayne was left to endure her mother's scrutiny.

"Now," Barbara said, hugging her closely once the men had left the room. "What don't I know?"

"Nothing," she replied and began collecting the mugs from the table. "The babies are doing fine and I feel okay other than a little morning sickness."

"I meant with the two of you," Barbara said and raised a brow. "He's awfully handsome, isn't he? And such nice manners."

Mary-Jayne smiled. "I know he isn't what you've imagined I'd bring home to meet you."

"Well, your track record hasn't exactly given us confidence."

"I know. And you're right—he's handsome and nice and has good manners."

"Are you in love with him?"

Love...

She'd not considered the word in regard to him. Falling in love with Daniel was out of the question. He'd never love her back. *He was numb.* There was nothing left in his heart. He'd love their sons and that was all.

"No," she said and heard the hesitation in her own voice. "Definitely not."

Barbara smiled. "It wouldn't be the end of the world, you know... I mean, if you did fall in love with a man like Daniel."

"It would," she corrected, suddenly hurting deep in her chest. "He still loves his wife. And she was very different from me. She was smart and successful and everything I'm not."

There...I said it out loud.

Her mother's expression softened some more. "You're smart, and your dad and I have every faith that your business will be a success one day. And sometimes being *different* is a good thing," Barbara added gently.

"Not in this," she said, her heart suddenly and inexplicably heavy. "I know you only want to see me happy, and I am happy about the babies. Really happy. Even though it's been something of a shock I'm looking forward to being a mother."

Barbara rubbed her arm comfortingly. "You'll be a good one, too, I'm sure of it."

"I hope so," she said. "Although I'm sure some people will think having twin boys is my medicine for being such a difficult child myself."

Her mother smiled. "You were spirited, not difficult."

"That's sweet of you to say so, but I know I caused you and Dad some major headaches over the years. Remember when I ditched school for three days to follow that carnival that had arrived in town?"

Barbara laughed. "Every kid dreams of running away and joining the circus at some point. Especially a strong-willed eleven-year-old."

Mary-Jayne giggled. "I had visions of being a trapeze artist."

They chatted for a few more minutes about her childhood escapades, and by the time her father and Daniel returned her mood was much improved. Daniel looked his usual self-satisfied self and her dad looked pleased as punch. Whatever had transpired in the garage, she was sure it had something to do her father giving Daniel his blessing and full support.

Typical...

Once they were back in the car, she strapped on the seat belt and pasted on a smile.

"Take a left at the end of the street," she instructed.

"Because?"

"You wanted to see my town, my home, right?"

"Well...yes."

"So we'll go to the beach."

He frowned a little. "We're not exactly dressed for the beach."

Mary-Jayne laughed. "Does everything always have to be done to order with you? Live dangerously, Daniel," she said and laughed again. "You might surprise yourself and enjoy it."

His mouth tightened. "You know, despite what you think, I'm not some overworked killjoy."

"Prove it," she challenged. "Get those extrastarched clothes of yours crumpled for a moment."

"Extrastarched?" he echoed as he started the ignition.

She chuckled. "Oh, come on, even you have to admit that you're a neat freak. You even folded your clothes that night we spent together." It was something of an exaggeration...but she had a point to prove. "My dress got twisted amongst the bedsheets and your suit was perfectly placed over the chair."

"I don't remember it that way."

"Hah," she scoffed. "You have a selective memory."

"I remember everything about that night," he said and drove down the street. "Left, you said?"

"Left," she repeated. "We'll drive past my sister's bed-and-breakfast."

"I know where that is already."

Her brows came up. "You do?"

He nodded. "Of course. I stayed there last night."

Daniel knew it would make her nuts. But he'd thought it was a good idea at the time and Evie Jones seemed to agree. After Mary-Jayne had kicked him out of her house the evening before, he'd driven around the small town for a while and come across Dunn Inn by chance. The big A-framed house stood silhouetted amongst a nest of Norfolk pines and the shingle out front had told him exactly who the place belonged to. So he'd tapped on the door and was met by Evie's much younger husband, Scott, and within minutes Evie herself was insisting he stay at the bed-and-breakfast while he was in Crystal Point.

"You stayed at my sister's place?"

She was all outraged, and it made him grin a little. "Sure. Something wrong with that?"

"Something? Everything! Of all the manipulative and conniving things I could imagine you—"

"I needed somewhere to stay," he said quickly. "You told me to leave, remember?"

"Ever heard of a thing called a hotel?" she shot back. "There are many of them in Bellandale."

"I wanted to stay in Crystal Point."

"Why?"

He glanced at her belly. "You have to ask?"

She glared at him. "Don't use the twins as a way of getting around this. How long do you intend on staying?"

"As long as I need to."

"You could stay for a lifetime and nothing would change. I will not marry you. Not now and not ever."

"We'll see," he said, with way more confidence than he felt.

The truth was, he was tired of arguing with her about it. She was as stubborn as a mule. Last night he could have stayed with her. He'd wanted to. A part of him had needed to. He'd wanted to spend the night making love to her. And her rejection had stung like a bucket of ice water over his skin.

"What about your job?" she asked. "You can't just pack that in for an indeterminable length of time."

"Sure I can," he said, and flipped a lazy smile and drove toward the beach. "I'm the boss, remember? I can do what I want."

She was clearly fuming. "Solana told me you never take vacations."

"This isn't a vacation," he said, and pulled the car into the parking area.

"No," she said, opening the door. "It's a hunting expedition...and I'm the prey."

Daniel got out of the car, ignoring the niggling pain in his temple. "Such drama. Let's just forget my marriage proposal for the moment, shall we?"

"It's all I can think about," she muttered.

"Well, that's something, at least." He locked the car. "So this beach?"

She crossed her arms and stormed off down the pathway. Daniel had to admit the beach was spectacular. The white sand spanned for several hundred meters until it met the pristine river mouth. No wonder she loved this place so much. It was early winter and a weekday, so there was no one about other than them and a lone dog walker playing chase with his pet. He watched as Mary-Jayne flipped off her sandals and strode across the sand until she reached the water. Daniel looked down at his shoes. They were Italian leather and not designed for the beach. He perched on a rock and took them off, stuffing the socks into the loafers. She'd called him an uptight neat freak on several occasions. Maybe she was right. When he was young he'd been impulsive and adventurous. Now he rarely did anything without considering the consequences. Taking over the helm of Anderson's from his grandfather had changed him. He felt the weight of responsibility press heavily on his shoulders 24/7. The most impulsive thing he'd done recently was go after Mary-Jayne. And even that he did with a tempered spirit. What he really wanted to do was haul her in his arms and kiss her senseless.

By the time he stepped onto the sand she was twenty meters in front of him. He quickened his steps and watched her as she walked, mesmerized by the way her hips swayed. She had a sensuality that affected him in a way that blurred the lines between desire and something else. Something more. He couldn't define it. Couldn't articulate in his mind what it was about Mary-Jayne that caused such an intense reaction in him. It wasn't simply attraction. He'd felt that before and it had always waned quickly. No, this was something he'd never experienced before. Not even with Simone. His wife hadn't driven him crazy. Loving her had been easy. She had never challenged him, insulted him or made him accountable for his beliefs. But Mary-Jayne did at every opportunity. She questioned everything and anything.

She made him think.

Feel...

It was a kind of heady mix of torture and pleasure.

Which was why making love with her had been so intense. They had chemistry and more. A connection that went beyond physical attraction. A mental attraction that defied logic.

Yeah, loving Simone had been easy. But loving Mary-Jayne... There would be nothing easy about that. Which was why he wouldn't. Why he'd keep it clear in his head what he wanted. His sons. A family. But where? It could never be here, he thought as he walked along the sand. Sure, it was a nice town. Peaceful and safe... Exactly the kind of place to raise children. The kind of place a person could call home. But not him. For one, Mary-Jayne would never agree to it. And he had his life in San Francisco.

She was walking at a leisurely pace now and stopped to pick something up, perhaps a shell. Daniel caught up with her and matched her slow strides.

"It's a beautiful spot."

She glanced sideways. "It's the prettiest beach along this part of the coastline."

"You're fortunate to have grown up in a place like this. To have made it your home."

She shrugged and tossed the shell in the shallow water. "What about you?" she asked. "Where's home for you?"

Daniel rubbed the back of his neck to ease the tension creeping up his spine. "San Francisco."

"That's where you live," she said quietly. "Where's home?"

He shrugged loosely. "When my grandfather was alive he and Solana had a place in the Napa Valley, and I used to go there for school vacations. Miles and Bernie moved around a lot, so my brothers and I always welcomed the stability of my grandparents' small vineyard. But when Gramps died things changed. Gran wasn't interested in the business end of things and decided to sell the place. Solana likes the warmer weather and divides her time between Port Douglas and San Francisco."

She stopped walking and faced him, her hair flipping around her face from the breeze. "So...nowhere?"

"I guess so," he replied, and started walking again.

She caught up with him quickly. "I don't want that for my babies. I want them to be settled. I want them to have a place they can always call home."

"So do I," he said, and stopped to look out over the water. "What's that called?" he asked, pointing to a land mass separated from the shore by an expanse of water that fed from the mouth of the river.

"Jays Island," she replied. "Years ago they used to bring sugarcane ferries up the river, so this was quite a busy spot. Now they use trains and trucks to transport the sugar so the river doesn't get dredged anymore. The sand banks built up and the island came about. Birds nest over there and at a really low tide you can wade through the shallows to get over there. When I was young I used to swim over there at high tide and come back when the tide went out." She laughed and the sound flittered across the wind. "Much to my parents' despair. But I loved sitting on that patch of rock," she said, and pointed to a ragged rock outcrop on the island. "I used to sit there for ages and just let the wind hit my face. It was the kind of place where a person could dream big and no one was around to make judgment. Where *I* could sit without worrying about other people's opinion."

"You mean your family?"

She shrugged. "My family are the best."

"But?"

Her green eyes glittered. "But everyone has a role, you know... My brother, my sisters. Noah took over the family business, Evie's the successful artist, Grace is the supersmart financial whiz who once worked on Wall Street."

"And you?"

Her shoulders lifted again. "I'm just the youngest. The one who got away with everything as a kid. I guess I have the role of being the one who hasn't amounted to anything."

Surely she didn't believe that. "A college education and a big bank balance don't equate to a person's value, Mary-Jayne. There's greatness in simply being yourself."

She offered a wry smile. "Is that why you've worked so hard to climb the corporate ladder? Because you believe it's enough to live a simple life?"

"An authentic life," he corrected, doing his best to ignore the growing throb in his head. "But I didn't really have a choice when I was drafted into the company. My dad wasn't interested, and my grandfather had a lot of health issues. I either joined or the company folded. Too many people were invested in Anderson's… I couldn't let it go down without a fight. So I made a few changes to the company's structure, sold off most of the mining interests and concentrated on the part that I enjoyed. Ten years later the resorts are now some of the most successful in the world."

"And if you hadn't joined the family business, what would you have done?"

"I'm not sure. Maybe law."

She laughed. "Oh, yes, I can see you as a lawyer. You do pose a good argument."

He reached out and grabbed her left hand, and then gently rubbed her ring finger with his thumb. "Not good enough, obviously. This is still bare."

She went to pull away but he held on. "You know why I won't."

"Because you hate me."

She shook her head. "I don't hate you, Daniel."

"No?" he queried as he turned her hand over and stroked her palm. "But you don't like me."

"I don't *dislike* you," she said quietly. "The truth is, I'm very confused about how I do feel about you. And it's not something I'm used to. Normally I know exactly how I feel about everything. I have an opinion and I usually express it. But around you..." Her words trailed. "Around you all I seem to do is dig myself into this hole and say things I don't mean. And I'm not like that. It's not a reaction I'm particularly proud of."

"So I wind you up," he said, still holding her, even though the pain in his head gained momentum. "We wind one another up. What's wrong with that? It'll keep things interesting."

"What things? A marriage where we're always fighting, always at each other's throats? That's not something I want our children to witness." She pulled away and crossed her arms tightly around her waist. "Because if you do, that's about as selfish and self-destructive as it gets."

Selfish? Selfish because he wanted to give his sons his name and the legacy that went along with it. She was the one being selfish—thinking only of herself. Like a spoiled brat.

"If you had any consideration for their future, for what they deserve, then you would see that I'm right," he said stiffly. "But right now you're acting like a petulant child, Mary-Jayne. Maybe this isn't what either of us planned. And maybe you're right, maybe we would never have seen one another again after that night if you hadn't gotten pregnant. But you did, and we are and I'll be damned if I'm going to let you dictate the kind of father I'm allowed to be. This might be a shock to you, but you're *not* the center of the universe, and right now the only thing that matters is the welfare of our sons."

She glared at him. "You're calling *me* self-absorbed? When you think you can simply snap your fingers and get what you want?"

Annoyance swept over his skin. He tried to keep his cool. Tried to get her to show some sense. But be damned if she wasn't the most infuriating woman on the planet!

In that moment a flashing light appeared out of the corner of his eye. And another. A dreaded and familiar ache clutched the back of his head. He recognized what was coming.

"We have to get back. I'll take you home."

And he knew, as he turned and walked back up the sand, that he was in for one hell of a headache.

Chapter Nine

Two days later Mary-Jayne got a call from her sister Evie. She'd had a peaceful two days. No Daniel. No marriage proposals. No insults. It gave her time to seethe and think and work.

"I think you should get over here."

She ground her teeth together. She didn't want to see him. She was still mad at him for calling her a petulant child. And she certainly didn't want her sister interfering or trying to play matchmaker. "What for?"

"He's been holed up in his room for forty-eight hours. No food or coffee or anything. I don't want to pry...but I thought you should know."

Mary-Jayne pushed down the concern battering around in her head. "He's a big boy. I'm sure he's fine."

"Well, I'm not so sure. And I have an obligation to my guests to ensure their welfare while they stay here."

"Good... You go and check on him."

"M.J.," Evie said, sterner this time. "Whatever is going on between the two of you, put it aside for a moment. *I* need your help."

Unable to refuse her sister's plea, Mary-Jayne quickly got dressed and headed over to the B and B. Evie looked genuinely concerned when she met her by the side door.

"So what's the big emergency?" she asked as she walked into the house and dropped her tote on the kitchen counter. "Maybe he's gone out."

"He's here," Evie said. "His rental car is outside."

"Maybe he's asleep."

"For two days?" her sister shot back. "Something's not right, and since you're the soon-to-be mother of his babies, it's your responsibility to find out what's wrong."

"I think you're under the illusion that Daniel and I have some kind of real relationship. We don't," Mary-Jayne informed her. "We barely tolerate one another."

Evie placed a key in her palm, touched her shoulders and gave her a little sisterly shove. "Go and find out. He's in the brown room."

There were four guest rooms at the B and B, each one styled in a particular color. Mary-Jayne left the family residence area and headed into the bigger section of the house. She lingered outside the door for a moment and finally tapped. Nothing. She tapped again.

She was about to bail when she heard a faint sound. Like a moan.

Did he have a woman in there?

The very idea made her sick to the stomach. He wouldn't…surely.

She stared at the key in her hand. What if she opened the door and found him doing who knows what with some random woman? She wouldn't be able to bear it.

Suck it up...

She pushed the key in the lock and slowly opened the door. The room was in darkness. The heavy drapes were shut and she couldn't hear a sound. There was someone on the bed, lying facedown.

"Daniel?"

She said his name so softly she wasn't surprised he didn't respond. She closed the door and stepped closer. He was naked from the waist up and had a pillow draped over his head. She said his name again and the pillow moved.

"What?"

His voice was hoarse. Groggy. Nothing like she'd heard before. She squinted to accustom her eyes to the darkness and spotted an empty bottle of aspirin on the bedside table. She took notice of everything, and a thought popped into her head.

"Are you drunk?"

He groaned softly. "Go away."

"You're hungover?"

He rolled slightly and took the pillow with him, facing away from her. "Leave me alone, Mary-Jayne."

She walked around the bed and looked at him. "Daniel, I was only wondering if—"

"I'm not drunk," he said raggedly, clearly exasperated. "I've got a headache. Now go away."

She glanced around the room. Total darkness. He hadn't eaten for two days. Empty painkiller bottle. She got to the edge of the bed and dropped to her haunches.

"Daniel," she said gently, and tried to move the pillow. "Do you have a migraine headache?"

He moaned and his hold on the pillow tightened. "Yes. Get out of here."

She got to her feet and headed into the bathroom, emerging a minute later with a cold, wet washcloth. He hadn't moved. She sat on the edge of the bed.

"Here," she said, and pried the pillow off him. "This will help." She gently rolled him onto his back and placed the cloth across his forehead.

"Stop fussing," he said croakily.

She pressed the cloth around his temples. "Let me help you."

"You can't."

"I can," she said and touched his hair. "My mother gets migraines. I know what I'm doing." She glanced at the empty medicine bottle. "When did you last take a pain-killer?"

He shrugged and then moaned, as though the move-ment took all his effort. "This morning. Last night. I can't remember."

She stroked his head. "Okay. I'll be back soon. Keep the cloth on your forehead."

Mary-Jayne was back in a matter of minutes. Evie had what she needed, and when she returned to his room she noticed he was still lying on his back and had his hand over his eyes. She fetched a glass of water from the bath-room and sat on the bed again.

"Take these for now," she instructed, and pressed a cou-ple of aspirin into his hand. "And I have some paracetamol you can take in two hours."

"Would you stop—"

"Take the pills, okay?" she said, holding on to her pa-tience. "You'll feel better for it." He grumbled again but finally did as she requested. Mary-Jayne took the glass and placed it on the bedside table. "It's important that you take in plenty of fluids."

"Yes, nurse."

"And drop the attitude for a while."

He didn't respond. Instead he rolled over and buried his face into the pillow. Mary-Jayne got up and pushed the drapes together as close as they would go. She knew many migraine sufferers had sensitivity to light. Countless times she'd watched her mother battle for days on end with the nausea and blinding pain.

She stayed with him for the next few hours. She gave him water and made him take some more medication. When she thought he could handle it, she sat on the bed and gently massaged lavender oil into his temples. There was a strong level of intimacy in what she did, but she couldn't let him suffer.

By late afternoon there was significant improvement in his pain level, and she left for a while to make him a sandwich and peppermint tea.

"How's the patient?" Evie asked when she came into the kitchen.

Mary-Jayne looked up from her task. "A little better. He's hungry, so that's a good sign."

Evie nodded and grinned. "Yeah… You were right—you two don't have a relationship at all. What was I thinking?"

"I'm helping someone who's in pain, that's all."

"That someone is the father of your babies. It's a bond, M.J. A strong bond that will forever keep you and Daniel in each other's life."

"I know it will," she said, heavyhearted. "I just don't know why he keeps insisting that we get married."

Evie raised her brows in dramatic fashion. "He lost a child once… I think it's easy to understand why he doesn't want to lose his sons, too."

"Lose them to what?" she shot back.

"Geography," Evie replied. "An ocean between you is a big incentive. Or the idea you might meet someone else one day and get married."

She wasn't about to admit she'd deliberately avoided considering any of that before.

"Marriage without love could never work."

"Are you sure about that?" Evie queried. "I mean, are you sure there's no love there? Looks to me as if you're behaving exactly like a woman in love would act."

She stilled instantly. Her sister's words rattled around in her head.

No, it wasn't true. She didn't. She couldn't.

"I'm not," she said, defiant.

Evie smiled gently. "I've never known you to be afraid of anything. What is it about loving this man that scares you so much?"

Nothing. Everything. Her sister was way too intuitive. "He's out of my league."

"Why? Because he has short hair and a job?"

The reference to her ex-boyfriend didn't go unmissed. "We're too different. And he'll want to shuffle me off to San Francisco. I don't want to live there. I want to live here. But he'll do and say whatever he has to in order to get his own way. I know he's handsome and can be charming and ticks all the boxes. But I know him... He's a control freak."

"So are you, in your own way," Evie remarked. "So maybe you're not so different after all."

Was that it? Was it their similarities and not their differences that spooked her? He'd called her a hothead. She'd called him arrogant. Were they both guilty of those traits?

Mary-Jayne ignored the idea for the moment and grabbed the tray. "I have to get back in there."

Evie smiled. "See you a little later."

When she returned to his room the bed was empty. The curtains were still drawn and there was a sliver of light beaming from beneath the closed bathroom door. He came out moments later, naked except for a towel draped around his hips, another towel in his hand that he used to dry his hair.

She pushed down the rush of blood in her veins. But his shoulders were so wide, his chest broad and dusted with a smattering of hair and his stomach as flat as a washboard that the picture was wholly masculine. A deep surge of longing flowed through her.

"You're back."

She swallowed hard and tried to not look at his smooth skin. "I'm back," she said, and placed the tray on the small table by the window. "How are you feeling?"

"Weary," he said, and smiled fractionally as he came toward her. "It takes me a few days to come good after."

Mary-Jayne poured some tea and made a determined effort to stop looking at him as if he was a tasty meal. "Have you always suffered from migraines?" she asked, eyes downcast.

He nodded. "Since I was a kid. They're less frequent now, but when one hits I usually just lock myself in my apartment with some aspirin for a couple of days and try to sleep it off."

"Have you tried stronger medication? Perhaps an injection of—"

"No needles," he said, and moved beside her.

He smelled so good. Like soap and some musky deodorant. She swallowed hard and glanced sideways. The towel hitched around his hips had slipped a little. "I should let you have some privacy and—"

"Shy?" he queried, reading her thoughts effortlessly. "It's nothing you haven't seen before."

Mary-Jayne swallowed hard. He was right. She'd seen every part of him. Touched every part of him. Been with him in the most intimate way possible. And still there was something unknown about him, something inviting

and extraordinarily sexy. There was nothing overt about
Daniel. He wasn't one of those constantly charming men
who flirted and manipulated. He was sexually confident
but not obvious. It was one of the reasons why she found
him so blindingly attractive. He could have her as putty
in his hands if he wanted to, but he didn't try to sway her
with sex. For sure, he'd kissed her a couple of times, but
even then he'd held back. When they'd been kissing in her
kitchen days earlier and she'd told him to go, he hadn't lingered. He hadn't tried to persuade her or coerce. Because
he possessed, she realized, bucketloads of integrity.

"You know," she said bluntly as she stirred the tea, "if
you kissed me right now you'd probably have me in that
bed in less than two seconds."

He chuckled. "I know."

"Except for your migraine, of course."

"I wouldn't let a lousy headache get in the way."

His words made her insides jump. She poured a second
mug of tea and sat down. "Shall I open the curtains?" she
asked, noticing that the only light in the room was coming from the direction of the open bathroom door. "Or are
you still too sensitive?"

"I'm okay now."

She pushed the drapes aside a little. "My mother can't
bear light when she has an attack. My dad usually bun-
dles her in the car and takes her to the doctor for a pain-
killer injection."

He flinched. "Bernie used to try acupuncture rather
than meds when I was young to combat the worst of the
pain."

"Did it work?"

He shrugged loosely and sat in the chair opposite. "At
times. Thank you for the tea and…everything else today."

"No problem. Glad I could help."

He sniffed the air. "I can smell flowers."

She grinned. "It's lavender oil," she explained. "I massaged some of it into your temples. It's something my dad does for my mother."

He rubbed his forehead. "Oh...well, thanks. It helped."

She sipped her tea and pushed the sandwich toward him. "You really should eat something."

He nodded and picked up the bread. "How are *you* feeling? Any nausea today?"

"No," she replied. "I've been okay for the past couple of days." She rubbed her belly and smiled. "And it's a small price to pay for having these two growing inside me."

He regarded her thoughtfully. "You're really happy about being pregnant, aren't you?"

"Ecstatic," she said and smiled. "I mean, it's not what I'd planned...but then again, I don't ever really plan anything. My work, my travels... It's always been a little ad hoc. But now I can feel them, I know I couldn't be happier."

"Except for the fact that I'm their father?" he queried, one brow raised.

Mary-Jayne met his gaze. "I've never wished for it to be any different. I think you'll be a really great dad." She sighed heavily. "And I get it, you know...about why you want to get married. You didn't get a chance, last time, to be a father. That was taken away from you. But I would never do anything to keep you from your sons, Daniel. They're a part of you, just like they're a part of me."

His gray eyes smoldered. "So you think all that, and you still won't marry me."

"No."

He tossed the untouched sandwich back onto the tray. "Okay. I won't ask you again."

It was what she wanted. No more proposals. No more pursuit. But somehow, in the back of her mind, she felt a strange sensation. Like…like disappointment. But she managed a tight smile. "Thank you."

"And custody?"

"We can share it. Of course, I'm going to live here and you'll be in San Francisco…but you can see them whenever you want."

"Don't you think that will confuse them?" he asked quietly. "Me randomly turning up to play daddy."

"At first," she said, and gritted her back teeth. "But it's going to be impossible to share custody when we live in two different countries."

"They could live here for six months and then in San Francisco for six months."

Fear snaked up her spine. "You wouldn't?"

"I wouldn't what?"

Mary-Jayne perched herself on the edge of the chair. "Try to get fifty percent custody. I couldn't bear to be away from them for six months at a time. I know you've got money enough to get the best lawyers, but I really couldn't—"

"You misunderstand, Mary-Jayne," he said, cutting her off. "I meant you and the twins could live in San Francisco for six months. Look, I know you love this town and don't want to be away from it permanently, but perhaps we could meet in the middle, metaphorically speaking. I'll buy you a house near where I live and you could settle there every six months."

"You'll *buy* me a house? Just like that?"

He shrugged. "Sure."

"And fly me and the twins back and forth every six months?"

"Yes."

Meet in the middle? Perhaps that was the only way to settle the tension between them. And as much as she protested, she knew she'd do whatever she had to do if it meant retaining full custody of her babies. "We'll see what happens. Anyhow," she said and got to her feet, "you should rest for a while. You look like you need it."

"Can I see you later?"

"No," she replied. "You need to get some sleep. And I have some work to do. I'm making some pieces for a friend of Solana's and I need to concentrate."

"My grandmother is very fond of you," he said, and got to his feet. The towel slipped a little more and she averted her gaze. It wasn't good for her self-control to keep staring at his bare chest.

"I'm fond of her, too."

"I know," he said, and then added more soberly, "and I apologize if I might have suggested you were not pure in your motives when you got to know her. She told me you turned down her offer to finance your business. I should trust her judgment... She knows people way better than I do."

Heat crawled up her neck. He was paying her a compliment. It shouldn't have embarrassed her, but it did. "I understand you only wanted to protect her. But I genuinely like Solana and would never take advantage of her in any way."

"I know that, Mary-Jayne. But if you need help getting your business off the ground, then I would be more than—"

"No," she said and raised a hand. "My business is mediocre because I'm not all that ambitious... I never have been. I like designing and crafting the pieces, but that's where my interest ends. I started selling them online almost by mistake. My friends Lauren and Cassie persuaded me to start a website showcasing the things I'd made and then all of a sudden I had orders coming in. I do it because

I have to make a living doing something, and why not earn money doing what I enjoy creatively."

He nodded as if he understood. She'd expected him to try to sway her some more, but to his credit he accepted her explanation. "I'll see you soon, then."

"Okay," she said, and shrugged lightly, even though the idea of spending more time with him tied her insides into knots. She liked him. A lot. And that made it increasingly difficult to keep him at arm's length. "I hope you feel better."

It took another two days for Daniel to get back to his normal self. He conference called his brothers to keep up with business and spoke to his grandmother. Solana was keen to know the details of his visit with Mary-Jayne, but he didn't tell her much. He certainly wasn't going to admit she'd turned him down again and again.

On Friday morning he headed to the kitchen and found Evie elbow-deep in some kind of baking.

"Good morning," she greeted, and smiled. "Coffee?"

He nodded and helped himself to a mug and half filled it with coffee. "Cooking for the masses?" he asked as he looked over the large bowls in front of her before he perched himself on a stool by the counter.

"For the fire station," she said cheerfully. "My husband, Scott, is a fireman. He's on night shift at the moment and I usually bake a few dozen cupcakes to keep him and the rest of the crew going."

It was a nice gesture, he thought. A loving gesture. "He's a lucky guy."

She smiled. "I'm the lucky one. He moved here, you know, from California. He'd come here for his sister's wedding to my older brother and we fell in love, but he left a few weeks after he arrived. When I discovered I was pregnant he came back and stayed. He knew I could never leave here… I had a teenage son and my family. So he changed his life for me. It was a very selfless gesture."

Daniel didn't miss the meaning of her words.

But live in Crystal Point permanently? He couldn't. It wasn't the place for him. He had a business to run. He couldn't do that from a tiny town that was barely a spot on the map. Plus, he had a life in San Francisco. Friends. Routine. A past. He'd known Simone there. Loved her there. Grieved her there. To leave would be like abandoning those feelings. And Mary-Jayne had made her thoughts abundantly clear. He was pretty sure she didn't want him anywhere near her precious town. That was why he'd suggested she come to San Francisco for six months of the year. It was a sensible compromise. The only way around the situation.

"I'm glad it worked out for you," he said, and drank some coffee.

One of her eyebrows came up. "Things have a way of doing that, you know."

"Or they don't."

She smiled. "I like to believe that anything is possible… if you want it enough."

It was a nice idea, but he didn't really agree. He'd wanted his wife and daughter to be safe. But fate had other plans. Things happened. Bad things. Good things. Sometimes it was simply a matter of timing.

"She's always been headstrong," Evie said, and smiled again. "Don't let that bravado fool you though. Underneath she's as vulnerable as the next person."

"I know she is. She's also stubborn."

"Perhaps that's because she thinks you shouldn't always get your own way?" Evie suggested.

He laughed a little. "You might be right. But I'm not out to change her. I only want to be a father to my children."

"Maybe that's where you're going wrong," Evie said. "Maybe you need to concentrate on her first and foremost."

"Nice idea," he said ruefully. "Have you met your sister? She's not exactly giving me an opportunity."

"She's scared of you."

Daniel straightened. "Of me? Why? I'd never harm her or—"

"Of course you wouldn't," Evie said quickly. "I mean she's scared of what you represent. You're…normal… You know…not a—"

"Unemployed musician?" he finished for her. "Yeah, we've already had the ex-boyfriend discussion. She's anti-wealth, antisuccess, anti-anything that gives her a reason to keep me out of the little bubble she's wrapped in."

"It's protection, that's all. Her first boyfriend was a deadbeat who stole her money. The one after that was a lazy so-and-so. If she's with you, it's as if she's admitting that she's not who everyone thinks she is. That all the other guys were just a phase…an aberration. That she isn't really a free spirit who does what she wants. It means that she's as vulnerable to a perfectly respectable and nice man as the rest of womankind is."

Daniel laughed. "So you're saying she won't marry me because I'm not a deadbeat?"

"Precisely."

He was still thinking of Evie's words when he was in town later that morning. Bellandale was a big regional town and had sufficient offerings to get what he needed done. By the afternoon he was back in Crystal Point and pulled up outside Mary-Jayne's house around five o'clock. She was in the front garden, crouched down and pulling weeds from an overgrown herb garden. She wore bright pink overalls that showed off her lovely curves and the popped-out belly. He watched her for a moment, marveling at her effortless beauty. His insides were jumping all over the place. No one had ever confounded him as much as Mary-Jayne Preston.

She stood up when she realized there was a car by the curb. She dropped the gloves and small garden fork in her hand and came down the driveway. Her crazily beautiful hair whipped around her face.

Daniel got out of the car and closed the door. "Good afternoon."

"You look better," she said as she approached. "Headache all gone?"

"Yes. How are you feeling?"

"I'm good," she said, and came beside the car. "Nice wheels. It doesn't look like a rental."

Daniel glanced at the white BMW and rattled the keys. "It's not."

Her eyes widened. "You bought a car?"

He nodded. "I did. Do you like it?"

She shrugged. "It's nice, I suppose. Very...highbrow."

A smile tugged at his mouth. "It's a sensible family car."

She looked it over and nodded. "I suppose it is. Since you had the rental, I didn't realize you needed a car."

"I don't," he said and grabbed her hand. "I still have the rental." He opened her fingers and rested the key in her palm. "It's yours."

Her eyes instantly bulged and she stepped back. "Mine?"

He nodded. "That's right."

The moment it registered her expression sharpened. "You bought me a car?"

"I did. I thought you—"

"I have a car," she said stiffly. "And it works just fine."

Daniel glanced at the beat-up, rusted yellow Volkswagen in the driveway. "Your car is old and not roadworthy."

Her hands propped onto her hips. "How do you know that? Have you taken it for a spin around the block?"

"I don't need to," he replied. "Take a look at it."

"I like it." She stepped forward and put the key back in his hand. "And I don't need another."

Daniel let out an exasperated breath. "Does everything have to be a battle between us? So I bought you a car. Sue me."

"I can't be bought."

Annoyance surged through his blood. "I'm not trying to buy you. I bought something *for* you. There's a significant difference."

"Not to me," she shot back. "First it's a car and then what…a house? Maybe one to match the house in San Francisco you want to buy? What then? A boat? What about a racehorse? Don't forget the jewels. I'll probably need a private jet, too."

"You're being ridiculous. It's just a car."

"Stop trying to justify this. Take it back. I don't want it."

He kept a lid on his simmering rage. "I want my sons to be safe, and they won't be in that jalopy," he said, and hooked a thumb in the direction of her old VW. "Be sensible, Mary-Jayne."

"I am sensible. And they'll be perfectly safe," she said hotly. "I would never put them at risk. But I won't let you tell me what to do. Not now, not ever."

He shook his head. "This isn't a multiple-choice exercise, Mary-Jayne. And I won't compromise on this issue. The car is yours." He took a few steps and dropped the key on top of the letterbox. "I want you to have it."

"I don't care what you want!"

Daniel stilled and looked at her. Her cheeks were ablaze,

her hair framing her face, her chest heaving. A thousand conflicting emotions banged around in his head. And he knew there was no reasoning with her. No middle road.

"No," he said wearily. "I guess you don't."

Then he turned around and walked down the street.

Chapter Ten

Bossy. Arrogant. Know-it-all.

Mary-Jayne had a dozen names for him and none of them were flattering.

He'd bought her a car. A car! Without discussing it with her first. Without any kind of consultation. He really did think he could do whatever he liked.

On Saturday afternoon she headed to her parents' place for lunch. The whole family got together once a month for a day of catch-up that included lunch, dinner and plenty of conversation and games with the kids. It was a Preston tradition, and since she'd missed the get-togethers while she'd been away, Mary-Jayne looked forward to spending time with them. Her father was manning the barbecue with her brother, Noah, while her brothers-in-law, Scott and Cameron, played pool in the games room, as Noah's wife, Callie, kept their kids entertained. Evie's toddler and Grace's newborn were the center of attention in the kitchen

while her mother fussed around making her famous po-
tato salad. Her best friend Lauren was there, too, with her
fiancé and her own parents. Lauren was Cameron's sister
and her fiancé, Gabe, was Scott and Callie's cousin. It was
a close-knit group. The blood ties alone made it a mammoth exercise to remember who was related to whom. She
cared for them all, but as she sat at the kitchen table, one
hand draped over her abdomen and the other curled around
a glass of diet soda, she experienced an inexplicable empty
feeling deep down, almost through to her bones.

She couldn't define it. She should he happy. Elated. She
had her babies growing in her belly and her whole family around her. But something was amiss. Something was
missing. *Someone was missing.*

She quickly put the idea from her head.

"Where's Daniel today?"

Her mother's cheerful voice interrupted her thoughts.
She shrugged. "I have no idea."

Barbara frowned a little. "I thought he might have liked
to come and meet everyone."

"I didn't invite him."

The room fell silent, and she looked up to see her mother's frown.

"I did," Evie added quickly. "But he said he wouldn't
come unless you asked him to be here."

Shame niggled between her shoulders. "Good. He's finally showing some sense."

Evie sighed. "What's he done now?"

Mary-Jayne couldn't miss the disapproval in her eldest sister's voice. It irritated her down to her teeth. "He
bought me a car," she said tartly. "A brand-spanking-new
BMW with all the trimmings." She laughed humorlessly.
"Imagine me driving around town in that."

The three women stared at her. It was Grace who spoke next.

"That was very thoughtful of him, don't you think? Considering how old and unreliable your current car is."

Mary-Jayne's jaw tightened. "I know it's old. And I know it's unreliable. But it's mine by choice because it's what I can afford. And he wasn't being thoughtful... He was being controlling."

Evie tutted. "Have you considered that perhaps he only wants you and the babies to be safe while you're driving?"

"That's what he said," she replied impatiently. "But I know Daniel and he—"

"Didn't his wife and baby die in a car accident?" Grace again, equally disapproving as Evie and their mother.

"Yes, they did," Evie supplied.

"And wasn't the other car involved an *old and unreliable* vehicle that had a major brake failure?"

"Yes," Evie said, looking directly at Mary-Jayne.

She sat up straight in the chair.

I don't care what you want...

Her careless words banged around in her head. Simone and their baby had died because the car that struck them had a broken brake line. She realized what he must have thought when he saw her old car—that history might repeat itself. That their sons' lives might be at risk.

It wasn't control that had motivated him to buy her a car. It was fear.

She stood up, her hands shaking. "I have to go out for a while." She looked toward Grace. "I'm parked behind you. Can you ask Cameron to move your car?"

Evie pointed to a set of keys on the counter. "Take mine," her sister suggested pointedly. "He's there alone, in case you're wondering, working in the office. My other guests left yesterday."

Mary-Jayne nodded, grabbed the keys and left.

The trip took just minutes, and she pulled the Honda Civic into the driveway. The gardens at Dunn Inn were like something out of a fairy tale, and she walked up the cobbled pathway, past the wishing well and headed up the steps to the porch. A couple of the French-style doors were open, and she slid the insect screen back. Her sister's artwork graced most walls, and the furnishings were well matched and of good quality. Evie had a style all of her own. There was a small office off the living room and when she reached the doorway she came to a halt.

Daniel sat in the chair, earphones on, tapping on the computer keys. She came behind him and touched his shoulder. He flinched and turned, tossing the earphones aside.

"Hi," she said, and dropped her tote.

He wore jeans and a blue shirt that looked as though it had been tailored to fit his gorgeous frame. His gray eyes scanned her face, his expression unreadable.

"I thought you had a family thing to go to?"

"I did," she said. "I do."

"Then, what are you doing here?"

"I left." She shrugged one shoulder. "I wanted to see you."

He swiveled the chair around and sat back. "So you're seeing me. What?"

Mary-Jayne swallowed hard. "You're working. I'm probably interrupting and—"

"What do you want, Mary-Jayne?" he asked impatiently.

She let out a long breath. "To apologize."

He stood up immediately and folded his arms. "Consider it done."

"I was wrong, okay," she said when she noticed his expression was still unmoved. "I shouldn't have reacted the way I did. I shouldn't have *overreacted*. I didn't stop to think about why it was so important to you that I have a new car." She rubbed her belly gently. "But I get it now... I understand that you need to know that our sons are safe because of what happened to your wife and daughter... You know, how the other car was old and had brake failure." Her throat thickened as she said the words. She looked at him and tried to read what he was thinking. But she couldn't. She wished she knew him better. And wished she understood the emotions behind his gray eyes.

The shutters were still up, so she pressed on.

"And I shouldn't have said that I didn't care what you wanted. I didn't mean it," she admitted.

His jaw was achingly tight. "I can't bear the thought of you driving around in that old car."

"I know," she said softly. "And I understand why you feel that way. I should have been more considerate of your feelings. But sometimes, when I'm with you, I react before I think about the consequences. It's not a conscious thing." She waved her hands. "But between you and me there's all this...tension. And getting mad at you is kind of like a release valve for that."

The mood between them suddenly altered. There *was* tension between them. Built on a blinding, blistering physical attraction that had never been truly sated. One night would never be enough for that kind of pull. Daniel had known it all along. She realized that as she stared up at him, breathing hard, chest heaving. That was why he'd pursued her for a month after Solana's birthday party. And that was why she'd refused him. She was scared of those feelings. Terrified of the way he made her feel. Because she still wanted him.

"Daniel..."

She said his name on a wispy breath. His eyes were

dark, burning and filled with desire. It was heady and commanding. It made her shake with longing and fear. Of course she wasn't afraid of him, only the hypnotic power he had over her.

He groaned, as though he knew he was about to do something he probably shouldn't. But Mary-Jayne didn't care. In that moment, with nothing between but barely a foot of space, all she wanted was to be in his arms.

"I'm trying so hard to fight this."

"I know. But it's me you're fighting," he said softly. "Not this."

He was right. She fought him. In her heart she felt she had to. But in that moment all her fight disappeared.

"Make love to me," she whispered and reached out to touch his chest.

He flinched against her touch as though it was poker hot. "Are you sure that's what you want?"

She shrugged lightly. "The only thing I'm sure about is that I'm not sure about anything anymore."

He reached for her shoulders and molded them with his hands. He fisted a handful of her hair and gently tilted her head back. "You drive me crazy, do you know that?"

She nodded a little. "I don't mean to."

"You can trust me, you know," he said and lowered his head toward her face. "I'm not your enemy. Even if it does feel as though most of the time we're at war with each other."

He kissed her then. Not gently. Not softly. But long and deep and fueled with heated possession. Mary-Jayne kissed him back and wrapped her arms around his waist. "Do you have any idea how sexy you are?" he whispered against her lips.

"No," she said, and smiled as she trailed her lips along

his jaw. "We've got the place to ourselves… Let's not waste any time."

He got her to his room in ten seconds flat. He closed the door and locked it.

They stood opposite one another by the bed. Last time there'd been no thinking, nothing but desire and pure instinct. This was different. This was conscious and planned and fueled by more than simple attraction.

"Do you know what I thought the first time I saw you?" he asked quietly.

Mary-Jayne shook her head.

"I thought," he said as he reached for her, "that I had never seen a woman with such beautiful hair in all my life."

He kissed her again, and she shuddered and tossed her head. When he pulled back she was breathing so hard she thought her lungs might explode. He slipped her T-shirt off one shoulder and trailed his mouth along her collarbone. There was such blistering intensity in his touch that it thrilled her to the soles of her feet. He kept kissing her, making her sigh and moan until finally she begged him to take her to the bed.

"What's the hurry?" he muttered against her neck.

Mary-Jayne ran her hands over his chest. His heart beat furiously behind his ribs and her hand hovered there for a moment. Last time they'd made love as if there was no time to waste. But now he seemed in no rush to get her naked and between the sheets. He was taking his time exploring her mouth with his own and gently smoothing his hands across her back and shoulders. They stood kissing like that for minutes. Or was it hours? She couldn't tell. She was too overwhelmed by the narcotic pleasure thrumming through her body at the seductive tone of his skilled touch. By the time they worked their way to the side of the bed she was a wriggling mass of need.

He stripped the T-shirt over her head and Mary-Jayne watched, fascinated as he slowly undressed her. It was intensely erotic and made her long for him with such urgency she could barely breathe. When she was naked, when her shirt was on the floor and her bra dispensed with, he hooked his thumbs under the band of her briefs and slowly skimmed them down over her bottom and legs. Then he was on his knees in front of her, touching her belly, pressing kisses across the curved, tightened skin. She'd never experienced anything more intimate or soul reaching in her entire life. He reached up to cup her breasts, and they felt heavy in his hands. As he gently toyed with her nipples, every part of her body felt more alive, more sensitive to his touch than ever before.

She whispered his name, and he looked up to meet her gaze. He was still fully dressed and she wanted nothing more than to feel his skin against her, to wrap herself in his embrace and feel his body deep within hers. Mary-Jayne curled her fingers around his shirt collar and found the top button. She flicked it open with eager hands.

"Take this off," she instructed with way more bravado than she felt.

He smiled, urged her to sit, and once she was settled on the bed he shrugged out of his shirt. Shoes and socks and jeans followed, and once he was naked he sat beside her.

"Better?" he asked, reaching for her again, kissing her neck and shoulders.

Mary-Jayne sighed heavily. "Much."

He palmed her rounded belly. "Pregnancy has made you even more beautiful, if that were possible."

It was a lovely thought. She'd never considered herself all that beautiful. Not like her sister Grace. Or Evie, with her dancing eyes and seductive curves. She was pretty at best. Not even particularly sexy. But beneath Daniel's glittering gaze she felt more beautiful than she ever had in her life.

She placed a hand on her belly. "Are we going to be able to do this?" she asked, smiling a little. "My middle is expanding at an alarming rate."

Daniel grasped her hand and spanned his own across her stomach. "I'm sure we'll manage just fine, darling."

Darling...

It was the first endearment he'd said to her. And it sounded so lovely coming from his lips that emotion unexpectedly gathered at the back of her eyes. She wanted that and more. Despite every argument and every rational part of her brain telling her it was madness—she wanted to be the woman he called darling every day of his life.

Because...

Because she loved him.

She'd fallen in love with the father of her babies. Wholly and completely. Even knowing that he didn't love her back and that he was all wrong for her and she for him. None of that mattered. Her heart had decided.

"What are you thinking?" he asked.

Mary-Jayne shook her head. "Nothing... Just...kiss me."

He smiled and found her mouth again. His kiss was long and slow and everything she wanted. She kissed him back with every ounce of feeling in her heart. He lowered her onto the bed and began to make love to her with such excruciating sweetness she could barely stop herself from calling out his name. He touched her, stroked her and worshipped her breasts with his mouth and hands until she was quivering in his arms. By the time he moved his hand between her legs to caress her she was so fueled with passion she rose up and over and found release almost immediately. It was wondrously intense, and when she came back to earth and the stars had stopped exploding behind her eyes she saw that he was staring down into her face.

"What's wrong?" she asked tremulously, pushing air into her lungs.

"Not a thing," he replied, and kissed her again. "So I guess we don't have to be too concerned about birth control?"

She grinned and stretched. "The horse has already bolted on that one."

Daniel laughed and rolled over, positioning himself between her legs. She relaxed her thighs and waited, so consumed with love for him in that moment that if he'd asked her for the moon she would had flown into the sky to catch it for him.

When they were together, when she couldn't tell when she began and he ended, Mary-Jayne let out a contented moan. He moved against her with such acute tenderness her heart literally ached. Nothing had ever felt so good. And she'd never been more connected to anyone than she was with him as he hovered above her, taking most of his weight on his strong arms, ensuring she was comfortable and relaxed. Release came to her again, slow and languorous and fulfilling, and when he shuddered above her she held on, gripping him tighter, longer and with more feeling than she ever had before in her life.

When he moved and rolled over onto his back, they were both breathing madly. Mary-Jayne closed her eyes and sighed. When her breathing returned with some normalcy she shifted onto her side and looked at him. His chest rose and fell, and he had his eyes closed. He reached for her hand and linked their fingers.

"You know," he said, and sighed, "we should do it down on the beach."

"Do what?" she asked, and kissed his shoulder. "This?"

"Get married. What else?"

Mary-Jayne stilled. A little voice at the back of her mind chanted that she should grab his idea with both hands and say a resounding *yes*. But she couldn't. He didn't love her. He never would. Sure, the sex was incredible and she had his babies growing inside her, but not even that was enough to sustain a lifetime relationship. He had to know that. Only a fool would believe otherwise. She loved him. But she wasn't about to become strapped to a one-side marriage.

"You said you wouldn't ask again," she reminded him.

He shrugged. "I can't help it. I want what I want."

"I can't."

"Or won't?" he asked.

"Both," she admitted, and rolled onto her back. "Can't we just get to know one another a little, Daniel? I mean, I hardly know anything about you and—"

"Because you've never asked," he said a little more harshly. "Okay—I'm thirty-four and recently had a birthday. My favorite color is yellow and I loathe brussels sprouts. When I was fifteen I chipped my two front teeth and now I have veneers. I was seventeen the first time I had sex and since my wife died I've slept with just over half a dozen women. I like imported beer but rarely drink. I haven't had a meaningful conversation with my dad in years and I still think it sucks that I never knew my real mom." He pulled himself up and draped the sheet across his hips. "Satisfied?"

Mary-Jayne sat up and covered her bare breasts with her arms. "That's not what I meant. I'm talking about time. We need time to get to know one another."

"We don't have it," he said flatly. "You live here. I live in San Francisco. I need an answer, Mary-Jayne."

She pulled herself across the bed and got to her feet. "Then, it's no."

* * *

No. Again.

Was there a bigger sucker than him?

Daniel sprang out of the bed and watched her as she snatched up her clothes. "You're being rash...as usual."

"I'm being honest," she said, and pulled on her underwear. "And sure, I'm impulsive and over the years it has gotten me into trouble every now and then. But in this I'm not being rash. I'm using my head," she said, and looked him over with deliberate emphasis. "And not the part of my anatomy that you are if you think having great sex is enough of a reason to get married."

"They're the reason," he said, and pulled on his jeans as he motioned to her belly. "Our children. The great sex is a bonus."

She tossed a shoe at him. And then another.

The first one hit him in the shoulder and the second sandal he caught midair. There was so much fire and spirit in her, so much passion. Daniel was inexplicably drawn to her like a moth to a flame. He liked that she wasn't a pushover, even though it drove him to distraction. "Stop throwing things at me."

"Well, you stop doing what you're doing and I will."

Daniel dropped the shoe and shrugged, holding out his hands. "What have I done now?"

"You know exactly what," she said on a rush of breath. "You know how I feel, Daniel. I don't want to get married and live somewhere else. I want to live here, in Crystal Point. I want our children to grow up in a home, not a house. And I want my family around me while I raise them."

"While *you* raise them?" he said flatly. "Which is exactly my point. *We* need to raise them, Mary-Jayne, together. And I think today proved that we can. We have a connection that's—"

"We had sex," she corrected. "But it's not enough. The truth is, you confuse me when you kiss me and touch me, and then I can't get any of this straight in my mind. I won't let you use sex as a way of—"

"*You* came here today, remember?" he reminded her, cutting her off. "*You* asked me to make love to *you*, remember? Not the other way around. I've left you alone these past few days…just as you asked."

She stilled. "But…"

Her words trailed and she glared at him, her eyes glittering with a kind of fiery rage. She was brash and argumentative and generally on the attack…but caught out, and she was as meek as a lamb. She was a fascinating contradiction. And he craved her more than he'd ever wanted any woman in his life.

"You came here today looking for me. For this," he said and gestured to the bed. "Because we have an insane attraction for one another that neither of us expected."

She sucked in a long breath. "I came here today because I felt bad for what I said the other day. I felt guilty, okay?"

"So today was about sympathy? Throw a crumb to the lonely widower whose wife and baby died?"

"No," she said quickly. "Of course not. I just thought we could…talk, that's all."

"Talk about what?" he asked. "You and me? There is no you and me, right? Or do you want to know about Simone? Or our daughter? What do you want to know? How long I sat in hospital the night my wife died? Eight hours," he said, feeling the memory of those hours through to the marrow in his bones. "Do you also want to know that I never got to say goodbye to her? I never got a chance to tell her what she meant to me—hell, I never even said it enough when she was alive. And yes, I held my daughter's lifeless body for a few moments before they took her away. Do you want to know if I cried? Once, after the wake when everyone had left and I realized for the rest of my life I'd be living with the fact that my daughter's birthday was the same day she and her mom died."

He stopped speaking and looked at Mary-Jayne. Her eyes brimmed with tears, and he immediately felt bad. He didn't want to upset her. He wanted to do the exact opposite, if she'd only let him.

"I'm so sorry…"

"You can't have it both ways," he said as he retrieved her skirt and T-shirt and passed them to her. "Yes, my wife and baby died. And yes, sometimes I feel alone *and* lonely because of that. Who the hell doesn't feel alone at times? But if you want to be here, then really be here, Mary-Jayne. Stop making excuses."

"I'm not," she said, wiping her eyes before she quickly slipped into her clothes.

"You are," he said, suddenly impatient. "And the next time you turn up on my door and ask me to make love to you, it'll only happen if my ring is on your finger."

"Then it will never happen again."

He shrugged, pretty sure she didn't believe that any more than he did. "You should get back to your party."

She shoved her feet into her shoes. "Would you like to come with me?"

He cocked one brow. "Are you sure that's what you want?"

"What I want is for us to get along for the sake of our children." She planted her hands on her hips and spoke in a quiet voice. "I'm trying to be rational and realistic. I don't want to be trapped in a loveless and empty marriage. And if you're honest with yourself, if you can think of only that and not about custody of the babies or how challenging it's going to be to raise them together when we live on opposite sides of the world, you'd realize that you don't want that, either. Especially after the way you loved your wife."

A loveless and empty marriage? Was that what she truly thought it would be? Were her feelings for him that hollow? He did his best to ignore the way that idea made him feel.

"I want," he said with deliberate emphasis, "my family."

"So do I," she said quietly. "But *my* family is here, Daniel. In Crystal Point. I like living a few streets away from my parents and having my sisters and brother close by. I don't come from a family where we greet one another with a handshake and live in different parts of the world. I like knowing that 'I love you' is the last thing I hear from my mother when I hang up the phone after I speak to her, and I like knowing that my dad would be there for me in a heartbeat if I needed him. And maybe that sounds like a silly TV movie to you, but it's what I want for my children."

For a second he envied her. It didn't sound silly at all. It sounded real and authentic and exactly what he'd hoped he'd have for his own children one day. Being around Mary-Jayne and her family had only amplified that need. He wanted to tell her that. But he held back.

I don't want to be trapped in a loveless and empty marriage.

That was what she imagined they'd have. Not a marriage like her siblings' or her parents'. But something less, something that would never measure up to the standards she witnessed in her life. It would never be enough. They would never be enough.

"We should get going," he said, and grabbed his shirt. "I would like to see your parents again."

She nodded and made her way across the room.

They drove separate cars to her parents' home. Him in his rental. She in her sister's Honda. He knew the BMW still sat outside her house. She hadn't driven it once, he was sure. She was stubborn and infuriating. When they arrived at the Preston house, he got out and met her by her car door, not saying a word about the old VW he spotted in the driveway, even though he hated the idea of her driving something so unreliable and potentially dangerous.

"I'm sorry about before," he said, and took her elbow. "I didn't mean to make you cry."

She sniffed. "Okay…sure."

He rubbed her skin. "I don't enjoy seeing you upset."

She nodded, eyes still glistening. "I know that. I don't mean to upset you, either. I just don't seem to be able to help myself sometimes."

Inside, he was welcomed by her family with the warmth he'd come to expect from them. They were good people, and it made him think about the dig she'd made about handshakes and living on opposite sides of the world. She was right. He was close to his brothers but not in the way she was with her siblings. And his relationship with Miles and Bernadette had been taxing most of his life.

He was by the pool talking to her brother and enduring a moderate kind of grilling about his intentions when his phone rang. He excused himself and picked up the call on the fifth ring.

It was Caleb.

Daniel listened to his brother's concerned voice, and once he ended the call went looking for Mary-Jayne. She was inside, in the kitchen with her mother and sister-in-law.

"I need to talk to you," he said, and ignored the thunder behind his ribs.

She must have picked up on his mood, because she

complied immediately and ushered him into the front living room.

"What is it?" she asked once they were alone.

"I have to leave."

"Oh, okay. I'll see you Monday, then. Remember I have an appointment with my OB at ten."

"I'm leaving Crystal Point," he said again, firmer. "Caleb just called me—Bernie's in the hospital in Cairns. She had a massive heart attack a couple of hours ago."

Mary-Jayne gasped and gripped his arm. "Oh, how awful. Is there anything I can do?"

Marry me and stay by my side...

He reached out and touched her belly, felt the movement of his babies beneath his palm and experienced such an acute sensation in his chest he could barely breathe. The connection was mesmerizing. Her green eyes glittered brilliantly, and he got so caught up in her gaze he was rooted to the spot.

"I could... I could..." Her voice trailed off.

"What?" he asked.

She shrugged a little. "I'm not sure... I just thought perhaps I could..."

She could what? Come with him? A part of him wanted that more than anything. But that couldn't be what she meant. She'd have to care one way or another. Daniel swallowed hard. "Take care of yourself, Mary-Jayne."

"You, too," she whispered. "Give your dad and Bernie my love."

But not you...

He got the message loud and clear.

"I'll talk to you soon."

"Please let me know how she is."

Daniel nodded, suddenly numb all over. "Sure." He

shrugged off her touch and walked to the door, but something stopped him. Then he turned and looked at her.

"What?" she asked softly.

"I've just realized that you're a fraud, Mary-Jayne," he said. "You walk and talk like some restless free spirit who can take on the world, but underneath all that talk is someone who's afraid to truly be who she is."

She frowned. "That doesn't make sense."

"Doesn't it? You've wrapped yourself up in this image of being a certain kind of person and it's as though you've locked yourself in a cage. Admit it, if I was some unemployed, tattooed and unsuccessful guitarist things would be very different. You'd have nothing to hide behind. You say you don't want to be trapped in a loveless marriage—but that's not it. You just don't want to marry *me*. Because if you did it would mean that everything you've ever stood for is a great big lie. It would mean that you've settled for the safe road, and then everyone around you would know that your boldness and bluster is just an act and that you're as mainstream and sensible as the rest of us. And that's what scares you—being like everyone else. That's why your last boyfriend was a deadbeat and why your business fails to get off the ground. You think that makes you a free spirit? You're wrong... All that makes you is a coward."

Then he turned on his heel and left.

Chapter Eleven

"Are you still feeling unwell?" Evie's voice cut through her thoughts.

Mary-Jayne battened down the nausea she'd been battling for a week. She'd spent the morning babysitting her niece while Evie and Scott attended an art show in Bellandale. She loved looking after Rebecca and considered it good practice for when her babies arrived.

"On and off. The crackers help a little, but yesterday I spent an hour bent over the toilet bowl. I saw my doctor the other day and we discussed some medication I can take to alleviate the nausea if it gets much worse. I just don't want to do anything that might harm my babies. But after yesterday I think I'm going to have to take his advice. I've got another doctor's appointment tomorrow at three."

Evie grimaced. "That's not much fun. Other than that, is everything going okay?"

"With the pregnancy? Yes, no problems. Except I'm getting as big as a house."

"You look lovely as always," Evie assured her. "Heard from Daniel?"

"Nope."

Evie's brows furrowed. "Everything okay on that front?"

"Nope," she said and sighed. "We sort of had a fight before he left."

"Just a fight? Anything else?"

Her sister was way too intuitive. Mary-Jayne shrugged. She wasn't about to admit he'd called her a coward, or that it was exactly how she felt. "Sex isn't enough to sustain a marriage...no matter how good it is."

Evie came around the kitchen counter and rested her hands on the back of a dining chair. "Why didn't you go with him?"

She shrugged, hurting all over. "He didn't ask me."

"Maybe he thought you'd say no."

She shrugged again, still hurting, and more confused than ever. She wasn't about to admit to her sister that she missed him like crazy. "I'm not part of his life in that way."

"But you're lovers?"

Heat crept over her skin. She could never lie to Evie. "I guess. Does one night and one afternoon together make us lovers? I'm not sure what that makes us. All it makes me is confused."

"But you're in love with him, right?"

"It doesn't matter what I am," she insisted. "I can love him until the cows come home and it won't change the fact that he doesn't love me back."

"Are you sure?"

"Positive," she replied, aching deep down. She pressed her hands to her belly and rubbed her babies as they moved inside her. "He's all one-eyed about what he thinks we should do. Which is get married and raise our children in San Francisco."

"He said that?" she asked. "He said he wants you to move there?"

She nodded. "Well, he offered to buy me a house so I can live there for six months of the year."

Evie tilted her head. "I thought he might have decided he liked it here."

Mary-Jayne's eyes popped wide. "Daniel live here? In Crystal Point?" She laughed shrilly. "Not likely. Too hometown for him. He's all business and logic. He'd be bored out of his mind in a place like this."

Her sister smiled. "Really? He looked pretty comfortable here to me. And since when did you get all stuck on Crystal Point as a be-all and end-all? You spent a good part of the past ten years away from here, traveling from one place to the next." Her brows came back up. "I can remember a certain nineteen-year-old telling me in no uncertain terms that it was the most boring, uneventful spot on the map before you hopped on a plane for Morocco. I think the folks thought you'd closed your eyes and pointed to a spot on an atlas and thought, 'Why not go there?' And then there was Thailand, and Cambodia, and after that it was Mexico. And wasn't it you who spent three months backpacking through Greece and working transient jobs and peddling your jewelry to patrons in sidewalk cafés to make ends meet? And didn't you recently leave here to bail out your old school friend in Port Douglas with only a day's notice?" Evie smiled. "What's happened, M.J.? Have you lost your restless spirit? Have you realized that this little town is not such a bad place after all?"

"I never thought it was bad. I love this town. I've just

always loved traveling and experiencing new places, that's all."

"New places except San Francisco?"

Mary-Jayne stilled. Evie had a point. "You think I should do it? You think I should marry him and move to another country?"

"I think you should do whatever your heart tells you is right."

"That's what I'm doing," she insisted.

"Your heart," Evie said pointedly. "Not your head."

But my heart will get pummeled, for sure...

"I can't." She stood and grabbed her bag. "I have to get going."

Her sister nodded. "Okay. Thank you for babysitting. Rebecca loves spending time with you."

Mary-Jayne smiled broadly. "It's mutual."

Evie reached out and hugged her tight. "By the way, I see you're driving the Beamer."

Mary-Jayne wondered how long it would take for her sister to remark about the car parked along the front curb. She shrugged. "Seemed silly to let it sit there, that's all."

"Smart move. Is it good to drive?"

"Like a dream," she admitted, and grinned. "And two baby seats arrived for it yesterday."

Evie's smiled widened. "He thought of everything, didn't he?"

"Pretty much," she replied, ignoring the jab of pain in her chest. "Anyway, I have to run."

"Let me know how things go at the doctor's."

"Will do," she said as she left.

By the time she got home it was after four. She fed the dog and parrot and took a shower and then changed into baggy sweats and flaked out on the sofa. She flicked channels on the television and stared absently at the screen for an hour. Later, she ate a grilled-cheese sandwich and attempted to do some work on a new bracelet for one of Solana's friends. But she couldn't concentrate. Her mind was filled with thoughts of Daniel and his parting words.

Four days after Daniel left, Mary-Jayne got a text from Audrey informing her that Bernie was finally off the critical list but still in intensive care. There was no word from Daniel. It had been a long, lonely week. Part of her was glad. Part of her never wanted to see him again. Another part missed him so much she ached inside.

Coward...

The word had resonated in her head for days. No one had ever called her that before. No one would ever dare. But not Daniel. He called it how it was. He made her accountable for her convictions. For the first time in her life Mary-Jayne felt as though she had met her match. Her *perfect* match.

If only he loved her...

But he didn't. He thought that physical attraction was enough to sustain a marriage. But in her heart she knew it wasn't. He was kidding himself. Sure, maybe for the first few years everything would be okay. They'd be busy raising their children and there wouldn't be time to think about how loveless their marriage was. But later, once the children were older and there was only them, their differences would be evident and insurmountable. It was an impossible situation. And she wouldn't do it. She couldn't. She owed her babies more than a life where their parents were together for the wrong reasons.

As much as she appreciated her sister's support, Evie didn't really understand. She'd fallen madly in love with Scott and he'd loved her in return. He'd wooed her and fought for her and laid his heart on the line as if nothing else mattered. But Daniel... There was no heart in his proposal. Only logic and his desire to share custody of their sons.

And that would never be enough.

Five days after arriving back in Port Douglas, Daniel and his brothers were still maintaining a rotating vigil outside Bernie's hospital room. Their father hadn't left his wife's side, and at seven o'clock on Thursday evening, Daniel headed for the small hospital cafeteria and returned with two double-shot espressos. Bernie had finally been taken off the critical list, and Blake and Caleb had gone back to the resort to get some much-needed rest while Daniel stayed with his father, ensuring Miles at least ate and drank something.

"Here," he said, and passed his father a take-out cup as he sat in one of the uncomfortable chairs outside the intensive care ward. "And don't let it get cold like the last one I gave you."

Miles managed a grin and then nodded. "Thanks."

His father's pain was palpable. "She's out of danger, Dad. That's good news."

"I know," Miles said, and sighed. "I don't think I could have taken another night of wondering if she was going to make it."

"You heard what the doctor said a few hours ago," he assured his father. "She's going to pull through and be back to her old self in no time."

His dad sighed again. "Who would have thought this might happen? I mean, she's always been so health conscious... I never would have guessed she had a weak heart."

"No one can predict the future, Dad."

His words felt hollow as they left his mouth. How often had he thought that? When his grandfather passed away?

When Simone and their baby died? When Mary-Jayne told him she was pregnant?

"Yeah, I know," his dad said, and tapped him on the shoulder. "Thanks for being here this week. It's meant a lot to me."

"I wouldn't be anywhere else."

Miles shrugged a little. "I know you've got a lot going on."

Daniel drank some coffee and stared at the wall ahead.

"You should go back," Miles said quietly. "You need to sort it out."

"Actually, I think a little time apart might be what we both need."

He wasn't about to admit that he missed Mary-Jayne more than he'd believed possible. But he hadn't called her, even though he craved the sound of her voice. And he was right about thinking they needed some time out.

"Nonsense," his dad said gently. "Time apart serves no purpose. Because one day you might find you have no time left, right?"

Daniel looked at his father. Miles had one of his serious expressions on his face, and as much as Daniel wanted to fob the other man off, he resisted. He'd seen that look once before, right after his grandfather had died and Daniel was preparing to step into the role of CEO. Miles had tried to talk him out of it. At the time, Daniel was convinced his father lacked vision and ambition and simply wanted to sell the company. And it had taken years for that idea to fade. It wasn't until the wake after Simone's death that he'd realized that there was more to life than business. More to life than seventy-hour weeks and meetings and racing to catch flights from one corner of the globe to the other. But still, he hadn't changed. He'd kept on doing the same things. He'd drowned himself in work to avoid thinking about all he'd lost.

"How about we concentrate on Bernie getting better and—"

"I'm very proud of you, you know," Miles said, uncharacteristically cutting him off. "I'm very proud of the man you have become."

Daniel's throat thickened. "Dad, I—"

"And I know I never say it enough." His father shrugged. "I guess I'm not sure if that matters to you."

"It matters," he said quietly. "The talking thing... It goes both ways."

Miles smiled. "Your mom was always telling me I needed to talk more to my own father. When you were born I promised myself I'd be a better father than Mike Anderson...but I'm not sure I have been. When your mom died I fell apart. Thankfully Bernie came along and picked up the pieces, even though she had every reason to run a mile. I was a grieving man with a baby, and I had so much emotional baggage it's a wonder she was able to see through all that and still give me a shot."

"She loved you," Daniel said, and drank some coffee.

"Not at first, she didn't," Miles said. "Some days I think she might have hated me. But we worked it out." His father nodded and grinned a little. "And you will, too."

Daniel didn't share his dad's optimism. Mary-Jayne opposed him at every opportunity. And he couldn't see a way out of it. He wanted her, sure. And sometimes...sometimes it felt as though he needed her like he needed air in his lungs. But it wasn't anything more than that. How could it be? They hardly knew one another. She was dreaming about some silly romantic notion that simply didn't exist. So maybe he did think about her 24/7. And maybe he did long for her in ways he'd never longed for anyone before.

But that was just desire and attraction. Add in the fact that he wanted the chance to be a full-time father to his sons...and of course it might seem like something else. Something more.

"I loved your mom," Miles said quietly. "But I love Bernie, too. It's not more, it's not less... It's simply a different kind of same."

A different kind of same...

He was still thinking about his father's words for hours afterward. And still when he tried to sleep later that night. His dreams were plagued by images of Mary-Jayne. He dreamed of holding her, of making love to her, of waking up with her hair fanned out on the pillow beside him. He awoke restless and missing her more than he'd imagined he could. And in the cold light of morning he realized one irrefutable fact.

He was in love with her.

And their relationship had just become a whole lot more complicated.

On Monday, with the nausea and lack of appetite still lingering, she went back to her doctor to discuss some medication and get her blood pressure checked. She was waiting for the doctor to come into the room when Julie, an old school friend and now the receptionist from the front desk, popped her head around the door.

"M.J.," she said and made a face. "There's someone out here who wants to see you. Who *insists* on seeing you."

She perched herself on the edge of the chair. "Who?"

Julie's eyes widened dramatically. "He says he's your fiancé."

The blood left her face. There could only be one possibility. "Oh...okay," she said, trying not to have a reaction that Julie would see through and then question. "Tall, dark hair, handsome, gray eyes?"

Julie nodded. "Oh, yeah, that's him."

She managed a smile. "You should probably send him through."

"Okay, sure."

She disappeared, and barely seconds later the door opened and Daniel strode into the room. Mary-Jayne looked him over. He seemed so familiar and yet like such a stranger. He wore dark chinos and a creaseless pale blue shirt. Her heart skipped a beat. She'd never found any man as attractive as him. And doubted she ever would. And deep down, in that place she'd come to harbor all her feelings for him, she was happy to see him. More than happy. Right then, in that moment, she didn't feel alone.

She took a breath and met his gaze. "Fiancé?"

He shrugged loosely. "Got me in the room, didn't it?"

She didn't flinch. "What are you doing here? How did you—"

"Your sister told me I'd find you here."

She nodded. "So you're back?"

"I'm back." He moved across the room and sat beside her.

"How's your mother?"

He rested back in the seat a little. "Out of intensive care. She had major bypass surgery for two blocked arteries. She's doing okay now. She'll be in the hospital for another week, though. So why are you here? Checkup?"

Mary-Jayne tried to ignore how her insides fluttered from being so close to him. "I haven't been feeling well and—"

"You're sick?" he asked and jackknifed up straight. "What's wrong? Is it the babies?" he asked and reached out to touch her abdomen.

She flinched a little from his touch, and he noticed immediately because he snatched his hand away. "Just nausea again. And I've lost my appetite."

He frowned. "Why didn't you call me? I would have come back sooner."

She pressed her shoulders back. "You needed to be with your family. It was important for your parents."

"I need to be here for you," he said with emphasis. "That's important, too."

"I'm fine," she insisted, feeling like a fool for thinking his concern must mean he cared. Well, of course he cared. She was carrying his babies. But caring wasn't love. And love was all she'd accept.

He inspected her face with his smoky gaze. "You look pale."

"Stop fussing," she said and frowned. "I'm fine, like I said. Just tired and not all that hungry because of the nausea. But I'm sure it will pass soon."

The doctor entered then, and she was glad for the reprieve. Until Daniel started barking out questions about her fatigue, her blood pressure and the likelihood of risks associated with the antinausea medication the doctor suggested she take if the symptoms didn't abate soon. She gave Daniel a death stare—which he ignored completely.

The doctor, a mild-mannered man in his fifties, just nodded and answered the questions in a patient voice. When he said he was going to draw some blood, Daniel almost rocketed out of his seat.

"Why? What's wrong?" he asked. "If you think there's a risk to her health then I insist we—"

"It's okay," she assured him and grasped his arm. "It's just a blood test. Remember how I told you that my sisters had gestational diabetes? It's only precautionary."

She thought he might pass out when the nurse came

in and took the blood. To his credit he sat in the chair and watched the entire thing, unflinching. When it was over and the doctor passed her a note with some more vitamins he wanted her to take, Daniel got to his feet and wobbled a little. She grabbed his hand and held on. Once they were in the corridor she slowed down and looked up at him, smiling.

"My hero."

He frowned. "It's not funny."

"Sure it is. Big, strong fella like you afraid of a little old needle... Who would have thought it possible?"

"I'm not afraid of them," he said, and grasped her fingers, entwining them with his own until their palms were flat against each other. "I simply don't like them. And just because you aren't afraid of anything, Mary-Jayne, doesn't mean you should make fun of people who are."

She grinned, despite the fact she was shaking inside. Holding his hand, making jokes and simply *being* with him shouldn't have made her so happy. But it did. Even though in her heart she knew it wasn't real. When they were outside he looked around.

"Where's your car?"

She took a second and then pointed to the BMW parked a few spots from the entrance. "Over there."

He glanced at the car and then to her. "Good to see you're coming to your senses."

She shrugged. "I hate waste, that's all. The car seats arrived, too... That was very thoughtful of you."

He gave her a wry smile. "Oh, you know me, an arrogant, entitled jerk and all that."

Mary-Jayne blew out a flustered breath. "Okay...so you're not all bad."

"Not all bad?" he echoed. "That's quite a compliment."

"All right, I'm an ungrateful coward who has been determined to see the worst in you from the moment we met. Satisfied?"

He smiled. "I shouldn't have called you that. I was frustrated and annoyed and worried about my mom and took it out on you. I missed you, by the way, in case you were wondering."

She nodded as emotion tightened her throat. "I might have missed you a little, too."

"I should have taken you with me."

She ached to tell him that was what she'd hoped for. But she didn't say it. "Well, I'm glad she's going to get well."

"Me, too," he said, and grinned. "So, truce?"

She smiled back at him. "I guess. Where are you staying this time? The B and B?"

He shrugged. "I'm not sure. I didn't get the chance to talk to your sister about it. Once she told me where you were I bailed and headed here."

"Would you like to stay for dinner tonight?" she asked.

He nodded. "I would. But I'll cook."

She gave him a colorful glare. "Are you suggesting that my cooking is below par?"

"I'm saying your cooking is woeful." He grabbed her hand and squeezed her fingers gently. "I'll stop at the supermarket and get what we need, and then I'll see you at home."

Home...

It sounded so nice the way he said it. The fluttering she'd had in her belly since he'd first walked into the doctor's office increased tenfold. "Okay, see you a little later."

And then he kissed her. Softly, sweetly. Like a man kissed a woman he cared about. Mary-Jayne's leaping heart almost came through her chest. And if she'd had any doubts that she'd fallen in love with him, they quickly disappeared.

* * *

Daniel pulled up outside Mary-Jayne's house a little over an hour later. He'd been all wound up in knots earlier in the morning at the thought of seeing her again, but the moment he'd opened the door and spotted her in the chair in her doctor's office, hands clasped together and her beautiful hair framing her face, all the anxiety had disappeared. She hadn't looked unhappy to see him. She'd looked...relieved. As if she welcomed him there. As if she wanted him there. Which was more than he deserved after the insensitive words he'd left her with, right before he'd returned to Port Douglas to be with his family.

He'd had a lot of time to think about their relationship in the past week. Sitting in the hospital waiting room with his father had been incredibly humbling and at times fraught with emotion. Memories of his own wife had bombarded him. Of the night they'd brought Simone into emergency and he'd arrived too late. She was already unconscious. Already too far gone for the doctors to try to save her. And then he'd waited while they'd delivered their baby and hoped that a miracle would happen and their daughter would survive. But she hadn't, and he'd lost them both.

And while he'd waited at the hospital after Bernie's surgery he'd really talked to his dad for the first time since forever. About Bernie, about his own mother, about Simone and their baby. And about Mary-Jayne. Miles had been strong, more resilient than he'd imagined. He'd wanted to comfort his dad, and in the end it happened the other way around. He was ashamed to remember how he'd always considered his father as weak. As a kind man, but one driven by his emotions. Daniel had mistaken Miles's lack of ambition as a failing. But he was wrong. His father's ambitions were simply different from his own. And yet, in some ways, very much the same. Because Miles had endeavored to be a worthy, caring dad to his sons, and Daniel was determined to emulate that ambition. He wanted to be around his sons and watch them grow into children and then teens and finally into adulthood. He wanted to share their lives and be the best man he could be for them. And for Mary-Jayne, too. He cared about her too much to simply let her be only the mother of his sons. He wanted more. He *needed* more.

And since he'd screwed up big time in the courtship department, he had to go back to square one and start all over again. Like he should have done in the beginning, on that first time they'd met. Instead of making that stupid, off-the-cuff comment about how they'd end up in his condo at some point, he should have asked her out. He should have wooed her and courted her like she deserved. He should have gone to see her while she was in South Dakota at her friend's wedding and pursued her properly, and not asked her to meet him on his turf as though all he was interested in was getting her into bed. No wonder she'd turned him down flat. And since then they'd been at war—arguing and insulting one another. She'd called him arrogant and she was right. He'd come out fighting on every occasion and hadn't let her really get to know him at all.

She wants romance and all the trimmings…

Well, he could do that if it meant she would eventually agree to marry him.

He walked up the path and saw that her old car had a for-sale sign propped inside the back window. It pleased him, and by the time he reached her door he was grinning like a fool.

"Oh, hi," she said, breathless and beautiful in a white floaty dress that came to her knees and buttoned down the front. Her belly had popped out more and she looked so beautiful he couldn't do anything other than stare at her. "Come inside."

He crossed the threshold and walked down the hall. Her little dog came yapping around his ankles, and he made a point of patting the animal for a moment before he entered the kitchen.

"So what are you making?" she asked when he put the bags on the counter.

He started unpacking the bags. "Vegetarian tagine... Spiced carrots...amongst other things."

Her green eyes widened. "Moroccan?" She laughed and the sound rushed over his skin and through his blood. "My favorite."

"Want to help?"

She nodded and tossed an apron at him. "Only if you wear this."

He opened up the garment and read the words *Kiss The Cook*. "Really?"

She shrugged. "You never know your luck."

He popped it over his head. "I already feel lucky."

She came around the counter and methodically tied it around the back. "You mean because of your mother? You must be so relieved that she's out of danger."

"We all are," he said, thinking how he was imagining he'd get to kiss her again and that was why he felt lucky. "My dad couldn't bear to lose her."

"I can imagine," she said, and pulled a couple of cutting boards from a drawer. "I mean, he already lost your mother, so to lose Bernie, too... I mean, I know your mother was the love of his life because Solana told me... but he loves Bernie dearly, you can tell by the way he looks at her."

Daniel stopped what he was doing and stared at her. Her green eyes shimmered so brilliantly it was impossible to look anywhere else. The awareness between them amplified tenfold, and he fought the urge to reach for her and take her in his arms. Instead he met her gaze and spoke. "Just because he loved my mom didn't mean he had less of himself to give to someone else."

She inhaled sharply. "I...I suppose so... I mean, if he was willing to open his heart."

"He was," Daniel said quietly. "He did."

The meaning was not lost on either of them. "And they've had a good marriage, Mary-Jayne. They got married quickly and didn't really know one another very well. But it worked. It *can* work."

She started to nod and then stopped. "But they love one another."

"They do now. They got married, had children, made a life together. So perhaps it did start out a little unorthodox...but in the end it's how it plays out that's important."

She didn't look completely convinced and as much as he wanted to keep pushing, he backed off and returned his attention to the grocery bags on the counter. They chatted about mundane things, like her new car and the weather. She asked after his grandmother and was clearly delighted when he told her Solana wanted to come to Crystal Point for a visit.

"She'd like it here," he said when the food was cooking. He stood by the stove, stirring the pot. "Once Bernie is assured of a full recovery, I'm sure my grandmother will come."

"I'd like that," she said as she grabbed plates and cutlery and took them to the table. "Um...how long are you staying for this time?"

He kept stirring. "I'm not sure. I have to get back to

work at some point. I need to go to Phuket for the reopening once the renovation is complete in a couple of weeks."

She nodded, eyed the salad he'd made and sniffed the air appreciatively. "That smells good. You really do know how to cook."

He grinned. "Told you," he said, and then more seriously, "There's a lot you don't know about me, Mary-Jayne. But I'd like to change that. You said we should take some time and you were right. But I don't want to pressure you. So if you want slow, then we'll go slow."

She stopped what she was doing and looked at him. "Honestly, I don't know what I want."

"How about you take some time to figure it out?"

"You said we didn't have time."

He shrugged loosely. "I was mad at you when I said that. We have time."

She nodded a little and took a couple of sodas out of the fridge. "I don't have any of that imported beer you like," she said, and placed the cans on the counter. "But I can get some."

"This is fine," he said, and cranked both lids. "I don't drink much."

They ate a leisurely dinner and she entertained him with stories of her youth, and when she was laughing hard and out of breath he did the same. It was interesting to learn they had both been rebellious as children and teenagers.

"I guess you had to rein in all that when you took over the company from your grandfather? Can't have a respectable CEO wreaking havoc, right?" she asked and laughed.

Daniel grinned. "I guess not. Although I wasn't quite the wayward teen that you were. No tattoos...so I was nowhere near as hardcore as you."

She laughed again. "That's only because you're scared of needles."

"No need to rub it in. I'm well aware of my weakness."

She rested her elbows on the table and sighed. "You don't have a weak bone in your body."

He met her gaze. "I have a weakness for you."

"That's not weakness," she said. "That's desire. Attraction. Lust."

Daniel pushed his plate aside. "Maybe it's more than that."

"More?"

He reached across the table and grasped her hand. "I care about you."

"Because I'm having your babies," she said, and went to move her hand.

Daniel's grip tightened. "That's only part of it."

She looked at him, her eyes suddenly all suspicious as she pulled her hand free. "What are you saying?"

He met her gaze. "Can't you guess?"

"I don't understand. Are you saying that you're... That you have feelings for me...?"

"Yes," he replied. "That's precisely what I'm saying."

Her gaze widened. "Are you saying that...that you're in love with me?"

Daniel nodded. That was exactly what he was saying. He *did* love her. The empty feeling he had inside when he was away from her was love. That was why he couldn't wait to return to Crystal Point. He wanted her. He craved her and ached thinking about it. She was the mother of his babies. And she was vivacious and fun and as sexy as anything.

He'd loved Simone. It had made sense. Loving Mary-Jayne made no sense at all. And yet, in the past few days it had become a clear and undeniable truth.

"Would it be so hard to believe?"

"Yes. Impossible," she said with a scowl and pushed the chair back. "I think you should leave."

Daniel got to his feet the same time she did. "Why are you angry?"

She glared at him. "Because you're lying to me. Because you'll say and do anything to get what you want and all of a sudden you seem to think that making some big statement about love will make me change my mind about getting married."

"I haven't mentioned marriage," he reminded her.

"It's on the agenda, though, right?"

"Eventually," he replied. "That's generally the result of a relationship between two people who fall in love."

"But *two* people haven't fallen in love."

Right. So she didn't love him. Didn't care. That was plain enough. His heart sank. Maybe she would... someday? If he tried hard enough to earn that love.

"We could try to make this work."

"Like your parents did?" she asked. "Maybe it worked for them because they actually liked one another to start with. I'll bet they didn't call one another names and look for the worst in each other."

Daniel expelled an impatient breath. "I apologized for what I said the last time I was here."

"You mean when you called me a fraud who had locked herself in a cage?" she enquired, brows up, temper on alert. "Don't be... You were right. I have been in a cage, Daniel. But as of this moment I'm out of it. And do you know what...I'm not going to trade one cage for another. Because being married to you would put me right back inside."

"I don't want to keep you caged, Mary-Jayne. I love your spirit and your—"

"Can you hear yourself? Three weeks ago you were calling me a flake and a gold digger and now you've miraculously fallen in love with me. I'm not stupid. I know when I'm being played. So you can come here with your sexy smile and make dinner and act all interested in my childhood and this town, but it doesn't change one undeniable fact—you want me to marry you because it suits you and your arrogant assumption that you can simply take whatever you want. Well, you can't take me."

He took a step toward her, but she moved backward. "What do I have to say to convince you that I'm serious about my feelings for you?"

"Say?" she echoed. "Nothing. Words are empty. It's actions that matter."

He waved an arm. "I'm here, aren't I? I came back. I feel as if I've been pursuing you for months."

"You first chased me because you wanted to get me into bed," she said hotly. "And now you're chasing me because you want your sons."

"I'm chasing you because I love you."

There… It was out on the table…for her and her alone.

She laughed, but it sounded hollow. "You're chasing me because you think it's a means to an end. Well, forget it. What I want for my life I can't get from you."

Pain ripped through his chest. "How do you know that? Just tell me what you want."

"I've told you in half a dozen ways. I want a man who carries me here," she said and put her hand against her breast. "In his heart. Over his heart. On his heart. Forever. And it might sound sentimental and foolish to you, but I don't care. I think I really know that for the first time in my life. And I have you to thank for it. You've shown me what I want…and what I don't."

"And what you don't want…that's me?" he asked, aching through to his bones.

"Yes," she said quietly. "Exactly."

He moved closer and grasped her shoulders, gripping her firmly. And then he kissed her. Long and hot and loaded with pain and guilt and resentment. When he was done he lifted his head and stared down into her face. She was breathing hard and her eyes were filled with confusion and rage.

He ran a possessive hand down her shoulder and breast and then down to her belly. "Nothing will change the fact that a part of me is growing inside you. Love me or hate me, we're bound together. And we always will be."

Chapter Twelve

The following Saturday, it was her niece's second birthday and Mary-Jayne didn't have the strength of mind to go, or to excuse herself. She'd exiled herself in her little house for five days, working on new pieces, revamping her website, thinking of her work, her babies and little else. She didn't spare a thought for Daniel. Not one. Not a single, solitary thought.

Big, fat liar...

He was in her dreams. She couldn't keep him out.

He'd said he loved her. It should have made her day. It should have...but didn't. It only made her angry. And achingly sad.

He hadn't contacted her. She knew from Evie that he wasn't staying at the B and B, and could only assume that he was at a hotel somewhere in Bellandale. It suited her just fine. She didn't want to see him. Not yet. She was still reeling from his declaration of love. Still hating him for it. And still loving him more than she had imagined she could ever love anyone.

Jerk...

Plus, her belly was getting bigger every day and now she waddled rather than walked. She went shopping for baby clothes with her sisters and cried all the way home because she felt as though part of her was missing. She considered buying furniture for the nursery and then put the idea on hold. The spare room needed significant work. In fact, she wondered how she was supposed to raise two babies in such a small house. Once she put two cribs, a change table and a cupboard in the spare room there wouldn't be much space for anything else. What she needed was a bigger house. With a large yard. With a swing set that the twins would be able to play on when they were old enough.

She felt a sense of loneliness so acute it physically pained her. And nothing abated it. Not her parents or her sisters. Not talking to her long-distance friends or cuddling with her dog on the lounge. Only her babies growing peacefully in her belly gave her comfort.

On the afternoon of the party she laid her dress on the bed, flicked off her flip-flops and started getting ready. The dress was a maternity smock in bright colored silk that tied in a knot at her nape, and the outrageously red sandals were low heeled and comfortable. Or at least they would have been, had she been able to get them on. Her body simply wouldn't bend like it used to. She twisted and turned herself inside out and still the darn sandals wouldn't clasp.

Frustration crept over her skin as she kept trying. And failing. Fifteen minutes later and she was ready to toss the shoes at the wall. Until the tears came. Great racking sobs that made her chest hurt. After a few minutes she couldn't actually remember why she was crying. Which only made her more emotional. More fraught. More miserable.

She considered calling Evie and then quickly changed her mind. Her sister had enough to do organizing the party. And Grace had a newborn and would be too busy. She thought about calling her brother, but once he saw she'd been crying he'd be all concerned and want to know why she was upset and then act all macho when she told him how much she hated and loved Daniel. He'd probably want to go and punch him in the nose. It would serve Daniel right, too. Although she was pretty sure he'd throw a punch as good as he got.

Not that she wanted to see him hurt. That was the last thing she wanted.

She sat on the edge of the bed and cried some more. And thought about how ridiculously she was behaving. And then cried again. She gave the shoes another try and gave up when her aching back and swollen feet wouldn't do what she wanted.

She flopped back on the bed and grabbed her phone. The battery signal beeped. She'd forgotten to charge it overnight. Typical. She flicked through the numbers and reached the one she wanted. After a few unanswered rings it went straight to message service.

"It's me," she said, and hiccupped. "Can you come over?"

Then she buried her head in the pillow and sobbed.

Daniel had been in the shower when Mary-Jayne called. He tried to call her back several times but it went to message. Unable to reach her back, he was dressed and out the door of his hotel in about two minutes flat. He drove to Crystal Point as speedily as he could without breaking the law. Pulling up outside her house, he jumped out and raced to the front door. No one answered when he knocked. He heard the little dog barking behind the door and panic set in behind his ribs. What if she was hurt? Perhaps she'd fallen over trying to lift something heavy? Or worse. He rattled the door but it was locked, and then saw that the front window was open. He pushed the screen in and climbed through, not caring if the neighbors thought he was an intruder. They could call the cops for all he cared. He just needed to know she was safe.

Once he was in the living room he called her name. Still nothing.

He got to her bedroom door and stilled in his tracks. She was on the bed, curled up.

He'd never moved so fast in his life. He was beside the bed in seconds. He said her name softly and touched her bare shoulder. Her red-rimmed eyes flicked open.

"Hey," he said and stroked her cheek. "What's wrong?"

She shook her head. "Nothing."

"You left a message on my cell."

"I know," she whispered. "I didn't know who else to call. And then you didn't call back and then my phone went dead and…" Her voice trailed off.

Daniel's stomach churned. He grasped her shoulders. "Mary-Jayne, what's wrong? Are you sick? Is it the babies?"

"I'm not sick," she said. "I'm fine. The babies are fine."

She didn't look fine. She looked as if she'd been crying for a week. But she'd called him. She'd reached out when he'd feared she never would. It was enough to give him hope. To make him believe that she did care. "You've been crying?"

She nodded as tears welled in her eyes. She hiccupped. "I couldn't…"

"You couldn't what?" he prompted.

"I couldn't get my shoes on!"

And then she sobbed. Racking, shuddering sobs that reached him deep down. He folded her in his arms and held her gently. "It's okay, darling," he assured her.

"I'm as fat as a house."

"You're beautiful."

"I'm not," she cried, tears running down her face again. "And my ankles are so swollen that my shoes don't fit. I tried to put them on but my belly got in the way."

Daniel relaxed his grip and reached for her chin. He tilted her head back. "Would you like me to put them on for you?"

She nodded, and he moved off the bed and found her shoes by the wall. He crouched by the bed and reached for her legs. He slipped the shoes on and strapped each sandal at the ankle. "See…they fit just fine," he said, and ran a palm down her smooth calf.

She hiccupped and some fire returned to her eyes. "Why are you being nice to me?"

"That's my job," he said, and sat beside her. "Isn't that why you called me?"

She shrugged helplessly. "I just called a number… Any number…"

He grasped her chin again and made her look at him. "You called *me* because you wanted me here."

She sighed. "I don't know why. Probably because I was dreaming about you and—"

"Good," he said, feeling possessive and frustrated. "I want you to dream about me. I ache to be in your dreams, Mary-Jayne," he rasped, and pulled her close. "I won't be kept out of them."

"I couldn't keep you out if I tried," she admitted, and then relaxed against him, despite her better judgment, he suspected. "I don't know what's wrong with me. I feel so—"

"You're pregnant," he said, and gently spread a hand over her stomach. "Your hormones are running riot. Don't beat yourself up about being emotional. It's perfectly normal."

Her eyes flashed. "Aren't you Mr. Sensitive all of a sudden?"

Daniel's mouth curled at the edges. "With you, absolutely."

"Only to get what you want," she said and sniffed. "Now who's the fraud?"

He tilted her chin again and inched his mouth closer to hers. "I really did screw up, didn't I, for you to have such a low opinion of me? I generally think of myself as a good sort of person, Mary-Jayne... Give me half a chance and you might, too."

She harrumphed. "Manipulative jerk," she whispered, but then moved her lips closer.

He kissed her gently. "I'm not manipulating you. I love you."

She moaned. "Don't say things you don't mean."

Daniel swept her hair back from her face. "I mean it. And I'll tell you every day for the rest of my life."

"I won't listen," she retorted, and tried to evade his mouth. "And one day I'll find someone who really does—"

"Don't do that," he said painfully, cutting through her words. "That would just about break me."

"I'll do what I want," she said and pulled back. "You don't own me."

Daniel held her still. "Oh, darling...I do. And you own me. You've owned me since the first time I saw you in that store window. And I'm not going anywhere, Mary-Jayne."

"You'll have to at some point," she remarked, all eyes

and fiery beauty in her stare. "You don't live here. You live in San Francisco. Then I'll be free of you."

"We'll never be free of one another. That's why you called me today. Admit it," he said, firmer this time. "You could have called any one of half a dozen people and they all would have been here in a matter of minutes. But you didn't," he reminded her. "You called me."

"It was the first number I pressed. It was random, and then my battery died. Don't read anything into it."

He chuckled, delighted and spurred on by her reticence. "Admit it... You're in love with me."

"I am not!" she denied, and pulled herself from his arms. "I don't love you. I never will. I'd have to be stark raving mad to fall in love with you. And you're only saying all this to get what you want."

"I am? Really?" He stood up and propped his hands on his hips. "Have I asked for anything? I've given you space. I've left you alone. I've holed myself up in a damn hotel room for a week, even though all I want to do is be here with you every day and hold you in my arms every night. I haven't sent you flowers or bought anything for the babies even though I want to because I know you'd accuse me of trying to manipulate you. I haven't gone to see your parents and explain to them what you mean to me and assure them I'll do whatever is in my power to do to make you happy even though my instincts tell me I should. I'm *trying*, Mary-Jayne... I'm trying to do this your way. Just... just try to meet me in the middle somewhere, okay?" He placed a hand over his chest. "Because this is killing me."

"So he's still in town?"

Mary-Jayne looked at Evie. Her sisters had come over to cheer her up and bring her some gifts for the babies. The tiny pair of matching baseball caps Grace gave her was so incredibly cute that she cried a little. Which seemed to have become a habit of hers in the past few weeks.

Crying... Ugh!

She had become a sentimental sap.

"I guess so."

"You've seen him?" Grace asked.

"Not for a week. Why?"

Her sisters both shrugged and smiled. It was Evie who spoke next. "It's only that...well... In the past few days he's come to see all of us and told us..."

"Told you all what?" Mary-Jayne asked, pushing up on her seat.

"That he's in love with you," Grace supplied. "That he wants to marry you."

Mary-Jayne saw red. "That no-good, sneaky—"

"It's kinda romantic," Evie said and grinned.

"It's *not* romantic," Mary-Jayne said hotly. "It's deceitful and underhanded. And do you know what else he did? He bought all this baby stuff and had it delivered. The garage is full of boxes and toys and baby furniture and—"

"Oh, how awful for you," Evie said and grinned. "Such a terrible man."

Mary-Jayne scowled. "You're on his side, then?"

"We're on your side," Grace said and smiled gently. "You seem unhappy, that's all."

"I'll be happier when he's gone."

"I don't think he's going anywhere any time soon," Evie said. "He told Scott he's going to buy a house here."

The color bled from her face. "I don't believe it. He wouldn't. He's got a business to run and he can't do that from here."

"Maybe he's found something more important than business," Grace said pointedly.

"Yeah—his heirs. He wants his children. Don't be blinded by the good looks and money."

"We could say the same thing to you."

Mary-Jayne stilled. Her sister's words resonated loud and clear. Was that how she appeared—as a judgmental and narrow-minded snob—and exactly what she'd accused him of being?

She'd resented his money and success without good reason. On one hand, she recognized his honesty and integrity. And yet, when he'd told her the very thing she wanted to hear, she hadn't believed him. She'd accused him of trying to manipulate and confuse her. But what proof did she have that he'd ever done that? None. He hadn't manipulated her to get her into bed. Their attraction had been hot and intense from the start. Not one-sided. She'd craved him and he'd made it abundantly clear that he wanted her. And then she'd convinced herself he was all bad, all arrogance and self-entitlement.

To protect herself.

Because he was nothing like any man she'd previously dated she regarded him as an aberration…someone to avoid…someone to battle. And she had at every opportunity. She'd fought and insulted and pushed him away time and time again. Because loving Daniel meant she would be redefined. He was rich and successful and all that she had professed to loathe. He'd asked her to marry him. He'd said he loved her. And still she let her prejudice blind her.

His parting words a week earlier still echoed in her mind. *This is killing me.* Real pain. Real anguish. And she'd done that to him. She'd hurt him. She'd hurt the one person she loved most in the world. She felt the shame of it through to her bones. He'd asked her to meet him in the middle.

But she could do better than that.

"You look as though the proverbial penny just dropped," Evie said.

Both her sisters were staring at her. "I think it just did. He asked me to marry him. He said he was in love with me."

"That's what he told us, too."

Tears filled her eyes. "I never imagined that I'd fall in love with someone like him. I thought that one day I'd meet someone like myself... Someone who wasn't so... conventional, if you know what I mean."

Evie came and sat beside her and grabbed her hand. "You know, just because he's not a bohemian poet, it doesn't make him wrong for you. If anyone had told me a few years ago that I would fall in love with a man nearly ten years younger than me I wouldn't have believed them."

"Same here," Grace said, and sat on the other side. "I never intended to fall in love with our brother's best friend. But I did. When you love, you simply love. That's the thing that's important, M.J. Not how successful or wealthy he is."

"He's a good man," Evie said quietly. "Give him a chance to prove it."

"What if he's changed his mind?" she asked, thinking of the terrible way they'd parted and how she'd told him she didn't love him and never would. "I said some pretty awful things to him the last time we were together. What if he doesn't want to see me?"

"You need a plan," Grace suggested.

"Leave that to me," Evie said, and she grabbed her phone from her bag.

Three hours later Mary-Jayne was at the B and B, sitting in the garden on a bench by the wishing well. She smoothed down the skirt on her white dress and then fluffed her hair. She'd always loved this spot. Through the vine-covered hedge she saw a car pull up to the curb.

Minutes later he was walking up the path, all purposeful and tight limbed. He wore jeans and a polo shirt and looked so good it stole her breath. When he spotted her he came to a halt midstride.

"Hi," she said, and smiled.

His expression was unreadable. "I didn't expect you to be here."

"I didn't expect me to be here up until a couple of hours ago."

His gaze narrowed. "Are you all right? No problems with the babies?"

She touched her abdomen gently. "No… Everything is fine. I feel good. The nausea is gone for the moment. I haven't seen you for a while… Where have you been?"

"I was under the impression you had no interest in seeing me." He took a step closer. "I had a call from your sister. Is she here?"

"No…just me."

His brows drew together. "Subterfuge?"

"Kind of," she admitted. "I wasn't sure if *you'd* see *me* after the last time."

"If you had called me, I would be here. Always. I've told you that before. What's this about, Mary-Jayne?"

He looked so good. So familiar. And she ached to be in his arms. "I'm sorry about what I said the last time we were together."

"Which part? When you said you didn't love me and never would?" he quizzed.

She nodded. "All of it. You came over to help me and I was thoughtless and ungrateful."

"Yes, you were."

She ignored a hot niggle of impatience that crept up her spine. "I hear you're looking at real estate?"

He shrugged loosely. "Do you disapprove of that, as well?"

God, he was impossible. "Of course not. I understand that you'll want to be close to the babies when they are born."

He nodded. "So anything else?"

Mary-Jayne sighed and grabbed the shopping bag by the bench. She stood up and extracted the two tiny baseballs caps. "I thought you might like these. They're cute, don't you think?"

He took the caps and examined them. "Cute. Yes. Is that it? You got me here to give me a couple of baseball caps?"

"I wanted to see you."

"Why now? Nothing's changed."

"Everything's changed."

His mouth flattened. "What?"

Her cheeks grew hotter by the second. "Me. This. Us. A week ago you told me you loved me."

"I know what I said," he shot back. "I also know what you said."

She took a breath. "Shall we go inside? I'd like to talk to you."

"So when you want to talk, we talk? Is that how this plays out? I don't seem to be able to get it right with you, do I?"

Mary-Jayne let her impatience rise up. "I'm going inside. You can stay out here in the garden and sulk if you want to."

She turned on her heels and walked up to the house as quickly as she could. He was about four steps behind her. Once she was through the French doors and in the living room she spun around.

He was barely a foot away, chest heaving. "Sulk?"

She shrugged. "Sure. Isn't that what you've been doing

this week? So I said something mean and unkind. I'm sorry. But you said yourself that I'm running on hormones because of my pregnancy. I should think it's about time you started making allowances for that."

"Allowances," he echoed incredulously. "Are you serious? I've done nothing *but* make allowances since the moment you told me you were pregnant. Nothing I do is right. Nothing I say makes any difference. You trust me, you don't. You need me, you don't. You want me, you don't. Which is it? I'm so damned confused I can barely think straight. I'm neglecting my business, my family, my friends…everything, because I'm so caught up in this *thing* I have with you."

Mary-Jayne watched him, fascinated by the heat and fire in his words. There was so much passion in him. She'd been so wrong, thinking he was some sort of cold fish who didn't feel deeply. He did. He just didn't show that side of himself to the world.

"I do trust you," she said, and moved toward him. "And I do need you," she said, and touched his chest. When he winced and stepped back she was immediately concerned. "What's wrong? Are you in pain? Have you had another migraine?"

"No. Stop this, Mary-Jayne. Tell me what I'm doing here and—"

"I'm trying," she said frantically. "But I need to know if you meant what you said."

He frowned. "What I said?"

"You…you said you loved me," she said, suddenly breathless. "Did you mean it?"

"Do I strike you as someone who says things I don't mean?"

"No," she replied, and blinked back the tears in her eyes. "It's just that…what you said about me being in a cage and about how things would have been different from the start if you hadn't been...well...*you*. If you'd been a dreadlocked, unemployed musician, I wouldn't have been so determined to keep my distance. Because that's what I thought I wanted. What I knew, if that makes sense. All that stuff you said, you were right." She touched his arm, gripped tightly and felt his muscles hard beneath her palm. "For as long as I can remember I've craved freedom and independence. But now I feel as if I've lived a life that isn't authentic. I left home at seventeen, but only moved three streets away from my parents. Some independence, huh? So you're right, I'm a fraud. I'm tied to this little town. I'm not a free spirit at all." She took a breath, not caring about the tears on her cheeks. "And you...you saw through that and through me. What you said about marriage makes sense. Each one starts out differently, like your dad and Bernie. And if this..." she said, and touched her stomach gently. "If this is what we start with, just these two precious babies bringing us together, then that's okay. Because if you do want me, and if you do love me, even a little bit, that will be enough."

He stared at her, holding her gaze captive. "But it's not enough for me, Mary-Jayne."

She froze. "I don't understand..."

"We both deserve more than some half-baked attempt at a relationship."

"But you said you wanted to get married and be a family," she reminded him, crumbling inside.

"I do," he said, and grabbed her hand. "But I want *all* of you, every beautiful, spirited, intoxicating piece. I had a good marriage once. But I want more than that this time. I don't want to leave at six in the morning and arrive home at eight. I don't want to eat out five nights out of seven because work always comes first. I don't want to miss family gatherings because I'm too busy landing some deal or flying from one country to the next. I've lived that life and I was never truly happy. I want us to raise our children together, like *they* deserve."

Tears wet her cheeks again. "I want that, too. You really... You really do love me?"

He grasped her chin and looked directly into her eyes. "I really do love you, Mary-Jayne. And I know they're only words, but they are what I feel."

"Words are enough," she said, happiness surging through her blood. "I love you, too."

"Words will never be enough," he said, and kissed her gently. "Which is why I did this."

"What?" she muttered against his mouth.

"This," he said, and stepped back a little. He tugged at the collar of his T-shirt and showed her what he meant.

Her name, in small but strikingly dark scrolled script, was now written on the left side of his chest. The ink was new and still healing, but she could see through all that to the beauty of what he had done.

"You got a tattoo?" she asked, crying. "I can't believe you did that. The needles... You hate needles."

He shrugged one shoulder. "I love you more than I hate needles." He grasped her hand and held it against his chest. "In my heart. Over my heart. On my heart. Forever."

They were the most beautiful words she had ever heard.

She reached up and touched his face. "I'm so much in love with you, Daniel. And I'm sorry I kept pushing you away."

He held her in his arms. "You had more sense than me. We needed to get to know one another. You knew that. I just arrogantly thought I knew how to fix things."

"At least you wanted to try," she said, and settled against

his shoulder. "I've been fighting this and you since the very beginning."

"I know," he said, and laughter rumbled in his chest. "You took off as if your feet were on fire after Solana's birthday party."

"I was in shock," she admitted. "I'd never had an experience like that before."

"Me, either," he said. "Making love with you is like nothing on earth." He kissed her nape. "But you never have to run from me again, Mary-Jayne."

"I promise I won't."

Seconds later they were settled on one of the sofas and he wrapped her in his arms. "There's something about you that draws me. You have this incredible energy...a life force all your own. I love that about you. And I love that our sons are going to have that, too."

She sighed, happy and content and so in love her head was spinning. "So where are we going to live? Here or San Francisco?"

He reached for her chin and tilted her face toward his own. "Darling, do you think I would ever ask you to leave here? This is your home."

"But San Francisco is *your* home."

"It's where I live," he said and kissed her gently. "I don't think I've ever considered anywhere as really home. Until now. Even when I was married to Simone and we had our apartment, most times it was simply a place to sleep."

She couldn't believe what he was saying. "Do you mean we can stay here permanently? I was imagining we'd do some time here and some over there."

He shook his head. "Your family is here. Your roots are here. And I like this town and I want to raise our sons here. If they turn out half as good as you then I'll be a happy man."

"But your business? How can you—"

"I need to let go a little," he admitted. "I need to trust Blake and Caleb more. They have just as must invested in Anderson's as I do… I think it's about time I lessened the reins. You see," he said, and grinned, "I'm learning to not be so much of a control freak."

"Don't change too much," she said, and pressed against him. "I like you just as you are."

He kissed her, long and sweet, and when he finally lifted his head he stared into her eyes. "You know something…I think it's time I proposed properly."

"What a great idea," she said, and laughed, so happy she thought she might burst.

Daniel grabbed her hand and brought it to his lips. "Mary-Jayne, I'm lost without you… Marry me?"

"Yes," she said, laughing, crying and loving him more than she had believed possible. "Absolutely, positively, yes!"

Epilogue

Three and a half months later...

At seven o'clock at night on a Monday, Mary-Jayne's water broke. Daniel was walking into the bedroom when she hovered in the bathroom doorway.

"What is it?" he asked immediately.

She grimaced. "It's time."

Panic flittered across his face. "You're in labor?"

"Yep," she said, and grinned.

He strode toward her. "But there's still nearly three weeks to go."

"We were told I'd probably go into labor early," she said and touched his arm. "Stop worrying."

"I'm not worried," he assured her. "How do you feel?"

"Better now I know what the niggling backache I had all day is about."

"You were in pain and you didn't tell—"

"Stop worrying," she said again, and ushered him out the doorway. "I'm fine." She rubbed her huge belly. "We're fine. Is my bag still in the car?"

He'd insisted they have her baby bag ready for when she went into labor. He'd also insisted on a trial run in the car and had organized Evie to be the backup driver just in case he wasn't around when the time came. Of course she knew that was never going to happen.

In the past few months so much had changed. Since their wedding two months earlier, he'd taken some much-needed time off from Anderson's. His brother Blake had taken on more global accountability, and general managers had been put in place in some of the resorts to alleviate the workload. Caleb was still recovering from an unexpected and serious boating accident and had been recuperating from his busted leg with Miles and Bernie for the past eight weeks. It had been a fraught time for the entire family, but since Bernie's heart attack, the family had become closer and they all rallied around to ensure Caleb had all the support he needed.

Despite all that, she knew Daniel had never been happier. She still marveled at how well he'd adjusted to not having such tight control over the company anymore. He'd learned to trust his brothers and share the responsibility. Of course, with Caleb out of action for a while, there were times when he was needed to fly back to San Francisco or one of the other locations, but he was never gone for more than a few days. And Mary-Jayne didn't mind.

He'd bought a house in Crystal Point just four doors down from Dunn Inn, and she loved the big low-set brick-and-tile home with its floating timber floors, racked ceilings, wide doorways and sprawling front deck that offered an incredible view of the ocean. She surprised herself by how much fun she had purchasing new furnishings. He was generous to a fault, and they had a wonderful time working on the nursery and getting the room ready for the babies.

Their relationship was amazing. *He* was amazing, and she'd never been happier.

The drive to the hospital took twenty minutes, and another five to find a vacant car space and get her into the emergency ward. She was quickly transported to maternity, and by the time she was settled in a room her contractions were coming thick and fast.

It was an arduous twelve hours later that her doctor recommended a caesarean birth. Mary-Jayne cried a little, and then agreed to do what best for their babes. William and Flynn Anderson were born a minute apart, both pink and screaming and perfect in every way.

Still groggy from the surgery, it was another few hours before she had a chance to nurse her sons. Daniel remained by her side, strong and resilient and giving her every ounce of support she needed. And when he held their sons for the first time, there were tears in his eyes. And he didn't seem to care one bit. Watching him, seeing the emotion and pure love in his expression made her fall in love with him even more.

"They really are beautiful," she remarked as William settled against her breast to nurse and Daniel sat in the chair by her bed and held Flynn against his chest.

Daniel looked at his son, marveling at the perfect beauty in the little boy's face, and smiled. When he returned his gaze to his wife he saw she was watching him. "You did an amazing job, Mrs. Anderson."

She smiled. "You, too. But then again, you do everything well, and I knew this wouldn't be any different."

Daniel reached for her hand and rubbed her fingers. "You know, we're going to have to start letting the masses in at some point. Your sisters are keen to spend some time with you. And Solana has been circling the waiting area with your parents for the past two hours. She's very excited about meeting her great-grandsons."

"I know," she said, and sighed. "I just selfishly want our babies and you to myself for as long as I can."

Daniel stood and gently placed their sleeping son into his mother's arm, watching, fascinated, as she held them both. It was the most beautiful thing he had ever seen. His wife. His sons. They were a gift more precious than anything he could have ever imagined. Love, the purest and most intense he'd ever experienced, surged through his blood.

"I love you," he said, and bent down to kiss her sweet mouth. "And, my darling, you have me to yourself for the rest of our lives."

Tears welled in her beautiful green eyes. "I never intended to love anyone this much, you know," she said, and batted her lashes. "I never thought it was possible."

"Neither did I."

"It's actually all Audrey and Caleb's doing," she said, beaming. "If they didn't have such a dysfunctional relationship we would never have met."

"Oh, I don't know about that," he said, and chuckled. "Audrey would have returned to Crystal Point eventually and Caleb would have eventually followed her, and since my brother is a hothead without any sense I would have had to come here and sort things out. So I'm pretty sure our paths would have crossed."

Mary-Jayne glanced at the twins. "Maybe you're right. Now they're here I can't imagine a world without these two in it." She looked up and smiled gently. "Speaking of Caleb and Audrey...any news?"

Daniel shrugged. "You know Caleb. He's refusing to get the marriage annulled."

They had all been shocked to learn that Caleb and Audrey were in fact married, and had been just a month after they'd met.

She sighed. "Well, I'm glad we don't have all that drama in our relationship."

Daniel smiled, remembering their own fraught beginnings. "Nah…we were a piece of cake."

She laughed, and the lovely sound echoed around the room.

"Shall I let them in?" he asked, kissing her again.

"You bet."

And he was, he realized as he opened the door, just about the happiest man on the planet. Because he had Mary-Jayne's love and their beautiful sons. He truly did have it all.

* * * * *

LET'S TALK

Romance

For exclusive extracts, competitions
and special offers, find us online:

f MillsandBoon

𝕏 @MillsandBoon

◎ @MillsandBoonUK

♪ @MillsandBoonUK

Get in touch on 01413 063 232

MILLS & BOON

THE HEART OF ROMANCE

A ROMANCE FOR EVERY READER

MODERN

Prepare to be swept off your feet by sophisticated, sexy and seductive heroes, in some of the world's most glamourous and romantic locations, where power and passion collide.

HISTORICAL

Escape with historical heroes from time gone by. Whether your passion is for wicked Regency Rakes, muscled Vikings or rugged Highlanders, awaken the romance of the past.

MEDICAL

Set your pulse racing with dedicated, delectable doctors in the high-pressure world of medicine, where emotions run high and passion, comfort and love are the best medicine.

True Love

Celebrate true love with tender stories of heartfelt romance, from the rush of falling in love to the joy a new baby can bring, and a focus on the emotional heart of a relationship.

Desire

Indulge in secrets and scandal, intense drama and sizzling hot action with heroes who have it all: wealth, status, good looks…everything but the right woman.

HEROES

The excitement of a gripping thriller, with intense romance at its heart. Resourceful, true-to-life women and strong, fearless men face danger and desire - a killer combination!

To see which titles are coming soon, please visit

millsandboon.co.uk/nextmonth

JOIN US ON SOCIAL MEDIA!

Stay up to date with our latest releases, author news and gossip, special offers and discounts, and all the behind-the-scenes action from Mills & Boon...

 @millsandboon

 @millsandboonuk

 facebook.com/millsandboon

 @millsandboonuk

It might just be true love...

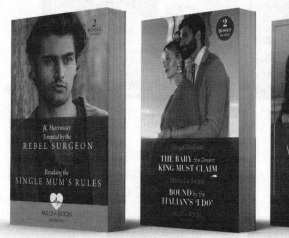

GET YOUR ROMANCE FIX!

Get the latest romance news, exclusive author interviews, story extracts and much more!

MILLS & BOON
True Love

Romance from the Heart

Celebrate true love with tender stories of heartfelt romance, from the rush of falling in love to the joy a new baby can bring, and a focus on the emotional heart of a relationship.

MILLS & BOON

Desire

Indulge in secrets and scandal, intense drama and plenty of sizzling hot action with powerful and passionate heroes who have it all: wealth, status, good looks…everything but the right woman.

MILLS & BOON

MEDICAL

Pulse-Racing Passion

Set your pulse racing with dedicated, delectable doctors in the high-pressure world of medicine, where emotions run high and passion, comfort and love are the best medicine.

MILLS & BOON

HEROES

At Your Service

Experience all the excitement of a gripping thriller, with an intense romance at its heart. Resourceful, true-to-life women and strong, fearless men face danger and desire – a killer combination!

MILLS & BOON

HISTORICAL

Awaken the romance of the past

Escape with historical heroes from time gone by. Whether your passion is for wicked Regency Rakes, muscled Viking warriors or rugged Highlanders, indulge your fantasies and awaken the romance of the past.

A MATCH TO FOOL SOCIETY

LAURA MARTIN

A LAIRD IN LONDON

CATHERINE TINLEY

ONE NIGHT WITH HER VIKING WARRIOR

SARAH RODI